TIB STREET BALLROOM

KEIRA WILLIS

MARMALADE PRESS

Published by Marmalade Press
www.marmaladepress.co.uk

First published 2024

A CIP catalogue record for this book
is available from the British Library

Printed and bound in Great Britain by
Clays Ltd, Elcograf S.p.A.

Typeset in Adobe Garamond Pro and Futura by Spike-E

ISBN 978-1-9997645-2-4

To D, B and M
with love

PROLOGUE

2nd January 1986

Rebecca was late.

Rebecca was actually *very* late, and Marnie was starting to regret her second measure of vodka. *Top of the Pops* blared loudly from the corner of the living room, but John Peel's face hadn't quite been in focus since he'd said something about Bronski Beat a little while earlier.

Okay, so maybe Marnie was *also* starting to regret not eating anything since the poor excuse for a lunch she'd created from the measly leftovers in the fridge. At least her parents had gone straight to the Odeon after they'd finished work, so there was nobody around to witness her laughably low tolerance for spirits. She knew that she'd be fine in a minute or two, and as long as she remembered to top up the Smirnoff bottle from the tap before she went out, her mother would be none the wiser.

'I need water,' she announced to the empty room as she rolled off the sofa, leaving her high heels lying on the floor by the pouffe with a brief look of disdain. She was going to break her neck in those shoes, she was sure of it, but Rebecca had practically bullied her into trying them on in Kendals a few days earlier.

'Oh, come on,' Rebecca had said, swinging them by their gold straps, right in front of Marnie's face, 'these are *perfect*.'

'They're too expensive.' Marnie had shuddered when she'd seen the price. There was no way she could spend that much money on one pair of shoes.

Rebecca had just laughed. 'I'm sure Rex will buy them for you after lunch. He *did* tell you to pick out anything you wanted.'

'I don't need them, Rebecca.'

Marnie had plucked the shoes from her best friend's hand and wedged them back onto the display before any of the perky salesgirls thought that she might actually be interested in buying them. They'd been following her around for the whole hour they'd been in the shop, and she wasn't enjoying the attention at all.

'Don't you want to make Janine horribly jealous, though?' Rebecca had whispered, grinning spitefully as she'd picked up the shoes again. 'She'd love these, you know she would. So, what better thing to wear to her stupid little party?'

Rebecca had then gleefully tapped the ring on Marnie's left hand. 'Well, not better than *that*, obviously.'

In the kitchen, Marnie spun the engagement ring self-consciously as she waited for the water to start running colder after rinsing out any dregs of vodka in the glass. On the occasions her younger self's imagination had drifted towards thoughts of engagement, she'd always fancied something a little more subtle than the enormous diamond-flanked ruby she now wore, but, then again, Rex with his flash car and his never-ending parade of new suits didn't seem to understand subtlety at the best of times. He was kind, though, and funny, and Marnie could cope with a little bit of showing off if it meant getting to spend the rest of her life with a man like that.

Marnie held her glass over the sink and sighed. Why was she even going to Janine's birthday party anyway? They hadn't been close at school, and even though they'd both been working at Lewis's for the past couple of years, Marnie could count on one hand the number of times Janine had spoken to her before Rex had strolled into the Perfume Hall last May looking for a present for his older sister. Janine had been much friendlier to her since then, which Marnie appreciated, but Rebecca – always suspicious – was convinced that Janine was just waiting to make a move on Rex when Marnie's back was turned.

'Janine's going to throw herself in the canal when you turn up with a huge sparkler!' Rebecca had shrieked down the phone when Marnie had called her on Christmas Day to tell her that Rex had proposed. 'It *is* a massive diamond, right? Rex seems like the massive diamond type.'

'No,' Marnie had said, still staring in surprise at her left hand. 'I mean, it's a paperweight, yeah, but it's a great big ruby. He said it's an antique.'

The weight of it still felt odd to Marnie a week later, with the gold band tapping against the glass as it filled slowly. Her hands felt unbalanced, and her mother couldn't resist grabbing at Marnie's arm any time she passed by, just taking another second to marvel at the fact her only daughter was marrying so well.

Marnie was due back at work the next day, and she hadn't yet decided whether she was going to leave the ring at home. It was far too flashy for a perfume girl, really. She sold bottles of *Beautiful* to women who wore jewellery like this every day, but she'd never thought she'd be one of those women herself.

Rex had told her that she wouldn't need to worry anymore, and that he'd make sure that her parents were taken care of if she wanted to hand in her notice, but Marnie enjoyed being out of the house and meeting new people every day. Rex hadn't seemed surprised when she'd told him that she was going to stick at the Estée Lauder counter for just a little bit longer. Instead, he'd only smiled as though he'd already known exactly what she was going to say, and then they'd carried on with their dinner date without either of them mentioning it again.

Shakin' Stevens was singing about Christmas for the umpteenth time on the TV, and Marnie knew every single word to that song now. She enjoyed December's joviality and the excuse for parties as much as the next person, but she was looking forward to something a bit less seasonal replacing the Christmas music that had been piped onto the shop floor since mid-November.

A brief flash of movement reflected in the window above the sink was the only warning Marnie had before something soft wrapped tightly around her throat.

Her eyes widened in surprise, and she dropped the glass of water when her hands came up to grapple with the material at her neck. The glass hit the lip of the sink, shattering into shards that rained down onto the tiled floor. The spray of water and slivers of glass that peppered Marnie's legs through her tights barely registered as she desperately clawed at the cord tightening around her neck; the fabric drawn taut enough to violently transform any delicacy of the fibres into unyielding steel.

Marnie struggled against the hold she was in, but the black spots dancing in front of her eyes were getting larger, derailing any efforts to escape with an eruption of sheer, unfathomable panic.

She had one final thought before her knees gave way beneath her and she tumbled heavily to the kitchen floor with a choked-off gasp of terror:

I would have made a beautiful bride.

ONE

3rd June 1986

Detective Inspector Andrew Joyce used to enjoy Mondays. He'd wake up just before his alarm clock rang, take a shower, eat breakfast, and still be in his car before anyone else on his street had even opened their front door to take the milk in.

But that had been in the time he now designated as *Before*.

He'd liked *Before*. *Before* had seen him steadily climbing the ranks at CID, exceeding everyone's expectations, and just being damn good at his job.

So, almost three months after he'd made Detective Inspector (at the age of thirty-three years and two days, thanks) Andrew had confidently assumed that DCI Chambers wanted to see him at the end of a fairly nondescript Monday because he was going to be commended for his exemplary case closure rate.

To be fair, Chambers had made it all *sound* like a reward.

'You'll be a good fit for the department,' Chambers had said from behind a cloud of blue-tinged smoke. 'Higson will appreciate your eye for detail.'

'A great fit where, sir?' Andrew had asked, because he'd had no idea who Higson was, or what department Chambers was referring to.

'DCI Higson's team,' Chambers had replied, as though that had helped in any way. 'The Case Re-examination Division.'

Andrew hadn't quite squawked in outrage as he realised what Chambers was talking about, but it was a near thing. 'The Graveyard?'

'I don't believe Higson likes that name very much,' Chambers replied nonchalantly. 'It was always known as 'the Ballroom' back in the day. I did a few years there myself in the sixties. It wasn't Higson then though; it was DCI Prentice. Now, *he* was a good man.'

Christ, Andrew had thought as Chambers had begun reminiscing about his time in Manchester City Police, *I'm finished. What the hell have I done to deserve this? Was I too smug about my exam results? Is this because I didn't stay late enough at the Christmas party last year? Oh God.*

'Sir!' Andrew had tried desperately to cut off Chambers' ramble through his personal history. 'With all due respect, I'm happy in my role here at CID.'

Chambers' expression cooled rapidly. 'DI Joyce, might I remind you that my regard for your 'happiness' is irrelevant here. The CRD's success rate has declined over the past few years, and I owe DCI Higson a favour. A very big favour. That favour has now been called in, and you're just the man for the job. You report to Tib Street at nine am tomorrow.'

'Tomorrow?' Andrew *had* actually squawked that time. 'But-'

'You have no active cases here as of this afternoon,' Chambers had replied, cutting off any further protest with a pointed tilt of his head. 'I therefore see no reason for you to delay your transfer. All the paperwork you need is on your desk. Good afternoon, DI Joyce.'

'Sir.' Andrew's choked-out reply had been as respectful as possible under the circumstances, and he'd risen from his seat when Chambers turned away in obvious dismissal.

It's fine, Andrew had told himself as he'd closed Chambers' door behind him and headed for the break room. *It will all be fine. It'll just be for a few months. Yeah, it's obviously just a temporary secondment. It's fine. Totally fine.*

Andrew had been relieved to find the break room empty. For once, the coffee sitting in the percolator looked like it might not actually have been languishing there for ages, so he'd poured himself a mug and leaned his forehead against the window, not really seeing the car park below.

For just a second, Andrew had thought that maybe he could walk back into Chambers' office and talk his way out of the transfer. If he could just go and offer up another name as an alternative to his, Chambers might go for it, and Andrew had a list of people he would be very happy to never have to work with again, so he wasn't lacking in suggestions.

The problem - and Andrew instinctively knew this - was that Chambers was probably the most stubborn bastard he'd ever met. He also knew that Chambers wasn't the type to owe anyone a favour, so whatever this DCI Higson had done to earn one must have been pretty spectacular.

Andrew had first heard of the Case Re-examination Division when he'd been at Bramshill for a training course a few years earlier. When he'd mentioned he was down from Manchester, another bloke at the lunch table – Jim, maybe? No, *Jez* - had asked if Tib Street was still standing. Andrew had shrugged, not knowing what that was supposed to mean, and Jez had laughed incredulously before launching into an explanation of the 'secret' department that had been running out of Manchester since the turn of the century. Andrew had given up trying to follow Jez's meandering tale of jewel thieves and a pirate, and instead had concentrated on sawing through the rubbery meat on his plate even when everyone else had continued to stare at the storyteller in awe.

'It's like the black magic of police work,' Jez had said as he'd shovelled cauliflower cheese into his mouth. He didn't pause to chew. 'They solve the cases that nobody else can solve.'

Andrew wasn't sure why Jez hadn't just led with that fact. 'Have you been there then? To Tib Street?'

Jez had shaken his head, crumbs spewing out onto the table. 'Nah. My uncle told me about it. He was in Salford for a couple of years.'

'So, it's not that much of a secret then, is it?' Andrew had said, frowning down at the lack of progress he was making with his lunch. What the hell was he eating that his knife wouldn't cut through it?

'Well, *you* hadn't heard of it,' Jez had replied steadily. He'd still been smiling slightly, but there was an edge to his tone that had very strongly hinted that he wasn't a man who liked to be questioned.

'I suppose not,' Andrew had said because *he* wasn't a man who particularly enjoyed confrontation at lunchtime.

That had been the last Andrew had heard about Tib Street until he'd arrived at CID, and certainly nobody had ever mentioned it with the level of reverence that Jez had. Instead, there'd been comments about 'The Graveyard' where unsolved cases lay waiting until they were eventually filed away in the archives, still as unsolved as the day they'd been transferred to the RCD. Why there was still funding for such a department was anyone's guess, but Andrew had just assumed that it served a purpose in providing a home for those who weren't very good at their jobs in the traditional departments.

Except now Andrew was one of them. He'd banged his head against the window twice, letting loose a torrent of expletives that would have had his girlfriend covering her ears and calling for a priest.

Oh God, Kate.

Kate wasn't going to be happy at all when he told her. Andrew was fairly sure that his girlfriend was genuinely proud of his achievements at work, but he was absolutely certain that she mostly just enjoyed telling her friends about how clever Andrew was, how he was so brave at that robbery in Ancoats last month, and how he was a *Detective Inspector* now, hadn't you heard?

Couldn't Chambers have waited just a few months longer to do this to him? Now Andrew was going to have to sit through three wedding receptions over the summer and constantly correct Kate's friends and colleagues about just what his job was.

Maybe he should just quit in protest. He'd probably be able to get a job somewhere else. Not in the police, no – there was no way that Chambers would give him a recommendation if he sacked off this transfer– but maybe he could do something else instead. Kate had always said that he would have made a good teacher.

Andrew didn't want to be a teacher though. He just wanted to get on with his job and not have to relocate to central bloody Manchester. He groaned loudly at the window.

'Are you alright there, Joyce?'

Andrew had spun around in surprise, coffee sloshing over the side of the mug and soaking into the cuff of his shirt. 'Jesus Christ!'

DI Fallon had been smirking at him from the doorway, obnoxiously chewing something. 'I heard you're leaving us.'

Andrew had only heard five minutes ago, but if Fallon already knew, then *everybody* knew. *Great.* Andrew realised that he'd been ambushed. He'd opened his mouth to reply, but Fallon had just snorted with laughter and left Andrew alone to have his breakdown in peace.

And that had been the end of *Before*.

In the fourteen hours that had followed Chambers' pronouncement, Andrew had been shouted at twice; once by Kate over their takeaway, which had resulted in her storming out of his house without finishing her dumplings; and once by a little old lady who'd answered his hesitant knock on the door at Tib Street a few minutes ago, when he'd finally decided that the weathered plaque next to the equally weathered door really did say *Cheryl Richard Dance Studios*. Why it said this he didn't know, but that was the address typed on the piece of paper in his hand, and so that was the door he'd knocked on.

"Oo are you?' the woman had asked with an expression that suggested that Andrew had wronged her terribly just by existing. She'd been holding a cigarette in her right hand, and a spray bottle in her left.

'I'm looking for DCI Higson,' Andrew had replied, automatically taking a step backwards just in case she tried to take a swipe at him. He fought the urge to nervously run a hand through his hair.

The woman's eyes had narrowed, pulling her obviously dyed jet-black fringe further over her wrinkled forehead. 'What do the likes of youse want with 'igson? 'Ow old are youse, anyways? Fifteen?'

Andrew had bristled. 'Excuse me, madam, but I-'

The woman had hooted with laughter. '*Madam*! Ha! Where the 'ell do youse think y'are?'

'Dolly, why on God's earth are you shrieking like a fishwife?' A woman called from inside the building. 'We can hear you upstairs!'

'This one 'ere is lookin' for 'igson,' the old lady – *Dolly* – replied as a smartly dressed, significantly younger woman appeared behind her, heels clacking on the tiles. Dolly crooked a wizened, yellowed finger towards Andrew as though the new arrival wouldn't see him otherwise.

'Oh!' The younger woman's face cleared, and she gently pushed Dolly out of the way with a hand on her shoulder. Andrew was surprised that this didn't end with Dolly immediately vaporising the woman for daring to touch her.

'You must be DI Joyce,' the woman said, smiling slightly even as Dolly scowled. 'Sorry, we weren't expecting you quite this early.'

'Traffic wasn't as bad as I thought it would be,' Andrew replied, which was only partially a lie. The truth was that he hadn't slept very well, and he'd actually got up at four when he'd heard the milkman outside and decided that it was probably close enough to breakfast time for a cup of tea. He'd then decided to drive into Manchester early for the lack of anything better to do, but that meant he'd arrived almost a whole hour before he'd originally intended to.

The woman nodded, accepting his explanation easily. 'I'm DS Cusack, sir. Follow me, I'll take you up.'

Andrew squeezed past Dolly, being very careful not to brush against her lest she somehow bestow a curse on him – she looked the type. *Well*, she'd look the type if Andrew believed in such nonsense.

This close he could see that while she was significantly older than Andrew's own grandmother, her eyes were as sharp as flint, and whereas Nana Joyce always smelled gently of lavender, Dolly was a potent mixture of bleach and cigarette smoke.

'I'll be seein' youse,' Dolly murmured quietly to Andrew, before baring teeth even yellower than her fingernails and heading out the door onto Tib Street with her cigarette held above her head like she thought she was Marlene Dietrich. 'Ta-ra Jen, love.'

'Bye, Dolly,' DS Cusack called back, as though Dolly wasn't even remotely terrifying. She closed the door gently before turning back to Andrew. 'Sorry about Dolly. She pops in most days to clean. You get used to her eventually. She's harmless, really.'

Andrew didn't respond to that. He'd only just arrived, so he probably shouldn't insult the cleaning lady before they'd even reached the top of the stairs. 'Why all the secrecy?' he asked instead. 'With the sign outside? For the dance studio?'

DS Cusack laughed lightly as she led Andrew down a short corridor before heading up yet another staircase. 'Once upon a time, it *was* for secrecy. These days, I'm not entirely sure.'

Andrew waited, but when DS Cusack still hadn't added anything to her explanation by the time they reached the second floor, he had to accept that this was all he was going to get, at least for now.

'Welcome to the Ballroom,' DS Cusack said as they paused outside a set of ornate double doors. She shot Andrew another small smile before twisting the handles and pushing both doors open.

Andrew blinked in surprise at the room in front of him. Even with everyone calling it the Ballroom, and the reference to the dance studios outside, Andrew hadn't been expecting an *actual* ballroom with a polished wooden floor. He glanced up at the ceiling, and his mouth dropped open at the sight, counting six chandeliers evenly spaced across a fresco of something vaguely biblical. 'It's like the Sistine Chapel in here.'

'Michelangelo's cousin was from Hulme; didn't you know that?' A gruff, male voice came from the opposite side of the ballroom.

Andrew looked over to see a balding man with a wiry grey beard pushing himself out of his desk chair. Andrew could practically hear the man's joints cracking in protest.

'Sir,' Andrew said with a curt nod, assuming that the man now shambling slowly towards him was DCI Higson. 'Detective Inspector Andrew Joyce.'

'Joyce,' repeated Higson, holding out a hand so enormous Andrew felt like he was shaking hands with a bear. 'Good to have you here. Chambers has assured me that you'll be a good fit.' He paused, almost glaring at Andrew. 'Don't prove him wrong.'

Higson then smiled, shark-like, and Andrew only just resisted the urge to gulp loudly. Christ, he was supposed to be a DI - and thirty-three years old at that – he wasn't supposed to be intimidated. But there was definitely something wrong with these people, Andrew thought as Higson finally released his hand. First, there was that mad woman at the front door, and now it seemed like his boss had seen *The Godfather* one too many times.

'Sir,' Andrew repeated, not entirely sure what else he could say that wouldn't run the risk of him ending up at the bottom of the Manchester Ship Canal before the day was out.

'Where's Parker?' Higson asked DS Cusack.

'I think I heard the door a second ago,' she replied, gesturing for Andrew to take a seat at one of the desks crammed into the opposite corner of the room to Higson's. 'You know what the queue's like at this time.'

Andrew sat at the only desk that wasn't covered in paper and looked around the room. Did nobody else think this was weird? The ballroom was enormous, and yet all the desks, barring Higson's, were bunched together on one side of the room. Why did they need all the space? This place wasn't actually the Cheryl Richard Dance Studio, was it? Was it some sort of *shared space*? Andrew had visions of trying to work while pensioners did the foxtrot around him.

'You'll get used to it,' DS Cusack said with a knowing grin as she took a seat at the desk opposite Andrew. Holding her hand out over the desks she waited for Andrew to clasp it. 'Jennifer Cusack, but everyone calls me Jen.'

'Andrew.'

Jen nodded. 'DC Parker will be here in a minute. Lloyd.'

'And that's it?' Andrew asked, still baffled by the enormous room. 'Just the three of you?'

'Four of us,' Jen said, pointing at Andrew. 'Our last DI left us a month ago.'

'Transfer?'

Jen grimaced slightly. 'Not exactly.'

There was something about the way that Jen looked away just a little bit too quickly that Andrew didn't like. None of the paperwork Chambers had left on his desk had mentioned anything about a predecessor, and it wasn't as though Andrew had been given time to ask.

'They didn't have any cheese and onion!' Andrew heard before something flew through the air across the ballroom. He looked over just in time to see Higson catch a white paper bag in one hand.

'Meat?' Higson asked the man who was heading towards Andrew and Jen. 'If this is vegetables again, Parker, I'll make sure you're in Ordsall nick by lunchtime.'

DC Parker smirked before he finally noticed that there was someone new in the room. 'Oh, hiya,' he said, grinning at Andrew. 'You're the new DI, yeah?'

Andrew nodded. 'Andrew Joyce.'

'Cool.'

Jen cleared her throat. When Parker stayed quiet she rolled her eyes. 'DI Joyce, this is DC Lloyd Parker, who has apparently forgotten how to behave around adults.'

'Right, yeah, sorry,' Lloyd said, brushing his too-long hair off his face. 'What she said, er, *sir*.'

'Nice to meet you,' Andrew replied, even though he didn't think it was that nice at all. He'd been calculating the distance to the door while Parker had been talking. He didn't think he'd be able to make a run for it before one of the others tackled him, but there was a pretty good-looking set of windows on the adjacent wall. The fall probably wouldn't kill him, but it would definitely get him out of whatever fever dream he'd found himself in. Because this *had* to be a dream.

'Right,' huffed Higson, 'if you're all ready to stop gossiping and actually do some work, get your arses over here. Cusack, bring your pick. Joyce, I'm expecting to be impressed.'

'Here we go,' said Jen encouragingly to Andrew as she picked up the file sitting atop the pile on her desk. 'Are you ready?'

Andrew shook his head. 'Impress him how? I have no idea what's going on. I was just told to show up this morning.'

'What?' Jen looked slightly taken aback. 'You didn't request a transfer here?'

Andrew shook his head. 'No, I was literally given this job last night.'

Jen's eyes bugged slightly, and she opened and closed her mouth a few times. She glanced quickly towards where Higson was inspecting his breakfast then ducked her head down and motioned for Andrew to move closer.

'Right, listen very carefully,' she hissed quickly. 'Higson has been looking for a suitable new DI, and so he called Chambers over at CID. A few days ago, Chambers called Higson back, to tell him that he'd had a request from someone in CID to move over here – that's you, obviously. Nobody *ever* requests a move to the Ballroom, so Higson probably thinks you're some kind of genius when it comes to difficult cases who's going to come in and seriously up our closure rate.'

Andrew made a noise somewhere between a question and a grunt of dissent.

'*Are* you some kind of genius when it comes to difficult cases?' Jen asked hopefully, waving the paper file towards him.

'I'm the youngest DI CID's ever had,' Andrew replied, although he managed to sound unsure about that fact, even as he knew it to be true. 'Does that help?'

Jen groaned quietly. 'I'm not sure what Higson will do if you don't go over there and say something useful.'

'Of course I'll say something useful.' Andrew bristled at the implication that he wasn't going to be good enough to work *here* of all places. 'I was at CID!'

'Yeah, CID, which is where *all* of the unsolved cases we get come from.' Jen rolled her eyes. 'Look, I don't know you at all, but I guess you must be a good copper, and I wouldn't want to see you thrown out of here on your first day. Higson really, *really* holds grudges, so you'd probably never work in Manchester again.'

'What am I supposed to do then?'

'Higson is seriously old school in a lot of ways,' Jen muttered as she pretended to look for something else on her desk. 'But he'll also listen if you have some sort of weird idea that might help. He loves weird ideas.'

'How weird?' Andrew asked, raising an eyebrow.

'We once spent a whole day rolling dice to make decisions on how to proceed.'

Andrew snorted, then stopped abruptly when Jen looked at him sharply. 'Christ, you're serious, aren't you?'

'Sorry, am I interrupting your mothers' meeting over there?' Higson bellowed across the room. 'This pasty's getting cold.'

'Sorry, sir,' Jen called, snapping her lips together in a tight smile. 'Just looking for a pen.'

Andrew trailed behind Jen and eventually found himself standing in front of Higson's desk with her on his left, and Lloyd to his right. It felt horribly familiar. It felt like standing in the headmaster's office at fourteen, waiting for him to dole out punishment for catching Andrew smoking on the playing fields with Paul and Mick.

'Well?' Higson asked, taking an enormous bite out of the pasty. Gravy coated his whiskers and slowly dribbled down his fingers.

'Marnie Driscoll, sir.' Jen said as she flipped open the file and placed it in front of Higson, just far enough away that he could read it, but without it immediately being endangered by any stray globules of grease.

'Twenty-two years old, strangled in her kitchen back in January,' Jen continued. 'Alone in her parents' house at the time, waiting for a friend to arrive before they were due to head onto a party together. No other injuries. The back door into the kitchen was forced open, and Marnie's engagement ring was missing from her body.'

Andrew remembered this case coming into CID. He'd been working on the spate of Post Office robberies in Salford back in January, but he couldn't avoid the Chester House gossip chain, not when the fiancé of the dead girl was Rex Hughes.

'She was engaged to a local businessman,' Andrew added, and Jen gave him a quick nod of approval. 'Rex Hughes. I assume you've all heard of him.'

'Isn't he an actor?' Lloyd asked with a frown. 'And really old?'

'That's Rex Harrison,' Jen sighed.

'*Rex Hughes*,' Higson said with a sneer, briefly forgetting about the pasty in his hand as his eyes narrowed, 'is a jumped-up little arse from out Heald Green way. Thinks he's some kind of Don Juan.'

Andrew nodded. 'His grandfather founded Hughes' Holiday Parks about forty years ago.'

'Oh yeah!' Lloyd's face lit up with a smile. 'I went to the Southport one a couple of times when I was a kid. Closed down now, I think.'

'It is,' said Jen. 'Rex's father, David, saw the writing on the wall for that type of holiday about a decade ago, and the family sold the parks to another operator, and funnelled the sale money into buying up loads of property around Manchester instead. Rex has managed most of the family investments since David died.'

'Rex Hughes is also heavily suspected to be part of Tony and Liam Byrne's network,' Andrew added. 'Since last summer, three drug raids with suspected links to the Byrne brothers have been at properties owned by the Hughes family. Nobody's managed to pin anything on Rex yet. He's always claimed that he has a property management company finding and managing his tenants for him.'

'Do you think the Byrnes had something to do with this girl's murder then?' Lloyd asked, looking round at the others. 'Some sort of warning to Hughes?'

'There was nothing at the scene that suggested this had anything to do with them,' Jen said, shaking her head. 'You know what the Byrnes are like; they're messy, and not afraid of letting people know they shouldn't cross them. If this had been anything to do with them, I think we'd know, even if we couldn't actually prove it.'

Andrew, and everyone else at CID for that matter, knew only too well how difficult it was to prove anything at all when it came to the Byrne brothers.

'Did you work this case, Joyce?' Higson asked suddenly as he dropped the empty paper bag on his desk, and Andrew flinched slightly at the unexpected direct question.

'No, sir,' Andrew replied curtly. 'I was assigned elsewhere.'

Higson nodded slowly before he leaned back in his chair and clasped his hands together. 'Alright. Well, go on then, astound me.'

'Isn't DS Cusack leading this briefing?' Andrew asked. Without seeing the file, he didn't even have enough information to list the basic facts of the case, for God's sake, let alone *astound* his new boss. If CID hadn't found anything useful, how the hell was Andrew supposed to just pluck a theory out of thin air?

Higson just raised an eyebrow and waited silently.

'Alright,' Andrew said, mostly to himself. 'Alright, fine. Witnesses?'

'None,' Jen confirmed. 'Marnie was found by her parents when they came home later that evening. Nobody had contacted the police before then. Neighbours across the road say they didn't see Marnie answer the front door to anyone.'

'What about the friend that was supposed to be calling for her?' Andrew asked, thinking back over everything Jen had said. 'Didn't she think it odd that Marnie didn't answer the door?'

Jen shook her head. 'No. The friend – Rebecca Silverman – was significantly late to meet Marnie in the first place. When she arrived and there was no answer she just thought Marnie had gone to the party without her. She didn't realise that this wasn't the case until she arrived in Fallowfield and Marnie wasn't there.'

'Any other evidence at the scene?' Andrew asked, slightly desperately. 'Anything at all?'

'Nothing,' Jen confirmed with a slight wince of apology. 'The Driscolls didn't report anything missing, besides the engagement ring.'

Think, Andrew, come on, he snapped at himself. 'How was she strangled? Bare hands?'

Jen shook her head. 'No, based on the marks on her neck, some sort of material was used as a garrotte. No sign of it at the scene and no identifiable fibres were found. There was broken glass in the sink and on the kitchen floor; it looked like Marnie dropped a tumbler of water.'

'Just the one glass?' Andrew asked.

'Yes,' Jen confirmed. 'One glass. There was a bottle of vodka on the table in the living room, so it looks like Marnie might have been drinking that first, and then went to the kitchen to get water, or to wash out the glass.'

'So, she's alone,' Andrew said, looking up at the ceiling as he thought aloud. 'Waiting for her friend to arrive. She has a drink – to what? Calm her nerves for some reason? Get a buzz before the party?'

The rest of the team stayed silent. Good, Andrew had meant them as rhetorical questions anyway.

'She goes into the kitchen, pours herself a glass of water, and is strangled.' Andrew frowned. 'She was facing the sink when it happened.'

'You can't be sure of that,' Lloyd said. 'Can you?'

'If there were shards of glass in the sink it means she was facing that way when she dropped the glass of water,' Andrew said, splaying out his fingers as though dropping something in surprise. 'So, whoever killed her was behind her. Where's the back door?'

'Er,' Jen picked up the file to flick through it. 'Here.'

Andrew looked over to see a photo of the scene, minus Marnie's body. Andrew assumed the photo had been taken from the kitchen door. The room was small, with the sink directly beneath a window that faced the back garden. The back door was just visible on the wall to the left of the sink.

'Where does that door lead?' Andrew asked, tapping at the photo where an internal door was just visible on the right-hand side of the room, closer to the photographer than the sink. 'Bathroom?'

Jen nodded, looking unsure of where Andrew was heading with this. 'Yeah. It's an old Victorian terrace. The bathroom looks like it was added on in the last ten years or so. There's a photo in the file of it. Tiny window, no door to outside.'

'I don't think the killer came through the back door and surprised Marnie,' Andrew said.

'What?' Jen asked in surprise.

'Yeah, what?' Lloyd added.

Andrew briefly glanced at Higson, but the DCI remained impassive. 'Look, if Marnie was standing at the sink she'd be looking right out into the garden. She'd see someone out there, right?'

'Well, yeah,' Lloyd said, frowning down at the photograph of the kitchen. 'But the killer could have been waiting at the side, by the door, yeah? She wouldn't have seen anyone there.'

'Right,' said Andrew. 'But the killer didn't come through the back door. At least not in the moments before Marnie was killed.'

'How do you figure that?' Lloyd asked, looking utterly baffled.

Andrew looked around the ballroom, blowing air loudly through his lips.

'Right, come over here,' he said to Lloyd, leading the way over to the double doors he'd come through earlier. 'You too, DS Cusack.'

Jen looked slightly apprehensive as she followed Lloyd more slowly to the other side of the room.

Andrew looked between them, before grabbing Lloyd and standing him just inside the door, facing the wall of windows. 'Right, pretend you're Marnie.'

'But I'm a bloke!' Lloyd protested.

'Yeah, well just for a minute you're actually a twenty-two-year-old woman filling a glass of water at a sink,' Andrew said, raising his eyebrows at Lloyd. 'Come on. Get on with it.'

'Do what he says, Lloyd,' Higson shouted from across the room. He'd made no move to join them, but he'd turned his chair towards the doors and was leaning further forward than he had been. Andrew took this as a positive sign.

Lloyd rolled his eyes and pretended to fill a glass of water.

'DS Cusack,' Andrew said as he opened just the left hand of the two doors and pointed into the corridor. 'I want you to go out there. Count to ten, and then open the other door as hard as you can. Imagine you're trying to force it open, yeah?'

'Alright,' Jen agreed, albeit slightly reluctantly, as she headed out of sight.

'Sorry about this, DC Parker,' Andrew said with a slight smirk.

'What?' Lloyd asked, confused as he continued to pretend he was fiddling with a tap.

A moment later, the door burst open, and Jen barrelled through shoulder first. The door hit Lloyd with enough force to send him staggering forwards. He didn't regain enough of his balance before he was then also hit by Jen, and he tumbled to the ground with a yell of surprise.

Andrew grinned slightly as Lloyd lay on his back, blinking up at the painted ceiling.

'Oh,' said Jen, her eyes growing wide as she met Andrew's. 'If the killer had forced the door open while Marnie was there, she'd have been hit pretty hard by the door because it's so close to the sink.'

'Exactly,' Andrew said as he reached down to pull Lloyd to his feet. 'And you said there wasn't another mark on her, right? No bruising to her arm or shoulder?'

Jen nodded slowly. 'So, the killer could have already been in the house without Marnie's knowledge. Maybe they had a back door key. So, they waited until Marnie went into the kitchen and then strangled her from behind. Is that what happened?'

'That's exactly what I think happened,' Andrew said, looking over to Higson. 'And if the lights were on in the kitchen, the window would have acted like a mirror.'

'Marnie would have seen her killer,' Jen breathed.

'She's our only witness,' Andrew said. The thrill he'd felt at knowing he'd spotted something that CID hadn't considered was already sinking into a well of disappointment. They were no closer to solving Marnie's murder. 'It's just a shame we can't ask Marnie.'

'Well, we could try,' Lloyd said, nodding before wincing and rubbing his shoulder slightly.

'What?' Andrew asked, staring in disbelief at the other man. Had Lloyd hit his head in the fall?

'We could try to ask Marnie. I've got a friend who might be able to help us with that,' Lloyd replied evenly.

Andrew looked at Jen and was surprised to see she just shrugged at Lloyd's suggestion. 'Seriously? You want to try and talk to a dead girl?'

'Do you have a better idea?' Higson asked mildly.

Andrew opened his mouth, frowned, and eventually shook his head. 'No, sir.'

'You'd better go see that friend of yours then, Parker,' Higson said, picking up the file from his desk. 'But be a good lad and get me another pasty first.'

TWO

It was fair to say that Peggy Swan wasn't having the most exciting day of her life.

She squinted at the stacks of paper and envelopes spread out all over her bedroom floor, grimacing at the chaos. She was certain that she'd seen something that looked vaguely like a vet's bill at some point in the past hour, but for the life of her, she couldn't see it now.

She glanced down at the notepad resting on her knees and sighed again. Even if she somehow managed to locate the bill again soon, she still had eleven more documents she really needed to find before the end of the day. At times like this, she wished she'd taken over the estate's paperwork before Charlie had so much as opened a single archive box. Her Father had always been fairly terrible at filing, but the complete lack of organisation she was up against now had her younger brother's fingerprints all over it.

'Peg? Peggy?'

Speak of the devil.

Peggy winced as her brother yelled her name again from somewhere else in the house. Charlie wouldn't actually think to just come and knock on the door to politely enquire if his sister was there, and he'd just continue calling for her as he sauntered around the house until Peggy eventually made herself known.

She uncrossed her legs and clambered off her bed, being careful not to step on any of the papers as she picked her way over the discarded invoices and statements to open the door. 'What do you want, Charlie?'

Charlie was sitting in the middle of the grand staircase, grinning up at her through the gaps in the balustrade. 'Oh! There you are.'

'Would it have killed you to come and knock on my door?' Peggy asked, rolling her eyes at him before wrinkling her nose. 'What on earth is that hideous thing you're wearing?'

Charlie beamed as though his sister had paid him the highest compliment. He swiped his hands reverently over the outrageously purple crushed velvet blazer. 'What, this old thing? I found it in a wardrobe in one of the guest rooms. Don't you like it?'

'You look ridiculous,' Peggy answered, shaking her head, but heading down the galleried landing to the top of the staircase anyway, 'but you already know that.'

'I look dashing,' Charlie replied as he patted the stair tread next to him in invitation. 'Charming, handsome, and desirable.'

'Which is, of course, why you're always single,' Peggy smirked as she sat down next to him.

'I'm very much in demand in town.' Charlie grinned again. 'Last night I met this girl called Linda, and she-'

Peggy held up her hand and clamped her eyes shut. 'Stop! Don't say one more word. I still don't want to hear a single thing about what you get up to in town.' She sighed loudly. 'Besides, I'm busy, Charlie.'

'Busy?' He frowned. 'Busy doing what?'

'The accounts,' Peggy replied, ignoring how her brother then rolled his eyes. 'The accountants are coming tomorrow, and I still haven't managed to find everything they've asked for.'

'Oh, come on,' Charlie replied petulantly, 'why are you even bothering? You know the accountants will just fudge it all to make sense anyway. One little missing invoice or another isn't going to make any difference, is it?'

'I probably wouldn't accuse Father's accountants of fraud in front of them,' Peggy said and then sighed again once more for good measure. 'Now, why exactly were you shrieking for me?'

'Oh right, yes,' Charlie said, nodding eagerly in that way that always reminded Peggy of the spaniel they'd briefly had as children. 'A friend of mine - well, more of an acquaintance, I suppose - needs a little bit of help.'

Peggy was shaking her head before Charlie had even finished speaking. 'No! Absolutely not.'

Charlie frowned. 'But I haven't said anything yet.'

'You don't need to,' Peggy replied, 'because the answer is *no*. You are not loaning any more money to 'friends'. You still haven't got a penny back from your 'very good friend' who wanted to take flying lessons before he decided whether or not to join the RAF.'

'I thought that seemed quite sensible,' Charlie argued, looking offended. 'Kit didn't want to commit to a life of service if he didn't actually like flying planes.'

'And did he?' Peggy asked patiently.

'What? Like flying planes?'

'*No*. Did he join the RAF?'

Charlie hunched down slightly. 'Well, no, not yet. He had to move to Spain quite suddenly after the first lesson. His Grandmother was very sick and needed the sun, and well – *oh*.'

'They're only ever after the money, Charlie,' Peggy replied quietly. 'You know they are.'

Charlie looked disgruntled for a long moment before brightening again. 'Well, this time it's got nothing to do with money.'

He sighed as his sister arched an eyebrow in judgment. 'Or cars, or land, *or horses*.'

'Then what *do* they want?'

Charlie somehow looked even more delighted. 'Well, Lloyd is a Detective Constable in Manchester. *No*, don't look at me like that, I wasn't arrested by him; he's been at a few of the same gigs, and he's always in Rotters on a Monday.'

Peggy twisted her lips in distaste. 'Charlie, you're thirty, why are you *still* going to Rotters?'

Charlie ignored her. 'A few months ago, Lloyd told me that he works for a department that takes a second look at cases that haven't been solved by the normal detective division. Apparently, they'd just closed this case - some gruesome murder or other - where his boss thought witchcraft might have been involved. They hired a shaman to consult on the investigation.'

'Oh my God, Charlie, you actually believe this utter bullshit, don't you?' Peggy hissed, pressing her fingertips to her forehead. 'You honestly think a police detective hired a shaman? Where the hell would you even *find* a consulting shaman?'

'Bolton,' Charlie replied seriously. 'And yes, I do believe what he said. *You* of all people can't be cynical about this sort of thing.'

'That's different, Charlie.' Peggy bristled. 'I'm not trying to con money out of an overgrown child.'

'I already told you, this isn't about money,' Charlie said, turning to fully face his sister. 'Look, don't get mad, but I might have mentioned to

Lloyd that you can, you know, communicate with dead people.'

'What?' Peggy shrieked, standing up so quickly she had to grab the bannister to stop herself from pitching down the stairs. 'Charlie, you promised me *twenty-odd years ago* that you'd never tell anybody else, and now you've gone and told the *police*!'

'I know, I'm sorry.' Charlie did actually look sorry as he stood up and patted his sister's arm. 'Lloyd was just telling cool stories about work, and I sort of said it without meaning to. Peg, really, I'm sorry.'

Peggy just pursed her lips and continued to stare at the floor. She was so angry with Charlie that she thought she might never stop berating him if she so much as opened her mouth.

Charlie had told precisely one other person about Peggy's 'gift' back when they were children, and it had ended with the siblings being split up and sent to different boarding schools. Nobody had believed what Charlie had said, of course, but the rumours about Charlie's 'crazy' sister had run riot for a summer, right up until their father had decided that the best course of action was to just send his two problems away, in opposing directions: Charlie up to Scotland, and 'Crazy Margaret' to Switzerland. For six years they'd only seen each other at Christmas.

'Peggy, look,' Charlie sighed unhappily, and Peggy knew that her brother hadn't done this to upset her. 'Lloyd called me this morning and told me that they really need your help.'

Peggy felt all of the blood drain from her face. 'No,' she shook her head. 'No, Charlie. I'm not having anyone else look at me like I'm lying. I don't want to be 'Crazy Margaret' again.'

'Peggy, a girl was murdered,' Charlie said pleadingly. 'You could help her. Help her family.'

'That's what the police are for,' Peggy replied, turning away, feeling sick to her stomach at the thought of murder. 'What help would I be, anyway? I can't bring her back from the dead. I can't control who responds and who doesn't, you know that.'

'Right, but-'

Whatever Charlie was going to say was cut off by the ancient doorbell chiming beneath them.

'Charlie!' Peggy hissed in betrayal as her brother bounded down the stairs before she could grab him. 'Charlie, wait!'

Peggy considered turning and running up the stairs to hide, but Charlie was already heaving the front door open to reveal three figures staring into the house in awe. She instead took a deep breath, straightened her spine, and tried to look as aloof as possible for someone who was effectively standing halfway up a staircase for no discernible reason.

'Lloyd!' Charlie said, sounding surprised, as though he hadn't been the one who'd invited the police to his home.

'I knew you were rich, mate, but this is something else,' Lloyd greeted him with a grin. He was a fair few years younger than Charlie, and definitely the most junior of the three on the doorstep, but Peggy could see how he held himself with confidence next to them. *Definitely a younger brother then,* Peggy thought. It was probably why Charlie liked him.

'Come in,' Charlie said, opening the door even wider and gesturing for them to enter.

Lloyd and the second man stepped back to allow the sole woman to enter first. *Well, well,* thought Peggy, *maybe chivalry isn't dead after all.*

The woman was probably closer to Charlie's age than Lloyd's, but she wasn't wearing a uniform. Detective then, Peggy concluded.

Lloyd was eventually followed by the taller man who'd been giving Charlie's outfit a similar look of horror to the one Peggy had shot him on the stairs. Peggy tilted her head and observed the way he stood slightly further away from the other two. He was dressed more smartly than Lloyd, and clearly lacked the younger man's obvious enthusiasm for this little jaunt. Peggy didn't know exactly what it was that gave him away, but she knew with the utmost certainty that this definitely wasn't the man who'd apparently consulted a shaman. Plain as day, this man was as sceptical as they came.

At that moment, Timothy, who was still refusing to take any sort of hint that maybe it was time to retire, slowly crossed the hall, gloved hands already reaching, ready to take any coats, capes, or top hats that should come his way. Peggy sighed as she watched the three guests take in the suited, skeletal form lumbering towards them in freshly polished shoes. Nobody ever expected a butler these days.

'It's like being in *Scooby Doo,*' Lloyd stage-whispered with a grin before turning to Charlie. 'Or *Batman*. Mate, do you have a secret lair?'

'Sadly not,' Charlie replied, sounding genuinely disappointed about it. 'Honestly, Timothy, I've told you a million times, we're perfectly capable of answering the door ourselves.'

Even though she couldn't see his face, Peggy knew that Timothy would now look like he had sucked on a particularly sour lemon. He'd never been a fan of the way Peggy and Charlie behaved, but he *was* a fan of rules and tradition, which was probably the only reason their father kept him around. Peggy paled again. Oh God, their father absolutely must not find out that they had the police in the house.

'Thank you, Timothy,' Peggy said loudly, causing everyone to look up at her. 'That will be all.'

Timothy looked ready to argue, but as that obviously would have been some infraction of the Secret Butler Code, or whatever rules he bound himself to, he simply nodded his head and left silently.

'I think we should move this somewhere else, *Charles*, don't you?' Peggy suggested, pointedly tilting her head in the direction Timothy had gone.

Charlie frowned slightly at his sister's unusual brusqueness, but then seemed to understand. '*Oh*, right, sorry. Yes, this way.'

Charlie took a few steps away and opened the door to the library. 'We won't be disturbed in here.'

The three police officers shuffled past Charlie and out of sight,

'Come on Peggy, *please*,' Charlie begged, looking up at where his sister still stood on the staircase. 'Just listen to what they have to say, and if you don't want to get involved then you don't have to. I just really, *really* think you might be able to do some good here. *Please*.'

Peggy was well aware that her brother was manipulating her into agreeing to help. She couldn't begrudge him for that really. Not when he'd spent most of the past year trying to get her out of the house and back into the world.

'Alright, fine,' Peggy sighed eventually as she descended the stairs and went to stand by her brother, 'but I'm not promising to do anything but listen.'

Charlie nodded and Peggy followed him into the library, closing the door firmly behind them.

'Right, first things first,' Charlie announced as he headed towards their guests and gestured for them to take seats. 'I'm Charles Swan, and this is my sister Margaret.'

'Detective Inspector Andrew Joyce,' the tall man said with a nod to both Swan siblings. 'This is Detective Sergeant Jennifer Cusack, and Detective Constable Lloyd Parker, who I believe you already know.'

'Just me,' clarified Charlie as he took a seat next to Peggy. 'Peggy wasn't aware that you would be visiting today.'

Peggy elbowed her brother and nodded towards the closed door they'd all just come through. Charlie nodded in understanding.

'Can I request that we keep this as informal as possible, please? Perhaps first names, and certainly no mention of rank from this moment on if you wouldn't mind. We've found that the walls have ears sometimes.' He looked at DI Joyce meaningfully.

DI Joyce nodded again in understanding and then turned his attention to Peggy. 'Miss Swan?' He stopped speaking and frowned. 'Er, or should it be *Lady* Swan?'

Peggy took pity on him before he could try to address her as Princess Swan. 'Peggy is fine, Margaret if you absolutely must.'

'Peggy then, thank you,' Joyce said, looking infinitely more relieved if not actually any more certain about why he was here at all. 'Would you mind answering a few questions for Jennifer here?'

Joyce looked over to DS Cusack next to him who was staring at him in surprise, and he shrugged one shoulder. 'Do you want to take this? Show me how it's normally done?'

DS Cusack looked taken aback for a long moment. *Odd*, thought Peggy. It sounded like DI Joyce wasn't usually part of this team. Maybe he'd replaced the shaman fan.

'Peggy, I apologise for our unexpected arrival,' DS Cusack said after she'd composed herself. 'I believe that your brother has suggested that you may be able to help us with one of our cases.'

Peggy nodded once but didn't offer any further information. She could hear the taunts of her former friends as clearly as though it were yesterday, and she'd meant it when she'd told Charlie that she wasn't interested in being laughed at again.

'I'm aware that this must seem like a strange request coming from the police,' DS Cusack added, 'but we do things a little differently in our department, and if there's anything you can do to help us, then I can assure you that we'll take anything you say seriously.'

It was obvious that DS Cusack understood that Peggy was hesitant. Peggy appreciated that, although she wondered how much of that was the DS's intuition, and how much came from stories Charlie had possibly spouted to Lloyd when they'd been out drinking together.

'I'm not sure how much help I can be to you, regardless of what Charlie's told you,' Peggy said eventually. 'What exactly is it that you want me to do?'

'Back in January, a young woman was murdered at her home in Cheadle,' Cusack continued, keeping her eyes on Peggy, even as her colleagues openly stared at their surroundings. 'Her name was Marnie Driscoll.'

'Yes, I remember it being on the news. Horrible,' Peggy replied with a shiver. 'Did they not find the person responsible?'

'Unfortunately, no, not yet,' Cusack answered with a grimace. 'Our department looks at cases from a different angle, and we sometimes find that we have to use slightly more *unorthodox* methods to try and help.'

'Like the shaman?'

'*Shaman?*' DI Joyce asked in disbelief. 'Seriously?'

Peggy huffed and folded her arms as she glowered at the Detective Inspector. 'Do you not subscribe to the same methods as the rest of your team, Det-*Andrew*?'

Andrew liked to think that he had developed a keen sense of identifying danger and threats over the years, and the glare Peggy Swan was sending him was definitely setting off particularly loud alarm bells.

On the drive out to Butterton House, Andrew had hoped that it was all going to be a case of discovering that Lloyd had believed some drunken bullshit he'd been fed on a night out and that once they rang the doorbell at the frankly *enormous* house they'd be told to kindly bugger off immediately. However, it was now obvious that, despite appearances, Peggy must be one of those hippie dippy mystic types who probably genuinely believed she was communicating with the dead. She probably had a room full of crystals and burned incense at all hours.

'I apologise,' Andrew said eventually, hoping that he sounded appropriately contrite. He was supposed to be a professional after all.

'He's new to the department,' Lloyd added, sounding unbearably smug to Andrew's ears. 'It can be a bit of a shock.'

Andrew turned to reprimand the junior officer but held his tongue when he realised that Peggy was still glaring at him.

'So!' Charlie said, far too loudly for the room. He clapped his hands together once and gave his sister a look of concern before turning to Jen. 'Jennifer, you were saying?'

Jen gave their host a look of grateful relief before she continued. 'Peggy, I was hoping that we could ask you to help us with progressing Marnie's case. Do you think you would be able to speak to her?'

Andrew leaned back slightly in the overstuffed chair. He was actually curious to see how Peggy responded to Jen's request. Lloyd and Jen had earlier made it clear to him that this wasn't the oddest line of investigation the CRD had ever followed, and, as far as Andrew could tell, Jen certainly wasn't addressing Peggy with anything less than full sincerity.

Who the hell were these people?

Peggy didn't reply for a long moment. Andrew watched her carefully as she crossed and recrossed her legs at the ankles before taking a deep breath and bracing her elbows on her knees.

'I'm not sure I'd be very helpful to you.'

Ah, here we go, Andrew thought, *this is where she backs down in the face of a test.*

'It's temperamental,' Peggy continued, worrying her hands. 'I don't often *try* to communicate with someone. It usually happens by accident, almost. It's not like this is a job, or even a hobby. Honestly, I'd prefer that nobody knew anything about it.'

She narrowed her eyes at her brother, who held up his hands in surrender.

'Well, thank you for your time anyway,' Andrew said, pushing himself forward, ready to stand. He wasn't going to waste any more time here, not when he could be back at the Ballroom, or, even better, trying to get back to CID where he could do some actual police work.

'Peggy, *please.*'

Jen's plea halted Andrew's attempts to leave.

'Let me be perfectly straight with you,' Jen said. 'We have no witnesses, we have no new leads, and this is the last chance we've got to try and find something that can help us. We think Marnie saw her killer, and if we could get *anything* from her, anything at all, it might just be enough to go on. Otherwise, it's over.'

'Won't you keep looking for her killer?' Peggy asked, frowning.

'If a case isn't solved in a reasonable amount of time it comes to us,' Jen replied. 'We do everything we can to find closure, no matter how strange our methods may seem to those on the outside, but without any leads, the case will remain unsolved. Marnie's killer will continue to walk free, and her parents and fiancé will likely never know why she was killed.'

Silence descended on the library once more, and Andrew tried to avoid catching anyone's eye. He wanted to get out of there, but he didn't want anyone to think that he was unfeeling towards Marnie or the plight of her family. He wanted to identify the killer as much as the rest of them, but to do that he needed to be able to do his actual job, and not waste time on some posh girl's parlour trick.

'What do you need me to do?' Peggy asked quietly.

Andrew practically threw himself off the chair in surprise. 'You just said you couldn't help us!'

Oh, that was possibly a little too accusatory if Jen's dark look was anything to go by. Andrew cleared his throat.

'Yes, well, I probably can't,' Peggy replied, not quite meeting his eyes. 'But who would I be if I didn't at least try?'

'Thank you,' Jen cut in quickly before Andrew could say anything else. 'I'm really grateful to you Peggy. Now, what do you need? Is there anything we can get for you?'

Peggy shook her head. 'I can't just *speak* to her.'

She sighed in frustration and crossed her ankles again. 'Look, it's not an exact science.'

It's not a science at all, Andrew thought mulishly. He was still standing awkwardly in the middle of the room.

'I'll try to explain.' Peggy said as she waved her hands around. 'So, this house, or some version of it, has stood here for hundreds of years. Most people would probably look at it and assume that if any house around here was going to be haunted, it would probably be this one.'

'They'd be right,' piped up Charlie, giving the back corner of the room a funny look.

Andrew tilted his head slightly to glance at the same spot out of the corner of his eye, but he couldn't see anything out of the ordinary besides the floor-to-ceiling shelves absolutely crammed with dusty, leather-bound volumes.

'Oh, you can speak to them too?' Jen asked in surprise, and Andrew only just refrained from rolling his eyes.

Charlie laughed slightly. 'Me? No way. But you can't grow up in a house this old and not be aware that there's something else here. I'd know I wasn't always alone even if I didn't have Peggy to tell me so.'

'I don't just walk around seeing ghosts absolutely everywhere. No matter what some people might suggest,' Peggy said pointedly, shaking her head at her brother again. 'The longer ago a person died the harder it can be to speak to them; I think that maybe they start to forget who they were, and eventually they're nothing more than a suggestion of the person they used to be.'

'Are we alone right now?' Lloyd asked, and Andrew was amused to see that the DC was looking a little pale.

Peggy shrugged 'Yes, and no. It's hard to ever really be alone in this house as it's so old, but there's nobody here right now that I could have a conversation with. I might be able to get an image or a single word if I concentrated hard enough, but nothing useful about who they are, or what they were like before they died. It's like trying to have a conversation with a person's shadow.'

Andrew shivered slightly, and he chastised himself immediately for it.

'Marnie died six months ago,' Jen said. 'That's not so long ago.'

'It's not,' Peggy agreed. 'But it's also worth bearing in mind that not everyone's spirit, or whatever you want to call it, remains after they've died. I know that I need to be somewhere the person spent a lot of time before they died, that's the main thing, but they also have to be willing to talk to me, just like any normal conversation.'

'So, Marnie's home might be a good location?' Jen asked. 'She was born there, and obviously, it's where she was killed too.'

'Absolutely not,' Andrew said, vehemently shaking his head. 'We are *not* going to turn up at the Driscoll house and ask them to entertain any of this nonsense.'

'Andrew, can I have a quick word?' Jen asked, getting to her feet. She narrowed her eyes dangerously. '*Now*, if you wouldn't mind.'

Andrew barely had time to blink before Jen grabbed his arm and manhandled him to the other side of the room. It turned out that she was far stronger than she looked, and Andrew had to save himself from stumbling into the fireplace by reaching out to grab the sliding ladder attached to the bookcase.

'What exactly do you think you're doing, Detective Sergeant?' Andrew hissed quietly. 'I'm the senior officer here, and I will *not* take some con artist to the home of a dead woman.'

'You're awfully quick to judge someone as a con artist, *sir*,' Jen replied, curling her lips and not looking even remotely cowed by Andrew. 'You haven't even given her a chance.'

'We're not doing this,' Andrew said, shaking his head. 'There's no way Higson would allow this.'

'This was practically Higson's idea! Look, if you don't want to take Peggy Swan to the Driscoll house then fine, as you said, you're in charge here.' Jen shrugged. 'But I will remind you what I said about Higson and grudges earlier. You work for him now, not CID, so you either play by his rules, or he'll have you thrown out of GMP so fast you won't even get a job writing parking tickets.'

Andrew scoffed, ready to argue that there was no way one man could have that much power, particularly one who'd clearly been side-lined into a completely pointless department. He was stopped, however, by Peggy appearing behind Jen.

'I'm fully aware that you don't believe a word I've said,' Peggy practically whispered to Andrew, 'and if I were you, I probably wouldn't believe me either. So, if you don't want me to help, then that's fine. I certainly won't argue with you.'

Jen looked crestfallen. 'No, Peggy, I really think you could help here. Marnie deserves justice.'

Andrew looked between the two women. What was he supposed to do now? If he said anything that suggested he didn't believe a criminal should be brought to justice then he was going to look like a complete arse, but he absolutely could not allow Marnie's parents to be taken for a ride. He also just wanted to get this case out of the way without pissing off Higson and losing any chance he had of getting away from the Ballroom.

'Fine,' Andrew agreed eventually, defeated for now. He narrowed his eyes at Peggy. 'You can have five minutes at the Driscoll house. You don't speak to Marnie's parents, and you're not to tell a soul about any of this.'

'I spend my days in a sixty-eight-room house with my brother, my father, and a butler who refuses to retire,' Peggy said drily. 'Who am I going to tell?'

This struck Andrew as a bit odd. From what Lloyd had said about Charlie being a well-known man about town, he'd imagined that Peggy would be similarly socially inclined. She was young and loaded, why wouldn't she go out and enjoy that?

'You have my word,' Peggy added before Andrew had a chance to comment further.

Andrew sighed loudly, pinching the bridge of his nose. 'Fine. Jen, how soon can we get into the Driscoll house?'

Jen perked up at last, clearly pleased with Andrew's response. 'If I can use a telephone, I could call Higson now. If he speaks to the Driscolls to let them know that we're re-examining the scene then I'm sure we could get into the house pretty much straight away.'

'There's a telephone on the desk over there,' Peggy said pointing beyond where Charlie and Lloyd were laughing about something. 'Please, go ahead.'

'Thank you.' Jen smiled and went to make the call.

'Five minutes,' Andrew repeated tightly to Peggy. 'That's all you get.'

Peggy nodded once and turned away. 'Charlie, we're going out.'

Charlie lit up like a small child on Christmas morning and practically jumped out of his seat. 'Excellent! I'll go and get one of the cars.'

'How many cars do you have?' Lloyd asked, laughing even as his eyes widened in disbelief at the very idea.

'Oh, you know,' Charlie shrugged nonchalantly, 'a few.'

Andrew sighed yet again. *Seriously, who* were *these people?*

THREE

Peggy followed Andrew's Vauxhall Belmont through the slightly heavier traffic they'd found themselves in as they approached Gatley, frowning when he indicated to turn right off the main road unexpectedly.

'I thought Marnie's house was in Cheadle,' she said to Charlie, who was idly flicking through an old edition of *Private Eye* that he'd found on the backseat.

'It is,' Charlie replied, not looking up from his reading.

'Then what are we doing here?' Peggy asked, as she gently pulled her car to a stop behind the Belmont. They were parked directly outside a pair of 1930s semi-detached houses, both with tidy front gardens and freshly painted windows.

'No idea,' Charlie replied, glancing at the house and throwing the magazine over his shoulder.

'Hey, can you not make a mess in my car?' Peggy cried.

'I wouldn't be making a mess in your car if you'd just let me bring the Aston,' Charlie replied with a huff. 'Jen and Lloyd would have thought it was awesome.'

'DI Joyce doesn't want us anywhere near his case as it is,' Peggy argued. 'What do you think he would have said if you'd turned up thinking you were James bloody Bond?'

'I could have brought the Jag then,' Charlie shrugged. 'Inspector Morse drives one.'

'Inspector Morse is also fictional, Charlie. Plus, you're not actually a detective, you know that, right? We're barely being tolerated here.'

Peggy watched as Andrew got out of his car, leaving the driver's door open, and jogged up the short garden path to the house. He pulled a keyring out of his pocket and seconds later pushed the front door open.

'Is this Joyce's house?' Charlie asked, frowning at his sister.

'Must be.'

Charlie pulled a crumpled pack of cigarettes out from a pocket inside the terrible purple jacket that he was still wearing and cranked open the window slightly.

'Don't even think about it,' Peggy warned dangerously.

'I opened the window!' Charlie protested as Peggy plucked the package from his fingers and shoved it into the driver's door pocket.

'No smoking in my car,' Peggy warned, prodding her brother in his chest. 'Those things will kill you, and I don't fancy having to put up with your ghost for decades before I eventually give up and die just to get away from you. Eat a bloody sweet or something instead.'

Peggy magnanimously ignored the mocking faces her brother made as he rifled through the glovebox to locate an open bag of Wine Gums.

'Oh God, how old are these?' Charlie moaned in horror as he put a sweet in his mouth and tried to chew. 'They're rock hard. Wine Gums aren't supposed to be *hard*.'

Peggy shrugged, then straightened. 'Hang on, DI Joyce is coming back.'

Andrew was putting something in his coat pocket as he locked the front door behind them. He didn't make eye contact with Peggy or Charlie as he climbed back into his own car and pulled away from the kerb.

'Good to know he's keeping us informed,' Charlie griped, opening the window wider so that he could spit the embalmed sweet out onto the road; it would probably burst someone's tyre in a minute.

'Just remember that this was all *your* idea, Charlie,' Peggy replied as they rejoined the main road and headed once more in the direction of Cheadle. 'If you hadn't said anything to your little friend I wouldn't be here right now, and you could be off doing whatever the hell it is that you do during the day.'

'You could have said no,' Charlie argued, and Peggy didn't need to look at him to know that he was pulling a judgemental face. 'In fact, you *did* say 'no', and then two minutes later you were agreeing to drive out here.'

'This is the right thing to do,' Peggy replied, hoping she sounded certain enough that Charlie wouldn't ask any more questions.

Truthfully, Peggy wasn't entirely sure why she'd changed her mind. It probably had something to do with how she'd decided that it was maybe finally time to actually get over what had happened last year and get on with her life. She wasn't going to tell Charlie that though. God no, he'd probably want to *talk about it*, and Peggy wasn't in the mood. She probably never would be.

'Hmm,' was all Charlie offered in response.

Peggy stayed silent and focused on the car in front. She could see Lloyd gesturing wildly in the backseat and Andrew shaking his head yet again. Why would a man so clearly sceptical about anything out of the ordinary be working with this department? Lloyd had outright said that Andrew was new, but as a Detective Inspector, surely that meant Andrew might have some sort of say in where he was stationed? Maybe he was just terrible at his job, but that seemed both uncharitable and unlikely when Peggy reasoned that he looked quite young for a Detective Inspector.

It wasn't long before Peggy followed the Belmont off Cheadle High Street and carefully parked behind Andrew on a narrow road with a neat row of terraced houses on the right-hand side, and a shorter row on the left that butted right up to the low stone wall of a churchyard

'Church Street,' Charlie said as he got out of the car and looked around. He eyed the gravestones directly across the road and wrinkled his nose slightly. 'I guess Graveyard View didn't have quite the same ring to it.'

Peggy hushed her brother as the three detectives walked over to join them.

'Right,' Andrew said sombrely, looking from one Swan sibling to the other. 'Mr and Mrs Driscoll have gone to their neighbour's house to give us some space. I'm going to go and collect the key from them, and then you have your five minutes. Not a second more, alright?'

Peggy nodded. She was ignoring the slight buzzing sound coming from across the road and was determinedly not looking towards the graveyard.

'What's wrong?' Charlie asked his sister quietly as Andrew was subsequently welcomed into the hallway of a house further up the street.

'Church, Charlie,' Peggy replied, avoiding Jen's questioning glance.

'Oh.' Charlie frowned at the gravestones. 'Noisy?'

Peggy nodded again.

'Is someone there?' Jen asked, nodding her head towards the graveyard. 'Is it Marnie?'

'No,' Peggy said as she shook her head. 'Graveyards are usually fairly quiet actually. Most people don't spend a lot of time there before they…'

Jen grimaced as Peggy trailed off. 'I see. So, what is it?'

'It's the church,' Charlie answered on her behalf, and Peggy was grateful. 'Churches are always noisy for Peggy. The devout seem to be the ones who want to be heard the most when they die, we don't really know why.'

'I used to be pretty good at switching off,' Peggy added, distracted as the door to the neighbour's house opened again. 'Otherwise, I'd never have been able to go anywhere near certain places without hearing voices trying to get my attention.'

'*Used to be*?' Lloyd asked. 'What happened?'

'Oh, nothing,' Peggy said, trying to wave it away. She'd already said more than she'd meant to. 'Just that I don't get out very much these days.'

Andrew's return thankfully halted the conversation there, and he quickly motioned for the others to follow him through the blue door of number three.

Peggy inhaled sharply as she walked through the door, and Charlie reached back to squeeze her hand gently. The sudden silence in the house after the cacophony outside was a shock.

Andrew was giving her a shrewd look from the front of the party as he stopped in the middle of the living room. Jen closed the front door behind them, and Peggy looked around.

Photographs of a baby with a shock of auburn hair hung over the television in the corner, and as Peggy turned her head she could watch the progression of Marnie growing up through the framed images. The final photograph, on the wall closest to the kitchen door, was of Marnie as a young woman, beaming at the camera as she posed in an emerald-green cocktail dress. Standing next to her was a tall, dark-haired man in a tuxedo, smiling not at the camera but directly at the woman next to him. They looked so happy that it made Peggy terribly sad just looking at it.

'That's Rex Hughes,' Jen said, seeing where Peggy was looking. 'Marnie's fiancé. He proposed on Christmas Day.'

Peggy looked away from the photo and swallowed down the sudden feeling that something was trying to crawl up and out of her chest. Now wasn't the time to dwell on any of that.

'Well?' Andrew asked impatiently, completely oblivious to Peggy's inner turmoil. 'You're running out of time.'

'Okay,' Peggy said. 'Can I go in any other rooms?'

'Here and the kitchen, that's all I'm allowing,' Andrew said.

Now that they were here in Marnie's house, Peggy could see how the DI's expression was more pinched than it had been earlier.

'And,' Andrew added, removing a black object from his coat pocket before putting it on the table, 'I just want you to know that I'm recording everything that happens here. If you say anything that turns out to be false and wastes police time then I will have evidence, and I *will* come after you.'

Peggy scowled and opened her mouth to remind Andrew that she didn't really want to be there at all.

'Three minutes,' Andrew said, obnoxiously tapping his watch and cutting her off. 'Tick tock.'

Peggy shook her head minutely at Charlie when it became obvious that the mutinous look he was throwing at Andrew might transform into physical violence if he continued to be unreasonably abrasive to his sister.

'Just stay still, all of you,' Peggy said as she closed her eyes.

She held the image of Marnie from the most recent photograph in her mind and took a measured breath through her nose before releasing it as slowly as she could manage. Peggy knew from previous experience that this all worked a lot better if she stayed calm.

Peggy blocked out the sound of traffic in the distance and focussed instead on the sound of Andrew's watch, which now sounded as though it was ticking obscenely loudly in the otherwise silent room.

For a long moment there was nothing at all except the rhythmic *tick, tick, tick*, and Peggy was ready to conclude that if Marnie *was* here, she didn't want anyone to know. But then there was a faint shuffling sound, so quiet that it was almost lost beneath the sound of

Peggy's own breathing.

'Marnie?' she asked quietly, the words not much more than a murmur.

Peggy's heart was hammering in her ears as she strained to hear the sound again, or to hear anything else out of the ordinary, but there was only silence.

Someone in the room shifted and Peggy dropped her chin to her chest in defeat. She'd lost her concentration, and she'd surely run out of time. She'd failed.

A sudden, crystal-clear image of the living room she was standing in appeared in Peggy's mind. It wasn't today though. There was a Christmas tree in the corner opposite the front door, and the fairy lights wrapped around it were glowing rainbow bright. A bottle of vodka sat on the coffee table next to a single glass tumbler, and John Peel was talking on the television.

There was a voice in her head for no more than a split second, and it was as though she saw the words rather than heard them.

Peggy's eyes snapped open, and she stumbled forward with a whisper of surprise. Andrew reached out a hand to her shoulder to steady her when she almost ploughed into him.

'What?' Andrew asked, looking just slightly apprehensive as Peggy blinked furiously.

'Did you hear Marnie?' Jen asked quietly, torn somewhere between surprise and disbelief. 'What did she say?'

Peggy shook her head as she tried to clear the shiver running up her spine and she pulled her arm away from Andrew's grasp. She felt off-kilter and really wanted to sit down, but she wasn't going to take a seat in the Driscolls' living room. She folded her arms tightly across her chest and firmly told herself to calm down.

'She didn't say anything?' Charlie asked as Peggy kept shaking her head. 'What happened, Peggy?'

'I saw this room,' Peggy said, and her voice was shaking. 'Exactly as it is now, but there was a Christmas tree. There was a bottle of vodka on the table just there, where the tape recorder is. *Top of the Pops* was on.'

Peggy saw Jen's head whip towards Lloyd and then Andrew in

surprise at the description.

'I heard Marnie,' Peggy said, scrunching her eyes shut again. 'Well, I felt it rather than heard her.'

'What did she say?' Jen asked, sounding a little desperate now. 'Peggy, what did she say?'

'Where are my shoes?'

* * *

'Shoes,' Andrew hissed to Jen as he watched Charlie carefully guide his sister back out to her car. 'Seriously? *Shoes*. She's making crap up, Jen. You know she is.'

'Shoes,' repeated Lloyd, and to Andrew's gratification, he also looked unconvinced. 'Why would a dead girl be worried about her shoes?'

Jen, however, looked thoughtful.

Andrew threw his hands up in frustration. 'Marnie doesn't care about shoes. She's *dead*, Jen. She's dead and we're absolutely no closer to solving her murder than we were this morning.'

He caught sight of his watch. Jesus Christ, it wasn't even three o'clock yet. He deflated even further when he realised that the end of the day wasn't going to mean the end of his time with these people. This was his life now.

'Hang on a second,' said Jen, frowning down at the carpet. She pointed at various objects in the room in silence, before looking to Lloyd. 'Case file?'

Lloyd held out the file to Jen. 'What is it?'

Jen flipped through the pages before turning the file around so to present her colleagues with the photo of Marnie's body on the kitchen floor. 'Look.'

Andrew shook his head. 'Look at what?'

'Her feet,' Jen replied, tapping the photo with her finger.

'She's not wearing any shoes,' Lloyd said slowly. 'Holy crap!'

Andrew held up a warning finger. 'That doesn't prove anything.'

Jen ignored him. 'Marnie's got her jacket on over her dress, so she's ready to go as soon as her friend arrives, right? They're already late for the party, but she's *not* wearing her shoes.'

'Why wouldn't she have her shoes on if she's ready to go?' Lloyd asked. 'Do you think the killer took them off her after she died?'

'Carpet,' Andrew said, pointing at the floor. 'She was probably waiting to put her shoes on at the last minute. They were probably by the front door. Mystery solved.'

'Mystery *not* solved,' Jen said, flicking through the case file again. 'There are photos of every inch of this part of the house, and the only shoes by the front door are a pair of old winter boots.'

'So, she was planning to wear boots to the party,' Andrew said, shrugging. 'It was January.'

Jen looked incredulous. 'Look around you. In any photo of Marnie, is she dressed anything less than impeccably? She was going to her friend's party, and she was all dolled up. She wouldn't wear a pair of ratty old boots outside.'

Andrew held his hand out for the file and took his time scanning each photo. Jen was correct; there was a photograph of every room downstairs, from every possible angle. There wasn't a single other pair of shoes to be seen.

'What about upstairs?' Andrew asked eventually. 'Maybe she left her shoes upstairs. She was going to run up and grab them when her friend arrived?'

'Seems unlikely,' Lloyd said, shaking his head. 'Her friend was already late, right? Why wouldn't Marnie be ready to go as soon as she called?'

Andrew ran a hand over his face. It did seem unlikely, even if it wasn't impossible. He still didn't believe that Peggy had 'heard' from Marnie - that really *was* impossible – but he couldn't quite forget the oddly vacant look on her face as she'd stumbled across the room towards him. There had been something unnatural about it, and he didn't care to see it again any time soon.

'Alright,' Andrew said. 'Jen, can you very quickly go upstairs and check Marnie's bedroom? Mrs Driscoll said that they haven't touched anything since before she died.'

Jen nodded and hurried up the staircase.

Charlie had left the front door open when he and Peggy had gone outside, and Andrew could hear the two of them talking quietly outside. Not loud enough to discern the words, but he could tell from the tone that Charlie was concerned about his sister.

Jen came hurrying down the stairs so quickly that Andrew was worried that she'd overshoot the living room and run straight out onto the pavement. She was clutching a white, cardboard shoebox in her hand.

'Sir, I think Peggy might be right,' Jen said, breathlessly waving the shoebox at Andrew.

Andrew took the box, frowning when he realised that it was empty. 'How does this help exactly?'

'Look at the label on the side,' Jen said pointing to an illustration of a shoe and a few lines of text next to it. 'One pair of gold strappy heels, size five.'

'And?' Andrew said, looking to Lloyd who only shrugged in confusion. 'It's empty.'

'Exactly,' Jen said. 'It's *empty*. That box was on the floor next to Marnie's bed, even though all of her other shoes were stacked neatly in their boxes by her wardrobe. I had a quick look around the room, and there wasn't anything even remotely matching the description of that label. Wherever those shoes are, they aren't in this house.'

Andrew lifted the lid on the shoe box, secretly hoping that the shoes would somehow magically appear and halt the train to Fantasyland that Jen and Lloyd seemed to have already boarded. No such luck though; the box remained stubbornly shoe-less. However, there was something underneath the tissue paper lining the box.

'What's that?' Jen asked as Andrew pulled a folded piece of paper out of the box.

Andrew unfolded the paper and huffed out a slight laugh of disbelief. They'd actually found something not mentioned in the crime scene report.

'It's a receipt from Kendals,' Andrew said, handing it over to Jen. 'These shoes were purchased on the thirtieth of December; only a few days before Marnie was killed.'

'So, she likely bought them to wear to the party,' Jen said, eyes scanning the paper in her hand. 'Look here, it says they were purchased on a Kendals credit account.'

'What is it?' Andrew asked as Jen's eyes widened almost comically.

'These shoes were really, *really* expensive,' Jen explained. 'There's no way that Marnie could have afforded these. This must be someone else's account.'

Andrew shook his head, trying to reign in the sense of excitement he always had when he'd spotted something that nobody else had. 'Well, I think we might have a pretty good idea of who that might be.'

'Rex Hughes,' Jen breathed in understanding as Andrew nodded at her.

'Right, let's get back to Tib Street,' Andrew said. 'Tomorrow we're going to pay a visit to Rex Hughes.'

'What about Peggy and Charlie?' Jen asked, gesturing towards outside. 'Peggy's really helped us out here.'

Andrew looked out through the front door and focused on the churchyard beyond. He couldn't accept that Marnie was communicating with them from beyond the grave. Maybe Peggy had just made a lucky guess, or maybe there was something more sinister about this whole situation. Either way, he needed to get to the bottom of it all.

'Let's take them to Tib Street too,' Andrew said eventually, his eyes narrowing slightly. 'Maybe Higson can get Miss Swan to tell us how she *really* knew about the shoes.'

* * *

'What *is* this place?' Charlie asked, clearly delighted as he followed Andrew up the first ornate staircase at Tib Street. 'It's actually a secret headquarters, isn't it?'

Andrew clenched his jaw to stop himself yelling at Charlie in frustration. Charlie's enthusiasm for anything and everything appeared to be boundless, and Andrew didn't understand why he couldn't just shut up for a second.

'This is the Ballroom,' Lloyd explained, because he was as irritatingly cheerful as Charlie about this whole place. 'The Division's been based here since nineteen-twelve. We only really use the Ballroom itself now. There's not much need for the other floors when the team is so small, and the other rooms are really just for storage.'

Well, that answered some questions Andrew had about the rest of the building. How odd that the Force would continue to pay for such an enormous building in the city centre though.

He looked over his shoulder as they reached the second-floor landing. Jen was talking quietly to Peggy, who still looked pale and drawn. Andrew wasn't feeling charitable and was content to assume that this was because Peggy wouldn't stand up to any interrogation from DCI Higson, and she knew it.

Andrew threw open the Ballroom doors and stalked through. He was disgruntled to see that Higson didn't so much as blink in surprise at the sudden intrusion.

'Ah, Joyce,' Higson greeted him, pausing with a biscuit mid-dunk in his Styrofoam cup of tea. 'And we seem to have some guests. I wasn't aware we were running a hostel.'

'Charles and Margaret Swan, sir,' Jen said, when it became clear that Andrew wasn't going to offer any information as he threw his coat over the back of his chair and took a seat at his desk. 'They're assisting with the Marnie Driscoll case.'

'Parker's friend,' Higson said, around a mouthful of Rich Tea, pointing at Charlie. 'Charles Swan, you say?'

'Yes, sir,' Charlie said chipperly, and Andrew rolled his eyes because the unfailing enthusiasm hadn't dimmed one iota.

'Any relation to William Swan?'

'Our father.' Charlie nodded.

'Hmm,' said Higson. He went back to his tea and biscuits.

'We have a lead on the Driscoll case, sir,' Jen said, gesturing for Peggy and Charlie to take a seat. 'We believe that a pair of shoes has been removed from the scene.'

'Shoes,' Higson repeated slowly, and for just a moment Andrew genuinely thought that Higson was going to laugh at them. Instead, the DCI eventually gestured for Jen to carry on.

'Peggy, er, Miss Swan-'

'I was under the impression that it should actually be Lady Margaret Swan,' Higson said conversationally as he plucked another biscuit from the ever-decreasing stack on his desk.

'And that one,' Higson then pointed at Charlie, 'I believe, is Viscount Ashley.'

Andrew looked over at the siblings again. He'd seen the sprawling house and grounds with his own eyes, and he'd tried to address Peggy properly earlier, but sitting here in Tib Street it seemed ridiculous that the two of them had titles. It was 1986, for God's sake. Then again, at least it meant that the force probably wouldn't have to pay them anything for their 'assistance'.

'Formalities aren't necessary,' Peggy said quietly, and Andrew thought she might actually sound embarrassed.

Peggy seemed to have lost all of the confidence she'd possessed back at Butterton. She wasn't glaring at Andrew, for a start, and seemed to be concentrating very hard on the polished wood of the floor. She looked more distracted than concerned, and Andrew found it quite off-putting.

'Peggy was able to briefly communicate with Marnie Driscoll,' Jen explained.

Higson dropped his biscuit and rubbed his hands together. 'Is that right?'

Andrew leaned forward, waiting for the DCI to tear Peggy to shreds. He almost felt bad for her. After all, she seemed nice enough underneath all the ridiculous lying. He wondered what sort of childhood resulted in someone growing up to pretend that they can speak to ghosts; the same sort of childhood that formed adults who thought purple velvet was appropriate casualwear, Andrew supposed.

'And how did you develop this talent?' Higson asked, looking at Peggy appraisingly.

'I don't know,' Peggy replied, eyes still downcast.

'Alright, how old were you when you first realised what you were doing then?'

Okay, this did *not* sound like Higson was about to turn Peggy inside out for being a liar and a fraud. Andrew rubbed his eyes thinking that maybe if he did it hard enough he'd just wake up in his bed and none of this would have really happened to him.

'Five,' Peggy stated. She obviously wasn't planning to elaborate on that simple answer.

Higson nodded. 'Hmm. The only true Medium I've ever encountered was in New Orleans, years ago now.'

Andrew dropped his head into his hands in disgust. Great, Higson was clearly off his rocker, and now Andrew knew that he needed to get out of there quickly. Jen and Lloyd were obviously already experiencing some sort of Stockholm Syndrome.

'I wouldn't call myself a Medium,' Peggy replied, finally looking up at Higson.

'Then what would you call yourself?' Higson asked, and now it seemed that his eyes were boring into Peggy and that the answer to this question was important.

'Nothing,' Peggy replied eventually. 'I wouldn't call myself anything. I don't usually talk about it, and I certainly don't seek out situations like this.'

'Yet, you agreed to help,' Higson continued. 'Why? We won't be able to compensate you.'

'I have no interest in money,' Peggy replied, and Andrew was surprised to hear how much resentment coloured that response.

Higson nodded, seemingly satisfied. 'Alright. DS Cusack, won't you continue?'

Peggy curled further in on herself as Jen explained what had happened at the Driscoll house. Andrew didn't miss the worried looks Charlie was shooting his sister, and even Lloyd looked like he might be about to offer help, or at least tea.

'Good work,' Higson concluded with a nod. 'What do you plan to do next? Joyce?'

Andrew straightened in his chair. He was going to solve this case, and he was going to do it without any more 'spiritual' intervention. 'I think we should pay Rex Hughes a visit first thing tomorrow, and we should follow up on the Kendals receipt.'

'I can go to Kendals before they open to the public in the morning,' Lloyd offered. 'Might make it easier to find the right person to speak to.'

'Fine,' Andrew agreed. 'DS Cusack, you'll come with me to question Mr Hughes then.'

'And what do we do?' Charlie asked, brightening slightly.

'Absolutely nothing,' Andrew replied steadily, moderating any glee out of his voice. 'Thank you for your time today, but we no longer require your services.'

'Hold your horses there, Joyce,' Higson said, reclaiming the previously discarded biscuit.

Andrew bristled. 'Sir, I fail to see how continuing to indulge any of this nonsense is going to find closure for Mr and Mrs Driscoll. Now, we may have had a lucky break with the shoebox today, but-'

'DI Joyce, if you don't wish to *indulge* my instructions any longer, then may I remind you that nobody is forcing you to be here, and you are more than welcome to leave at any point.' Higson's face was impassive, but the words were cold and sharp.

'Sir,' Andrew gritted out. It wasn't apologetic, but it was as non-combative as he could stomach at that moment.

'Tell me,' Higson said, turning back to Peggy, 'can you see him?'

'Who?' Peggy asked, sounding almost guilty as her eyes went back to the floor.

'Try again, Miss Swan.' Higson's expression hardened. 'I've watched you glance at the wall behind my desk six times in the past few minutes.'

She had? Andrew hadn't noticed that at all, and he usually prided himself on noticing *everything*.

If it were possible, Peggy paled further under Higson's scrutiny.

'Peggy?' Charlie asked carefully. 'Are you alright?'

Peggy met Higson's gaze. 'He says you need to stop eating so much crap for breakfast. He saw the third pasty, even if nobody else did.'

Higson, to Andrew's great surprise, laughed loudly, slapping his hands on his knees. 'I *knew* it was him!'

'What?' Lloyd looked at everyone in confusion. 'What's going on?'

'Anything else?' Higson asked, and now he was *smiling*.

Peggy glanced guiltily at Andrew for just a split second, and Andrew frowned.

'Well?' Higson asked, still grinning. 'Come on, he never could shut up, so that can't be all of it.'

'He said your new DI has quite the stick up his arse,' Peggy said quietly, wincing as Andrew's eyes widened in outrage.

Higson roared with laughter again. 'Well, he's right about that.'

Andrew's mouth dropped open. Twenty-four hours ago, he'd thought he'd commanded a perfectly normal amount of respect from his colleagues. He didn't expect special treatment, but this was unbelievable.

'I think he'll be alright eventually though,' Higson added, still smiling at Peggy before turning to the wall behind him. 'Good to hear from you, you old bastard.'

'Could someone please explain what's going on?' Lloyd asked, looking between Higson and Peggy in confusion.

Higson waved towards Peggy as though granting her permission to explain, even though she hadn't asked for anything of the sort.

'DI Benson sends his regards,' Peggy said in a small voice. She had started picking at her fingernails and it was making Andrew twitch.

Jen and Lloyd looked at each other, dumbfounded.

'Who the fu-' Andrew cut himself with a deep, calming breath. 'Who the *hell* is DI Benson?'

Higson looked over and grinned at Andrew. 'You're sitting in his chair.'

FOUR

When Andrew woke on Wednesday morning, he was surprised that it was to the sound of his alarm clock ringing. When he'd finally climbed into bed the night before, after a long evening of Kate continuing to ignore his calls, he'd been utterly convinced that there was no way that he'd be able to fall asleep. The sheer absurdity of everything else that had happened at Tib Street and in Cheadle had been crowned by learning that his predecessor – one Detective Inspector Chris Benson – had died a few months earlier, and, according to a certain *Lady* Margaret Swan, said predecessor was still present in the Ballroom.

Andrew had left Tib Street shortly after Peggy's declaration. He'd practically run to his car and barely stopped for red lights the whole way to Gatley. During the drive home, he'd managed to convince himself that this must be some sort of elaborate prank by Higson. The DCI must have called Peggy Swan and given her the information about Benson. Maybe even Jen or Lloyd had been feeding her notes about the case throughout the day.

But *why*?

He hadn't been able to answer that, and so he had gone off to the pub for a solitary pint to try and take his mind off all of it.

In the light of a new morning, he decided to take the only rational course of action left available to him: he would simply call CID to request a meeting with Chambers. Surely if Andrew explained what was going on at Tib Street he'd be welcomed back to CID with open arms.

Decision made, Andrew felt much lighter as he drove to the address written on the piece of paper Jen had handed to him just before he'd left the day before.

Rex Hughes's house was only ten minutes or so from Andrew's own, but the difference was stark. The neat, semi-detached house that Andrew had inherited from his mother was dwarfed by the building hiding behind the enormous electric gates. Doric columns on either side of the front door reminded Andrew of the Swans' house, albeit this was on a significantly smaller scale. The house had clearly only been built in the past few years, but everything about it suggested that the inhabitants had a taste for the finer, older things in life and the building aspired to be just so.

A hand lightly rapped on the passenger window, and Andrew jumped, clutching his chest in surprise. Jen was peering in at him, and he could see her own car parked a little further up the road behind her.

'Morning, sir,' she said with a nod. The easier familiarity of yesterday had obviously cooled slightly, perhaps due to Andrew all but storming out of the Ballroom.

Andrew gestured for her to take the passenger seat. 'Good morning. Have you been here long?'

'No, just a few minutes,' Jen replied as Andrew slowly directed the car towards the gate. 'I don't live too far away from here. I checked in with Lloyd before I left the house. He was just about to head to Kendals, so hopefully he'll have something useful for us by the time we get back into town.'

Andrew nodded. He rolled down his window and reached out to press the intercom button. It buzzed loudly, but after a few seconds, there was still no answer.

'Four cars in the driveway,' Jen said, peering through the gaps in the gate. 'Surely that means someone is home.'

Andrew agreed. He pressed the button again, holding it for a good second or so longer than could be considered polite.

'For God's sake, have some patience,' came a clipped, condescending female voice a moment later, static crackling at the edge of every word. 'What is it?'

'Greater Manchester Police,' Andrew replied calmly. 'We'd like to speak to Reginald Hughes.'

'Oh, I'm terribly sorry,' the woman said after a short pause, although Andrew didn't think she sounded terribly sorry at all. 'I didn't mean to be rude. Do come in.'

An extended buzz, followed by a distinct clanking sound came a moment later, and the two gates began to swing inwards. Andrew slowly drove forwards, eventually parking behind a bright red Ferrari Testarossa.

Jen let out a low whistle. 'Someone's doing well for himself.'

'Isn't he just?' Andrew replied, trying to work out how much the four cars on the driveway must have cost to buy. Every figure he came up with just made him uneasy.

Back in CID, everything Andrew had heard about Rex Hughes had led him to firmly believe that Hughes was tied up with the Byrnes and their network of drugs, guns, and violent crime, but it was impossible to find anything concrete on him. It had pissed Andrew off then, and now, sitting here on the driveway, it pissed him off even more.

Any idea who the utter delight that buzzed us in could be?' Andrew asked, nodding towards the file in Jen's lap.

'Rex's mother, Rosa, and his sister, Athena, both live here too,' Jen replied, checking her notes carefully. 'I suppose it could have been either of them. Or a girlfriend, maybe?'

Andrew thought back to the photograph of Marnie lying on the kitchen floor. 'I hope not.'

The front door opened, and a statuesque blonde appeared. She was dressed in white from head to toe, and with strings of pearls draped around the high neck of her dress she reminded Andrew of a photo of Lady Di he'd seen in one of Kate's magazines a few weeks earlier. It was only eight-thirty in the morning though, so it all seemed a little much to him for this time of day.

'I think that's the sister,' Jen said out of the corner of her mouth as she prepared to open the car door.

'Good, because I was really hoping it wasn't his mother.'

Jen snorted slightly before composing herself and following Andrew's lead of stepping out of the car.

'Good morning, officers,' the woman said primly, elegantly sweeping down the front steps to stand before them. 'So sorry again about my abruptness. I'm not much of a morning person.'

'Not a problem,' Andrew replied, with a polite smile. 'Detective Inspector Andrew Joyce, Greater Manchester Police. This is Detective Sergeant Jennifer Cusack.'

'Good to meet you both,' the woman said as she nodded at each in turn. She shot them the barest hint of a smile. 'I'm Athena Hughes. Rex is my younger brother. Can I ask what this is about?'

Andrew nodded for Jen to take over; she knew this case better than him, after all.

'We're from the Case Re-examination Department, Ms Hughes,' Jen explained. 'We're going back over anything and everything related to Miss Driscoll's death, and we just have a few follow-up questions for your brother about some of Marnie's belongings.'

Athena's face crumpled slightly at the mention of Marnie before she tilted her jaw up defiantly. 'Of course. Rex was just taking a phone call when you arrived, but if you follow me, you're very welcome to wait in the house.'

'Thank you,' Jen said graciously.

Athena led them into the entrance hall. Andrew didn't think he'd ever seen so many reflective surfaces in one place before. An enormous chandelier hung above their heads, and the white-tiled floor was practically glowing beneath his feet.

The room Athena eventually paused in was a large living room, with two pristine, cream-coloured sofas, and a matching armchair. A marble fireplace even larger than the one in the library at Butterton took up most of the far wall, and the shelves opposite were filled with an eclectic mix of ornaments. The room screamed 'expensive', and Andrew was half-convinced that they probably wouldn't be allowed to sit on the furniture without a plastic sheet between their clothes and the cushions.

'Please make yourselves comfortable,' Athena said, gesturing towards the sofas. 'I'll see if Rex is off the phone yet, and I'll ask Mary to send a pot of coffee through.'

'Please don't go to any trouble,' Andrew replied. 'We really just need a few minutes with your brother and then we'll be on our way again.'

Athena smiled and left them to it.

'Same photograph as at the Driscolls',' Jen said, nodding towards the framed photo of Marnie and Rex on the mantlepiece as she sat down. Marnie's green dress was the only real flash of colour in the whole room.

'It doesn't feel very lived in, does it?' Jen asked as she wrinkled her nose at their surroundings,

Andrew had to agree. When he'd been considering whether or not to sell his mother's house, he'd gone to have a look around a couple of show homes on the new estates that seemed to be popping up everywhere, and even they had felt more inhabited than this room. This place was more like an exhibition of affluence than a home.

Athena reappeared a moment later, this time with her brother in tow.

'I'll leave you to it,' Athena said, gently squeezing her brother's shoulder. 'Let me know if there's anything I can do to help.'

Andrew nodded his thanks and gave his full attention to the new arrival.

Rex Hughes looked nothing like the smiling, handsome man in the photograph with Marnie. His hair was longer than it had been then, but it seemed more likely the product of missed cuts rather than any attempt at style. His eyes were puffy, and the bags beneath them discoloured his skin with a bruise-like purple. In contrast to his impeccable sister, Rex Hughes looked absolutely terrible, and Andrew was somewhat taken aback.

'Detectives,' Rex said, and even his voice was hoarse and brittle. 'I'm sorry to have kept you waiting. If I'd known you were coming, I would have rescheduled my call.'

'Not at all, Mr Hughes,' Andrew said, rising to his feet to shake Rex's hand as he introduced himself and Jen again. 'I'm sorry that we've arrived unannounced.'

Andrew wasn't actually remotely sorry, but Rex didn't need to know that, did he?

'Athena says you're here about Marnie?' Rex's voice shook slightly. 'Have you found something?'

'We're not sure at this stage, but we hope so,' Andrew replied steadily. 'Our team is re-examining all evidence that's been gathered up to this point, so we're hoping to speak to everyone involved with the case again. I apologise if this means that you're giving answers to questions that you've already been asked.'

Rex shook his head and took a seat in the armchair. He ran his hand over his chin and looked imploringly at Andrew. 'Ask me anything at all, Inspector Joyce. If anything I say can help you find who did this to my Marnie I'll answer your questions a hundred times over.'

Andrew hadn't been expecting such direct compliance, and that, coupled with the dishevelled state of the man before him, was almost enough to make Andrew doubt himself. It made sense that Marnie could have been a target because of Rex's connections to the Byrnes, and, if Rex himself didn't already have a rock-solid alibi for the night of the murder, he would be a prime suspect himself. Andrew had been expecting resistance to any further questioning, or maybe just a half-arsed impersonation of gradually fading sorrow, but he hadn't actually anticipated that he might need to consider that perhaps Rex Hughes genuinely didn't know anything about Marnie's murder. Andrew liked to consider himself quite decent at reading people's true intentions, and right then he wasn't getting anything more than sincerity and raw grief from Rex Hughes.

Jen raised her eyebrows at Andrew, silently asking if she could start questioning Rex. Andrew nodded and kept his eyes firmly on Rex.

'Mr Hughes, would you mind taking us through the circumstances of meeting Marnie for the first time?' Jen asked.

Rex nodded slowly. 'I'd gone into town to meet an old friend for lunch. Afterwards, I thought I might have a quick look for a birthday present for Athena before heading home. I popped into Lewis's as I was that side of the city.

'Athena's great at buying gifts, and I'm crap at it, so I thought that if I went to the Perfume Hall I'd probably find a salesgirl who could help me choose something Athena would like. I saw Marnie as soon as I walked in. She was laughing with another girl, and I knew I wanted to go over there and talk to her.

'I did just that, and when I left twenty minutes later I had a bottle of *Beautiful* for Athena, and a date with Marnie for the following Saturday.'

Rex paused and looked down at his hands. 'I wonder sometimes, you know, about what might have happened if I hadn't gone to Lewis's that day, or if I hadn't met Marnie. Would she still be alive?'

'Why do you say that, Mr Hughes?' Jen asked. Her voice was still gentle, but Andrew could hear the suspicion colouring her words. 'Do you think Marnie's death had something to do with you?'

'I don't know,' Rex said quietly as he looked up again. 'I don't know.'

Jen narrowed her eyes. 'Mr Hughes, is there something you're not telling us? Is there anyone you can think of who might have wanted to hurt Marnie because of her association with you?'

'No,' Rex said, shaking his head more vehemently.

Andrew wanted to outright ask Rex if he thought Marnie's death was the work of the Byrnes, but he had no grounds to do that here, besides, if Rex shut them out now they might miss out on learning something useful.

'What I meant,' Rex continued, 'was that everyone knows my family. They know *me*, and they know how much money we have. What if that was the reason? What if they didn't actually mean to kill Marnie? What if they were just going to kidnap her and ask for ransom money?'

It wasn't actually a terrible theory, Andrew thought, but Jen's case file showed that they had found no evidence that this was a kidnapping gone wrong. It could easily be the desperate musings of a grieving man looking to find a reason for his fiancée's death, or, as Andrew was more inclined to believe when it came to anyone suspected of being involved with organised crime, it was a conscious effort to divert the police's attention elsewhere. Andrew would not be diverted.

'Obviously, we're looking into all possibilities, Mr Hughes,' Andrew said levelly, 'but at this time it doesn't seem likely that a kidnapping was planned.'

Rex sighed tiredly and gave one short nod.

'Mr Hughes, did you often buy Marnie gifts?' Jen asked.

'Of course,' Rex confirmed, slightly nonplussed. 'What's that got to do with anything?'

'When we visited Marnie's home yesterday, we noticed that there were a couple of items missing from her bedroom,' Jen said, carefully watching Rex's face for a reaction.

Rex sat up straighter, looking surprised. 'What was missing? Why has nobody mentioned this before?'

'As I said, we're re-examining everything in detail,' Jen replied, keeping her voice even. 'Did you buy anything for Marnie in the days before her death?'

'Probably.' Rex frowned before his eyes widened suddenly. 'Yes, yes, I did. I met her and her friend Rebecca for lunch. The girls had been to Kendals, looking for outfits to wear for the party they were going to later that week.'

Rex crumpled again. 'That was where Marnie was supposed to be the night she was killed.'

'Do you need a moment?' Jen asked quietly.

'No. No, I'm sorry, no.' Rex shook his head and cleared his throat. 'The girls had found a pair of gold shoes. I bought them for Marnie, even though she thought they were far too expensive. I liked spoiling her. She was special, and she deserved to know that.'

'Did you buy anything else for her that day?' Jen asked. 'Or in the weeks leading up to then?'

'Not the same day.' Rex shook his head again. 'Just lunch for the three of us. I gave her a pair of pearl earrings for Christmas, and some leather gloves. Oh, and the CD player too. She really liked that Dire Straits song. Oh, what's it called? The one with the opening bit that everyone knows?'

'*Walk of Life*,' Jen and Andrew answered simultaneously.

'Yeah, that one,' Rex said, and his smile lingered for a couple of seconds before his face fell. 'She loved that song. I thought she was probably going to wear out the tape from listening to it on the way to work. I bought her the CD player so that she could listen to it at home instead.'

Jen frowned as she flipped through the file on her knee.

'Is there a problem?' Rex asked.

'Where did Marnie keep the CD player?' Jen asked, running her finger down each piece of paper. 'In the living room?'

'No,' Rex said, shaking his head. 'Her Mum prefers watching television, so Marnie kept it up in her bedroom. I always told her that when we got married she'd be able to listen to her music as loud as she wanted.'

'DS Cusack?' Andrew asked pointedly, as Jen's frown deepened.

Jen looked up and handed the file to Andrew. 'Sir, there's no record of a CD player in Marnie's bedroom listed in the case file, and I didn't see one yesterday.'

'Well, that can't be right,' Rex said.

'Where did you purchase the CD player, Mr Hughes?' Andrew asked as he skimmed the papers in his hand.

'Kendals,' Rex replied. 'It's near my office. I have a credit account there.'

'Do you think you can remember everything you purchased from Kendals for Marnie?' Andrew asked sharply.

'I can try,' Rex said, still looking baffled. 'They should have all of the records held at the shop, though. Why?'

'I have a theory, Mr Hughes,' Andrew said, closing the case file and handing it back to Jen, 'and I need you to help me prove it.'

* * *

Peggy shook her head at the sign proclaiming *Cheryl Richard Dance Studio*.

'Remind me how you got me to agree to come back here?' she asked her brother as he knocked on the door, and then pressed the doorbell for good measure; it didn't ring.

'Oh, come on,' Charlie grinned, 'you can't tell me that you aren't delighted that people actually believe you for once. Plus, we get to help solve a murder. How cool is that?'

'I'm not sure 'murder' and 'cool' are supposed to go together in a positive sentence, you know,' Peggy muttered as Charlie rang the doorbell again.

Before Charlie could reply, the door swung open to reveal a short, elderly woman with what Peggy would only be able to describe as a bird's nest of hair surrounding her face. Her eyes narrowed as they darted between the Swans before her face suddenly broke into what was probably supposed to be a friendly smile. It looked much too like a snarl for Peggy's comfort.

'Hello there, madam,' Charlie said politely, looking positively thrilled to have discovered yet another person connected to the Ballroom.

'Madam!' The woman howled with laughter. 'That's two of youse callin' me *madam* now. I'm not the bloody Queen.'

'Oh, aren't you?' Charlie grinned. 'I could have sworn you were.'

The woman practically hooted. 'Yer a cheeky one, ain't youse?'

Peggy noted that Charlie did nothing to deny it; in fact, he only smiled even wider.

'I'm Charlie, this is my sister Peggy. We're here to see DCI Higson.'

'Youse must me the poshos,' the woman said, looking between the two of them again. 'Lloyd mentioned ye on his way out to Kendals this mornin'.'

'Yes, I suppose that would be us,' Charlie replied gleefully. 'And *you* are?'

'Dolly,' she replied, before turning to stare directly at Peggy. 'And girlie 'ere speaks to ghosties? Isn't that right?'

'Well,' Peggy started 'I-'

'Me auntie used to do that too,' Dolly butted in. 'Used to light a bloody load of candles and then yell at 'er 'usband. 'E were dead then, obviously.'

'Brilliant!' Charlie said, still grinning.

'Oh God, not her.'

Peggy turned in surprise at the new voice. Andrew was looking at Dolly warily as he walked up Tib Street towards them with Jen at his side.

'Charmin'!' Dolly yelled, before letting out such a hacking cough that Peggy thought one of Dolly's lungs might actually be making a break for freedom. After a long moment, the coughing subsided, and Dolly pounded her fist against her chest a few times.

'Good morning.' Jen smiled at everyone and then nodded to Peggy. 'Thanks for coming back.'

Andrew muttered something too quietly for Peggy to hear.

'Oi!' Dolly snapped at him. 'Is you bein' rude over there, Pretty Boy?'

'*Pretty Boy*?' Andrew was the very picture of appalled.

'That's what I said,' replied Dolly dangerously. 'If I c-'

'Alright!' Jen announced brightly, stepping slightly in front of Andrew and grasping Dolly's arm at the same time. 'We do need to be getting on, Doll. If you wouldn't mind, that is?'

'Course not, Jen, love,' Dolly said, tone much cheerier again. 'Yer a busy girl.'

Dolly stepped out of the doorway and graciously waved everyone through. She grabbed Peggy's arm as she walked by.

'Bit of a curse about you, ain't there?' Dolly's eyes darkened as her bony fingers tightened around Peggy's wrist. 'You be careful, girlie. Youse don't want to end up like the ones you talk to.'

'Um,' Peggy replied stupidly. For a split second, she had the unsettling feeling that Dolly was somehow seeing straight through her, and she shivered despite the warmth of the morning.

'Oh, just ignore her,' Andrew said, sidestepping the pair of women. 'She's mad as a box of frogs.'

Dolly growled, letting go of Peggy in an attempt to lunge at Andrew. He was saved only by Charlie grasping Dolly's two hands.

'Delightful to meet you, Dolly,' Charlie said enthusiastically. 'May we meet again soon.'

'Lovely manners, this one,' Dolly said delightedly, reaching up to pat Charlie on both cheeks before heading off down a corridor behind the main staircase with just a short, final glare at Andrew.

'You can thank me for saving your life later, DI Joyce,' Charlie laughed as Andrew stared at him in horror.

Andrew shuddered and waved for everyone to go ahead up the staircase ahead of him.

Peggy watched Dolly until she disappeared through a door in the distance. There was something about her that set Peggy on edge. It was something more than Dolly just being a somewhat terrifying old lady, but Peggy, for the life of her, couldn't say what.

'She's probably got a whole witchy hovel back there somewhere,' Andrew said suddenly from behind her, making Peggy jump in surprise.

'I thought you didn't believe in that sort of thing, DI Joyce,' Peggy replied primly, following Jen and Charlie up the stairs.

'Oh, I don't,' Andrew scoffed, 'but that doesn't mean that *she* doesn't believe it. Totally mad.'

Peggy felt that the comment was probably aimed at her as well as Dolly. She was under no illusions about DI Joyce and his obstinate refusal to accept anything out of the ordinary. Once, perhaps not even that long ago, Peggy would have revelled in finding ways to prove him wrong, but right now she just didn't have the heart to try.

'Oh, come off it, Dolly's completely harmless,' Jen laughed as they rounded the final corner. 'She just likes unsettling people.'

Well, she's managed that beautifully, thought Peggy.

When they'd arrived the day before, Peggy hadn't really taken in her surroundings. Her stomach had been twisted in knots since they'd arrived at the Driscoll house, and she'd felt like she'd needed to sleep for a week by the time they'd reached Tib Street. The further surprise of seeing the recently deceased DI Benson standing by the window had felt like the final straw.

Today though, DI Benson didn't seem to be in the Ballroom, and

Peggy finally took in the surprisingly ostentatious surroundings. How had this weird little department sprung up in the first place, and why on *earth* were they in this building now?

Peggy was surprised to be back here at all, but the fact that Higson seemed to believe her, along with Jen and Lloyd, had bolstered her confidence in a way that she hadn't experienced in a long time.

'Ah, good. You're all here,' DCI Higson said, waving a half-eaten Eccles cake around as he rotated his desk chair to face the new arrivals. 'Now maybe Parker here will stop acting like he's about to wet himself in excitement and share what he's learned this morning.'

Lloyd looked a little bit outraged.

'I wanted to tell you as soon as I got back from Kendals, but you sent me out to get your breakfast!' He pointed at the Eccles cake. 'Then you told me to sit down, shut up, and wait for everyone else to get here!'

'Did I?' Higson mused, contemplating a stray currant that had abseiled down his beard onto his desk.

'Yes!' Lloyd rolled his eyes but immediately adopted a much more contrite expression when Higson's gaze sharpened slightly. 'I mean, yes, *sir*.'

'Well, get on with it then,' Higson said as he scrunched up the now empty paper bag and threw it towards the wastepaper bin. It missed spectacularly, but nobody moved to pick it up.

'Right,' said Lloyd, shaking out his shoulders and looking down at the notepad he was holding. 'The accounts department confirmed that it was Rex Hughes's credit account used to purchase the missing shoes, just like we thought.'

Lloyd paused and looked around the group. 'What's weird, though, is that the shoes were returned to the shop about a month after Marnie was killed.'

'What?' Jen asked in surprise. 'Rex returned them?'

'No. Not personally anyway,' Lloyd replied. 'I looked back at all the paperwork they had for his account and compared signatures. The only two people who had previously returned items for that account are Rex himself, and his sister Athena once or twice. The signature matches neither.'

'Rex could have just disguised his signature if he thought the return might somehow be traced back to him,' Jen said, looking to Andrew for confirmation. 'Right?'

'Maybe, but why return the shoes in the first place?' Andrew asked, frowning. 'Surely disposing of them would be easier.'

'They were really expensive though, weren't they?' Jen said.

'I don't think Rex Hughes would be worried about losing a few hundred pounds,' Andrew replied. 'Jen, you saw that house this morning. He doesn't need to worry about money.'

'It definitely wasn't him anyway,' Lloyd said, tapping his notebook. 'The girl I spoke to said it definitely wasn't Rex or Athena Hughes. She remembered her boss dealing with the return, but only because of the special circumstances.'

Andrew tilted his head in question. 'What special circumstances?'

'It was a larger than usual return, and the person returning the items wanted the refund paid in cash rather than as credit,' Lloyd explained. 'That meant someone from Accounts had to go down to the shop floor and confirm everything.'

'It wasn't just the shoes?' Jen asked in surprise.

'Nope.' Lloyd checked his notes again. 'Besides the shoes, there were seven other items.'

'Was there a CD player?' Andrew asked.

Lloyd looked taken aback. 'Yeah, there was. How did you know?'

'Do you want to have a guess at what else might be on the list, Jen?' Andrew asked.

'Leather gloves?' Jen offered.

Lloyd's eyes widened further. 'Seriously, *how* do you know that?'

'Jesus, you were right, sir,' Jen said, shaking her head at Andrew.

'Gold shoes, CD player, leather gloves, pearl earrings, cashmere blanket, gold bracelet, black beaded necklace, and an emerald brooch,' Andrew said, handing over his notes to an astonished Lloyd.

'What? No cuddly toy?' Higson deadpanned.

'Are you psychic, DI Joyce?' Charlie asked, clapping his hands together.

'Charlie, hush.' Peggy elbowed her brother in the ribs.

'Go on then, Joyce,' Higson said, shooting his officer a speculative look, 'amaze us. How did you know what Lloyd was going to say?'

'When we spoke to Rex Hughes this morning, he mentioned that he'd purchased a CD player as a Christmas gift for Marnie,' Andrew explained. 'DS Cusack noticed that the inventory of the crime scene, and indeed of Marnie's bedroom, didn't list a CD player among the items.

'Marnie had lots of trinkets in her bedroom, along with a few other items of obvious value, but we knew that only very specific things had been taken; the engagement ring, the shoes, and the CD player. We asked Hughes to give us a list of everything he'd bought on his Kendals credit account, and that list matches the return receipt DC Parker uncovered this morning.'

'So, the killer took everything that Rex Hughes bought Marnie?' Lloyd asked, looking between the two lists. 'Then returned it all to Kendals?'

'Good catch, Cusack,' Higson said approvingly.

'Thank you, sir.' Jen's smile was small but pleased.

'Do you have anything on who actually returned the items?' Higson asked Lloyd.

'Not that much,' Lloyd replied. 'The girl I spoke to said that she remembers it was a young woman with long dark hair, fairly short, and she only remembers seeing her at all because she kicked up a massive fuss when the manager wouldn't let her return the earrings. Oh, and apparently she was wearing expensive clothes.'

'Hmm.' Higson turned to look at Peggy. 'Miss Swan, do you think you'll be able to get anything else from Miss Driscoll?'

Peggy chose to ignore whatever it was that DI Joyce muttered under his breath. 'Perhaps. If she *wants* to talk, that is.'

'Then I suggest you do everything you can to make her want to,' Higson said evenly. 'Right, Joyce, take Miss Swan here back to the Driscoll house. Cusack, I want you and Lloyd to go back to Kendals and question everyone who might remember anything about the woman we're looking for.'

'We can't go back to the house,' Andrew protested. 'Marnie's parents want answers, not hocus pocus.'

'What they *want*, DI Joyce, is for us to find whoever murdered their daughter,' Higson replied sharply. 'I believe I made it quite clear yesterday, but just in case you've forgotten, I'll remind you that if you don't like how we do things here then you're perfectly free to return to CID whenever you choose.'

Peggy was surprised at how quickly Andrew deflated. There was definitely a story there then.

'It doesn't have to be the house,' Peggy said quietly. 'As long as it's a place where Marnie spent a significant amount of time, I might be able to reach her there.'

'Place of work, maybe?' Jen suggested. 'Marnie had been at Lewis's for years. She got a job there straight out of school.'

'That could work,' Peggy replied.

She turned to face Andrew, who still looked completely against the idea. 'Well?'

'Fine,' Andrew replied eventually, 'but don't even think about making a scene.'

Peggy curled her lip in distaste. 'Trust me when I say that making a scene is about the last thing I want to do.'

FIVE

The first time Peggy realised that she could see things that other people couldn't, it had been her fifth birthday. She'd been sitting on the old swing in the garden, hoping that nobody would notice that she'd disappeared from her own party.

Peggy hadn't been enjoying herself as it was, but then horrible Elizabeth Cleverley had snatched the plate of birthday cake right out of Peggy's hands, and, *really*, that had been the last straw. She'd retreated to the garden and had been morosely swinging backwards and forwards when she'd heard the voice.

'Isn't it your birthday today, Miss Margaret?'

Peggy had looked up in surprise. A lady in a funny-looking dress had been smiling down at her. She'd looked a little bit familiar, but Peggy had been unable to place her. She'd thought she might have been a friend of her mother's, perhaps.

'It is,' Peggy had replied grumpily, 'but Elizabeth took my cake, and my little brother keeps crying. It's nicer out here.'

'I think so too,' the woman had agreed, smiling wider. 'I saw you taking a plum from my tree last week. Was it ripe enough?'

'Your tree?' Peggy had frowned in confusion. 'I'm only allowed in this part of the garden. Where's your house?'

'This is my home too,' the woman had replied, nodding towards Butterton House, where Peggy could just about make out Charlie's distraught wailing again.

'Oh,' Peggy had said slowly, trying to understand. 'Do you work here?'

The woman had just laughed and gently patted Peggy on the shoulder. 'Happy Birthday, Miss Margaret.'

'Peggy! What are you doing out here?'

Peggy had turned towards the house in surprise as her mother had shouted from the doorway.

'Come inside at once,' her mother had ordered sharply, striding across the lawn. 'Your friends are missing you.'

This was unlikely, Peggy had thought, given that she didn't really know any of the children her parents had invited.

Peggy had wriggled off the swing, resigned to the fact that she was going to have to spend at least another hour with terrible Elizabeth. She'd glanced behind her, but the woman who'd wished her a happy birthday had disappeared.

Peggy had then forgotten all about her encounter in the garden due to a particularly vicious round of pass the parcel, which ended when awful Elizabeth tugged the winning girl's hair so forcefully she'd still been clutching a clump of it as she'd been pulled, screeching, from the room by her own furious mother. That had rather spectacularly ended the party, much to Peggy's relief.

Later that night, when Charlie's plaintive, colicky yowls had woken Peggy again, she'd clambered out of bed intending to make her way down to the kitchen to locate a slice of her birthday cake. As she'd crossed the galleried landing towards the main staircase she'd looked up to her right and had stopped, stock still in the semi-darkness.

In the line of portraits that she'd never really cared to look at in great detail – after all, they were stuffy, old, dead members of the family and therefore terribly uninteresting to five-year-olds– she'd seen the woman from the garden. She'd been painted in a dress similar to the one that she'd been wearing that afternoon. The painted woman was sterner looking than the lady in the garden had been but, even still, Peggy had been certain that it was her.

So, in that particular way that only a young child can be entirely certain of something, regardless of any evidence whatsoever to the contrary, Peggy had concluded that she'd seen a ghost.

If she'd known then how much trouble any of it would have caused in the years that followed, she might have just pretended that it had never happened. She might have just ignored any further sightings of the woman – Great-great-great-great-aunt Emmeline – and she might have pretended that she hadn't been able to see or hear any of the other things that Charlie had never noticed.

But she hadn't known, and now, after almost thirty years *and* everything that had happened in the preceding two in particular, Peggy was standing on a street corner in Manchester, trying to reassure a horribly sceptical *police detective* that she wasn't actually a fraud.

'You're not to tell anyone why we're here,' Andrew said, rolling up his shirt sleeves as though this would somehow make him fit in better with the early-summer shoppers around him. It didn't. He still looked terribly tense and awkward to Peggy.

'I'm not going to say anything to anyone,' Peggy replied. 'Except maybe Marnie.'

Andrew rolled his eyes, and Peggy had to take a deep breath to stop herself from berating him for his insufferable behaviour. Honestly, he was more annoying than even Charlie could be, which was a fairly spectacular feat.

'Detective J-'

'*Andrew*,' he hissed, looking around quickly.

Peggy had to stop herself from rolling her own eyes this time. 'Jesus, who do you think is listening to me? It's barely ten in the morning on a Wednesday. It's not exactly packed out here right now, is it?'

'Look,' Andrew snapped sharply, before seeming to remember that he wasn't supposed to be raising his voice.

He sighed. 'Look, I don't really know what Higson is playing at, and I have no idea what your game is either, but I want to find the person who murdered Marnie. So, for now, I'll play along with whatever the hell it is that you're up to because those are my orders, but when we go in here we're doing things *my* way. That means that nobody is going to have a clue that this has anything to do with a police investigation. I didn't work my arse off to end up in some joke division, so I want this case solved so that I can go back to doing the job I actually signed up for. Clear?'

Peggy wanted to say something about Andrew's career chances but held her tongue. She knew Marnie and her family deserved justice, and she was going to help them get it, even if Joyce didn't believe a single thing she said. '*Crystal*.'

Andrew considered her for a long moment before turning away and heading towards the main entrance of Lewis's.

Peggy ran a hand through her hair and followed him after only a moment's hesitation. She could do this. It would all be fine.

'I hate shops,' Andrew griped as he held the door open for Peggy to enter before him. 'There's always too many people.'

Peggy agreed with the sentiment but didn't think her comments would be welcomed.

Being early in the day it wasn't actually that busy at all when they reached the perfume counters, but the chattering of staff and customers bounced off the tiled walls and floors in the relatively open space of the ground floor in a way that made the shop feel more crowded than it was.

Andrew wrinkled his nose at the combination of perfumes mingling together. The rich, musky sort of fragrance he knew Kate liked mingled with enough flowery scents to rival Interflora. It was claustrophobic, and he had no idea how anyone could stand it long enough to work here.

'How does anyone actually smell enough of one thing to pick it out and buy it?' Andrew asked, arching an eyebrow at Peggy.

'Don't tell me you've never bought a girl perfume, *Andrew*?' Peggy said, mock horror colouring her words. 'How very surprising. You seem like *such* a romantic at heart.'

'I like to think I have a few more original ideas than perfume or chocolates,' Andrew shot back. 'But I *have* actually bought perfume if you must know.'

'So how did you pick it out then?' Peggy asked, throwing his own question back to him.

'I asked my girlfriend which one she wanted,' Andrew replied, shrugging.

'Guess I was right about the romantic thing then,' Peggy said, rolling her eyes again as she wandered off towards the Estée Lauder counter where she knew Marnie had worked, occasionally stopping to make a show of considering some other brands. She tried to keep Marnie in her mind as clearly as she could, hoping that by concentrating her thoughts she might be able to let Marnie know that she was here and ready to listen.

As Peggy got closer to the counter, Andrew slowly closed the distance between them again in increments. She really would have preferred if he'd just waited outside, but it was clear he wasn't going to let her out of his sight. By now, she was fairly certain that Marnie and a whole host of other ghosts could manifest right in front of Andrew Joyce and he would *still* choose not to believe it.

Standing in front of the bridal-themed advertisement for *Beautiful* was a woman in her early twenties wearing a deep blue dress. Her long, blonde hair was cascading down her back in perfect waves, and Peggy felt horribly underdressed in comparison.

'Good morning,' the woman – her name badge said Rosemary - said, smiling toothily at Peggy, her hands already elegantly proffering the scalloped bottle of deep-golden perfume towards her potential customer. 'Can I interest you in a spray of *Beautiful*?'

'Absolutely,' Peggy replied with a smile. She immediately feared that she might have come across as too enthusiastic. 'Sociable Peggy' hadn't really had to make an appearance in a while, but the woman didn't make any comment. Instead, she waited patiently for Peggy to hold out her arm so that she could spritz the inside of her wrist with the perfume.

'It's perfect for summer,' Rosemary said as Peggy held her wrist up to her nose, 'and it's really the only choice for an elegant wedding fragrance.'

Andrew made a slight choking noise as the woman shot him what she clearly thought was a knowing look.

Peggy had to bite her lip to keep from laughing as she inhaled the scent again.

The sudden force of the intrusion in her head made Peggy gasp sharply in surprise. The screaming voice echoing in her mind and bones was high-pitched and forceful, but the words weren't clear, sounding almost as though they were underwater.

'Are you alright?' Rosemary asked as her features drew together in concern.

Peggy nodded hesitantly, fighting the urge to clutch at her head even as the volume of the screaming subsided slightly. 'Migraine,' she croaked out.

'Poor thing,' Rosemary cooed, already pulling a wooden, three-legged stool from behind the sales counter. 'Here, sit down. I'll get you a glass of water.'

Peggy had no chance to protest before Rosemary pushed down on her shoulder until she dropped unceremoniously onto the stool.

Rosemary tottered off into the distance without another word.

'Marnie's here,' Peggy croaked to Andrew, where he was hovering a safe distance away. 'She's here, and she's really not happy.'

'Why do you look like crap all of a sudden?' Andrew asked.

'Wow, thanks,' Peggy snapped pressing her hand to her forehead. She held in the whine of frustration as well as she could.

'Let's just imagine that I believe you for a second,' Andrew replied, still keeping his distance but looking at Peggy far more warily than he had been. 'What exactly is she saying?'

'I can't understand most of it,' Peggy muttered. 'I think she knows I can hear her though.'

Peggy looked around and grimaced slightly. A few people were glancing in her direction and murmuring quietly to each other. *Great*, she'd managed to make that scene she'd promised to avoid, and all without even trying.

'Andrew?' Peggy hissed quietly. 'Could you just come over and stand next to me for a minute?'

'Why?' Andrew asked cautiously even as he stepped towards her anyway.

'Well, for starters you look like a bit of a dickhead standing six feet away from the woman you came perfume shopping with,' Peggy replied, raising an eyebrow and then immediately regretting the pull of it across her tender brow. '*And*, I want to actually try and talk to Marnie, but I can't do that if everyone is looking at me and thinking that I'm talking to myself.'

'Fine,' Andrew acquiesced eventually, 'but don't bloody pass out. I'll leave you here if you do.'

Peggy nodded and closed her eyes as Andrew faced away from her to scan the shop floor, blocking her from the view of other shoppers as he did so.

This didn't feel at all like the friendly chats Peggy often had with Emmeline, or even like communicating with any of the other spirits she'd ever come into contact with. Marnie had been violently ripped from the world, and Peggy instinctively knew that she was going to have to tread carefully. She had no intention of telling Andrew – not that he'd believe her anyway – but Peggy was a bit worried about how Marnie's spirit had just aggressively intruded on her thoughts. That's not how things usually worked for Peggy.

'Marnie?' Peggy whispered as quietly as she could, bracing herself for whatever may come next.

Peggy experienced one unsettling second of pure silence before the screaming started again. Her fingers tightened around the edge of the stool.

'Marnie?' Peggy tried again. 'Marnie, I need you to calm down. I can't understand what you're saying. *Please.*'

The screaming stopped abruptly, but the subsequent quiet held an obvious threat.

'Thank you,' Peggy whispered. 'Marnie, we're so, so sorry that this happened to you. We want to help.'

A wave of sadness rolled over Peggy, and she nearly sobbed out loud. Jesus, what was happening here? She'd never really *felt* anything from a spirit before, but she knew that the grief and fear weren't hers - she could tell that they were slightly detached from her own emotions, even as they caused her heart to clench in her chest.

'Shit,' Andrew hissed suddenly, spinning around to face Peggy. 'Rex Hughes just walked in. I can't let him see me here right now. He'll recognise me and the jig'll be up.'

It was as though just the mention of her former fiancé's name gave Marnie the strength to grip onto Peggy and the world around her even more tightly. The fog shifted, and suddenly Peggy found herself staring straight at Marnie Driscoll, standing only a few feet away.

Marnie looked as solid as anyone else in the Perfume Hall, but there was a slight shimmer to her outline that reminded Peggy of a mirage she'd seen in a film once. She was dressed exactly as she had been in the crime scene photograph that Andrew had in the case file; her shoes were missing, but here in Lewis's, she was still wearing her engagement ring.

'Oh my God,' Peggy breathed in astonishment.

'Oh my God,' Marnie repeated, her own eyes going wide. 'You really *can* see me, can't you?'

'What?' Andrew asked sharply, glancing cautiously over Peggy's shoulder for any sign of Rex. It was obvious that he couldn't see Marnie at all.

'Marnie's here,' Peggy replied, keeping her eyes on the other woman lest she disappear.

'What? Where?' Andrew almost spun around entirely but caught himself just as Rex crossed the Perfume Hall. He also had to remind himself that Marnie couldn't actually be there, considering she was *dead.*

'She's about three feet to your left,' Peggy replied, and she *almost* enjoyed Andrew's comical little stagger backwards.

'Well, whatever you're doing, hurry it up,' Andrew muttered quickly. 'The salesgirl is on her way back with your water.'

'Wait. What the hell?' Marnie hissed, and Peggy felt a detached surge of anger flood her own body.

Marnie was staring across the room. Peggy followed her gaze and saw Rex Hughes embracing a petite brunette in towering heels. As he pulled back, Rex kissed the woman lightly on the cheek.

'I knew she was up to something.' Marnie's brittle voice shook. 'How could she do this to me?'

'Who? Who is she?' Peggy asked, concerned as Marnie seemed to flicker out of focus for a moment.

'Rebecca,' Marnie growled, and Peggy flinched when the stool beneath her wobbled of its own accord.

Marnie's outline guttered again as she let out a plaintive howl of anguish. '*Why*?'

'Er, Peggy?' Andrew asked cautiously as a strong breeze rippled through the Perfume Hall even though the doors to the street remained firmly shut. 'What's happening?'

'I don't know,' Peggy replied, practically throwing herself from the stool as it slid out from beneath her. 'I think this is Marnie's doing.'

Staff and customers alike were looking around in confusion as the wind picked up speed. Even Rosemary had paused only a few feet from Rex and Rebecca, still clutching Peggy's glass of water.

'Can't you stop this?' Andrew asked, poleaxed by even asking such a question about something he *absolutely did not believe in.* Andrew realised that it was much harder to have conviction in something when all evidence pointed to the contrary.

Peggy shook her head as the breeze grew to a howling gale. 'I don't understand what's happening.'

The screaming started when a woman on the far side of the room had her shopping bag blown from her hand. Seconds later people were tripping over each other in their haste to reach an exit.

'Marnie, stop!' Peggy cried, but her request was lost to the wind as the Perfume Hall emptied around them.

'We need to get out of here,' Andrew said, blindly reaching for Peggy's hand and starting to tug her away from the Estée Lauder counter.

Peggy saw Rex do the same to Rebecca, and then the wind abruptly died away as the couple ran for the door.

'It's stopped,' Andrew said, blinking in surprise as he looked around the otherwise empty space.

Peggy couldn't see Marnie anywhere anymore, but she could feel the beginnings of the screaming in her head again. 'No, I don't think it has.'

It started with a low hum that quickly built to an ear-splitting whine, and Andrew warily eyed the bottles of perfume on the countertops around them as they started ratting dangerously, knocking against each other with the unsettling clink of glass on glass.

'Marnie, stop!' Peggy yelled as the wind whipped around the room again.

Andrew didn't even care that Peggy might actually be shouting at a ghost, he just wanted her to do whatever she needed to do to make it stop.

The whine reached an impossibly higher pitch, and Andrew knew deep in his bones what was about to happen.

He yanked on Peggy's arm, pulling her heavily against his chest. He only just managed to drop his own head down to protect them both before the bottles of *Beautiful* on the display immediately behind them exploded in a shower of glass and perfume. Andrew winced as something sharp hit his face just below his right temple.

The silence that followed was oppressive, bearing down on Andrew like a physical weight. It released him only when Peggy cautiously pushed back against his arms, which were still wrapped tightly around her back.

Peggy was even paler than she had been back at the Driscoll house, and her expression grew more horrified as she surveyed the chaos around them.

Shards of coloured glass littered the tiled floor, and if Andrew had thought that the scent of perfume had been stifling when they'd first entered the shop, it was now positively toxic as pools of liquid collected and merged together around their feet.

'We should leave,' Andrew said, glass crunching beneath his shoes as he turned towards the exit. He ran a hand through his hair, grimacing as his fingers brushed against shards of glass. Part of him wanted to stay and take a look around in a professional capacity, but he knew that the police would have been called by now and there was no way it would reflect positively on him if anyone from CID found him at the centre of this mess.

'I'm sorry,' Peggy said, almost under her breath, as she followed Andrew carefully out of the Perfume Hall. Andrew just shook his head silently in response, even though he wasn't entirely sure the apology was meant for him.

Customers and Lewis's staff alike were congregated on the pavement outside the shop, all looking shell-shocked.

Andrew caught sight of Rex Hughes almost immediately. He was at the edge of the crowd consoling the same young woman he'd been with inside the shop.

'That's Rebecca,' Peggy explained quietly, following Andrew's gaze as they manoeuvred their way through the crowd. 'Marnie's best friend. I think Marnie believes that there's something going on between Rebecca and Rex.'

Andrew stopped so suddenly that Peggy walked right into him.

'It was a short brunette woman who returned the gifts,' Andrew muttered at the pavement, thinking aloud.

Peggy was startled as Andrew suddenly darted across the road and started running up Tib Street at speed. Peggy hurried after him, catching up just as Andrew skidded to a halt next to the dance studio plaque.

Andrew pounded on the door with his fist.

'You really should get a key,' Peggy said, breathing heavily.

'I don't plan on being around long enough to need one,' Andrew replied, hitting the door again.

A surprised-looking Jen appeared seconds later. 'What the hell happened to you two?'

Andrew didn't reply as he pushed past the DS and sprinted up the stairs to the Ballroom.

'What do we have on Rebecca Silverman?' he asked, bursting into the room with Peggy and Jen only a second behind him.

Higson raised one eyebrow at the sight of his dishevelled Detective Inspector, but after a long moment, he gestured towards Lloyd in an obvious invitation for him to give Andrew any relevant information.

Charlie, who was lounging on the ratty blue sofa against the far wall, frowned first at Andrew, and then at his sister. 'Why do you two smell so fabulous?'

Lloyd sniffed loudly as he handed a file to Andrew. He wrinkled his nose. 'Why do you smell like my sister, sir?'

'There was an incident at Lewis's,' Andrew said vaguely, flicking through the pages in his hand, only pausing briefly to idly rub at the thin trail of blood drying on his face with a grimace.

'An incident?' Jen asked, askance, as she reached over to pluck a small chunk of glass out of Peggy's hair.

'DI Joyce, are you planning on sharing some great revelation with the rest of us?' Higson asked impatiently.

'We have possible reason to believe that Rex Hughes may have been having an affair with Marnie's best friend, Rebecca Silverman,' Andrew replied, eventually closing the file and laying it on Higson's desk. 'Rebecca also fits the description of the woman seen returning Marnie's gifts to Kendals in February.'

Higson leaned forward to rest his elbows on his desk. 'And where, may I ask, did this information about the possible affair come from?'

Andrew briefly glanced at Peggy and steeled himself. 'Miss Swan has offered some insight into the situation.'

'Oh really?' Higson replied slowly, drawing out each syllable in a clear taunt. 'And you trust Miss Swan's 'insight', do you, Detective Inspector?'

Andrew cleared his throat and looked at the floor. What had he been reduced to? He'd been here for under twenty-four hours, and he was already buying into the madness, even if only a little. 'I have no reason to doubt the assumption, sir. We saw Hughes and Miss Silverman together at Lewis's.'

'Miss Swan?' Higson asked, turning his attention to the woman now sitting next to her brother. 'Do you have anything to add?'

Peggy shrank back slightly as everyone's attention landed squarely on her. 'Um, I was, er, briefly able to connect with Marnie.'

'Connect?' Jen asked. 'So, you spoke to her?'

'I did. I also saw her,' Peggy replied, nodding as Jen and Lloyd looked at each other in surprise. 'She knows I can hear her. Marnie's actually the one who raised suspicions about Rebecca and Rex. She made her displeasure at the thought quite clear.'

'Made it clear *how*?' Higson asked, looking unreasonably delighted.

'Let's just say that Lewis's will probably be closed for at least the rest of the day.' Andrew replied, looking towards the window as he heard the faint sound of sirens. 'Quite a few bottles from the Perfume Hall are now in pieces all over the floor.'

'Wait, *what*?' Charlie asked, gripping his sister's arm and looking at her in concern. 'Marnie did that? Peg, are you alright? Did she hurt you?'

'I'm fine, Charlie,' Peggy replied. 'I just got a bit of a fright, like everyone else.'

'Do ghosts usually behave like that?' Lloyd asked so simply that Andrew wondered what it must be like to just accept anything you were told as fact. 'I mean, if they're angry about something?'

'No.' Peggy shook her head again, sagging slightly against a cushion. 'Not in my experience, anyway. Marnie's different somehow though; I can feel her emotions so strongly, and what I felt when she saw Rex and Rebecca was definitely something like betrayal.'

'Fascinating,' Higson said, and the smile he shot Peggy was tinged with something manic. 'Did Marnie say anything about her killer?'

'No,' Peggy replied. 'I wasn't able to ask her anything specific before Rex and Rebecca arrived. At first, she seemed surprised that they would be together, but then she said that she'd thought that Rebecca had been up to something.'

'Fascinating,' Higson repeated slowly. 'Do you think you'd be able to find her at Lewis's again if you went back?'

Peggy's face fell further, and Andrew frowned at his DCI. 'Sir, I don't think that's necessarily a good idea at this juncture.'

'I don't believe I asked for your opinion, Joyce,' Higson snapped. 'You've already made it quite clear that you don't take the methods of this department seriously, and if Miss Swan can get information that nobody else can, then it would be in everyone's best interests to access that information sooner rather than later.'

'Rebecca Silverman's alibi is flimsy at best,' Andrew shot back, ignoring Higson's jibe and tapping the folder on the desk. 'She claims that she was late getting to Marnie's house because she missed the bus. According to that file, the driver of the bus she apparently took to Cheadle can't say for certain that he saw her.'

Higson considered Andrew's reply and pursed his lips. 'All the more reason to ask Marnie herself right now. '

'Sir-'

'We have *nothing* on Silverman,' Higson snapped. 'We have a description that could fit half the girls in the city, and as far as your precious CID was concerned, her alibi was tight enough to keep her above suspicion. We need more from Marnie herself, so we need Miss Swan to get back to Lewis's and find her.'

Andrew clenched his jaw in frustration, and he tried to pretend that he couldn't see Jen's pity.

'I don't think I'll be able to find Marnie today,' Peggy piped up quietly, and Andrew looked over at her in surprise. 'The way it was explained to me is that it takes a lot of energy for a spirit to communicate in any way, and it takes time to build up the strength to be able to do it for prolonged periods of time. Marnie seems to find communicating easier than most - I don't know why - but the display at Lewis's is going to have taken a lot out of her.'

Higson contemplated Peggy carefully. 'Is Benson here?'

Peggy inclined her head towards the far side of the room by the door. 'He is.'

Higson turned to face where his previous DI ostensibly stood slouched against the wall just as he always had, and addressed him directly, 'Well, what do you have to say about all this?'

Peggy shrugged after a long moment. 'He's not saying anything.'

'Fine, be like that, you useless sod,' Higson growled. He looked around at the motley crew assembled in the Ballroom.

'Wait.' Peggy held up her hand and squinted at the wall again before looking at Higson. 'DI Benson isn't anywhere near as clear as Marnie, but I think he's saying 'Tabitha'.'

Higson blinked once before he threw his head back in a guffaw so loud Andrew nearly got whiplash from wheeling around in surprise.

'Of course,' Higson said, pointing at the wall and laughing to himself. 'Of course. How could I forget about bloody *Tabitha*? Brilliant! We'd get information without spooking the suspects.'

'Who's Tabitha?' Lloyd asked, looking at Jen, whose answering shrug confirmed that she had no idea who the mysterious Tabitha was either.

'Tabitha,' Higson began, rubbing a hand over his moustache, 'was a psychic from just outside Paris. She did a little work for us back in the day.'

Andrew pinched the bridge of his nose when Higson chuckled again. He didn't need to be a psychic from just outside Paris to know that he probably wasn't going to like wherever this train of thought was headed.

'We were looking into gang recruitment, and we needed an inside man – or woman, in that case,' Higson explained, grinning again. 'Tabitha went undercover as a nun in Moss Side for us.'

'A nun?' Lloyd asked in surprise.

'Sister Lucilla,' Higson confirmed. 'Surprisingly handy with locks and weapons.'

'This is incredible!' Charlie practically howled in joy.

'Why are you still here?' Andrew snapped at the elder Swan, before immediately chastising himself for letting himself get wound up.

Charlie just smiled toothily in reply.

'You want a psychic fake nun to help us?' Lloyd asked Higson, scratching his head.

'Don't be so dense, lad,' Higson replied. 'Tabitha would be eighty now if she were a day. We need a younger woman on the inside at Lewis's. Someone to get close to Rebecca, and to keep an eye on Rex Hughes in case he's still chummy with the Byrnes.'

'Oh,' Lloyd drew the word out as he processed Higson's meaning. 'I get you now. You mean Jen.'

Jen shook her head, frowning at Higson, who was staring intently at Peggy. 'No, Lloyd, I don't think he means me.'

'Peg!' Charlie virtually whooped in delight, completely ignoring his sister's horrified reaction. 'Peg, you get to go undercover! How awesome is that? Do you want her to pretend to be a nun too?'

'No way!' Andrew interjected. 'Absolutely not!'

'DCI Higson, I can't do that. I'm not a police officer,' Peggy managed to choke out, and Andrew was pleased that he wasn't the only one who thought this whole idea was completely insane.

'Precisely,' Higson replied calmly. 'Nobody would have any reason to suspect you, and we know it's a good place for you to be able to contact Marnie.'

'Sir,' Jen cleared her throat. 'Sir, with all due respect, I do think that I'm more qualified for this than Miss Swan here.'

'Yes,' Peggy gratefully agreed. 'Much, *much* more qualified.'

'Oh, I'm sorry DS Cusack,' Higson said, holding his hands up, 'I wasn't aware that you could communicate with the dead these days. Oh no, wait, you *can't*. Plus, Rex Hughes would recognise you the second he saw you.'

'DCI Higson, I will respectfully have to decline,' Peggy said, pushing herself to her feet. 'I'm sorry, but I don't think I can help any further. Good luck with the case. I truly do hope you find Marnie's killer.'

Higson looked surprised as Peggy practically hightailed it from the room.

'Well, gentlemen, DS Cusack,' Charlie added nodding at each of them as he slowly rose from the couch, 'I believe that's my cue. Lloyd, I'm sure I'll see you at Rotters on Monday.'

Charlie then trailed after his sister, out through the doors and down the stairs with a small wave of farewell.

'I don't know why you're still standing here like the last bleeding sausage roll at Greggs!' Higson barked at Andrew. 'You'd better go convince her royal highness downstairs to get her arse on board with this plan, or you can make your way back to CID in the morning.'

'But I-'

'*Final chance*, Joyce.' Higson snapped.

He then shot Lloyd a dark glance as he sank back into his desk chair. 'Speaking of sausage rolls, go and get me a bag of them. They'd better be *hot*.'

Lloyd gave Higson a quick salute before he shrugged at Andrew and followed the Swans down the stairs.

'I don't think you've got a choice here, sir,' Jen said quietly, briefly patting Andrew's shoulder, before she retreated to her desk to flick through the measly information they had on Rebecca Silverman.

Andrew glanced out of the window and thought longingly for even just a week ago. With a deep sigh of resignation, he turned, trudged out of the Ballroom, and traipsed down the stairs.

He wasn't delighted to see that Dolly was in the foyer, scrubbing at an oddly shaped dark spot on the wall, cigarette hanging limply from her lips even as she sprayed cleaning product again.

'Leaving are ye?' she hissed at him without turning around.

'Not quite yet,' Andrew retorted sharply.

'Death follows you around too, don't it?' Dolly mused. 'Youse should tell him to leave ye alone. He would. It's been long enough.'

Andrew stopped in front of the door to the street and stared at Dolly in surprise. She couldn't know anything. *Nobody* knew anything about that. It was a box that Andrew had locked up tightly when he'd left home the first time. *No*, she knew nothing, she was just a mad old bat who wanted to have the last word.

Without replying, Andrew stepped out onto Tib Street and caught sight of Peggy and Charlie arguing over the roof of their car. Jesus, was that a Rolls Royce? Andrew was surprised it still had *wheels* given that it had been sitting out there for hours.

'Oh, don't be ridiculous, Charlie,' Peggy sighed in exasperation. 'Higson's obviously completely mad. Now, open the bloody door before I come over there and take the keys myself.'

'Peggy, this would be *good* for you,' Charlie replied. 'You can't just hide in the house forever. Peg, I *know* you don't want to talk about what happened, but-'

'You're right, I don't,' Peggy snapped. 'And certainly not *here*.'

Charlie drooped; the argument clearly lost.

Well, this is it, Andrew thought with depressing clarity. If the Swans drove away without agreeing to Higson's frankly insane plan Andrew could probably kiss the rest of his career goodbye. He hated himself a little as he raised his hand and jogged towards the car. 'Miss Swan. *Peggy*, wait a minute!'

Peggy looked up in surprise as Andrew headed towards her and Charlie. He was the last person she'd expected to follow them out of the

Ballroom.

'Look,' Andrew said, as he reached them, 'I don't like Higson's plan any more than you do, but perhaps it does have some merit to it.'

'No, it doesn't,' Peggy replied scathingly. 'I'm only here because my brother can't keep his mouth shut when he's out drinking. I tried to help, and it ended in disaster. I don't want to be involved any further. Goodbye, Detective Inspector Joyce.'

Andrew had been raised by a proud mother, and he'd seen what too much pride could do to a person when they were unwilling to compromise. He gritted his teeth. '*Please*. If you don't do this I'm going to be out on my arse by morning.'

'Your job isn't my responsibility,' Peggy replied, and it was almost apologetic.

'No, it's not,' Andrew agreed with a sigh, 'but you wanted to help Marnie, and you can still do that if you just agree to do this one thing.'

'You don't even believe in ghosts, DI Joyce. Even after what happened earlier, I'd bet that you're still trying to explain it all away *rationally*. You want to save your career? You need to do that by yourself.' Peggy turned her glare on her brother. 'Let's go, Charlie.'

'I'm good at my job!' Andrew threw his hands up in frustration. 'I'm bloody *good* at my job, and right now I can't do it. I'm stuck here in this weird department that I didn't ask to be assigned to, and I've got a DCI who thinks it's perfectly normal to have a shaman on speed dial. I am asking you, no, I am *begging* you, to agree to Higson's plan. Just try it, even for a day, and if you don't get anywhere then we'll pull the whole thing, I swear.'

Peggy pursed her lips. 'I see how this helps *you*, but you're asking me to do something I have no training for, and I don't see how any of this is of benefit to me.'

'Well, it would probably get Father to stop complaining that you never leave the house,' Charlie piped up.

The look of utter betrayal that flashed across Peggy's face as she whipped her head towards her brother was startling in both its ferocity and the sheer *depth* it seemed to contain. Andrew was very glad he wasn't the one on the receiving end of such an expression.

Charlie didn't seem remotely concerned though, and simply added, 'I also think you'd be good at it. You were always so good at talking to people, Peggy. People trust you; they tell you things. Plus, if you do this, I swear I'll never touch even a single piece of the estate paperwork again. *Ever.*'

Peggy actually looked like she might be considering that as a good deal, and Andrew took another quick moment to wonder just how weird life must be when you were as rich as the Swans were.

'Not a single thing?' Peggy asked her brother after a long moment, eyes narrowed in suspicion.

'Not a sausage,' Charlie replied, hands raised in surrender.

Peggy turned to Andrew. 'And *you* swear that if I don't want to do it after one day that will be the end of it? You won't try to persuade me again?'

'I swear,' Andrew replied solemnly, already feeling relief flooding through him.

'Ugh, fine,' Peggy sighed unhappily, swiping a hand through her hair, and grumbling as she found another few stray shards of glass. '*One* day.'

'Maybe we'll only need one day,' Andrew replied, crossing his fingers behind his back.

He wasn't hopeful.

SIX

By the time Andrew returned to Acacia Road on Wednesday evening, he'd already had enough of the whole week. He sighed tiredly as he parked the Belmont outside of his house and dropped his head onto the steering wheel. If he let out a low moan of despair then, *well*, there was nobody around to hear it.

He ran his hands over his face, grimacing when his fingers scraped over stubble and briefly nicked the corner of the thin scab that had formed over the cut next to his eye. He hissed as the sharp, unpleasant stab of a disturbed wound briefly set his skin on fire, and he valiantly tried not to think about how he'd received the cut in the first place. He was going to stick to the facts, even if everyone else around him was disappearing off into thoughts of the fantastical. He'd seen where that had got his mother in the end, and he hadn't even the slightest intention of repeating her mistakes.

As he looked up at the house he'd grown up in, Andrew wondered, not for the first time, what his father would have made of his youngest son choosing to join the police.

Back when Andrew was still just a baby, Jack Joyce might have considered it a perfectly respectable career path for a boy from a perfectly respectable home. Yet, by the time Andrew's fifth birthday had rolled around, Jack's business interests had long since taken a turn to the other side of the law, and only weeks later had been the last time Andrew had seen his father alive. Privately, Andrew had always thought that it was seeing his father cold and laid out at the wake that had spurred on his childish desire to be a detective when he grew up, accelerating him towards a pre-destined inevitability. Back then, he'd believed he'd be able to clean up the city; that he could somehow stop the festering rash of crime from infecting the suburbs and taking other kids' fathers away.

Andrew never quite dared to think about what path his life might have taken if Jack hadn't died. It certainly wouldn't have been the path to Tib Street anyway, of that Andrew could be certain. Jack had wanted his sons' feet to stay firmly on the ground, forcing Andrew and his brother to keep their imagination to themselves. Jack had been a man who'd put more stock in corporal punishment than divine judgement which, coupled with Andrew's mother's aggressive brand of militantly devout Catholicism, hadn't fostered the happiest of homes at times; or ever, really.

Still, the house was his now, and Andrew was well-practised at keeping the ghosts of his past at bay. His eye caught the small window at the top left of the house, where the curtains remained resolutely drawn, and his stomach clenched slightly, just as it always did.

Maybe not *all* of the ghosts then.

Andrew sighed again and shook off his increasingly morbid thoughts as he opened the car door and stepped out into the early summer evening. As he leaned into the backseat to pick up the files he'd brought home from Tib Street he caught sight of the small yellow car trundling up the road towards him. He groaned and smacked his head on the car door as he dodged backwards in an attempt to get out of sight before the driver saw him.

No such luck, of course. Kate was staring right at him as she parked across the road. She had a face on that suggested Andrew was still in trouble for his *demotion* as she had taken to calling it. The fact that she was here at all was honestly a bit of a surprise in itself.

The realisation of just *why* Kate was there hit Andrew a second later. Oh God, they were supposed to be going to the pictures with Kate's best friend and her husband; he'd agreed to it almost under duress. Andrew hated double dates at the best of times, but he *really* hated them when the other pair was the incessantly chatty Roz and Paul.

'You're back late,' Kate called over to him as she climbed out of her car, elegant as always.

'Well, I have to drive from bloody central Manchester now,' Andrew grumbled under his breath, before adding, louder, 'I got stuck in traffic.'

'You didn't forget about the film, did you?' Kate asked as she crossed the road in bright pink heels. Andrew had once suggested to her that she might want to consider driving in more sensible shoes, but she'd just told him to keep his nose out of her footwear decisions. He hadn't mentioned it again.

'Course not,' Andrew replied, forcing a smile onto his face. He wasn't actually sure how he'd forgotten about facing the hell that would be sitting through two hours of Michael Douglas and Kathleen Turner running around another exotic location while Kate and Roz giggled their way through every scene. It might have had something to do with the fact that his professional life was going to hell.

He hoped that Kate was just spectacularly early for once, because he couldn't go out in public smelling like a perfume explosion. He hadn't actually been able to smell himself at all since about two o'clock, but he was fairly certain that this was because his nostrils had been permanently damaged by the scent of gardenias, or roses, or whatever the hell it was that they put in perfume, rather than the scent had just faded away. He felt like a walking chemical weapon.

Kate stopped short a metre away from him. Her mouth dropped open and her eyes narrowed. 'Are you kidding me?'

'What?' Andrew asked. He looked down at himself, and, okay *yes*, maybe his shirt was filthy and his tie was missing, but he had actually been planning on changing his clothes before subjecting himself to their evening plans.

'What the hell have you been up to?' Kate asked, before inhaling loudly. She took a step closer and sniffed Andrew again. 'Oh my God, why do you smell like *perfume?* Where have you been?'

'I was at work, Kate,' Andrew sighed again. He vaguely remembered his aunty telling him that you should always cough after sighing. He couldn't remember why, and he also thought that Kate probably wouldn't appreciate being coughed at right in that moment. *God, he was so tired.*

'*That* is not my perfume, Andy,' Kate said, voice dangerously low.

Andrew hated it when she called him Andy.

'Whose perfume is it?'

'It's nobody's!' Andrew waved his free arm around. 'It's basically every perfume they stock in Lewis's.'

'Ugh,' Kate said, turning on her heel. She turned back suddenly and slapped Andrew's cheek like they were rehashing a scene from *Coronation Street.*

'Ow,' Andrew whined, rubbing his face. 'What the hell was that for?'

'How could you do this to me?' Kate cried, her cheeks growing rosier by the second.

Andrew clenched his jaw, tightening his fingers around the paper file in his hand. 'Kate, don't be ridiculous. I was at *work*.'

'You don't normally come home stinking of another woman's perfume when you're at *work*!'

'Kate,' Andrew replied, trying to be patient, 'there was an incident in Lewis's. The perfume bottles all exploded. Jesus, no woman would choose to smell like this!'

Kate shook her head slowly. 'Unbelievable. Is that really the best you can come up with?'

'It's true!'

'You disgust me,' Kate spat, stomping back across the road to her car. 'No wonder you got demoted.'

'I didn't get demoted!' Andrew yelled, before catching himself and lowering his voice. 'Look, just stop it. I'll take a quick shower and we'll head off to the pictures then, alright?'

Kate laughed, disbelief evident on her face. 'You seriously think I'm going anywhere with you? Go find whatever piece of skirt you've got yourself in the city, Andy.'

'What?' Andrew blinked. 'You seriously think I'm cheating on you?'

Kate's eyes narrowed further. 'I knew it! You utter pig!'

'I'm not doing anything!' Andrew shouted in frustration, no longer caring that his curtain twitcher neighbours were no doubt thoroughly enjoying the spectacle. 'Kate, stop being ridiculous.'

'I'm *not* ridiculous, Andy!' Kate yelled back. She turned and unlocked her car. 'Don't bother calling me, I won't answer. Neither will Mum. You're dumped, Andrew Joyce, you utter, *utter* bastard.'

Andrew just stood there, staring after the little yellow car as Kate drove - *far too fast* - up Acacia Road, shooting a very creative but viciously unpleasant hand gesture at her boyfriend. *Ex*-boyfriend now, Andrew supposed.

Jesus Christ. It was only *Wednesday*, and he'd been demoted (he could admit that to himself), he'd been assaulted by what was allegedly an angry ghost, he had a new boss who was completely mad, and now he'd been dumped. Oh, and Mrs Roberts across the road was staring directly at him from her living room window and not even bothering to pretend that she hadn't seen everything that had just happened.

Deciding that he didn't have the heart to go inside the house to have a much-longed-for shower, Andrew instead grabbed his suit jacket from the car, locked the door and trudged up the road.

He needed a pint. *Again.*

* * *

Peggy looked at the three dresses on her bed with a vague sense of trepidation. She hadn't worn any of them since the previous summer, and it was only a very, very deeply ingrained sensibility that had stopped her from just building a bonfire in the formal gardens and committing every single nice dress she'd ever bought herself to a spectacular public burning.

That, and the fact that the groundskeeper would have come after her with a pitchfork for ruining the lawn.

After she'd agreed to at least give Higson's plan a go, she'd spent a couple of hours with Andrew and Jen, talking through the ins and outs of what she was going to have to do. Lloyd and Charlie had hovered at the periphery, making occasional asinine comments and generally behaving like a pair of eight-year-old boys playing detectives. She'd breathed a sigh of relief when Higson had taken himself off home – or, as she strongly suspected, to the *pub* – at five o'clock.

It had been shockingly easy for Andrew to make a phone call to the shop manager and spin a yarn about a police investigation into the 'unexplained events in the Perfume Hall earlier that day'. Peggy had suddenly found herself with a new job, starting at eight am sharp the next morning.

'Going somewhere nice, dear?'

Peggy jumped in surprise as Aunt Emmeline appeared in the corner of her bedroom.

'I did knock, darling,' Emmeline added, patting Peggy on the arm, 'but it was obvious that you were somewhere else entirely. *Again.*'

'Believe it or not,' Peggy replied, ignoring Emmeline's mild jibe, 'I have a job.'

'A job?' Emmeline looked perplexed. 'Why would you need a job?'

'I'm helping the police with an investigation.'

Emmeline blinked, opened her mouth to say something, paused, and then just blinked again without further comment.

'I know it sounds strange,' Peggy said, wrinkling her nose. 'It *is* strange, but they think that I might be able to help them find out who murdered a young woman back in January.'

'Peggy, that all sounds terribly unsavoury,' Emmeline replied. 'Is that why your brother is in such a good mood? I assume he is involved in some way.'

'Of course he is,' Peggy muttered. 'Yes, Charlie sees the whole opportunity as an excuse to play pretend. You know how he always wanted to be a policeman.'

'Yes,' Emmeline said with a moue of distaste. 'I do remember those noisy toy cars.'

'Well, I think this might be him living out his dream,' Peggy replied as she picked up the black dress to frown critically at it.

'But that doesn't really explain why *you're* involved. It doesn't seem very like you, of late at least.'

Peggy sometimes forgot that Emmeline knew about everything that had occurred within the grounds of Butterton, stretching back generations. She probably knew more about everything that had happened the previous summer than even Charlie, who was the only person Peggy had explained the situation to in any detail.

'Yes, well…' Peggy shrugged and picked up the black dress again. 'I thought perhaps it was time to get back to myself.'

'Good for you, my girl.' Emmeline was the very picture of a proud older relative. 'Then perhaps you can forget all about that terrible-'

'Don't!' Peggy held up her hand desperately. 'I don't want to talk about it. Look, what do you think of this dress?'

Emmeline tilted her head and scrutinised her very great grandniece for a long moment. 'I think the blue suits your colouring better, but I do see that the black one is a sensible choice, if not a little maudlin for my taste. I still don't understand why you girls choose to wear the colour of mourning when you have such fabulous choices available. Just last week I saw a photograph in one of your magazines, and the girl there was wearing head-to-toe bright pink. Why can't you embrace that?'

Peggy bit back a laugh. Emmeline was so strait-laced in so many ways, but she had fostered a real love of fashion since Peggy had first shown her one of her mother's magazines when she was a child. Emmeline believed that everyone on the planet should be truly fascinated by the concept of coloured Lycra, so Peggy was somewhat grateful that Emmeline couldn't change her clothes at will, even if it was a constant source of disappointment for Emmeline herself.

'I think I'll stick with the black,' Peggy replied with a small smile.

'Then you must wear my emerald ring,' Emmeline said, pointing towards Peggy's ancient jewellery box. 'It will add some colour.'

Peggy felt instantly sick at the thought. 'No.'

'Peggy,' Emmeline sighed, 'it belongs to *you*. No matter what significance was ascribed to it by someone else, it remains *yours*, and I want you to wear it. I insist.'

'I can't.' Peggy's voice cracked slightly. 'You know I can't.'

'Yes, you can,' Emmeline replied, utterly no-nonsense as always. 'You are Margaret Susan Emilia Swan, eldest daughter of the Earl of Acresfield. That ring belongs to you, and I forbid you to think of it as anything other than *my* gift to you.'

Before Peggy had a chance to protest further, Emmeline had drifted across the room and retrieved the emerald ring from where Peggy had all but thrown it at the end of last August. She held it out towards Peggy. 'Here, take it.'

'I don't want to,' Peggy replied, voice trembling slightly.

'You're a Swan, dear,' Emmeline said with a slight grimace, 'and that sometimes means doing things that we don't necessarily want to do. You know how I wish that I'd been able to do more to help, but I made sure that they were unable to take this one thing from you. Wear it, and find yourself again, my girl.'

Peggy gingerly took the ring and tried to ignore the gnawing ache of betrayal in her chest. It felt a lot like what she'd experienced from

Marnie earlier that day. She slid it onto the ring finger of her right hand and sternly told herself not to cry.

'There we go,' Emmeline said. Her smile was brittle. 'That wasn't so hard now, was it?'

Peggy remained silent.

* * *

Thursday morning found Andrew in the Ballroom at just before seven-thirty, cradling his aching head in his hands. His skull throbbed any time he moved too quickly, in a visceral reminder of why he never usually drank more than two pints. If he were still in CID, he'd probably care that he might be judged for coming into work with a mild hangover, but given that Higson had a hip flask on his desk all day, every day, it didn't seem worth even thinking about. At least Lloyd had answered the door instead of Dolly.

'Here.'

Andrew looked up, squinting slightly as Lloyd deposited a large mug of coffee on the desk in front of him.

'No milk, and strong enough to kill a giant,' Lloyd added. 'Allegedly.'

'Thanks,' Andrew said croakily. He cleared his throat and took a sip of the steaming coffee. He winced as the bitter liquid hit his tongue. 'Jesus Christ, you weren't kidding.'

Lloyd grinned. 'It's how I make it for the boss most mornings.'

Andrew took another tentative sip. 'Where is he anyway?'

'He doesn't usually get in until closer to nine.' Lloyd shrugged.

'But we have an operation starting this morning,' Andrew replied aghast, somehow still surprised that Higson acted so differently to any DCI he'd encountered before. 'It's *his* operation.'

Lloyd shrugged again, even more nonchalantly this time. 'Well, it's yours now, I guess. Benson ran any ops when Higson wasn't here, and I suppose you're the new Benson, aren't you, sir?'

Andrew wasn't terribly comfortable with the idea of being the 'new Benson' in any way, but on some level Lloyd was correct; with Higson absent, Andrew was in charge, and he didn't intend to waste any time getting this sideshow on the road. If it failed spectacularly – as Andrew firmly believed it would – he wanted it over and done with as soon as possible.

The external door opening and closing downstairs signalled the arrival of Jen. From the mingling voices that floated up the stairs, it was clear that the Swans had also arrived. Andrew grimaced at the thought of dealing with Charlie's eternal exuberance on a morning like this.

Jen was laughing at something Charlie was saying as the trio entered the room. Peggy looked more sombre than the other two, but even she had a small smile on her face, which surprised Andrew given the resistance she'd shown to the whole plan the previous afternoon.

'Morning, sir,' Jen said brightly as she deposited her jacket and bag on her desk. 'Lloyd.'

Andrew groaned again when he saw Charlie look at him knowingly and then grin.

'*Oh dear*, did someone have a heavy night?' Charlie asked, sticking out his bottom lip in fake sympathy.

Andrew, with a strength of character known only to saints, somehow managed to both bite back a torrent of swearing and refrain from throwing something at the other man. He forced a tight smile for Peggy instead. 'Alright?'

Peggy nodded with a barely audible sigh. Andrew had noticed that she seemed to do that a lot, which he assumed was a side-effect of dealing with her younger brother for a lifetime.

A quick glance at his watch confirmed that it was almost time to head to Lewis's. If everything had gone to plan, Rebecca Silverman would be waiting at the staff entrance for her newest colleague to arrive. Andrew surreptitiously looked over at Peggy again; she looked a little nervous, but no more so than could easily be attributed to first-day nerves.

He'd probably been a little uncharitable with his initial assumption that Peggy had spent her whole life being work-shy in the way that only the truly rich could, and a few things that she'd said the day before had left him with the impression that Peggy ran the financial side of Butterton Estate without any useful assistance from either Charlie or their father.

'Right, shall we run through this one last time?' Andrew asked as he leaned back in his chair. He held in the wince of discomfort when his headache violently reminded him that it was still there, no matter how hard he was trying to ignore it. He took another sip of his coffee. 'Jen?'

Jen shifted into professional mode instantly. 'Mr Jenner, store manager, believes that we are conducting an investigation into the events of yesterday afternoon. He is under the impression that we have grounds to believe that it may have been the work of a disgruntled employee. Officially, the case is actually closed. The officers who visited the scene yesterday concluded that the damage was caused by a temporary issue with the ground-floor air ducts.

'Peggy is taking on Marnie's previous role as a salesgirl at the Estée Lauder counter. The girl who has been working at the counter – Rosemary Chater – was doing so in a temporary capacity, and she has this morning returned to her previous role in Fashion Accessories.

'In a stroke of good luck, Rebecca Silverman, Marnie's best friend, has been selected by Mr Jenner to train Peggy in her new job. She remains unaware of our investigation.'

Jen paused to give Peggy an encouraging smile. 'All you need to do is get Rebecca talking. See if you can get her to give you anything useful about her relationship with either Marnie or Rex Hughes. DI Joyce, DC Parker and I will pop in over the course of the day to check in with you, but if you need to tell us anything that you think is urgent then you've got permission to use the telephone in Mr Jenner's office to call the Ballroom. The number's here.'

Jen handed a small card over to Peggy who repeated the short number under her breath before slipping the card into the small handbag she was carrying. She then repeated the number aloud perfectly, twice.

Andrew raised one eyebrow in surprise. Maybe this wouldn't be a *complete* disaster after all.

'Time to go,' he said, standing up and grabbing his jacket from the back of the chair. 'Come on, I'll walk you to the corner.'

'Alright.' Peggy didn't sound terribly enthusiastic.

'Hang on!' Jen reached down to pick up a carrier bag from by her feet. From inside it, she produced a denim jacket and a pair of plain black high-heeled shoes, which she then handed to Peggy. 'Sorry, they might be a little big for you, but they're the most sensible black ones I had.'

'Thank you,' Peggy said, sitting down to pull off her own flat shoes and replace them with Jen's heels.

'Don't you have enough shoes of your own?' Charlie laughed, looking a little perplexed.

Peggy gave her brother a sharp look. 'Mother,' was all she said.

Andrew was astonished at how quickly Charlie's face fell as he immediately lapsed into uncharacteristic silence.

The silence that followed was strained and was only broken when Peggy stood up and shrugged off her coat to switch it with Jen's jacket.

'I'll meet you outside,' she muttered to Andrew before leaving the room.

Andrew tilted his head in surprise as he watched her walk away. Now that she was no longer hiding beneath that ridiculous trench coat she'd arrived in, Peggy looked as well-dressed and polished as the salesgirls they'd encountered in Lewis's the day before, which was…surprising.

Yes, he'd stick with 'surprising'.

Jen held her hands out towards Andrew and Lloyd. 'Here.'

'What's that?' Lloyd looked down at Jen's empty hands.

'Your jaws,' Jen replied, rolling her eyes. 'You both seem to have dropped them on the floor.'

Andrew cleared his throat. 'That's not appropriate, *Sergeant*.'

Lloyd snorted.

'Of course,' Jen replied, but she was clearly suppressing another eye-roll. 'Sorry, sir.'

Andrew glared briefly at Charlie, who was smirking at him in a terribly insufferable manner.

'I don't want you here when I get back, Mr Swan. Is that clear?'

Without waiting for an answer, Andrew pulled on his jacket and headed down the stairs to catch up with Peggy.

When he reached the pavement, she was leaning against the wall, lightly chewing on her thumbnail.

'Let's go then,' Andrew said, and Peggy fell into step beside him for the short walk down Tib Street.

'What do I do if Marnie has another episode like yesterday?' Peggy asked quietly after a few moments.

'Do you think she will?' Andrew asked, still unsure that he really believed that Marnie had done anything at all. Really, why couldn't it have just been a malfunctioning air duct? A very coincidentally timed malfunctioning air duct, obviously.

'I don't know,' Peggy replied despondently. She was worrying a ring on her right hand, spinning it around and around in an obvious nervous tic.

Andrew supposed that it was his job to ensure that their asset – for that's what Peggy now equated to in an official capacity – was calm and prepared. 'You'll be fine.'

As they turned the corner onto Market Street, Andrew stopped Peggy with a light hand on her arm. 'Look, Rebecca's already outside.'

Peggy followed his gaze, and sure enough Rebecca was standing outside Lewis's chatting to another woman, tilting her face up towards the weak early summer sunshine.

'Here I go then,' Peggy said with a frail impression of a smile. 'I'll see you after five.'

Despite himself, Andrew decided then that he actually preferred the sharp edges of the Peggy Swan he'd seen in the days before to this polite, nervous wreck before him.

'You'll be fine,' he repeated, more forcefully this time, hoping that she might believe him if he said it enough times. 'I promise.'

Peggy was almost across the road when Rebecca looked over to her, obviously trying to gauge whether or not this was the woman she was waiting for.

Peggy smiled, hoping that she looked confident and poised, rather than like how she actually felt. Grasping for any thread of reassurance she could get, she glanced back across the road to where Andrew still stood. He only gave her a short nod before turning on his heel and disappearing back down Tib Street, but it felt like enough.

'Hi. Peggy?' Rebecca asked, smiling widely as Peggy approached.

'That's right,' Peggy replied, holding out her hand for Rebecca to shake. 'You must be Rebecca.'

Rebecca nodded and then inclined her head towards the woman she'd been speaking to. 'This is Bette. She's in Haberdashery.'

Bette reminded Peggy a little bit of the short, shouting woman who'd been at Tib Street the day before. The creepy one. *Dolly*.

'Hello there, dear,' Bette said. Thankfully her voice was higher and smoother than Dolly's. She also didn't seem to have any odd comments that she wished to make about Peggy and death, so Peggy was enormously grateful for that.

A smartly dressed man wearing the old-fashioned Lewis's uniform unlocked the door from the inside and the small crowd of staff waiting outside was ushered into the darkened foyer.

Peggy followed Rebecca and Bette down a long corridor before they reached the first staircase. They twisted and turned through doors and hallways until they finally stopped in a fairly large cloakroom.

Rebecca pointed at the row of lockable cupboards on the far wall, all covered in varying degrees of chipped walnut veneer.

'You can take any of the empty ones,' Rebecca explained. 'Leave your coat and bag. If you bring anything for lunch, it's best to keep that in there too. It makes it more difficult for the stockroom boys to steal your sandwiches!'

'Little snipes,' Bette muttered under her breath as she hung up her coat. 'They stole two meat pies from George last week, you know.'

'I'm sure George will dole out a suitable enough punishment for them come Saturday,' Rebecca said, laughing a little.

Peggy shoved her jacket and handbag haphazardly into the nearest empty cupboard and locked the door. She then slid on the rubber wristband holding the key and pulled the sleeve of her dress down over it.

'Most of us get chains to put the key on,' Rebecca said, pointing to a delicate chain around her neck. 'It saves trying to always wear dresses with long sleeves or pockets.'

'She's full of good ideas, that one,' Bette said, patting Rebecca on the shoulder as she passed by and left the cloakroom.

'Nervous about your first day?' Rebecca asked as she gestured for Peggy to follow her back down the stairs. 'Mr Jenner didn't tell me much beyond your name.'

'A bit nervous,' Peggy replied, which was quite a spectacular understatement. 'And there's not much to tell, I suppose.'

Rebecca had the sort of tinkly laugh that Peggy had always wished she'd possessed, if only so that she could sprinkle it throughout conversation with dull people and immediately sound as though she were entirely engaged. Rebecca's accent rounded the edges of her words warmly, and, if based on that alone, Peggy didn't think the friendly woman in front of her seemed particularly murderous in any way. Then again, Peggy supposed she'd never knowingly encountered a murderer before, so what did she know?

'Where were you before here?' Rebecca asked. 'You don't sound like you're quite from round this way.'

Peggy thought back over what she'd discussed with Andrew and Jen in the Ballroom the day before. 'Oh, I was staying with family in Norfolk for a bit. I worked in a little clothing shop near the seaside for a while when I was there.'

Rebecca nodded, easily accepting the fiction. 'Well, I imagine this might all seem a little different to you then. Busier, maybe. It's fine, though, I promise. The customers are mostly nice, and all the girls in Perfume are pretty good at warning each other when there's a difficult customer around. As long as you're polite and cheerful every minute you're on the shop floor you'll be fine. You can then go scream into oblivion in the break room at lunchtime.'

Peggy blinked, and it took her a second too long to realise that Rebecca was expecting her to laugh. She forced a giggle and felt completely moronic. She was glad Aunt Emmeline couldn't see her right now.

'Was that your husband dropping you off this morning?' Rebecca asked, craning her head to take a peek at Peggy's left hand as she held open the door to the Perfume Hall.

Peggy nearly choked. *Jesus Christ.* 'No,' she croaked. 'No. Not my husband.'

'Ah,' Rebecca said, nodding sagely. 'Just waiting for him to ask then. I know that feeling.'

Peggy dearly wanted to get off this topic but given that she was supposed to be actively finding out about Rebecca's relationships that was going to be a little difficult.

Rebecca sighed loudly, obviously pleased to have found an

opportunity to talk about her own life. 'I've been waiting an absolute age to get a proposal, but I'm hoping that it might happen soon. It's my birthday next month. Birthdays are good for proposals, don't you think?'

Peggy made a fairly non-committal noise in reply – she was too distracted by the all-too-familiar smell of the Perfume Hall incident of the day before – but Rebecca accepted it in her stride.

'It doesn't usually smell quite like this,' Rebecca said, wrinkling her own nose as she saw Peggy looking around. 'There was a bit of a problem in here yesterday. Some bottles were broken.'

'Oh, right?' Peggy asked as nonchalantly as she could manage.

'Yeah,' Rebecca said. 'It was really weird, actually. There was this big gust of wind and then the bottles all smashed. There were people running around all over the place and screaming.'

Rebecca interpreted Peggy's look of horror to mean that she was scaring away the new employee, and she backtracked hurriedly. 'No, I mean, it wasn't *that* bad. Nothing like that has ever happened before. I'm sure it won't happen to you.'

'Let's hope so,' Peggy said, eyeing the Estée Lauder counter with apprehension.

'Rebecca?' a voice called from across the hall.

Rebecca looked apologetic. 'Sorry, Peggy, can you give me two minutes? I just need to run over there to speak to Cathy and then get some paperwork for you to sign. We can talk about what you need to do this morning when I get back. Yeah?'

'Of course,' Peggy replied. 'I'll just wait here.'

Rebecca smiled and then dashed off across the Perfume Hall towards the woman who'd shouted for her, calling out greetings to others as she went.

As Peggy approached the bridal-themed display of perfume, which had already been carefully reset after yesterday's disaster, albeit with far fewer bottles, she felt a presence behind her. 'Marnie?'

'You came back,' Marnie said, sounding vaguely accusatory, but also quite pleased. 'What are you doing here?'

'I'm trying to help you,' Peggy hissed, keeping her voice as low as possible while she pretended to inspect a bottle of *Beautiful*. 'I can't do that if you start blowing things up around me.'

'Sorry,' Marnie replied, and she sounded sheepish. 'If it helps, I didn't actually mean to do that. I didn't hurt you, did I? Or that man you were with?'

Peggy shook her head. 'No, but you did scare the hell out of a lot of people, didn't you?'

'Who are you anyway?' Marnie asked, clearly choosing to take Peggy's question as rhetorical.

'My name's Peggy. I'm working with the police to try and find out what happened to you.'

'You're a detective?'

Peggy turned around and was surprised to see that Marnie looked as solid as she had done the day before. *Weird.* Peggy hadn't been expecting Marnie to be able to materialise so soon after expending what must have been an awful lot of energy the day before.

'No, I'm not,' Peggy whispered, careful not to move her lips too much. 'I'm just helping them.'

'But the handsome guy with the great hair *is* police, right?' Marnie asked, grinning slightly. 'I was always good at picking out coppers a mile away.'

Peggy wondered how pleased Andrew would be to know that Marnie thought he was handsome. She might have to try and drop it into conversation at some point just to see what happened. He'd probably drop dead in horror.

Another group of salesgirls entered the hall. They were all laughing together before splitting off to head for their respective workspaces.

'Marnie, listen, I want to talk to you, but I can't do that too easily here,' Peggy said, looking around shiftily. 'Not unless I want everyone to think I'm stark raving mad on my first day. Is there somewhere you can get to where we can talk later?'

Marnie looked at Peggy questioningly. 'How do I go to different places?'

'Well...' Peggy trailed off. 'I don't know. How did you get *here*?'

Marnie looked slightly pained. 'I don't really know. I remember being at my house, and you were there with some other people. Then I was here, and you could see me, but then, I don't really know. I know time has passed, but I don't know where I've been.'

Peggy didn't remember Emmeline ever saying anything that sounded similar, but she'd have to check with her once she got home to make sure. Maybe it had something to do with how little time Marnie had actually been a ghost in the scheme of things. Maybe not, though.

'Well, is there anywhere that you'd meet a friend if you wanted to confide in them at work?' Peggy asked. 'Where's a good place not to be overheard?'

'Maybe the ladies toilets on the fifth floor?' Marnie suggested after a few seconds of thought. 'Nobody really goes up there anymore.'

'Alright,' Peggy agreed. 'Look, I don't mind if you stay around here this morning. I might not always be able to talk back though. I know that what happened yesterday was because of Rebecca, but she's showing me around today, and if you do anything like that again I'm not going to be allowed to stay and help, alright?'

Marnie sighed, sounding sadder now. 'Alright.'

'Peggy!'

Peggy turned and saw Rebecca striding back towards her, clutching a sheaf of paper.

'So sorry about that,' Rebecca said, still smiling cheerily as she reached Peggy's counter. 'Are you ready to get started?'

Peggy looked at Marnie out of the corner of her eye, watching as the younger woman glared at her former best friend.

'Absolutely.'

SEVEN

Charlie Swan had been called many things in his life, but 'patient' had never been one of them. So, while he appreciated that the police had procedures in place for when it came to conducting investigations, he was overwhelmingly disappointed by how boring most of the job seemed to be.

He'd hoped that when DI Joyce returned from depositing Peggy at Lewis's there might have been some level of action. Perhaps a raid on a suspect's house, or maybe even a dramatic car chase, but other than being chastised by Joyce for still being in the Ballroom, nothing interesting had happened to Charlie at all. Everyone in the Ballroom seemed to be content to sit in near silence and read files.

Nobody gave Charlie a file.

After ten long minutes, he'd taken his leave with a promise to catch up with Lloyd for a drink at the end of the day. What was he supposed to do now though? He couldn't go and bother Peggy at work because she might actually kill him, but then he didn't really fancy driving all the way back out to Butterton either; he'd only have to come back into town again later anyway.

Charlie looked at the Jaguar parked slightly further up the road. What would Morse do? Go to the pub and drink alone, he supposed. He wasn't in the mood for that.

He thought about his favourite car languishing in the garage at home. The poor car that his killjoy sister had refused as an option again that morning. What would *Bond* do?

Charlie grinned when he realised that he *could* be Bond in this situation. Peggy was obviously another double-oh agent, on a mission in deep cover, and Andrew was quite clearly 'M' because he was just a dull pencil-pusher at the end of the day.

If DI Joyce wanted information on Rex Hughes and Rebecca Silverman, then Charlie Swan was the man for that job. With a newfound spring in his step, Charlie pulled his sunglasses out of his pocket and whistled merrily as he headed down Tib Street towards the city centre.

Anyone who was anyone wouldn't be out at this time of the morning; it was *far* too early, after all. Those who'd spent the night partying would be sleeping it off, and those in gainful employment would already be sequestered away in their plush offices waiting for the first meeting of the day to start without them.

That didn't mean all was lost, though. Charlie had learned over the years that the people who were the most useful when it came to collecting information in any social situation were the ones who were always watching from the sidelines. It was the waiters, the barmaids, and the hotel concierges who were the real stars of the show. They made it their business to know everyone and *everything,* and they could bring down a dynasty if they chose to weaponise the information that they'd gathered from the loose lips of the wealthy and drunk.

Charlie knew exactly who he needed to speak to first.

Ed Templeton had been a fixture behind the counter at Howth's for as long as Charlie could remember. He had a permanent scowl on his face, which, given that he spent six mornings a week serving chip butties to hungover twenty-somethings and grumpy council workers, probably wasn't all that surprising.

Ed did, however, perk up dramatically any time he saw Charlie wander into his establishment. Not because Charlie was a particular friend, but usually because Charlie was willing to hand over an extra few pounds if Ed swore not to tell anyone who Charlie had stumbled in there with on any given morning. Charlie had been handing over notes for a decade, and Ed had kept his mouth shut for just as long.

'Charlie Boy,' Ed said with a wink as he looked over Charlie's shoulder. 'Wait, all alone this morning, are we?'

'Morning, Ed,' Charlie replied with a grin, taking a seat at the sticky counter. 'Today I thought that maybe you could help me with a little project. Very top secret.'

Ed raised his eyebrows and Charlie rolled his eyes before handing over a five-pound note.

'One breakfast special it is then,' Ed said with a grin, turning back to retrieve an overdone fried egg from the griddle behind him. He slid it onto a thick slab of buttered toast and covered it in lashings of ketchup.

'Yummy,' Charlie said drily but shrugged and grabbed the paper-wrapped knife and fork next to the plate anyway. Peggy did always tell him that he was basically nothing more than a dustbin with legs.

'What is it you want exactly?' Ed asked, leaning down so that his head was level with Charlie's.

Charlie wasn't terribly worried about being overheard. Howth's wasn't exactly packed to the gills at eight-thirty on a Thursday morning.

'I want to know if there's anything interesting you can tell me about Rex Hughes.' Charlie shrugged again as he stuffed a forkful of egg and toast into his mouth and was delighted to discover that it wasn't actually that terrible.

''Ughes?' Ed said, grimacing. 'Why? What are you doing getting yourself mixed up with the likes of 'im for?'

'Oh, I'm not,' Charlie replied, sawing at the toast. 'I just need to know a few things about him, that's all.'

'I don't know anything about 'im,' Ed replied, far, far too quickly to be even remotely believable.

'What? Is a fiver not enough?' Charlie asked. 'Because, honestly, I'm feeling pretty ripped off here, Ed. This ketchup is knockoff Heinz, I can tell.'

'A fiver's definitely not enough for me to say a single word about 'ughes,' Ed replied, lowering his voice even further. 'Rumour has it that he's mixed up with the Byrnes now that they've pushed over into Danny Craigson's patch. I don't want no part of any of that.'

'What about for another ten?' Charlie asked, already reaching for his wallet. Let it not be said that Charlie Swan was above using money to get what he wanted sometimes.

'For ten, I'll tell you *one* thing,' Ed said, 'but then you're getting out of 'ere and not coming back for at least a week. Alright?'

'Alright,' Charlie agreed. He passed the note to Ed, who quickly stuffed it in his pocket with more speed than even the five had disappeared with.

'You know 'ughes' Daddy had that 'oliday business? The camps?' Ed asked, pretending to wipe at a stain on the counter with a horribly greasy rag. 'Well, when 'e sold them 'e kept a couple of seaside 'ouses that they owned. One's over Wallasey way. The other one's down south.'

'And?' Charlie asked, failing to see how this was worth the money.

'Well,' Ed growled, leaning even closer, 'that one down on the south coast 'as apparently caught the eye of the Byrnes, what with it being near Dover and all.'

It took a second for him to process what Ed was implying, but when he did, Charlie's mouth dropped open in a combination of glee and surprise. 'Ed, are you telling me that Rex Hughes is involved in drug smuggling?'

'Shut yer big mouth,' Ed hissed dangerously, smacking Charlie in the face with the greasy rag. 'You'll get yourself killed if you're not careful, kid.'

'Oh, come on, don't be so dramatic.' Charlie laughed lightly but sobered when he realised that Ed wasn't even remotely amused.

'The Byrnes are dangerous, Charlie Boy,' Ed muttered, 'and they've got eyes and ears everywhere. They're mixed up in all sorts. Keep your 'ead down, alright?'

'Alright,' Charlie agreed. He pushed the uneaten remains of 'breakfast' across the counter. 'See you around, Ed.'

Ed didn't reply. When he turned his back and started cracking eggs into a large, metal bowl Charlie knew that he'd been silently dismissed.

He briefly considered heading back to Tib Street immediately to share the information he'd gained about the possible link between Rex and the Byrnes but he had one more place he wanted to visit before he did his grand unveiling.

He checked his watch. It was still too early for Gio to have opened up at *Osteria* yet. Apparently, the eldest of the three Ceccarelli brothers didn't think Manchester was quite ready to embrace the idea of languid Roman breakfasts yet, so he was happy to wait to entice the lunch crowd in with the promise of large glasses of Italian wine instead. Good for business, but less good for Charlie when he needed information.

There were a few other places that might be a good shout, but Charlie knew that the girls who worked at Kendals could often be found in *Osteria* at the end of the work day. So, if Rex frequented the department store it was likely Gio knew him as a customer too. Charlie hoped that he'd also be able to get something on this Rebecca girl if she really *was* having an affair with Rex.

Wait, *Kendals*! Of course, he could just go there and do a little more investigating first. Yes, that seemed like a very good idea.

As long as he avoided Violetta in the Linens department he'd be fine.

Charlie pushed his sunglasses down over his eyes as he stepped back out into the bright morning feeling almost overwhelmingly pleased with himself.

EIGHT

Peggy's cheekbones ached from the amount of smiling she'd been forced into over the course of her first morning in the Perfume Hall. She'd smiled through endless customer queries about what had happened the day before ('I'm afraid I only started this morning'); through conversations with well-meaning, but fairly inept husbands ('I'm so sorry, but 'smells like flowers' isn't quite enough for me to work out exactly which perfume your wife usually wears'); and genuinely *beamed* all the way through her tea break with Haberdashery Bette ('Dear God, yes, I would *love* another cup of tea!').

By the time lunchtime rolled around, she hadn't had a single opportunity to talk to Marnie, even though the other woman had been hovering around the *Beautiful* display for hours, demonstrably moping even as she'd remained silent. She also hadn't seen Rebecca for more than a few minutes at a time once the shop had opened and the customers had started arriving.

She thought longingly about escaping out into the sunshine to find some lunch, but instead found herself trudging up a poorly lit staircase that wound up and around until she finally popped out on what was, according to the sign on the wall, the fifth floor. It was immediately obvious that up here had seen better days.

The air was cool and smelled slightly damp. In direct contrast to the airy, well-maintained ground floor, the paintwork, which had obviously been glorious in the store's heyday, was now faded and peeling. There were a few other people around, drifting in and out of sight in Peggy's peripheral vision, and she knew just from their dated clothing that only she could see them.

Of course the fifth floor was haunted. *Just great.*

Peggy kept her head down and made sure not to look at any of the figures directly. It was a trick that Emmeline had taught her years ago, and for the most part, it worked, particularly if the spirits weren't that strong. Apparently, ghosts naturally assumed that nobody could see or hear them, so unless you made direct contact they were pretty likely to leave you alone. Being mithered by ancient shop workers wasn't high on

Peggy's to-do list for the day, so she walked as quickly as she could towards the far wall where the sign for the ladies toilets was just visible behind a stack of trestle tables.

'Marnie?' she asked quietly into the darkness as her hand groped against the wall, to search for a light switch in the windowless room.

The dim overhead lights flickered on, reflecting eerily off the bottle-green tiles on the walls. Above the enamel sinks, the mirrors were smoky and cracked, and Peggy felt a vague sense of sadness emanating from the walls, as though the building itself longed for its past.

Marnie appeared in front of her only seconds later, beaming when she saw Peggy.

'I did it!' Marnie was clearly delighted with herself.

'Well done,' Peggy replied, hoping that she came off as more encouraging than patronising. It felt a little like dealing with a small child, which, Peggy supposed, wasn't too far off the mark given that Marnie had only been like this for six months.

'You did alright this morning,' Marnie said, grinning at Peggy. 'As a perfume girl, I mean. Everyone definitely believed you.'

'Oh.' Peggy was slightly taken aback at the unexpected compliment. 'Thanks.'

Marnie shrugged. 'It took me months to feel confident, you know, with all that smiling and talking to strangers. Mum always worried that I was too quiet back when I was at school, so I think she was more surprised than anyone when I got a Saturday job here.'

'Did you like working here?' Peggy asked. She was uncomfortably aware that she hadn't actually had to have a proper conversation with someone who wasn't either related to her or who worked for Greater Manchester Police, in quite a long time.

'I did.' Marnie smiled, although it had a sorrowful edge to it now. 'I really did. Rebecca already worked here. She's a year older than me, see. She thought it would be good for me to get a bit of experience here before I left school.'

'Had you always been friends?'

Marnie sighed, and Peggy felt that horrible gut-wrenching misery from her again.

'Always,' Marnie said. 'Our mums were best friends, so it was natural that the two of us would be the same, even with a year between us.

'She was always cooler than me, you know, but that was alright because if you were friends with Rebecca you sort of got to hang onto her coattails a bit and just go along with everything.

'I just can't believe that she'd go behind my back with *Rex* though.'

Peggy could hear a slight whine somewhere in the background, and her eyes widened. They couldn't have a repeat of yesterday. Not when Peggy was acutely aware of the enormous plate-glass mirrors in front of her. 'Marnie, I need you to stay calm, okay?'

'Yeah,' Marnie said, sucking in the ghostly approximation of a deep breath. 'Sorry, yeah.'

The whine faded away, and Peggy's shoulders drooped in relief. 'Thanks.'

'How come you can see me when nobody else can?' Marnie asked, scrutinising Peggy closely. 'Are you some sort of witch, or something?'

'No,' Peggy replied, then frowned. 'At least, I don't think so.'

'But how come you're helping the police? I mean, that's not something that happens a lot, right?'

'Honestly, I'm here because my younger brother has a big mouth and there's an odd Detective Chief Inspector in a ballroom on Tib Street. Apparently, this sort of thing is his speciality.'

'That's a bit weird,' Marnie replied before her eyes widened. 'I mean, not that I'm not grateful to you for being here at all!'

She then paused before sheepishly asking, 'I don't suppose you know how to make me, um, not be like this?'

Peggy scrunched up her face apologetically. 'Sorry.'

Marnie sighed again. 'That's alright. I just thought I'd ask. So, how do you think I can help you?'

Peggy looked at the young woman in front of her, with that flashy engagement ring sparkling even under the terrible lighting conditions of the toilets. It didn't seem fair that any of this had happened to Marnie, and it didn't seem right to have to ask her to try and relive something so unfathomably traumatic. She had to though, that's why she was here.

'I need to ask you about that night,' Peggy said quietly, 'and I know how hard that must be to think about.'

Marnie looked frozen, and there was something akin to terror in her eyes. Peggy hated herself.

'Marnie,' she added, 'DI Joyce – Andrew, who was here with me yesterday – he thinks that you might have seen who broke into your house. A reflection in the window, maybe?'

Marnie shook her head vehemently. 'I don't remember.'

Peggy nodded. 'Okay, that's okay.'

'I don't remember,' Marnie repeated, and she dug her fingernails into her palms as her voice grew tremulous. 'I don't remember.'

'Marnie, it's okay,' Peggy said, keeping her tone as even as she could, seeing Marnie growing more hysterical by the second. 'It's okay. We can try again another time, alright? It's okay. I promise.'

Marnie sniffled and kept shaking her head. Peggy knew that she needed to diffuse this situation as quickly as possible.

'Marnie, it's alright,' Peggy said softly. 'You'll be fine. I promise.'

Marnie was quiet for a long moment. 'He said that to you this morning.'

Peggy frowned. 'Who said what?'

'The policeman,' Marnie replied. 'What did you say he was called?'

'Andrew.' Peggy thought back to that morning. Andrew *had* said that to her, but how did Marnie know that when she hadn't been there? 'How d-'

'I don't remember anything about what happened to me,' Marnie said, cutting Peggy off. 'I was waiting for Rebecca.'

Marnie scowled darkly. 'Maybe if she hadn't been late this wouldn't have happened.'

It probably wasn't quite the moment to mention that back at the Ballroom they were working on the potential theory that Rebecca was the murderer. Peggy changed tack. 'Why was Rebecca late?'

'I don't know.' Marnie shrugged petulantly. 'She'd been late for things a lot recently. Oh God, do you think she was with my Rex?'

'I don't think so,' Peggy replied. 'I don't really know the details, but I think DI Joyce said that Rex was at an event somewhere over near Wilmslow.'

'That's what Rex told me too,' Marnie muttered. 'He asked me to be his guest, but I'd already promised to go to Janine's birthday party.' She paused. 'Oh my God, what if I'd gone with him instead? I wouldn't be here, would I?'

Marnie was flickering a little, and it was setting Peggy on edge.

'What do you mean Rebecca was late a lot recently?' Peggy asked, trying to get Marnie back on topic. 'Had she seemed different to you? Been acting strangely?'

Marnie frowned. 'Why are you asking so much about Rebecca?'

Peggy hoped her shrug was passably nonchalant. 'No reason, just trying to understand the situation, and how everyone fits in.'

For a long moment, Marnie stared back, eyes ever so slightly narrowed.

'Well,' she began eventually, 'a few weeks before Christmas, Rebecca started cancelling some of our plans. First, she said she wasn't feeling well, but then it turned into running errands for her mum, and by the time Christmas came around I'd barely seen her.

'The weird thing was that I popped over on Christmas Eve with Mum to drop off presents, but Rebecca wasn't there.' Marnie frowned. 'Her mum said that she hadn't seen much of her over the past few weeks, what with all the extra shifts she was doing. What extra shifts though? If she was doing extra work, it wasn't here.'

That was odd, Peggy thought. It was also probably the sort of thing that Andrew wanted to know about.

'I tried to ask her about it when we met up to go shopping,' Marnie continued, rubbing her hands together, 'but she just laughed and clammed up. We were in Kendals, shopping for party outfits, and she kept finding excuses to duck off to go look at something any time I asked her a question.'

'Had she ever been like that before?' Peggy asked.

Marnie shook her head. 'No. Rebecca wasn't the flighty type. One of the things I liked most about her was how straight-talking she was. You know, she'd always tell you what she really thought about you, unlike awful Janine. At least I *thought* that's what she was like.'

'And you've got no idea what she might have been keeping from you?' Peggy asked. She glanced surreptitiously at her watch. She didn't have much break time left, and she still needed to sneak back down the stairs without being seen. She didn't fancy answering questions about why she was wandering about upstairs on the fifth floor.

'No,' Marnie said. Then she tilted her head suddenly. 'No, wait, hang on. The day of Janine's party she called me at home. I'm sure she did.'

'What did she say?' Peggy asked. Okay, this could be good. If Marnie was starting to remember things about the day she died, then maybe there was still some hope of getting some useful information that Peggy could take back to Tib Street.

Marnie squinted down at the floor, and it was obvious that she was thinking hard about what had happened. 'I didn't speak to her. I was out. She spoke to Mum. Apparently, she had something that she really wanted to tell me, but that it was okay, and it would keep until that evening.'

Marnie looked up, helpless. 'I don't know what it was.'

'We'll figure it all out, Marnie,' Peggy said gently, ignoring the little voice in her head warning her that she probably shouldn't be making promises like that.

Marnie cleared her throat and straightened her shoulders. 'You should get back downstairs. Someone will notice if you're late, and if it's Janine she'll definitely tattle on you.'

'Janine, as in Janine Turner? She works here too?' Peggy asked in surprise. Nobody had mentioned that to her before now.

'Unfortunately.' Marnie rolled her eyes. 'She's over on the other side of the hall, where she bloody well belongs.'

Peggy laughed before she even realised what she'd done, and oh my God, *what* did it say about her life that the first 'friend' she'd made in an absolute age was a dead woman who might be able to bring down the building around them if she tried hard enough?

'You're right though,' Peggy said, looking down at her watch again. 'I'd better go. Are you coming downstairs?'

'I'll be there,' Marnie replied. 'When I work out how to get there.'

Peggy gave her a small smile and turned away to switch off the light.

Marnie's voice stopped her. 'Peggy?'

'Yes?'

'What happened to you?' Marnie asked quietly.

Peggy flinched. 'What do you mean?'

'I don't really know,' Marnie replied. 'You just seem...*sad*.'

'I'm fine,' Peggy replied, hastening to turn away again. 'I'll see you in a minute, alright?'

The obvious lie that was 'I'm fine' was underscored heavily by the way Peggy practically ran from the ladies toilets. She clattered back down the stairs towards the break room and over to the staff staircase that would take her back down to the shop floor.

She was in such a hurry that she only just managed to stop herself from crashing headfirst into a woman in a deep red dress who was standing at the top of the staircase.

'Watch it,' the woman snapped.

'S-sorry,' Peggy stammered. 'My fault.'

'Of course it was your fault.' The woman raised an eyebrow. 'Oh, you're the new one.'

Peggy bristled at the icy tone. 'I suppose I am, yes. And you are?'

The woman didn't reply, she just smiled sharply and sailed down the stairs as though she wasn't wearing five-inch heels.

'*That's* Janine.'

Marnie's whisper surprised Peggy so much that she nearly fell down the stairs herself.

'Great,' she muttered back as she grabbed the handrail, and watched as Janine sashayed down the corridor beneath them and out of sight.

'I wouldn't take it personally,' Marnie said with a shrug. 'She just hates everyone.'

'Which counter does she work at?' Peggy asked, hoping it really was as far away from her as possible.

'Over at Christian Dior,' Marnie replied, pursing her lips. 'She sells *Poison.* Which is rather fitting, don't you think?'

Peggy, regrettably, felt she might be inclined to agree.

* * *

Andrew pressed the heels of his hands into his eyes hard enough that spots of colour flashed in the darkness. Charlie Swan had *not* just told him that he'd wandered off around Manchester looking for information on Rex Hughes. He couldn't have done. It must be a stress-induced hallucination.

Andrew opened his eyes. Charlie Swan was still there.

'Please tell me that you're joking,' Andrew said, and he was dimly aware that his voice was oddly emotionless given how angry he was. 'Please tell me that you did not jeopardise this entire investigation because you were bored.'

'I don't think of it as 'jeopardising' anything,' Charlie replied blithely. 'I was being helpful.'

Andrew wondered how long they'd jail him for if he murdered an aristocrat.

'What the hell did you think you were doing?' *Ah*, and now Andrew had remembered how to yell. 'Do you have any idea how bloody stupid that was?'

'I can't see how it's any stupider than sending my sister undercover to have a friendly chat with a ghost,' Charlie replied, raising one eyebrow. 'Anyway, I've learned some *very* interesting things about our friend Rex.'

'I don't want to hear anything you've heard on your little walkabout,' Andrew snapped. 'Jesus Christ, how dense do you have to be? You're *not* police.'

'Neither is Peggy,' Charlie replied more sharply. 'That's not stopped you from sending her off to Lewis's, has it?'

'*I* didn't send her anywhere!'

'Excuse me!'

Both men turned towards the door in surprise. Higson was standing there, jacket draped casually over one shoulder like he'd just been out for a long lunch, which he probably had. It was the first time he'd shown his face in the Ballroom all day.

'Why exactly are you giving the posh boy a bollocking?' Higson asked Andrew, frowning as he lumbered towards his desk. There was no sense of urgency about his movements, despite being almost four o'clock in the afternoon.

'Mr Swan took it upon himself to investigate Rex Hughes himself,' Andrew explained, gritting his teeth.

'Using his initiative,' Higson replied with a nod of approval.

Andrew briefly wondered how long they'd jail him for if he murdered an aristocrat *and* his superior officer at the same time.

'If Rex Hughes gets wind that people are out asking questions about him it could jeopardise the whole operation,' Andrew said tightly, putting his murder plans firmly on hold. Momentarily, at least. 'Mr Swan is not a member of this department.'

Charlie didn't look remotely bothered by this fact.

'Well,' said Higson, gesturing towards Charlie, 'did you get anything useful?'

Charlie beamed, and Andrew felt his heart sink.

'Actually, yes. I can give you one reason why the Byrne Brothers are so interested in Rex Hughes,' Charlie said, pulling his legs up to sit cross-legged on the blue sofa.

Andrew baulked. CID hadn't been able to confirm a link between Hughes and the Byrnes, no matter how hard they'd tried, so there wasn't a hope in hell that Charlie had been fed anything but utter crap by some time-waster.

'The Hughes family own a property down near Dover,' Charlie explained. 'A leftover from their holiday camp days. I called a few friends of mine - the ones who know about these sorts of things - until I found one with knowledge of the Hughes' portfolio.'

That was news to Andrew. He'd looked over the list of property owned by the Hughes family, and there was no mention of any houses outside of the Greater Manchester area. Oh God, had Charlie *actually* found something useful? Andrew would never live it down.

'The house is about half a mile from the ferry port and sits on a couple of acres bordering an access road used by port workers,' Charlie continued. He shot Andrew a sharp look. 'So…'

Andrew sighed and ran a hand over his face, understanding exactly what Charlie was getting at. '*So*, if the Byrnes are importing anything from Europe – which we strongly suspect they are - they'd have a pretty easy route out of the port to a storage facility. Shit.'

How the hell had CID missed that?

'Well, well, well,' Higson said, one corner of his mouth quirked up. 'Looks like his lordship has done a better background check than our esteemed colleagues over at your place, Joyce.'

Andrew pursed his lips. So, he was considered part of the Ballroom when Higson wanted him to convince Peggy to go undercover, but he was CID again when he'd missed something. What did Higson want from him?

'I have something else,' Charlie announced, clearly pleased with himself.

Higson held out his hands as if to say, 'Please continue' and Andrew braced himself.

'I went to Kendals to see if any of the girls there knew anything useful,' Charlie replied, 'but nobody could remember much about the woman who came in with Marnie's things. I did learn that Rex has been engaged twice before though.'

'*Twice*?' Andrew coughed out.

'Marnie was lucky number three,' Charlie said. His face fell. 'Well, *unlucky* number three, I suppose.'

'What happened to the first two girls?' Andrew asked, his mind already pulling out information on any unexplained deaths of young women that had occurred in the previous few years.

'Oh, nothing,' Charlie replied, shaking his head, instantly derailing Andrew's serial killer theory. 'It sounds like the girls were the ones who called it off both times. Maybe Rex just isn't the marrying type, no matter how much he thinks he is.'

'We need to look into who these women are,' Andrew said, reaching for his notepad behind him. 'Did you get the names?'

Charlie nodded. 'But there's one last thing you should know first.'

'Go on,' Andrew said, rolling his eyes, because what was the point in trying to stop Charlie now?

'I popped into *Osteria*, you know, on St Ann's Square,' Charlie said. Higson looked nonplussed, but Andrew nodded. Kate had often pestered him to take her there for dinner, but he never had.

'Well,' Charlie continued looking a little less sure of himself, 'I know the guy who owns it. Well, *one* of the guys who owns it. He says that Rex Hughes used to be in there all the time, sometimes with Marnie after work, and sometimes at lunchtime for what were, apparently, 'business meetings'.'

'Okay, *and*?' Andrew asked when Charlie trailed off.

'Apparently, Rex hasn't been in since the end of January,' Charlie said. 'The last time he was there – blind drunk, apparently - he had an argument with another customer.'

'Not entirely surprising,' Andrew said with a shrug. 'His fiancée had been murdered a few weeks earlier.'

'Right,' said Charlie, 'but the other customer was Liam Byrne.'

Andrew caught Higson's eye, and for just one moment they were united in something.

But then Higson had to add, 'I see CID missed something else then.'

Andrew ignored him and focussed on Charlie. 'Did your guy hear what the argument was about?'

Charlie screwed up his face apologetically. 'Not really, but apparently Rex did sound like he was blaming Liam Byrne for something, calling him a liar.'

'Looks like you might need to go and have another chat with Mr Hughes,' Higson said pointedly to Andrew. 'If Marnie Driscoll's death has something to do with the Byrnes, then I want enough on them to put them away for a good long time. Those scumbags always manage to wriggle free, and we're not going to let that happen this time. Got it, Joyce?'

'Sir,' Andrew replied with a nod, because he couldn't argue with that, could he? Putting the Byrnes away would definitely be enough of a coup to allow him to waltz back into CID.

'Good work, Mr Swan,' Higson said, looking mildly impressed. He stretched back in his chair, clasping his hands on his sizeable stomach. 'Now that you're here though, can you do me another favour?'

'Of course,' Charlie agreed eagerly.

'Be a good lad and go get me a coffee.'

Andrew snorted into his hand as Charlie's expression fell. He threw his notepad towards the disappointed man.

'Write down the names of Rex's previous girls before you go,' Andrew said, sending a pencil sailing through the air a second later.

The door downstairs clanged open, and Charlie fumbled the pencil, almost dropping it in surprise.

A few seconds later Jen arrived. She'd just been over to Lewis's to check that everything was fine with Peggy, and Andrew wasn't delighted to see that his sergeant looked a little harried.

Higson was now frowning down at a crossword on his desk, so Andrew assumed that this show of indifference meant that *he* was still in charge.

'Everything alright?' he asked, holding out his hand to collect the notepad from Charlie.

'Kind of,' Jen replied, biting her lip. 'Probably.'

Andrew sat up straighter, and he could tell that Higson was listening even though he hadn't looked up from the paper. 'What's happened? Is Peggy alright?'

'Yeah, yeah, she's fine,' Jen replied. 'I mean, she looks a bit dead on her feet, but she's okay.'

'Then what's the problem?' Andrew asked slowly. If Peggy was fine then it couldn't be anything major, but the thought of a wrinkle in their plan bothered him more than it would have done an hour ago, back when he'd far less evidence that a connection existed between Rex and the Byrne Brothers.

'While I was there, one of the customers recognised Peggy,' Jen said, wincing slightly.

From the corner of his eye, Andrew saw Charlie stop dead on the way out of the door and turn back towards them.

'Who was it?' Charlie asked, eyes wide.

Andrew was slightly taken aback by the look of panic on Charlie's face. He could see how it might be a little odd for anyone who actually *knew* Peggy to see her in her new job as a perfume girl, but he couldn't understand the potency of her brother's anxiety.

Jen, however, didn't look perplexed at all. She looked uncomfortable. 'Peggy said her name was Charlotte Bamford.'

'Fucking hell,' Charlie muttered in dismay. 'What did she say? Charlotte, I mean.'

'Enough that the entire Perfume Hall now knows that they have a *Lady* in their midst,' Jen replied with a wince.

'Nothing else?' Charlie asked, looking slightly desperate.

Jen screwed up her face, and Andrew could tell that whatever she was about to say wasn't going to please the younger Swan at all.

'She told Peggy that your mother had been over for dinner last week,' Jen explained quietly. 'That she'd brought Edgar with her.'

Charlie swore loudly and colourfully enough that even Higson looked over in interest. 'I need to go and talk to my sister.'

'Whoa, hold on. What's this about?' Andrew asked, his curiosity more than getting the best of him. 'Who the hell is *Edgar*?'

Charlie shook his head mulishly. 'I'm not going to gossip about my own sister, Detective Inspector. If Peggy wants you to know anything she can tell you herself; and only if she *chooses* to.'

There wasn't even the barest hint of the ever-present levity in Charlie's tone, and Andrew instinctively knew that he was deadly serious.

'Peggy's fine, Charlie,' Jen said reassuringly. 'I promise. Charlotte was only around for a few minutes. I think Peggy just got a bit of a shock, that's all.'

Charlie shook his head. 'You don't understand. If Charlotte 'Big Mouth' Bamford knows that Peggy's working in Lewis's, you can bet that everyone in a three-mile radius will know by the end of the day.'

Andrew still couldn't really see why this was so problematic. 'So?'

'So?' Charlie repeated, his voice icy. '*So*, I can guarantee that my father will want to know what exactly his daughter is up to, and conversations with our father are something Peggy and I usually prefer to avoid unless absolutely necessary. She doesn't need this. She needs someone to make sure she really is alright. *So*, if you'll excuse me.'

'Oh, Jesus Christ, *fine*,' Andrew sighed in exasperation, holding up his hand to stop Charlie from leaving.

He pointed to Charlie, then the blue sofa. 'You, sit there and shut up. Jen, can you get the boss a coffee, please? I'll go and check on Peggy. Also, where the bloody hell is Lloyd?'

'He's trawling the jewellery shops within walking distance of Kendals,' Jen replied, already picking up Higson's mug. 'We figured that maybe whoever returned Marnie's gifts to Kendals tried to get rid of the earrings somewhere nearby. Plus, we still have no idea where the engagement ring went, and that's got to be the most valuable thing Marnie owned, by miles.'

Andrew nodded approvingly. 'That's a good idea.'

'Thanks, sir,' Jen replied, with a small but genuine smile as she left to get the coffee.

'Seriously, do *not* move from that sofa,' Andrew warned Charlie as he stood up and shrugged his jacket on again. 'If the Byrnes are anywhere near this, you need to stay the hell out of it.'

Charlie nodded silently.

Higson looked mildly approving as Andrew glanced towards him and then headed for Lewis's.

* * *

Peggy was sitting on the counter between the two sinks in the fifth-floor ladies toilets, clutching the large mug of sweet tea that Rebecca had forced on her.

Rebecca hadn't really had any idea why Peggy had looked so shellshocked after Charlotte's surprise appearance, but the tea had been almost as gratefully received as the extra fifteen-minute break Peggy had been sent off to take.

She'd run straight up the stairs, barely stopping before she'd closed the door behind her. Marnie had materialised a few seconds later, but she hadn't actually said anything, for which Peggy was exceedingly appreciative.

'Think I still have a job?' Peggy asked eventually, only half joking.

'Of course you do,' Marnie replied, frowning. 'Can't believe you're a *Lady* though. Well, no, I suppose a can. I mean, you don't exactly sound like you're from round here most of the time.'

Peggy took a sip of her slightly too-hot tea. 'Andrew's going to kill me. He made me swear I wouldn't make a scene. Technically I've now made *two*.'

'This wasn't your fault though, was it?' Marnie said, scrunching up her nose. 'Plus, it wasn't that bad. The girls will gossip for a few days, you'll just have to accept that, but it's not like it's a bad thing for them to know, right?'

'It's who else will find out I'm here that's the problem,' Peggy muttered, blowing gently over the rim of the mug.

'What did that Charlotte woman mean about your mother?' Marnie asked, tilting her head.

Peggy had been expecting that question, yet it still made her flinch. 'Nothing really.'

Marnie raised her eyebrows in disbelief. 'You went white as a sheet. You can't tell me that it's nothing. Come on, it's not like I'm going to be able to tell anyone if you've got a great big secret, is it? Plus, my mum always said it's best to talk about your problems, you know.'

'Oh, Marnie, trust me when I tell you that people have talked about my problems enough over the past year.'

'That's not the same as *you* talking about them though, is it?' Marnie asked gently.

Peggy sighed. Marnie was right, but it didn't mean that she just wanted to have a sharing session right here in the ladies toilets. Oh God, she *was* going to have to tell Andrew though, wasn't she? That wouldn't be mortifying at all…

'Not right now, Marnie,' Peggy replied tiredly. 'Sorry.'

'That's alright.' Marnie shrugged. 'I get it. When I first started seeing Rex, I didn't want anyone to know; it just seemed too weird, you know, me being me, and him being who he is. I thought that maybe if I kept it to myself it would last longer. Drove Janine mental when she found out though, so I sort of wish I'd told her earlier.'

Marnie's triumphant laugh actually made Peggy smile slightly. Then she frowned. Everyone had been so focused on Rebecca fitting the vague description of the woman in Kendals, that nobody had stopped to consider Janine.

'What?' Marnie asked, her jollity slipping away as she watched Peggy.

'Nothing,' Peggy shook her head. 'Well, probably nothing. Look, don't worry about it.'

She checked her watch. 'I should get back downstairs. Thank God there's only half an hour left.'

Marnie laughed again, quieter this time. 'You get used to it pretty quickly. The questions are always the same, but it's fun to help people, you know? Perfume's not important, but it's nice to think that you're going to make someone's day a little bit brighter when they get a present that they like.'

Peggy was as surprised by Marnie's optimistic view of life as she was saddened by the thought that someone who seemed so genuinely *pleasant* had met such a tragic fate. It perhaps helped to put Peggy's own mishaps into perspective; a little, at least.

By the time she reached the Perfume Hall again, Peggy was well and truly braced for the whispering. She tilted her chin up and kept her face as impassive as possible. As Emmeline had reminded her the night before, sometimes being a Swan meant doing things you didn't want to do.

'Feeling better?' Rebecca asked, quickly coming over from where she had been helping a customer.

'Much better, thanks,' Peggy replied. 'Sorry about that.'

Rebecca looked like she was bursting with questions, but she held her tongue and Peggy had never been more grateful in her life.

However, any appreciation lasted only the full three seconds it took for Andrew Joyce to walk through the door.

Oh God.

'Oh, look,' Rebecca smiled, spotting him too. 'Your 'not-husband' is here.'

Peggy blanched and really hoped that Andrew's fairly impassive expression as he approached them meant that he hadn't heard what Rebecca had just called him.

'Hi!' Andrew said brightly, and Peggy only managed to stare at him in witless surprise. Where on earth had this agreeable version of DI Joyce come from? There wasn't even the tiniest suggestion of the slightly abrasive tone he usually possessed.

'I was just passing by,' Andrew added with a small shrug, *still smiling*. 'So, I thought I'd come and see how you were getting on.'

He turned towards Rebecca as though he hadn't been aware of her presence. 'Oh, hi, sorry. I know I probably shouldn't just be coming in like this.'

Rebecca beamed at him. 'No, it's fine.'

'Andrew,' came the reply, along with another charming smile as he shook Rebecca's hand.

Peggy's confusion must have shown on her face because Andrew shot her a look that clearly told her that she might want to dial down the disbelief a few notches.

'Oh, um, yes, all fine,' Peggy managed to choke out eventually. This did not improve Andrew's expression. 'Small incident. Not a big deal.'

Rebecca patted Peggy's arm sympathetically. 'Peggy's big secret is out, I'm afraid.'

Peggy had to clamp down on the hysterical laugh that was trying to fight its way out of her chest. Peggy's previously undisclosed position as a member of the nobility wasn't even *approaching* her biggest secret, but Rebecca didn't have to know that, did she?

'Oh?' Andrew asked, eyes wide.

Peggy thought that Andrew's impression of surprised concern was sufficiently believable, even when she knew full well that Jen would have gone straight back to the Ballroom to relay the story of the encounter with Charlotte.

'Are you okay?' Andrew added. His manufactured concern had morphed into something more genuine.

'Fine,' Peggy replied shortly. She wished that Andrew would just leave now that he knew Peggy hadn't done anything to give away their ruse. She had half an hour left before she was finished work and due at Tib Street again, and she'd prefer to get her thoughts fully in order before she had to explain herself to him.

Rebecca bestowed another sympathetic glance on her newest colleague. 'You know, there's only half an hour left, and you've had quite the day. We're not too busy, so why don't you head off now?'

'Oh no, I couldn't do that.' Peggy shook her head in slight desperation. 'I'm fine. I'm very happy to stay.'

'No, really,' Rebecca said, nodding seriously as she squeezed her arm in a show of support. 'Just think of it as a first-day perk.'

'She never let me go home early, and I was supposed to be her best friend,' Marnie muttered darkly from behind Peggy, and *that* wasn't helping either.

Andrew smiled directly at Peggy, and now that she looked closely enough, she could see the edge to it. Andrew Joyce wasn't actually happy at all. *What a surprise.*

'Come on Peg,' Andrew said cheerfully, as though he couldn't quite believe their luck. 'This is probably the only time this will ever happen.'

Peg! The only person allowed to call her 'Peg' was Charlie, and she narrowed her eyes at Andrew before remembering that she was supposed to be pleased about getting the chance to skip out of work early.

'Thanks so much, Rebecca,' Peggy said gritting her teeth. 'That's really kind of you.'

'No problem,' Rebecca replied, blushing slightly as Andrew smiled at her again. 'We're all family here, so we look out for each other.'

Marnie snorted in disgust and Peggy fought the urge to roll her eyes at the ghost.

'I'll meet you outside,' Peggy said to Andrew. 'I just need to go get my things.'

'I'll wait here,' Andrew replied, still beaming at Rebecca. 'If Rebecca here doesn't mind.'

Rebecca didn't look like she minded at all, so Peggy headed off to the break room. Marnie trailed behind her the whole way.

'I hope you're not actually into that man in any way,' Marnie said, leaning against the neighbouring locker as Peggy retrieved her handbag and jacket, 'because apparently Rebecca doesn't care about that sort of thing.'

'Marnie,' Peggy hissed, looking around carefully to ensure that they really were alone, 'can you stop saying things like that, please?'

'Ugh, fine,' Marnie replied, sounding petulant. 'But it'll be your fault if you get back down there and Rebecca's draped herself all over him. Look, I'm just saying, that if I didn't have Rex - and I was still alive, *obviously* - I wouldn't say no to *that*.'

'Jesus, I am not having this conversation with you,' Peggy replied, putting the key back around her wrist. 'I'm actually perfectly content with the idea of growing old and dying alone, thank you very much.'

Peggy stalled as she thought about what she'd just said and cringed. 'Sorry, I didn't mean to say that. That wasn't fair.'

Marnie just rolled her eyes again. 'See you tomorrow, *Lady* Peggy.'

Peggy grimaced as she slung the handbag strap over her shoulder and headed back downstairs to the Perfume Hall, where Andrew and Rebecca now appeared to be deep in conversation.

'I need to go out the other way,' Peggy said to the detective, pointedly tilting her head towards the back of the shop floor. 'So, I'll see you outside, alright?'

'Alright,' Andrew replied, sparing her no more than the briefest of glances. 'See you in a sec.'

'Bye, Rebecca,' Peggy added and was pleased when the other woman actually turned around to say goodbye properly. She clearly had more manners than Andrew.

It took Andrew another five minutes to meet Peggy outside the main entrance.

'Having a nice time with your new friend?' Peggy asked, and her tiredness made her tone sharper than she'd intended.

Andrew just raised a single eyebrow. 'I think you mean *your* new friend.'

'Hmm,' Peggy replied, folding her arms.

Andrew, to Peggy's surprise, actually laughed, and there was nothing forced or false about it.

'What?' she asked, deeply suspicious.

'You really are horribly anti-social, aren't you?' He laughed again and still looked amused when he eventually sighed. 'Come on.'

Peggy deflated. She didn't really fancy going back to Tib Street for a debrief right now but she turned, shoulders hunched, and made to cross the road.

'Where are you going?' Andrew asked.

Peggy pointed across the road. 'The Ballroom?'

Andrew shook his head and gestured over his shoulder. 'No, we're going this way.'

'Why?'

'I'm taking you for a drink because you look like you need one,' Andrew replied with a shrug. 'Just think of it as a first-day perk.'

NINE

Andrew had always been good at noticing things.

When he'd been very young, he'd noticed that when his father would disappear for days on end, his mother would develop lines at the corner of her mouth as her lips pulled together tighter and tighter. The appearance of these lines usually signalled the worst of his mother's moods, which then led to him and Rob crouching together under the tree at the end of the garden, doing their best not to draw attention to themselves.

He'd noticed the way some of the other children who'd lived on their road would never ask him and Rob to play; and how those same children would whisper to each other when Andrew joined their class in primary school, always looking over at him as though he'd done something terrible to offend them. He'd noticed their parents behaving similarly.

Yet, he'd never quite been able to notice the little tells his father gave before one of his absent stretches though, so it had always come as a surprise to see the armchair empty for days and nights at a time. By the time Jack would eventually come home again, the boys and their mother had almost forgotten what it was like to live with him.

When Andrew looked back at his childhood, he thought that there were probably obvious clues to his father's activities, but you couldn't have expected a small child to foresee the descent of a decent family man into a one-way spiral of drink, debt and crime. In reality, he'd barely known the man, and perhaps that was why Andrew had grown up wanting to know how to read people better; needing to know what they were really thinking beneath the veneer they presented to the world.

His attention to detail was what had fast-tracked him through the earliest hoops of his career and hurtled him down to Bramshill for further training. It's what had pitted him against older, more experienced officers when it came to promotion considerations. It was what made him an exceptional detective when he was allowed to actually do his job; when he was free of cantankerous DCIs, undercover civilians, and the constant undercurrent of the supernatural.

When he'd arrived at Lewis's earlier that afternoon, Andrew had noticed two things almost instantly. First, that Peggy had looked like she'd seen a ghost - if he excused himself the pun; and second, that Rebecca Silverman smiled far too widely and far too frequently. Andrew never trusted people who doled out smiles so freely, as more often than not it was because there was something darker there, lurking just beneath the mask of affability.

This second observation had finally given him the chance to do his job, and in the ten minutes he'd spent with Rebecca he'd learned three things:

1. Rebecca was an incorrigible flirt. This probably made her excellent at her job but did also ratchet up the likelihood of Rebecca having crossed a line in her relationship with Rex.

2. Rebecca was definitely digging for information on Peggy. Andrew suspected that this was probably due to the revelation of Peggy's aristocratic connections rather than anything more sinister, but Andrew couldn't call himself a detective if he didn't keep this under close examination.

3. Rebecca had a secret. Andrew didn't know what it was yet, but there were odd little stops and starts in her speech and her movements, which suggested that she was being particularly careful about what she revealed.

He hoped that Peggy had managed to get something useful from her stint in the Perfume Hall, but right now he was actually more interested in Peggy herself.

Since he'd met her, he'd been watching her flip from reserved and aloof one minute, to sharp and scathing the next; and whereas he'd already decided that he needed to get to the bottom of all of that anyway, the appearance of the mysterious, and apparently dreaded, 'Charlotte Bamford' that afternoon had ignited his insatiable desire to *know*.

So, he'd decided as he'd headed out of Lewis's and back onto Market Street, that he was going to take the opportunity to actually do a bit of investigating.

Which was how he found himself carrying a glass of brandy and a pint of beer across the slightly manky carpets of *The Pelican*. The pub was unfashionably empty, partly because it wasn't even five o'clock yet, but mostly because *The Pelican* probably hadn't been considered 'fashionable' even for a single moment in its long existence. Incidentally, this was why it was the perfect place for Andrew to do a little digging out of the way of any prying eyes. He couldn't imagine any of the well-dressed shop girls of central Manchester popping in here post-work, nor any of the nouveau-riche posers like Rex Hughes. More to the point though, it was still a frequent haunt of the city's old guard of police, and retired or not, the very possibility of their presence made *The Pelican* an unattractive prospect for the likes of the Byrnes and their associates.

'Here you go,' Andrew said, placing the brandy snifter in front of Peggy, before taking the seat opposite.

'Thanks,' Peggy said quietly. She didn't take a drink, but she wrapped her hand around the glass and began nervously drumming her fingers against it. The slight clink of her ring's band on the glass reminded Andrew a little too much of the sound of perfume bottles clacking together, and he unconsciously raised his fingers to lightly touch the scab on his face.

Up close, Andrew became uncomfortably aware that the jewels on Peggy's right hand were unlikely to be the costume jewellery that Kate had favoured on nights out and were probably worth more than his house, plus maybe his car as well.

He lifted his glass and held it out, waiting for Peggy to tap her own glass against it half-heartedly.

'Cheers to your first day,' Andrew said, as he took a drink. 'How was the world of gainful employment?'

'Far too cheerful.' Peggy sighed tiredly.

'Rebecca seems to like you, which is good.' Andrew nodded to himself. 'She's more likely to open up to you now.'

'So, you do actually want me back in there tomorrow?' Peggy asked uncertainly.

'Why wouldn't I?' Andrew asked, frowning. 'Today went fine. Rebecca has no reason to suspect that you're anything other than what she thinks you are.'

Peggy started picking at the corner of a beer mat with her free hand. 'Look, I know that Jen will have told you about this afternoon. I wasn't expecting to bump into anyone I knew, but now that Charlotte's seen me everyone within twenty miles will already know that poor old Margaret Swan can be found in Lewis's Perfume Hall.'

'Why's that such a problem? Are you worried people will think less of you for working in a shop?'

Peggy visibly bristled. 'What? *No*. No, that's not it at all. It's…'

'What then?' Andrew asked carefully after a long moment of Peggy just looking deeply offended by his suggestion. Really, he'd known full well that the thought of the great and good of high society looking down on Peggy for having a job wouldn't have inspired such a dramatic reaction from both Swan siblings. Peggy had already made it clear on a number of occasions that she couldn't care less what the rest of 'high society' thought about her, and Andrew suspected that Charlie, despite his ridiculous clothes and cars, and his fondness for a social life, was similarly inclined.

When Peggy eventually resumed talking, her eyes drifted downwards and remained firmly trained on the table. 'Charlotte's mother and my mother have been friends since before we were born. They were both young, pretty girls who'd married rich old men with titles. Let it never be said that the landed aren't a complete cliché.'

Peggy twisted her lips in self-deprecation. 'Anyway, my mother left us for the first time when I was six, and Charlie was barely walking. She took herself off around the world, spending my father's money, and generally leaving a trail of destruction in her wake, or so I've been reliably informed.

'Every few years, she'd appear at Butterton again, begging clemency from my father. He'd be a little bit harder to convince each time, but eventually, she'd always be let back into the fold, and our lives.

'My father probably thought he was doing the best for me and Charlie, by assuming that we needed our mother close to us. It was never about us for her though. As it always has been, it was about *money*, and her access to it.'

Andrew was surprised at the bitterness in Peggy's voice. This was also the most he'd heard her speak in one go since he'd met her, and he was worried that if he interrupted to ask a question she might just clam straight back up again.

Peggy sighed again. 'After a few years of radio silence, she turned up at the house, Christmas Eve before last.

'My father surprised us all by instantly agreeing to let her stay in the house, but the next day, in the middle of the world's most awkward Christmas lunch, he announced that he'd finally had enough of the whole situation and wanted a divorce.'

Peggy took a sip of brandy. 'As I'm sure you can probably imagine, my mother didn't take this announcement well. After that moment, she made it her business to cause as much trouble as she possibly could, for all of us.'

Andrew quirked his mouth in sympathy. He supposed that this explained why Peggy and Charlie weren't delighted to hear that their mother was back in the area. He thought back to what Jen had told him about the encounter with Charlotte, and before he could stop himself asked, 'Who's Edgar?'

Peggy closed her eyes with a grim smile. 'Ah, so she heard that bit, did she?'

Andrew suddenly felt less like he was investigating, and more like he was prying. 'You don't have to tell me,' he said quickly, holding his hands up.

'I know I don't,' Peggy agreed as she opened her eyes again, 'but, someone recently told me that I probably *should* talk about it.'

Andrew briefly wondered who she meant as he picked up his pint glass to take a drink.

'Edgar was my fiancé,' Peggy said simply.

Andrew tried to swallow his drink and say something at the same time, which only resulted in him choking on both words and beer. He coughed loudly as his eyes watered.

'Putting two and two together now, are you?' Peggy asked pointedly.

Charlotte had said that Peggy's mother had been visiting and that Edgar had been with her. *With* her.

'Christ,' Andrew spluttered, clearing his throat.

'Last August, I came home from a meeting with the Estate's accountants to find that my rooms had been ransacked. Any item of clothing that my mother hadn't deemed unworthy of her was gone, along with all of my jewellery; most of which had been family heirlooms.'

Andrew nearly dropped his beer glass as he tried to put it back on the table without taking his eyes off Peggy.

His mouth ran away from him when Peggy tapped her ring finger against the brandy glass again, drawing his attention instantly. 'But not that?'

Peggy put down her glass and twisted the emerald on her right hand. 'This belonged to someone very dear to me. Edgar didn't have a ring when he proposed. He said that it was because I wore this one so often anyway there was no way he could do any better.

'I didn't really care about him giving me a ring, so I was happy to keep on wearing this one, just on a different finger, and with a new meaning attached to it.'

Andrew thought it a miracle that this 'Edgar' hadn't been tracked down and murdered by a vengeful Charlie Swan by this point.

'Anyway,' Peggy continued, dropping her hand, 'it turns out that he planned on stealing it and giving it to my mother when they made their great escape. Thankfully, someone who *does* care about me made sure that didn't happen.'

Peggy took another large sip of brandy. 'So, there you go. That's my tragic backstory; my fiancé and my estranged mother ran off together, taking most of my possessions with them. Bit hard not to be the talk of certain sections of society when that sort of thing happens to you. So, maybe you can see why I don't really want people to know where they can find me.'

Andrew couldn't quite believe what he was hearing. He had a terrible suspicion that he might have been gawping. 'What did your father do? Did you call the police?'

Peggy's laugh sounded like it hurt. 'No. My father prefers to pretend that it had nothing to do with him. As everything taken was mine personally, it wasn't something he felt he needed to concern himself with. He couldn't stop people talking about my mother and Edgar, of course, and the blame for that rests solely on me. I introduced Edgar to our family, and therefore the scandal is of my own making.'

Peggy smiled bitterly as she parroted her father's words, and then gave a shrug that was far too practised to actually be a show of true indifference. 'Sorry. I know that you asked me not to make a scene.'

Andrew realised again that he might have been more than a little harsh in his previous assessment of Peggy. His own mother had been fairly terrible, and then virtually non-existent after what had happened to Rob, but she hadn't *actively* tried to ruin his life. As for Peggy's father; Andrew couldn't imagine how detached from reality you would have to be to prioritise protecting your reputation over your daughter.

'I'm sorry,' he managed eventually. It was underwhelming and unsatisfactory, but he didn't know what else to say.

'You really have nothing to be sorry for.'

She shook her head, hair finally escaping from where it had been neatly pulled back all day and sat up straighter, as though she could throw off any remaining vulnerability. 'Anyway, enough about me. Do you want to know what I found out today?'

Actually, Andrew had a good few hundred more questions for Peggy on the subject of her life and that of her mother. He was also actively wondering if he could conceive any grounds that would allow him to seek out and arrest Edgar on sight. Peggy, however, clearly wanted to move on, so in the end he just nodded his agreement.

Peggy sighed in obvious relief. 'Well, Marnie can't tell us anything more about her killer. Not yet anyway.'

'What do you mean 'not yet'?' Andrew frowned.

'She can't remember her actual death,' Peggy explained quietly, 'which I think is probably fair enough really. But she has started to remember the day she died in a bit more detail.'

'Go on,' Andrew encouraged, once again choosing to ignore the fact that he was buying into the whole 'communicating with the dead' lark.

'Marnie said that Rebecca had called the Driscoll house earlier in the day. She had something important that she wanted to tell Marnie.'

'What was it?' Andrew asked, silently hoping that it was something that could help them.

Peggy shook her head. 'Marnie wasn't at home when Rebecca called. She did say, however, that Rebecca had been acting strangely for a while leading up to that point.'

'Acting strangely how?'

'Mood swings,' Peggy said, tapping her glass again. 'Changing or cancelling plans with Marnie at the last minute, or telling people she was somewhere where she clearly wasn't. She'd been lying not just to Marnie but to her mother as well.'

'And Marnie has no idea what this was all about?'

'No. Although, she is still quite stuck on the idea that Rebecca and Rex were seeing each other behind her back.'

'What do you think about that?' Andrew asked, glancing over at the door when it opened so he could check who was coming into the pub.

'I don't know yet, but Rebecca seems nice enough.' Peggy paused to get her thoughts in order. 'I know I don't know her at all, and I know that I'm not trained like you, but I just can't see Rebecca being involved in Marnie's death.'

'People can surprise you,' Andrew replied. 'Some are just better liars than others.'

'Tell me about it,' Peggy said darkly, finishing her drink and checking her watch. 'I should probably go and get Charlie.'

'Higson's probably sent him out another coffee run,' Andrew said and was gratified when Peggy's lips quirked slightly.

He downed the rest of his pint and stood to leave. 'Alright, let's go.'

Peggy stopped him with a hand on his arm. 'Thank you.'

Andrew nodded once, not entirely sure what the gratitude was for. 'You did well today, you know.'

Peggy scrunched her face up slightly in embarrassment but seemed to accept the compliment as she pulled her arm back.

'Your *brother* on the other hand…' Andrew trailed off, rolling his eyes as he held open the door and gestured for Peggy to walk through.

'Oh God,' Peggy groaned, 'what has he done now?'

On their short walk back to the Ballroom, Andrew relayed Charlie's movements, and, in the spirit of being fair to the errant Swan, he also shared that the information he'd recovered had actually proved useful to the investigation, giving them a strong possible connection between Rex and the Byrnes.

'I'm still going to kill him,' Peggy said quietly, as they slowly ascended the staircase.

'Get in the queue,' Andrew muttered in reply as the man in question came into sight, sitting exactly where he'd been told to stay when Andrew had left.

Jen and Higson were nowhere to be seen, but Lloyd was scribbling furiously on a piece of paper at his desk. He didn't even look up at the new arrivals.

'Peg!' Charlie called brightly, throwing himself off the sofa and flinging his arms around his sister. 'Are you alright?'

'I'm fine, Charlie,' Peggy said, extricating herself carefully. 'I'd just quite like to go home now.'

'You're sure you're okay?' Charlie asked, 'because-'

'Charlie!' Peggy held up one hand. 'Stop. I'm fine, alright?'

Andrew could see that Charlie didn't quite believe that his sister was 'fine', and that an argument may be about to break out in front of him.

'We'll see you in the morning,' Andrew said, raising his voice slightly more than necessary. It did the job of cutting off any further comment from Charlie though.

Peggy nodded, shooting him a grateful look. Then her eyes widened. 'Oh, wait, I forgot to tell you something! About today, I mean. It could be nothing, of course.'

'What is it?' Andrew asked as he leaned his hip against the edge of his desk.

'Janine,' Peggy replied. 'You know, the girl who was having the party the night Marnie was killed?'

Andrew nodded in recognition.

'Well, she works at Lewis's too,' Peggy replied. 'I mean, you probably already knew that, *but* she also fits the description of the woman who returned Marnie's presents to Kendals. Maybe it was her, and not Rebecca.'

Andrew pulled his notes across his desk towards him with a frown and looked for Janine's name. 'According to this, Janine worked her last day in Lewis's at the end of December and was starting a new job in January. It doesn't say where she was moving to.'

'Well, she's definitely back at Lewis's now,' Peggy replied. 'I've seen her.'

'Alright, I'll take another look at her,' Andrew said. 'Maybe tomorrow you could try and strike up a conversation with her.'

'*Ah*, that probably won't happen, I'm afraid,' Peggy replied sheepishly. 'I nearly knocked her down a flight of stairs today, and she didn't take it too well. Although Marnie did say that Janine's like that with everyone.'

'Is she now?' Andrew mused consideringly. 'Well, let's see if we can work out why CID gave up on her so quickly.'

If he was honest with himself, Andrew was going to have to admit that

CID had done a pretty piss-poor job with Marnie's case in general. The interviews looked slapdash to begin with, and he knew that if he'd had anything to do with the investigation he would have had plenty of follow-up questions for quite a few of the people involved.

'Thanks, Peggy,' Andrew said, underlining Janine's name.

'No problem. See you in the morning, Andrew,' Peggy replied. She looked over at the other occupied desk. 'Goodnight, Lloyd.'

'Huh? Oh, goodnight,' Lloyd called back, finally looking up from his scrawled notes.

He then pointed at Charlie. 'Are you coming to the Troubadour tonight? Fiona's coming with me, and she said that she might bring a friend.'

Charlie considered for a moment. 'Yeah, yeah, sure. I'll be there around ten.'

'Cool,' replied Lloyd, and immediately went back to his notes.

Andrew couldn't think of anything worse than heading back out into the city at ten o'clock at night, and judging from the way Peggy was shaking her head at her brother, neither could she.

* * *

Peggy had never been so glad to see the looming chimneys of Butterton House in the distance.

'Oh, thank God,' she sighed, lifting her head off the passenger window as Charlie turned the car down the short, bumpy lane that would take them to the village.

'Peg,' Charlie said quietly, turning off the music he'd had blaring since they'd driven away from Tib Street, 'you know that she might come looking for you now, don't you? Him too.'

'I know,' Peggy replied, and her stomach twisted at the thought. 'There's not much I can do about that though, is there?'

'Look, I know you don't like talking about what happened, and I really don't blame you, you know I don't,' Charlie continued, turning right onto the long driveway to the house itself, 'but maybe you should consider telling DI Joyce what happened, even if it's just a condensed version. You know, just in case they turn up while you're at work.'

'I already told him.'

Charlie slammed on the brakes so suddenly that Peggy shrieked in surprise.

'You *told* Joyce?' Charlie asked, mouth open wide enough to catch a bird, never mind flies. 'You actually told him? *When*?'

'After work today,' Peggy replied before she punched her brother's arm. 'And don't bloody stop the car like that!'

'*When* after work?' Charlie made no move to continue their journey, staring at his sister in gormless shock. 'It's barely a three-minute walk from Lewis's to the Ballroom.'

'Rebecca let me leave a bit early after what happened with Charlotte,' Peggy explained. 'Although mostly I think it's because she was flirting with Andrew. Anyway, we went for a quick drink.'

'Wait, wait, wait. You went for a quick drink?' Charlie's eyes grew even wider. '*You*, Peggy Swan, went for a drink with Joyce?'

'Oh, come off it, Charlie,' Peggy said, rolling her eyes. 'I do actually know how to behave like a normal human being sometimes. Plus, you're the one who told me to stop hiding in the house.'

'I know I did,' Charlie replied. Then he huffed out a laugh. 'I'm actually proud of you, you know.'

'Well, thank you,' Peggy said, ducking her head, 'but can we please just get back to the house now?'

'Alright.' Charlie put his foot back on the accelerator. 'Hang on, what do you mean Rebecca was flirting with Joyce? I thought she was involved with Rex Hughes.'

'Well, nobody knows that for certain,' Peggy replied. 'Also, *you* criticising anyone else for flirting is the most ridiculous thing I've ever heard.'

'Fair,' Charlie acquiesced. 'Though should I suppose that you weren't doing any flirting of your own?'

'No, I bloody well wasn't!'

'Course not,' Charlie grinned, and Peggy knew she was about to be teased mercilessly. 'What with the way you were all 'Goodnight, *Andrew*' instead of 'Detective Inspector' by the time we left.'

'Not listening.' Peggy replied airily as the car rolled to a stop next to the steps up to the house. She grabbed her handbag and started climbing out but paused to turn back to her brother. 'And, *not that it matters*, but he has a girlfriend anyway. One he buys perfume for.'

'Oh, you mean the one who dumped him last night?' Charlie asked smugly, laughing slightly at Peggy's obvious surprise. 'Yeah, he was telling Lloyd all about it this morning. I don't think he came out of it well, just in case that sways your opinion at all.'

'*Still* not listening,' Peggy said primly. 'Now, I'm going to find something to eat, and then I'm going to bed. You're driving me to Tib Street in the morning, so don't suddenly find yourself at some house on the other side of town, alright?'

'Spoilsport,' Charlie replied, sticking his tongue out. 'Alright, fine, I'll be a good boy and be back by three.'

'*Goodnight*, Charlie,' Peggy said, closing the car door just before her brother drove off towards the garages.

Peggy let herself into the house quietly, hoping that Timothy wouldn't make an appearance to retrieve her coat, or worse, to inform her that her father wanted to see her immediately.

The coast looked clear but that didn't stop Peggy from quickly pulling off her borrowed heels and hurrying up the staircase, shoes in hand. She only stopped for breath when she reached her bedroom and closed the door behind her.

'Oh, hiya. Why've you got all these wedding magazines?'

For the second time in five minutes, Peggy shrieked in surprise. She stumbled backwards and her head hit the wall with a solid thump.

There, sitting casually on the carpet and flipping through a copy of *Brides*, was Marnie.

* * *

In the midst of everything, Andrew had forgotten what day of the week it was. He didn't actually remember until he'd tiredly climbed into his car at seven-thirty and heard Janice Long announce that it was, in fact, *Thursday* evening.

He'd sworn loudly, and the Belmont's engine had screeched in protest as he'd hurtled out of Tib Street towards Gatley.

He'd known full well that he didn't have a hope in hell of making it to Hollyhedge Park in ten minutes but figured that if he wasn't *that* late, Mike might still let him play the second half. He'd missed the two previous Thursday night matches as he'd been busy with cases, which Mike understood being a DS himself. Missing three in a row, however, meant that Andrew was at risk of being replaced by that little upstart DC Wallace who'd turned up at training a couple of months back and referred to Andrew as 'Old Man'. *Little arse.*

Andrew had already lost his job at CID, his girlfriend, and most of his sanity, all by Thursday evening. He damn well wasn't going to lose his football team too.

When he'd finally reached the park, after first stopping to assist a woman in a broken-down car, and then getting stuck behind an ancient caravan, the pitch was empty, save for Mike and a few others tidying things away.

Mike had politely explained that they were too over-subscribed to keep places open for players who'd missed so many matches and that he really was very sorry to have to let Andrew go, but not to worry as there was always next season. He did think, however, that Andrew would be pleased to know that they'd beaten Peel Hall one-nil and that Wallace had scored the winning goal.

Massive arse.

Andrew had trudged home, stopping briefly to pick up a takeaway at *Tung Sing.* He'd then proceeded to eat his body weight in egg fried rice and satay chicken while sitting on the sofa only half-watching the new episode of *Moonlighting* and wondering how much better his life would be if he ran his own fictional detective agency in Los Angeles. Or, if he'd been born as Bruce Willis instead of Andrew Joyce.

So, it wasn't any wonder that he was still wide awake at one in the morning, laying on the sofa in complete darkness, uncomfortably full, and dissecting every single second of his miserable week. He'd just reached the point where he was reliving the moment Higson had made him chase after Peggy when the telephone rang.

He held up his left arm and squinted at the green glow of the watch face on his wrist, just checking that he wasn't having an MSG-induced hallucination. His Casio confirmed that it was far too late for anyone to be calling, but it still took a good few rings for the realisation to dawn that a call at this time of night probably wasn't someone looking for a friendly chat. He rolled off the sofa and groped for the cordless receiver on the coffee table.

'*Hello*?'

Andrew could hear strains of music and conversation in the background.

'Hello?' Andrew tried again, louder this time.

'Sir? Hello? Sir, is that you?'

Andrew frowned. 'Lloyd?'

'Yeah, yeah, it's me,' Lloyd replied, clearly yelling now. 'Can you hear me?'

'No, not really,' Andrew said, pinching the bridge of his nose. Why the hell was Lloyd calling at one am? Was this some other weird quirk of working at the Ballroom?

'Hang on, I'll see if I can find somewhere quieter to call from,' Lloyd replied just before the line went dead again.

After ten minutes of silence, Andrew was getting close to just giving up and finally going to bed but then the phone rang in his hand and he almost dropped it in surprise.

'Lloyd?'

'Yes, sir, sorry about that,' Lloyd replied, and Andrew could hear him perfectly this time. 'They've let me use the phone in the back office.'

'Who's 'they', and where the hell are you?' Andrew snapped. 'You *do* realise what time it is?'

'Yes, sir, I do, and I'm sorry,' Lloyd said, sounding contrite. 'I wouldn't have called if it wasn't important. Oh, and I'm at the Troubadour, you know, down the other end of Oxford Road.'

Andrew thought back to earlier that day. 'Lloyd, are you out in town with Charlie Swan?'

'Yeah, that's right,' Lloyd replied. 'We were watching this band that Fiona likes, and I went back to the bar to get a round in, but when I was there I saw that Rebecca Silverman girl.'

'Alright,' Andrew replied slowly, trying to second guess where Lloyd was going with this. 'It's a Thursday night, and there's a band on, so there's not really anything special about Rebecca being there.'

'Right,' Lloyd said, 'and normally I'd agree with you. The thing is, though, she isn't here on her own.'

Andrew perked up immediately. 'Rex Hughes?'

'Worse, sir,' Lloyd replied. 'She's all over Liam Byrne.'

'Shit,' Andrew hissed, immediately wide awake. 'How sure are you?'

'Completely certain, on both of them sir. I went right over to the bar again and stood near them for a bit, just to make sure,' Lloyd said.

Andrew had no reason to doubt Lloyd's certainty. Rebecca being involved with Liam Byrne was yet another connection to Rex, and therefore Marnie.

Had he really been right from the beginning? Was Marnie killed because of Rex's association with the Byrnes? How had CID missed so many things?

'There's also one more thing,' Lloyd added apprehensively.

'I'm listening.' Andrew held his breath.

'I heard Rebecca telling Liam all about the new girl at her work,' Lloyd replied.

Andrew let out his breath in a whoosh of surprise. 'You don't think she could have been talking about someone else?'

'Unless there's another girl called Peggy, who just so happens to also have a title, then I'd say we can be fairly sure she's talking about our girl. Liam was pretty interested in it all.'

'Shit,' Andrew said again. He winced as a thought struck him. 'Oh Christ, does Charlie know about any of this?'

'No, sir,' Lloyd said. 'I took the drinks back to the table and then excused myself again. I called you straight away.'

'Right,' Andrew said, as he paced around the coffee table, running a hand through his hair. 'That's good. Okay, I need you to get Charlie out of there without his and Byrne's paths crossing. He'd just open his big mouth and end up dead in some gutter in Ancoats before morning.'

'Got it,' Lloyd confirmed. 'Band's nearly done, so I'll make sure we all leave sharpish.'

'Make sure you do.'

'Sorry again for disturbing you at home, sir,' Lloyd added. 'I didn't know what else to do.'

'It's fine, Lloyd, don't worry about it.' Andrew frowned again. 'Although, why didn't you call Higson?'

'What exactly was he going to do?' Lloyd asked, and he sounded genuinely baffled.

What indeed? thought Andrew as Lloyd ended the call.

Well, there was no chance he was going to sleep now. Andrew turned on the light and went in search of some paper and a pen.

It was time to get some work done.

TEN

'Peggy, dear, I really do think that you should have some breakfast before you leave,' Emmeline said, frowning over at where Peggy was battling with a pair of tights. 'It's the most important meal of the day, you know, and you've barely slept.'

Peggy actually did need a coffee more than she'd ever needed anything in her life, but she didn't have the energy required for the trek across the house to the kitchen. She was planning on sleeping the whole way into Manchester and Charlie would just have to put up with any snoring from the passenger seat.

It had been enough of a surprise to find Marnie at Butterton the night before – a place that, by all rights, she should not have been. But then, Marnie had behaved like the ghostly equivalent of a teenage girl at a friend's sleepover and kicked the whole situation into a whole new level of surrealism. She'd barely paused for breath all night, talking about anything and everything, until she'd finally faded away sometime around three am. Peggy had been left feeling somewhere far beyond exhausted.

Emmeline had noticed Marnie's presence almost immediately the night before and had spent most of the evening as baffled as Peggy. Peggy had spoken to many ghosts in her life, but never once had one followed her home.

'I don't understand,' Peggy had muttered to her aunt while Marnie was waxing lyrical about the latest episode of *Moonlighting* she was watching on TV.

'Neither do I,' Emmeline had replied with stark honesty.

It had taken almost ten years of interaction with Peggy for Emmeline to appear completely solid all of the time, and another ten before she was able to interact with objects as though she were completely human again.

Marnie simply didn't make sense.

Peggy let out a tired whine as she hauled herself to her feet so that she could look in the mirror. She'd done a passable job covering up the bags beneath her eyes, but she didn't look as polished as she'd managed to appear the day before.

The doorbell chimed and Peggy looked at Emmeline in surprise. It was barely past six-thirty. Who on earth would be here at this time?

Peggy grabbed her shoes and jacket before she headed out onto the landing with a quick goodbye to Emmeline. As she approached the top of the staircase, she saw her brother already shuffling towards the door, car keys grasped in one hand.

When the door opened it revealed a rumpled Andrew Joyce standing on the doorstep and wearing a slightly manic expression.

'Jesus, that's too bright,' Charlie whimpered as he covered his eyes against the assault of the early morning sunshine.

'You'd better not tell me that you drove yourself back here last night,' Andrew said to Charlie accusingly, narrowing his eyes. 'And you really better not tell me that you thought you were going to be driving your sister anywhere this morning. You smell like a brewery.'

'I won't tell you anything then,' Charlie grumbled. He turned back into the house and spotted Peggy. 'Oh good, you're up. He's *your* detective, *you* can deal with him.'

'Where are you going?' Peggy asked in surprise as Charlie started trudging up the stairs towards her. 'You're supposed to be driving me in. I wanted to sleep in the car!'

'Get DI Buzzkill over there to take you then,' Charlie replied mulishly, pulling a pair of sunglasses out of his jacket pocket and shoving them over his eyes hurriedly. 'I'm going back to bed.'

Peggy watched her brother disappear around the corner. The sound of his bedroom door closing firmly came a few seconds later.

'Charming,' Andrew said, rolling his eyes.

'Yes, he's always at his most enchanting when he has a raging hangover,' Peggy replied drily. She covered her mouth as she yawned widely.

'Sorry, am I keeping you up?' Andrew looked amused.

Peggy sighed. 'No, that would be the overly chatty ghost.'

Andrew's brows knitted. 'I'm sorry, what?'

'I'll tell you in the car,' Peggy said moving to grab her handbag. She paused. 'Wait, why are you here?'

'GMP's paying my petrol,' Andrew said, shrugging but missing casualness by a mile.

Peggy shook her head slowly. 'No. Try again.'

Andrew deflated slightly. 'Fine. Not here though, alright?'

Peggy caught the faint sound of footsteps heading towards them. 'Oh God, let's get out of here before Timothy sees you.'

It seemed that Andrew didn't need telling twice and he made an immediate beeline for the Belmont. As he turned back to the house, Peggy saw him do a double take.

'What's wrong?' she asked as she closed the door behind her and hurried towards the car.

Andrew was silent for a long moment before he shook his head. 'Nothing. No, nothing. Seeing things.'

'Seeing what?' Peggy asked with no small amount of trepidation. She looked up and scanned the many windows that overlooked the driveway but couldn't spot anything out of the ordinary.

Andrew ran a hand over his face and huffed out a nervous laugh.

Now that they were out in the daylight, Peggy could see that Andrew hadn't shaved that morning, and his hair was sticking out at slightly odd angles, as though he hadn't been able to just leave it alone to dry. Peggy was oddly pleased to discover that she wasn't the only one looking slightly shambolic that morning.

'I thought I saw Marnie there for a second,' Andrew replied with a disbelieving laugh, opening the car door and climbing in. 'I clearly spent far too long looking over the file last night.'

Peggy froze. Andrew couldn't have seen Marnie. That wasn't possible.

Noticing that Peggy hadn't entered the car as expected, Andrew climbed back out a few seconds later and stared at her in confusion. 'What is it?'

'Marnie,' Peggy whispered. 'Marnie *is* here, Andrew. I don't know how, but she was here when I got home last night.'

'What?' Andrew asked, eyebrows flying up in surprise. 'I thought you said you had to be somewhere where the, you know, *person* had spent a lot of time.'

'I know I did,' Peggy replied, glancing back at the house where she could now see Emmeline staring worriedly at her. 'That's how it's always worked in the past. You definitely shouldn't be able to see her though, unless there's something you've not been telling us.'

Peggy frowned then and pointed at the window Emmeline was visible in. 'Look up there for me, would you?'

Andrew came and stood next to her, looking up at the house as instructed. 'Where? The big window in the middle?'

'Yes. See anything?' Peggy asked, watching Andrew carefully for any reaction.

Andrew shook his head, pursing his lips. 'Just a big bloody window. Why?'

'Because standing right there is someone a lot older than Marnie. Someone who's very much part of this house, and even *she* doesn't understand why Marnie is here, or how she managed to get here in the first place.'

'You're serious?' Andrew asked, staring at Peggy unblinkingly. 'Are you trying to tell me that Marnie's actually haunting *you*?'

'I don't know,' Peggy said slowly, watching as Emmeline turned away, 'but something's definitely not right here.'

Andrew nudged her shoulder lightly a few seconds later. 'Come on, we need to go.'

'Will you tell me why you really came all the way out here this morning?' Peggy asked, finally opening the passenger door.

'I will,' Andrew replied as he buckled his seatbelt and started the engine.

Peggy, for all her acceptance of life beyond death, had never really been one to put much stock in gut feelings, but as Andrew drove them away from the house and towards the main road, Peggy felt, with terrifying certainty, that everything was about to go terribly wrong.

* * *

When she walked into the Perfume Hall, Peggy was disappointed to discover that quite a few of the Lewis's salesgirls hadn't yet recovered from the grand reveal of her 'secret identity' the day before. Four or five of them were leaning against the *Calvin Klein* advertisement in a clump of hairspray and gossip, openly staring and whispering to each other as Peggy turned her head the other way and headed for her counter.

'Hi, good morning!'

Peggy looked around in surprise to see Janine tottering towards her in another pair of towering heels – yellow this time. Even more of a surprise was the fact that Janine was *smiling* at her.

'Oh, hello,' Peggy replied, not even remotely sure of where she stood in this interaction.

'I'm really sorry about yesterday,' Janine said, making a face. 'We got off on the wrong foot. I'm Janine. Janine Turner.'

'Peggy Swan.'

'Yes, I know,' Janine replied. She beamed as they shook hands.

Ah, there it was. Janine wanted to be Peggy's 'friend' now that she thought Peggy might be somebody worth knowing. Well, Janine was going to get quite the shock when she found out that wasn't true, wasn't she?

'How did you find yourself here?' Janine asked, and it was obvious that her brand of friendliness co-habited with blatant snooping. Peggy would have to put her in touch with Charlotte Bamford; she thought they'd probably get on like a house on fire.

'Oh, you know,' Peggy trailed off with an affected shrug. 'I just needed a change of scenery.'

Janine looked so disappointed that Peggy hadn't immediately regaled her with tales of tragedy and scandal it was almost comical.

Peggy concluded that this was her one and only opportunity to have a conversation with Janine, so she steeled herself and said, 'Oh, yes! I'm sure you'll know all about this! I heard something *terribly tragic* happened to a girl who used to work here. Is that true?'

Peggy gamely upped the crispness of her pronunciation to really hammer home the image of a blue-blooded aristocrat and tossed her hair in a spot-on impression of a snobby girl Charlie had (*very briefly*) been seeing a while ago.

Janine looked disturbingly delighted at the opportunity to gossip, and Peggy was appalled on poor Marnie's behalf.

'Oh, yes,' Janine hissed, '*terribly tragic*. Poor thing was murdered right there in her parents' kitchen.'

Peggy did her best to keep her expression of indifference, silently praying that Marnie wouldn't make an appearance just yet. 'Oh, that's awful.'

'Oh, it was,' Janine replied. 'You know, she was actually supposed to be at *my* birthday party, so I feel really, really connected to the whole thing. To be so close to such a tragedy, I mean, I often think that it could have been *me*. Right?'

That seemed terribly unlikely, but Peggy wasn't going to argue when Janine was on a roll. 'Oh, so she was a friend of yours then?'

Janine's non-committal noise told Peggy everything she needed to know. 'I wouldn't say *friend*, exactly. I mean, I don't want to speak ill of the dead or anything, but she wasn't really my kind of person, you know?'

'Mmm,' Peggy replied, and she was privately very glad that Marnie wasn't Janine's kind of person.

'Her poor fiancé though,' Janine simpered. 'Rex is such a darling. I hope he finds someone better for him soon.'

'Janine, shouldn't you be getting your promotional material ready?' Rebecca snapped, coming up behind the two women.

Janine smiled coldly at Rebecca and walked away. No love lost there then.

'Was she bothering you?' Rebecca asked warily. 'Janine's the kind of person that tends to rub others the wrong way. Alright at her job though, I suppose.'

Peggy thought that you should probably go through life hoping that people didn't think that the best thing about you was that you were 'alright at your job'. Yet, as uncharitable as the thought was, she did have to wonder whether it really *was* the best thing about Janine. She hadn't seen anything to contradict that theory so far, after all.

'No, no, it's fine,' Peggy replied airily. 'She just wanted to tell me about the girl who used to work here, or something.'

Rebecca's face fell immediately, and Peggy felt like a complete cow for putting an expression like that on someone else's face. Even though Andrew had told her in the car that she had Rebecca to thank for sharing her identity with a 'complete bastard of a criminal' (Andrew's words, not Peggy's), she couldn't feel good about throwing Marnie's death in her face like that.

'*Oh*,' said Rebecca, and really it was more of an exhalation than a word in its own right.

'Sorry,' Peggy said, meaning it. 'Have I said something wrong?'

'No, no,' Rebecca whispered, shaking her head in denial, even as her eyes filled with tears. 'No, you're fine. I just need to…'

Rebecca swiped at her face, 'If you'll please excuse me for a moment, Peggy.'

Marnie appeared just as Rebecca turned her back and hurried away.

'Crocodile tears,' said Marnie, crossing her arms across her chest, but she actually looked upset too. 'She just wants you to think she's a decent one, and not like Janine. You know, I can't believe it was *Rebecca* that I should have been worrying about the whole time.'

'Rebecca's not in a relationship with Rex,' Peggy whispered out of the corner of her mouth as she busied herself with a polishing rag,

'And how are you so sure about that?' Marnie asked, fixing Peggy with a sharp look.

'Because this morning, Andrew told me that Rebecca's actually in a relationship with someone else.'

'Who?'

'Do you know who Liam Byrne is?' Peggy asked quietly, crouching down as if adjusting her shoe.

'*Liam Byrne*?' Marnie shrieked incredulously.

The lights hanging from the ceiling flared ominously brighter for a second.

'Marnie, for Christ's sake, calm down,' Peggy hissed, glaring up at the other woman.

'Sorry,' Marnie said sheepishly. 'Sorry, you just surprised me. Yeah, I know who Liam Byrne is. Who *hasn't* heard of him?'

Well, I hadn't, thought Peggy. Then again Peggy not being quite up to date with current affairs wasn't entirely surprising, given that she'd practically lived as a hermit for the past year.

'He's a wrong 'un,' Marnie continued, looking over to where Janine was lining up a row of perfume bottles. 'But your Andrew must be wrong because Rebecca wouldn't touch Liam Byrne with a barge pole.'

'Well, h-'

'She wouldn't,' Marnie replied mulishly. 'Not least because Liam Byrne used to be Janine's boyfriend.'

Peggy briefly remembered when she'd thought her own life was dramatic.

'You didn't know that, did you?' Marnie asked with just a hint of petulance. 'My God, it's like nobody actually bothered to do any proper police work.'

Peggy felt inclined to agree. 'Okay, no, I didn't know that, but I do trust Andrew.'

'Course you do,' Marnie drawled, raising one judgemental eyebrow. 'But I trust my best friend not to be that stupid.'

Rebecca chose that moment to re-enter the Perfume Hall. She looked directly over to where Peggy and Marnie were standing together, and her face went ashen in an instant. Her mouth dropped open in an 'o' of pure surprise, and she had to reach out to steady herself on the counter next to her.

Peggy quickly glanced at Marnie, who seemed to have also realised that Rebecca must have seen her. Marnie gave Peggy a quick look of horrified surprise before disappearing entirely. Had Rebecca just seen Marnie? If she had, that meant that Andrew *must* have seen her at Butterton earlier that morning too. But, if that were true, why hadn't the other salesgirls screamed in terror when Marnie had first appeared?

Rebecca was staring in terror at the space Marnie had just vacated, and Peggy was genuinely concerned that she was about to witness a very public - and very confusing - breakdown.

Peggy hurried across the tiles as quickly as her borrowed heels allowed. 'Are you alright, Rebecca?'

Rebecca shook her head, blinking furiously. She looked directly at Peggy. 'Did you see her?'

'See who?' Peggy asked, playing dumb. 'One of the other girls?'

'Marnie,' Rebecca replied desperately. 'Did you see *Marnie*? She was standing right next to you.'

'Who? There was nobody next to me,' Peggy replied quietly, and she felt even more horrible than she had before as she watched Rebecca's eyes widen again before her face completely shut down.

'Sorry, sorry,' Rebecca said, tucking her hair behind her ears and sniffling. 'Sorry, I'm just tired. I'm seeing things that aren't there.'

'Why don't you go and have a cup of tea?' Peggy suggested quietly. 'Do you want me to get one for you? Is there anyone I can call for you?

Boyfriend, maybe?'

That's a bit sly, said Marnie's disembodied voice.

Peggy ignored her and gave Rebecca her most sympathetic look.

Rebecca just shook her head again. 'No, no, I'll be fine. Best not to bother Liam when he's at work anyway.'

Peggy was too distracted by the lights flickering again to feel even the slightest bit of triumph at proving Marnie wrong. Then, one of the lightbulbs popped blindingly before fizzing out of existence. A few girls squeaked in surprise and Rebecca ran from the Perfume Hall, tears streaming down her face.

Sorry, came Marnie's whisper.

Sure you are, thought Peggy, as she rolled her eyes and headed back to her counter.

* * *

Andrew pressed the buzzer on the gate intercom at the Hughes house for the second time and tapped his steering wheel in frustration. 'Why do people have these things if they don't plan on ever answering them?'

'I guess that's sort of the point,' Jen replied, shrugging one shoulder. 'Nobody can get close enough to the house to see if you're actually in, so you can always pretend you're out if you don't fancy seeing someone.'

The speaker on the wall finally crackled to life. 'Can I help you?'

Andrew didn't recognise the voice, but he was pleased that it wasn't a stroppy Athena Hughes this time – he was far too tired to deal with *that*.

'Detective Inspector Joyce, here to see Mr Hughes.'

'Goodness!' exclaimed the voice. 'That was quick. Yes, come in, come in.'

Before Andrew could ask exactly what that was supposed to mean the intercom disconnected and the gates began to slowly open.

As soon as the gap was wide enough, Andrew carefully drove the Belmont through and onto the drive. He counted two more cars than on their previous visit.

'It's like a bloody NCP,' he grumbled as he parked behind a gleaming Porsche.

Jen quickly stifled a laugh, before the front door burst open and a harried Rex Hughes bounded towards them.

'Now, what the hell do we think this is this about?' Andrew muttered as he and Jen climbed out of the car.

'Detectives!' Rex skidded to a halt in front of them. He was still wearing his slippers. 'Were you in the area? I've only just called it in.'

Andrew exchanged a baffled look with Jen. 'Mr Hughes, we're here to ask a few follow-up questions. Has something happened?'

Rex nodded as he swallowed heavily.

'Shall we, Mr Hughes?' Jen gestured towards the house.

'Of course, yes, come in,' Rex replied, standing aside to let the two detectives pass him.

Andrew and Jen found themselves in the same room as on their previous visit, though this time Athena Hughes was wedged into the corner of one cream sofa, knees pulled up to her chin. Trails of ash-grey tinted tears covered her cheeks and she wiped hurriedly at her face when she realised that she had company.

'Detectives,' Athena said in surprise, quickly unfurling her legs and smoothing out her black trousers. Her eyes were puffy and red, and very little makeup remained.

Andrew was taken aback. 'Are you alright, Miss Hughes?'

'Yes, I'm fine,' she said, her voice shaking. Her stoic expression dissolved into tears almost immediately. 'I mean *no*, no, I'm not fine.'

'Sweet tea, perhaps. For your sister?' Jen asked, looking pointedly at Rex.

Jen then took a seat next to Athena, keeping her distance so as not to spook the other woman further, but retrieving a tissue from the small, bejewelled box on the coffee table and handing it over.

Athena took the tissue gratefully as her brother left the room. 'Thank you. I'm so sorry. I didn't expect you to get here so quickly.'

'Your brother said something similar,' Andrew said, standing by the fireplace. 'Would you mind explaining what's happened, Miss Hughes?'

Athena frowned. 'You're not here because of the note?'

Andrew shook his head. 'What note, Miss Hughes?'

Athena paled even further, and with shaking hands, she picked up a piece of paper from where it was lying on the carpet next to her feet. She held it out to Andrew, who took it wordlessly.

The paper was slightly crumpled at the edges, but the sharp creases that segmented it suggested that it had been folded very carefully by someone in the first instance. The writing wasn't much more than a scrawl, but the words were clear:

Empire Street. He stops or you're next.

Andrew frowned down at the paper and handed it over to Jen. The words themselves were fairly meaningless without additional context, and the threat was a bit heavy-handed in the 'I've seen too many gangster films' sort of way.

'It came through my window this morning,' Athena said quietly.

'*Through* your window?' Andrew asked, eyebrows raised. So, the note was meant specifically for Athena, which suggested that the 'He' was indeed Rex.

Athena nodded. 'I was about to go out to meet my cousin, so I'd just gone back into my bedroom to get my purse. Then a rock came through my window and nearly hit me. The note was tied onto it with some string.'

'Show me?' Andrew was already heading for the door.

'Oh, yes, of course.'

Athena led Andrew and Jen up the staircase, and Andrew couldn't help again thinking that whoever had designed this house had been aiming for a sort of modern-day Butterton.

Athena's bedroom was as neutral as the rest of the house, although there were pops of colour everywhere in her overstuffed walk-in wardrobe. Shards of glass covered the carpet near the window, and there, lying on the floor next to the dressing table, was a large grey rock. A piece of butcher's twine was discarded nearby.

Andrew stepped over the glass so that he could look out of the window. Athena's bedroom was at the back corner of the house, and the lane that ran along the side of the property meant that it would have been easy enough for someone to aim at the window over the wall without even coming into the garden.

'Okay,' Andrew said, 'we can go back downstairs now.'

'Have you noticed anyone suspicious outside the house recently?' Jen asked as they descended the stairs.

'No,' Athena replied, pulling her jacket tighter around herself. 'We get very little in the way of foot traffic on the lane. It's mostly just farm vehicles. It's one of the reasons my father built the house here; my mother wanted to live somewhere quieter. Thank God she'd already gone out this morning before all this happened.'

'Do you know what the note means?' Andrew asked as they sat down again. 'Empire Street?'

'We own property on Empire Street in town,' Rex explained as he came back from the kitchen. He handed the cup and saucer over to his sister before sitting in the armchair he'd favoured last time. 'Right next to Strangeways.'

'So, what does 'he stops' mean? Stop what?'

Rex sighed loudly. 'We've got two big old warehouses, up the other end of the road to the brewery. Our grandfather bought them decades ago – it's where he used to store all of the out-of-season stuff for the camps that wouldn't fit anywhere else. You know, so during the summer it was full of all the Christmassy crap they decorated the places with, but in the winter you couldn't get in there for the kayaks and deckchairs.

'The warehouses have been empty for years, and we've got no use for them these days. Full of holes, water and rats, so it's not like I could lease them to anybody for good money. I've been thinking of selling them to a developer who's buying up a load of old property around there. He wants to build these big prefab commercial units in their place.'

Athena put her cup and saucer down forcefully enough that the porcelain rattled ominously. 'Rex, you need to tell them about the other notes.'

Rex looked at his sister sharply. '*Athena*.'

'Other notes?' Andrew asked quickly. He knew that if Rex had called the police just before he'd arrived with Jen it wouldn't be long before another unit turned up.

Rex sighed again. 'There have been a few other notes in the past couple of weeks. A couple left on my car, and then one at the bar for me when I went out for dinner. They all say the same sort of thing. If not Empire Street, then somewhere else that we've earmarked for sale.'

'Have you told the police about this?' Jen asked. 'You didn't mention these notes the other day, Mr Hughes.'

Rex stood quickly. 'Look, this isn't the first time someone's tried to intimidate me when it comes to business affairs. This city's full of scum who think they can just take whatever they want. They can't.'

'Scum who don't think twice about threatening your sister,' Andrew said darkly. 'Mr Hughes, I'm sure I don't need to remind you that Detective Cusack and I are here because we're looking into what happened to Marnie.'

'This has nothing to do with what happened to Marnie,' Rex said, and he sounded more desperate than certain of himself. 'It was a burglary gone wrong, that's what the police said. *You* were even asking me about things missing from Marnie's house the other day.'

'Mr Hughes, I'm going to ask you once again, do you have any reason to suspect that *anyone* you've had dealings with would have wanted to harm Marnie?' Andrew kept his voice low and steady even as he thought that Rex Hughes might just punch him for mentioning Marnie's name again. This was the question he'd come here to ask, after all.

'No.' Rex replied, deflating instantly.

'Rex,' Athena said warningly. 'Rex, you should tell them about-'

'There's nothing to say,' Rex snapped at his sister.

Andrew held his hands out placatingly. 'One final question then?'

'One,' Rex agreed still glaring at his sister. Athena was glaring back.

'Why were you arguing with Liam Byrne back in January?' Andrew asked. He watched as Rex's eyes bugged in shock before he quickly rearranged his features into indifference.

'I don't know what you're talking about,' Rex muttered eventually.

'Okay, let me remind you then. It was the end of January, only weeks after Marnie had been killed,' Andrew continued, knowing that he was laying it on a little thick. 'You were seen in *Osteria* on St Ann's Square, and apparently, you were having quite the row with Liam Byrne.'

'It was nothing,' Rex replied, pursing his lips.

'Who?' Athena asked, baffled. 'Who's Liam Byrne?'

'Someone very dangerous,' Andrew explained, all the while keeping his eyes on Rex. 'Someone who would be very interested in making sure that things went his way. Someone who wouldn't be afraid of removing anything that stood in his way, whether that was through threatening someone's fiancée or a member of their family. Or *worse*.'

'Rex, what is he talking about?' Athena asked, staring at her brother in open horror.

'I think it's time for you both to leave now,' Rex said, and his hands were clenched tightly against his thighs. 'I'm sure you have everything you need.'

'I hope so, Mr Hughes,' Andrew replied, mouth set in a grim line. 'I really hope so. We'll see ourselves out.'

Andrew and Jen had just made it back to the Belmont when Athena came out of the house, quietly closing the door behind her.

'I'm sorry about my brother,' she said, looking back at the house sadly. 'He hadn't really recovered from our father dying when Marnie...'

She trailed off, shaking her head. 'Sorry.'

'It's alright, Miss Hughes,' Jen said. 'We know that it's been a difficult time for your brother.'

'Do you really think Marnie was killed because of something to do with Rex?' Athena asked carefully.

'We're just looking at all possibilities,' Andrew replied, noncommittally.

Athena nodded slowly. 'Okay.' She looked back at the house again. 'Look, I don't want to cause problems for my brother, but if this helps him to find out what happened to Marnie, I need to say it.'

'Say what, Miss Hughes?' Jen asked.

'Last night, someone called the house looking for Rex,' Athena all but whispered. 'I don't know who it was, Mary answered the phone.'

'Mary?' Andrew frowned.

'Sorry, yes, she's our housekeeper,' Athena explained. 'I was watching TV with Rex and Mum, *Moonlighting* was on, you know. Anyway, Mary came in to say that there was a man on the phone for Rex, but he hadn't given his name.

'Rex was gone for maybe five minutes, but when he came back into the room he seemed off. Like, he usually can't shut up when we're watching something – it drives Mum mad – but he didn't say a single word. I don't think he was really watching it by that point anyway.'

Athena glanced at the house one more time. 'Mum went off to bed at the end of the show, and Rex said he was doing the same, but he didn't. I heard him go out about twenty minutes later. He took the car, and he still hadn't got back by the time I went to bed, which was just before midnight.'

Athena looked at Andrew imploringly. 'Do you think that might help you?'

'Thank you for the information, Miss Hughes,' Andrew said with a nod.

'I really want you to find out what happened to Marnie.'

'We will,' Andrew replied with all the certainty he could muster.

Athena smiled weakly at them and pointed to the gate. 'Thank you both. I'll buzz you out.'

Andrew waited for the gates to start opening before he reversed the Belmont carefully, avoiding the staggering amount of expense around him. As he crossed over the threshold a white Ford Capri turned sharply towards the drive. Andrew swore loudly and slammed on the brakes. The Belmont and the Capri stopped with only an inch of space between their noses.

Andrew glared at the other car, his expression darkening further when he recognised DI Fallon from CID in the driver's seat.

'Move!' Andrew shouted as he gestured at Fallon with a shooing motion.

DI Fallon sent a gesture of his own back, only his was much ruder.

'Bloody idiot failed the advanced driving course three times,' Andrew muttered to Jen when Fallon finally started reversing his car back onto the main road. 'I hope Rex Hughes doesn't care all that much about those cars in his driveway.'

Fallon rolled his window down as the Belmont drew level with him.

'What the hell are you doing here?' Fallon asked Andrew with a sneer. 'Aren't you supposed to be tucked away in the Graveyard? This is CID business, Joyce, and you're not CID anymore.'

Andrew pursed his lips. He wasn't going to rise to this. 'Goodbye, Fallon.'

Fallon snorted with laughter. 'Aw, did I upset little Andykins? Some people just can't hack real police work.'

Andrew's only answer was to put his foot on the accelerator and drive away, the back end of the car swinging out momentarily as it struggled to keep up.

'Absolute dickhead,' Andrew grumbled, ignoring the side-eye he was getting from Jen. 'The thing is, if CID had done its job properly, then maybe this would have been solved by now.'

'We'll get there,' Jen said soothingly.

'And the *Byrnes*,' Andrew continued, now that he was on a roll, 'the fucking *Byrnes*! It's looking increasingly likely that Marnie was killed because the two people she was closest to had got themselves tangled up with those scumbags, yet the most CID has ever got the Byrnes on was fencing stolen goods, *once*, ten years ago! They were practically still teenagers then.'

'This could be the thing that finally gets them put away,' Jen said, eyeing the speedometer with apprehension.

'Yeah, it *could* be,' Andrew scoffed loudly as he rounded a corner a little too fast, 'but what if it's not? What if we're just heading towards finding Athena Hughes dead in her kitchen too?'

'It won't come to that. Sir, maybe you should slow down a little bit though.'

'And then there's Peggy. Liam fucking Byrne knows who she is now.' Andrew swiped violently at the indicator but barely slowed at the junction.

'Sir, you really do need to slow down now,' Jen said sternly.

'What's he going to do with the information, Jen?' Andrew carried on, ignoring Jen's comment. 'What if they skip over Athena and go straight to Peggy? I reckon Athena is probably scarier in a fight, and Peggy's got enough money to kill for.'

'Nobody's going to kill Peggy!' Jen protested.

'But what if they do, Jen?' Andrew cried. 'That would be on *me*! I can't have another death on my conscience. I can't. I said this was all a terrible idea, and now I'm seeing bloody ghosts! Ghosts that can't be there, because ghosts aren't real!'

'Stop this car right now, Detective Inspector!'

Jen's shout surprised Andrew so much that his foot, completely separated from his consciousness by that point, slammed on the brake pedal and the Belmont skidded to a stop.

Andrew stared at the steering wheel, breathing hard.

'Okay, sir,' Jen said. Her voice had dropped back into that soothing register again. 'I think that maybe I should drive for a while. We'll go back to the Ballroom and get you a nice big mug of Lloyd's deadly coffee, alright?'

Andrew slumped in his seat. God, what if Fallon was right? What if Andrew really *wasn't* cut out for police work?

'Sir?' Jen prompted.

'Yeah, sorry.' Andrew winced in apology. 'Sorry, Jen.'

'It's alright,' Jen replied with a small smile. 'The job gets to you sometimes, that's all. You'll solve Marnie's murder and Peggy will be fine. I have faith.'

At least someone does.

Andrew got out of the car.

ELEVEN

After scaring the living daylights out of Rebecca, Marnie had made herself scarce for most of the day, which Peggy was quite thankful for. Marnie's presence at Butterton was still inexplicable and would require some quite serious investigation, but somehow that wasn't actually Peggy's priority right now. It couldn't be her priority when both Andrew the Unbeliever *and* Rebecca had caught a glimpse of Marnie. Even Charlie had never successfully managed to actually *see* a ghost, and he was fairly surrounded by them any time he was at home. None of it made any sense to Peggy whatsoever.

Lloyd had popped into Lewis's to see her around lunchtime, muttering something about Andrew being on a warpath and Jen behaving like a psychiatrist. Peggy had quietly passed on the information about Janine's relationship with Liam Byrne when Lloyd had pretended to have a very detailed question about the scent profile of *Beautiful*.

After he'd gone, Rebecca had come over to Peggy and smirked conspiratorially. 'Another admirer there, I'd say.'

'What do you mean?'

'He was over here yesterday too,' Rebecca had replied, brows knitting together. 'Did you really not notice?'

'Oh, no, I hadn't.'

Oh God, Rebecca was far more observant than anyone had given her credit for. Peggy had blinked furiously, trying to look distressed. 'Although, I suppose yesterday was a little *eventful*.'

Rebecca had shot her a sympathetic look. 'Oh, yeah. Sorry, I didn't mean to bring that up.'

Peggy had sighed over-dramatically. 'It's okay, really. How about you though? I really am sorry about this morning. I didn't mean to upset you.'

Rebecca had given her another sad smile. 'It's not your fault, you weren't to know. Janine really shouldn't have been gossiping, but you should probably know that the girl who used to work here was my best friend. I'm not sure I'll ever get over her being gone, you know?'

Peggy hadn't really known what to say in response, so she'd given

Rebecca the best compassionate expression she had.

'Sorry,' Rebecca had laughed self-deprecatingly, 'I'm being a downer again when actually the reason I came over was to let you know that some of us are going out after work for a few drinks, and I wondered if you wanted to come with us.'

All Peggy really wanted to do was go home and hide under her duvet until she had to get up again for work in the morning, but Andrew was counting on her to get as much information out of Rebecca as possible. She'd smiled, praying that she'd looked sincere. 'That sounds lovely, thanks.'

Peggy had taken advantage of the fact that she had access to the phone in Mr Jenner's office and phoned Tib Street to let them know. Andrew had answered and even offered to call Butterton and let Charlie know that his sister would need picking up slightly later than had previously been agreed.

Peggy wasn't sure whether Andrew still thought Rebecca was capable of murder, or whether it was just her association with Liam Byrne that had him on edge, but he hadn't been delighted to hear that Peggy was out with Rebecca. He was only slightly mollified when she'd explained that there were other people with them.

And so, Peggy had found herself squashed into a booth in *Osteria* on St Ann's Square with Rebecca on one side and a girl named Laura, who apparently worked in Homeware, on the other. Haberdashery Bette was across from them, sitting next to the final member of the group, Matthew. Mathew looked to be about nineteen and seemed, to Peggy's eyes at least, to be slightly confused by his presence in this group of women from work.

'Well, thank God that week's over,' Bette announced loudly, raising her glass of white wine in front of her. 'To the weekend!'

'It's alright for *you*,' Rebecca grumbled, clinking her own glass. 'Some of us have to work Saturdays too.'

'Now hang on, you get Tuesdays off,' Bette replied, stabbing at an olive with a cocktail stick.

'I'd still rather be off on a Saturday,' Rebecca grumbled. 'That place is mad on a Saturday afternoon.'

She gave Peggy an apologetic glance. 'Sorry, but there's really no point in me sugar-coating it. You'll see what I mean tomorrow.'

Peggy winced. How could it possibly be worse? She'd thought that the last hour before her shift finished had been busy enough.

'Oh, come on Rebecca,' Laura laughed, 'don't scare the new girl away. She'll call in sick if you're not careful.'

'Oh my God, *please* don't do that,' Rebecca groaned, taking a gulp of her wine. 'Jesus, I'm still not over that time four of the girls called in with food poisoning. I spent two days running around like a blue-arsed fly trying to cover everything.'

'But that's why you're such a good floor manager,' Bette said as she gave Rebecca a motherly look. 'You've got a good head on your shoulders.'

'Hmm,' Rebecca replied, but she looked pleased. 'I'd still rather have Saturdays off.'

'And, Bette, you're not overrun by desperate husbands trying to buy presents on their way home from work,' Laura said. 'Even *I* don't have to put up with that like these two do in Perfume. And you *certainly* don't.'

Bette laughed loudly and then nudged the teenager next to her. 'Well, Matthew here's going to take over Haberdashery when I'm dead and gone. Isn't that right?'

'Yes, Auntie Bette,' replied Matthew in resignation.

'And by the time that happens, you'll all be in on Sundays too,' Bette said, selecting another olive. 'Mark my words.'

'Working on a Sunday?' Matthew asked, horrified. 'Never going to happen.'

'Well, work hard now, and that way, when Rebecca's running the whole shop, she'll make sure you get weekends off.' Bette patted her nephew on his shoulder.

Rebecca rolled her eyes at Peggy. 'Sorry about Bette. She likes to get these very grand ideas into her head when she's had a glass of wine. She's convinced that we're all destined for greater things and lives of luxury.'

'Well, speaking of lives of luxury…' Laura said, quirking her head towards the entrance.

Everyone turned to look as a man and woman entered the restaurant. The man was instantly recognisable from his photograph at Marnie's house as Rex Hughes, but he was accompanied by a tall blonde woman

Peggy couldn't place.

'Who's that?' Peggy asked, playing dumb.

'That's Rex,' Rebecca said quietly. 'Rex Hughes. He was engaged to my friend.'

Rebecca placed such emphasis on the word 'friend' that even if Peggy didn't already have the knowledge she had, she'd know that Rebecca meant Marnie.

'And his sister, the Queen of Sheba,' Bette giggled.

'Oh, stop it, Bette,' Rebecca hissed, making sure to keep her voice down. 'Athena's lovely, and she was so kind to Mar-' She cut herself off. 'Just stop, alright?'

'They've seen us,' Laura whispered against her wineglass. 'They're coming over.'

'Rebecca,' Rex greeted her warmly and smiled at the others. 'Ladies. Oh, and a gentleman too.'

Matthew looked a bit put out.

'Rebecca, darling,' Athena added, blowing a kiss. 'How are you?'

'Well, thank you,' Rebecca replied. 'Are you having dinner?'

Rex nodded and Peggy thought that he looked a little troubled. 'Yes. We've had quite a day and thought it might be nice to get out of the house.'

'Oh?' Rebecca asked, clearly wanting to pry but without seeming too obvious about it. 'Is everything alright?'

'Nothing to worry about,' Rex said, forcing a smile.

Athena's smile was more genuine. 'Would you all like to join us? Heaven knows we could do with the company.'

Bette quickly finished her wine. 'I'm afraid I need to get this young man home before his mother accuses me of leading him astray. Thanks though, love.'

'I'd best be off too,' Laura said, looking at her watch. 'Ben's taking me to the pictures.'

'Oh, for the new Michael Douglas one?' Athena asked as her eyes lit up.

'Yes!' Laura agreed with a grin. 'Can't wait.'

'Peggy?' Rebecca asked. 'How about you?'

As much as she wanted to say 'no' so that she could go home and deal with whatever the hell was going on with Marnie, this could be the perfect opportunity to observe Rebecca and Rex together to see if there really had been something going on between them. Andrew wouldn't necessarily be happy about it as a plan, but then again, was Andrew ever really happy about anything?

'Sure,' Peggy agreed, smiling at the Hughes siblings. 'That sounds great, thanks.'

* * *

'You know, you really don't have to stay,' Andrew called over to Jen. 'I know this isn't most people's idea of a fun Friday evening.'

'It's fine, honestly,' Jen replied, only briefly looking up from her notes. 'I *want* to stay. Honestly.'

It was gone half-eight and the Ballroom was quiet, save for the occasional scratch of a pen, or the hum of the traffic wafting in through the open windows. Higson had disappeared just after four again, and Lloyd had left at five-thirty on the dot because apparently it was against the law to stay at work for a second of overtime when the sun was actually out on a Friday evening. He knew that Jen really did want to stay and help for the case's sake, but also that she'd been keeping a close eye on him since his little episode in the car that morning.

Andrew stood to stretch his shoulders, uncomfortably aware that the early summer humidity was helping his shirt cling to his back. He rolled his sleeves up as he headed over to the open window in search of a hint of breeze. As he took a deep breath of cooler air, the smell of something garlicky caught Andrew's nose and made him instantly aware of how hungry he was.

'Do you want some dinner?' Andrew asked, staring out over the city. Tib Street was in greying darkness below them, but the lights and buzz of elsewhere were visible in streets beyond. 'I'll pop out and get a takeaway.'

'Are you sure, sir?' Jen asked. 'I can go if you want.'

'I'd enjoy the walk,' Andrew replied. 'And it's the least I can do to make up for this morning.'

'I already told you that you don't need to apologise about that,' Jen said. 'I know how much of a shock it can be to come here and find out that we do things so differently. I can only guess that it's probably even weirder when you've come here from CID.'

Andrew nodded his thanks. 'Chinese?'

'If you want,' Jen replied, 'or there's Bombay Palace over on Cross Street if you'd prefer Indian.'

'Actually, yeah, that sounds good,' Andrew said, deciding that even as terribly as his week was going he probably shouldn't repeat meals two nights in a row.

He reached for his jacket but changed his mind and just picked up his wallet instead. 'Any requests?'

'I'm not fussy,' Jen replied with a shrug, 'but make sure you get a big pot of mango chutney.'

'That I can do,' Andrew said as he headed for the door. 'I won't be long,'

Tib Street during the day could be pretty grim, but at night there was an unseen and inexplicable sense of threat lurking just beneath the surface. Andrew thought that it had something to do with the way the buildings seemed to hem you in, and then funnel you down towards the looming, dirty-grey Portland stone of Debenhams on the corner. Andrew couldn't imagine anyone ever actually coming down the street to attend a tea dance at any point in time, which just made the location of the Ballroom even more bizarre.

Crossing Market Street, Andrew looked up at Lewis's. The shop was closed, but there were still lights on inside as the unseen night staff busily prepared the shop for Saturday's customers. All those people keeping the world ticking over and yet remaining faceless, and nameless, to those who visited the shop during the day.

When they had heard that Peggy was on the rota for Saturday morning, Andrew, Jen and Lloyd had all agreed to come into the Ballroom at the same time. Higson had rolled his eyes and informed them that if they needed him for anything they'd just have to bloody well wait until Monday.

When this case was over, Andrew was going to have to do a little bit more digging into DCI Higson's background. He still couldn't understand what sort of favour Higson had called in to get CID to agree to just handing over a DI. He should probably also ask a few questions about his predecessor DI Benson too; DI Benson, who apparently casually haunted the Ballroom and made occasionally helpful comments.

Andrew sighed loudly as he turned onto Cross Street. He was wildly aware of the fact that he'd just got used to hearing people chat about ghosts as though it were all terribly normal, which led him to conclude that one of three things had happened:

1. He'd entered into some sort of training exercise dreamed up by his superiors at CID without realising. They were actually monitoring him to see how he dealt with the unusual and stressful situation. (Unfortunately, this was the least likely explanation.)

2. He was suffering from some form of Stockholm Syndrome, possibly compounded by overwhelming peer pressure.

3. He actually believed what Peggy Swan was telling him.

Whichever one it turned out to be, Andrew wasn't going to be pleased with himself.

He'd spent the afternoon poring over everything Lloyd had collated about the possible whereabouts of Marnie's earrings from his tour of Deansgate jewellers and pawn shops the day before. In total, seven pairs had closely matched the description on Rex's Kendals account, so Lloyd had taken himself back to the four shops involved that afternoon, armed with a disposable camera. He had then dropped the film off to be developed before he'd diverted into Lewis's to check on Peggy on his way back to Tib Street.

Up until that point, it might almost have been possible for Andrew to entirely forget about ghostly interactions and concentrate solely on the hard facts that usually underscored his job, but then Lloyd had come bursting in to announce that, according to Marnie, Liam Byrne had previously been in a relationship with yet another person of interest in his investigation.

So straight back to ghosts it had been.

Only a few yards from the door of Bombay Palace, Andrew paused. There, parked right outside the door to the restaurant was a pristine, silver-grey Aston Martin DB5.

'You have got to be fucking kidding me,' Andrew muttered, with a deep and terrible certainty that he knew exactly who owned that car.

His suspicions were confirmed a few seconds later when a head of floppy blond hair appeared through the open driver's side window.

'Joycie!' Charlie Swan crowed as Andrew glared back at him. 'Fancy seeing you here. Have you cheered up since this morning?'

Andrew shook his head and carried on walking past the car as though he hadn't heard a thing.

'Hey, hey, wait, *hang on*!' Charlie called, unfolding himself from within the car, and brushing what looked to be shards of poppadom off his shirt before he turned to lean casually against the door. 'Seriously, what *are* you doing here?'

'Getting some dinner, what does it look like?' Andrew rolled his eyes. '*Some of us* are working, even though it's Friday night.'

'Technically I *am* working.' Charlie grinned impishly. 'I'm in the employ of the Greater Manchester Police, same as you.'

'What's that supposed to mean?' Andrew asked as he moved out of the way of a large group of men and women heading into the restaurant.

'Well, someone has to ferry my sister around now that she's very busy and important,' Charlie replied.

Andrew looked up sharply. 'You mean you've not picked her up yet? Why not? She was supposed to be only going out for a quick drink!'

Charlie rolled his eyes. 'Calm down, she's a big girl, and she'd have your head if she thought you believed otherwise. She's fine. She called the house from *Osteria*. Peg said that she and Rebecca had just accepted an invitation to have dinner with Rex Hughes and his sister.'

Andrew's eyes bugged. '*What*?'

Charlie raised one eyebrow. 'Are you alright, Joyce? I'll be honest, you look a bit mental right now.'

'Peggy's having dinner with Rex Hughes?' Andrew asked, voice low and entirely disbelieving.

'Oh, Christ,' Charlie rolled his eyes, guffawing. '*Please* don't tell me you're jealous.'

'I'm not fucking jealous, you *idiot*,' Andrew snapped. 'Someone threatened Hughes's sister this morning, and it very well may be the same person responsible for Marnie's murder.'

Charlie's face fell instantly. 'Is my sister in danger?'

'I don't know,' Andrew admitted. 'I *do* know that I don't want her anywhere near Rex Hughes, or his sister; not when they could be targeted again at any point.'

'Shit,' Charlie said, his eyes widening.

'Yeah, I know,' Andrew replied.

'No,' Charlie hissed, gesturing further up the road with his head. 'I mean, *shit*, here comes my sister, and Rex Hughes is with her.'

Andrew didn't turn around. He had no reason to doubt what Charlie was saying and all hope of keeping this whole thing quiet would be lost if Hughes saw him. Instead, he tucked his head down and hurried into the restaurant, ducking just out of sight of the open inner door. The group from a moment ago was still blocking the main entrance into the dining room as they divested themselves of jackets, so Andrew pressed himself against the wall, hoping he'd be just out of sight from anyone on the pavement.

'Can I help you, sir?' a smartly dressed man asked him, raising an eyebrow at the strange half-crouched position Andrew was in.

'Yes, sorry, I wanted to order some food to take away,' Andrew said, keeping his voice only slightly above a murmur.

'You have to order at the bar,' the man replied, and *really* all credit to his professionalism for not just asking the person behaving incredibly strangely to leave immediately.

'Yes, I know that,' Andrew replied. He peered around the door furtively, and, *bugger*, there was Peggy, closely followed by Rex Hughes. Hughes was gesturing towards Charlie's car with a grin.

'Sir?' The man tried again, and Andrew could sense that his patience wouldn't last forever.

Andrew reached into his pocket for his identification and held it up. 'Detective Inspector Andrew Joyce. Sorry about this, I'm actually just following someone right now, but I *will* order in a minute.'

'Oh, are you undercover too?' The man's face switched from rightfully suspicious to deeply delighted in an instant.

'Undercover *too*?'

'Yeah,' the man said, his voice dropping to a whisper. 'Like Charlie out there. He's always in here, but I didn't realise he was police.'

'Charlie told you he was undercover?' Andrew asked, utterly outraged.

'Oh, sorry,' the man apologised sheepishly. 'I wasn't supposed to say anything, was I?'

'I'm going to kill him,' Andrew muttered, looking back out the door. The noise from inside the restaurant made it impossible to hear what Rex was saying, but he was smiling at both Swans warmly.

'If you tell me what you want, I'll order it for you, but just this once, alright?' the man offered, distracting Andrew again. 'I can see that you're busy.'

Andrew sighed. 'Enough food to feed two hungry people, please. Whatever you recommend, as long as there's a vat of mango chutney involved.'

'Yes, sir,' the man replied. 'I'll be back in a minute.'

Andrew looked out just in time to see Rex shake Charlie's hand and then lean over to kiss Peggy chastely on the cheek. Andrew reflexively tightened his grip on the doorframe.

Charlie caught his eye for the briefest second as he turned to get back into the car and there was a definite sense of '*what the hell are you doing*?' about the look he gave him.

Andrew glanced to the other side of the car and flinched when he saw Peggy staring at him in surprise. She quirked her lips in something that was perhaps supposed to be an apology, but possibly just an echo of her brother's confusion, before also climbing into the car.

Andrew stayed where he was until the car had driven away, and then waited a good few more minutes until he was certain that Rex was completely out of sight before he stood up. He winced at the beginnings of pins and needles in his right foot.

'Oh, done now, are you?' The man had reappeared and was holding a bulging plastic carrier bag out towards Andrew. 'Perfect timing.'

'Thanks,' said Andrew, taking the bag. He paused just as he went to pull his wallet out of his pocket. 'Hey, does Charlie have a tab?'

'Yes, sir,' the man replied. 'Like I said, he's a regular. Good tipper too.'

'Great,' Andrew beamed. He was going to take what he could get from this disaster of a day. 'Could you add this to his tab, please? Plus a *really* big tip.'

'Of course, sir.'

Andrew didn't feel even a tiny bit guilty as he thanked the man again and headed back out into the evening, the carrier bag hanging heavily from his hand.

* * *

'Where've you been?' Marnie asked as soon as Peggy opened her bedroom door.

Peggy groaned internally. She was tired, and she really wasn't in the mood to deal with a disapproving ghost. 'Out. Drinks, dinner, you know.'

'Ooh!' Marnie grinned. 'Who with? *Andrew*?'

'No, *not* Andrew.' Peggy shook her head as she hung her jacket up and dropped her shoes just outside the wardrobe. 'Rebecca and some of the others from work.'

'Hmm,' Marnie's eyes narrowed as she stepped closer to Peggy. 'Hang on, I smell aftershave. I recognise it.'

Oh God, here we go. Might as well explain before I'm busted anyway, Peggy thought. 'Yes, well, Rex and Athena turned up at the same place for dinner.'

'What?' Marnie screeched. 'Are you telling me that you had dinner with Rex?'

'Well, not dinner with Rex *by himself*,' Peggy said as casually as she could. 'But yes, there was dinner, and yes, he was there.'

Marnie looked poleaxed. She drooped slightly and sat on the edge of the bed.

Peggy was inordinately pleased about that. Not because she wanted to see Marnie upset, but because she'd become increasingly concerned on the drive home that Marnie might just vaporise the entirety of Butterton – the house *and* the village - in rage when she found out about Rex.

'How was he?' Marnie asked quietly after a long moment.

'Sad,' Peggy replied, and it was true. Rex had been very charming with everyone he encountered, telling stories, and laughing in all the right places, but there was a sadness that Peggy recognised on a primal level. 'He misses you.'

Marnie's lower lip wobbled, and she sniffled quietly a few times. 'It's not fair, Peggy.'

'I know,' Peggy said, and, in a way, she truly did understand.

'Do you?' There was a hint of judgement in Marnie's voice.

'Do I know what it's like to die and leave everything behind?' Peggy shook her head as she sat down next to Marnie. 'No, I don't know about that. But I do know what it's like to lose someone, and I know what it's like to feel like everything and everyone is conspiring against you. I know how it feels to imagine that there's no way to ever be happy again.'

'Is that why you seem so sad too?' Marnie asked carefully. 'Did someone you love die?'

'They didn't die.' Peggy shook her head. 'Someone I cared about betrayed me. Actually, *two* people I cared about, if I'm honest about it. It's why I haven't left the house much in the past year; I've been busy wallowing.'

'There's nothing wrong with a bit of wallowing,' Marnie said sternly.

'No, I know,' Peggy replied. 'I know that. I *needed* it, but I think it's time for me to do something else.'

'Is that why you're helping the police?' Marnie asked.

Peggy shrugged. 'That's part of it. But I also want to keep helping because I think that you deserve to know what happened to you, and so do all of the people who care about you.'

Marnie sighed. 'Can you answer a question for me, please? I want you to be completely honest.'

'Alright,' Peggy agreed, bracing herself anyway.

'Do you think there's anything going on with Rex and Rebecca?' Marnie asked. 'Or if anything ever *has* happened?'

Peggy shook her head without hesitation. 'Honestly, no. They're close, I can see that, but the way they talked about you tonight…'

She trailed off and shook her head again. 'They both love you, Marnie. I don't think they would have done anything to betray your trust in them.'

Marnie's lip wobbled again, and then she was crying in earnest.

'Oh Marnie, I'm sorry,' Peggy said, as Marnie stood up and started pacing around the room. 'I didn't mean to upset you.'

'It's okay,' Marnie whispered brokenly. 'It's okay. They're friends. It's okay.'

'Look, Marnie, I know you don't want to think about it, but Rebecca really *is* in a relationship with Liam Byrne,' Peggy added softly.

'I still can't believe that, you know,' Marnie said, shaking her head. 'I'm surprised Rex hasn't given her a piece of his mind about that one. He never liked him.'

Peggy frowned. 'You know, I don't think Rex actually knows about Rebecca and Liam. Rebecca was really cagey when we were all talking over dinner; she didn't say much about her personal life at all, come to think of it.'

'She knows what Rex would say, that's why!'

There was a knock at the bedroom door, and Peggy hauled herself to her feet to answer it.

'Peg, who the hell is in there with you?' Charlie asked, peering around the doorframe.

It was hard to say who screamed the loudest out of Marnie and Charlie as they stared at each other in surprise.

'Shut up!' Peggy hissed, grabbing Charlie by his collar and hauling him into the room. 'Jesus, are you *trying* to get Timothy's attention?'

Charlie didn't answer, he was still staring wide-eyed at an equally stunned Marnie.

'Can you see me?' Marnie asked, blinking furiously.

'Peggy?' Charlie asked slowly. 'Peggy, why can I see a dead girl in your bedroom?'

Peggy looked between the two of them and closed her eyes. 'I haven't got a bloody clue.'

TWELVE

'Morning, sir,' Jen said brightly as she draped her jacket over the back of her chair.

'Jen,' Andrew replied with noticeably less enthusiasm. He was tired (again), grumpy (again), and lamenting the sad downward spiral of his professional and personal life (again).

'Here you go!' Lloyd was annoyingly chipper as he presented Andrew with a mug of coffee. 'That'll sort you out in no time, sir.'

'I don't have a hangover, Lloyd,' Andrew grumbled, but he picked up the mug anyway.

'Then what's wrong with you?' Lloyd frowned and looked back over his shoulder at Jen. 'What's wrong with him?'

Andrew didn't have the energy to tell Lloyd off for being insubordinate. 'Did you get the photographs?'

'Yep,' Lloyd announced, popping the 'p' with gusto as he pulled the envelope out from where it was wedged under his arm, and handed it to Andrew. 'Seven pairs of pearl earrings, all of which were brought into, and subsequently purchased, by the shops at some point in the past six months. All match the description we have from the Kendals' receipt. There are also three pairs that have since resold, so unfortunately there are no photos of those ones.'

'Good work, Lloyd,' Andrew said, flipping through the photos quickly. He wasn't pinning all his hopes on finding the correct earrings, but just maybe they would catch a break and get a better description of the suspect than they had so far.

'Thanks, sir,' Lloyd said. 'Oh, and I did what you said. I asked all the jewellers where they'd take a high-value piece if they wanted to sell it through a broker, and all of them came back with the same two names: Boodles, here in town, or French & Son in Hale.'

'Good,' Andrew nodded. 'Jen, can you follow up with Boodles, please? You're due to check in with Peggy this morning, so it makes sense for you to stay here. Lloyd, you can come with me to Hale. These are our two best bets if someone tried to sell that engagement ring locally, so we need to keep our fingers crossed that one will know exactly which ring we're talking about.'

'I've also got the information on the two girls Rex was previously engaged to,' Jen said as she handed Andrew a sheet of paper with names and addresses on it. 'Amy Hawke and Ruth Wallace. Amy is the daughter of a former business associate of Rex's father, and Ruth went to school with Athena Hughes.

'There isn't much else to say on either of them, to be honest. It sounds like the breakups were quite amicable, and neither one has any ill feeling towards Rex, or Marnie for that matter.'

Andrew tapped his pen against his desk. He'd sort of been expecting that, but it was still disappointing to hit a dead end. 'Alright, thanks Jen. I guess we can rule out any involvement on their part then.'

'Hey, did you guys get Bombay Palace without me last night?' Lloyd piped up, pointing accusingly at a napkin on Andrew's desk.

'Perk of working a Friday night, Lloyd,' Andrew said with a shrug.

Lloyd sighed dramatically, but before he could start complaining in earnest, Andrew threw him the keys to the Belmont. 'Let's go. I'll even let you drive.'

'What, really?' Lloyd asked, grinning. 'Nobody ever lets me drive.'

'Oh, Christ, am I going to regret this?' Andrew asked as he rubbed his temples. 'If you drive like Nigel Mansell, I *will* throw you out. I won't care whether we're on the M56 or not.'

'Lloyd actually has the opposite problem,' Jen said, one side of her mouth pulling down as Lloyd threw Andrew a salute and bounded down the stairs. 'He drives like my granny when she's forgotten her glasses.'

'Oh, good,' Andrew replied, gulping down some more coffee before turning more serious. 'Jen, when you go to Lewis's, can you ask Peggy to come back here when she's finished her shift? And if either Hughes or Byrne makes an appearance I want to know immediately, alright?'

Jen studied him closely for a moment. 'You're really worried about her, aren't you?'

'There's too much that doesn't quite make sense. I'm worried we're missing something.' He'd stayed up most of the night again trying to straighten out everything they had so far and see how it might fit together; he hadn't been any closer to the answer by the time he'd finally fallen asleep on the sofa around four. At least he'd remembered to shave before work this time.

'Peggy won't do anything to put herself in danger,' Jen said. 'I'm sure of that.'

'It's not *Peggy* doing something unexpected that I'm worried about.'

Jen opened her handbag and pulled out a yellow plastic pencil case decorated with flowers and glittery fairies. Jen caught him frowning at it and laughed.

'I was going to do a bit more digging into properties owned by the Hughes family before heading to Boodles,' Jen explained, unzipping the pencil case and tipping brightly coloured pens all over her desk. 'One of my nieces left this at my house last time I babysat. She has a pretty decent collection of felt tips, so I thought I'd borrow them for colour-coding property on the map. Don't worry, I wasn't planning on having some sort of Tony Hart moment while you were out!'

Andrew laughed slightly, despite his dark mood. 'Wouldn't be the weirdest thing to happen round here.'

'True.' Jen grinned. 'Now, sir, not to worry you, but the last time Lloyd was left alone with a car he managed to break a key in the lock.'

Andrew took off at a run, with the sound of Jen's laughter following him down the stairs.

He half-tripped off the bottom step and nearly careened straight into Dolly, who didn't seem to be doing anything but smoking.

'Watch it!' Dolly yelled at him, as though Andrew would ever try to consciously go anywhere near her.

'Sorry,' Andrew mumbled while avoiding eye contact, side-stepping Dolly and heading for the pavement.

'Worried are ye?' Dolly asked, sniffing loudly before another hacking cough escaped.

Do not engage, Andrew told himself sternly. *Do **not** engage.*

Dolly snorted.

'What's that supposed to mean?' Andrew snapped, turning around, because apparently even he was no longer listening to himself. 'Are you eavesdropping on police business? I could have you for that you know.'

Dolly smiled in a way that may have been serene on others but on her cracked and cratered face it appeared as coldly predatory. 'I don't give a rat's arse what youse are talking about up there, but I do like the creepy girl.

And her brother knows how to treat a lady right, unlike *some* people.'

'This is absolutely none of your business.' Andrew clenched his fists at his sides. He had too much to do to get drawn into a pointless argument with the resident lunatic. He was going to have a word with Higson about Dolly's presence as soon as he had an opportunity to do so. The Ballroom was under a permanent sprinkling of dust, so she clearly wasn't up to scratch as a cleaner.

'I'd worry about the creepy girl,' Dolly said, pointing at Andrew with the hand holding the cigarette, ash salting the tiles. She narrowed her eyes at him. 'Oh, I'd be worried if I were you.'

Andrew shook his head at her and went to find Lloyd.

He slammed the door of the Belmont behind him and scrabbled for his seatbelt with more force than necessary. He pulled hard enough that the retractor clamped the belt in place.

Lloyd blinked in surprise as Andrew swore at the seatbelt and let go. 'You alright there, sir?'

'That bloody old crone is a menace,' Andrew growled, outraged. 'Why is she even here? It's not like she actually cleans anything. Telling *me* what I should be worrying about!'

'Uh oh.' Lloyd grimaced. 'Has Dolly been doing her spooky voodoo thing on you?'

'Her *what*?'

Lloyd shrugged. 'See, Dolly sometimes just *knows* things. It's really weird. You can have a secret, something that you've never told anyone, and one day Dolly will just bring it up. Why, what's she said to you?'

Andrew opened his mouth and then closed it again firmly. No, he was already going along with the ghost thing, he wasn't going to accept that Dolly was anything more than a crazy old woman who did her best to wind Andrew up. 'Nothing.'

Lloyd nodded slowly. 'Alright, look, I know it's weird, but this whole place is weird, right? So, just, whatever Dolly's said to you, maybe don't just ignore it. Yeah?'

Andrew couldn't exactly ignore something he'd already been thinking about, so he just gave Lloyd a short nod. He looked straight down the street, Lewis's just visible around the corner at the end, and he tried to ignore the slight prickle under his skin. Andrew had built his career on trusting his instincts, and no matter how hard he tried to explain away his thoughts as irrational, he couldn't help but feel like something had shifted and they were all about to face the consequences.

'Sir?' Lloyd asked, turning the key in the ignition. 'Are you ready to go?'

'Yeah, go for it,' Andrew replied, tearing his eyes away from the distant building. He reached down into the footwell and picked up the notes he'd made the night before as Lloyd guided the car out of Tib Street.

'Do you mind if I ask you a question?' Lloyd piped up a few minutes later.

'Go ahead,' Andrew replied, hoping that it had something to do with the case and not just Lloyd mining for personal information.

'Do you think it's a bit weird that whoever returned Marnie's gifts to Kendals knew exactly what to take?' Lloyd asked. 'I mean, even if Hughes organised the whole thing it seems strange that you'd send someone to kill your fiancée and then take her presents back. Right?'

Andrew sighed. This was exactly what he kept coming back to himself. If Rex had organised Marnie's murder, then why would he risk incriminating himself by removing certain items and then returning them to Kendals? And for what? Money? He was practically swimming in cash as it was.

The theory that either Rebecca, or indeed Janine, had made the return still made sense if you pinned Marnie's death on Liam Byrne instead. It was easy to theorise that the Byrnes wanted to send a message to Rex, and also make some money out of the situation.

Yet, *how* would Liam Byrne know exactly which of Marnie's possessions had been purchased for her by Rex? Sure, Rebecca might have been shown each gift by Marnie as she received them, but what was Andrew supposed to think then; that Rebecca kept a list just in case she was ever employed by her criminal boyfriend? That didn't seem even remotely likely.

'It is strange,' Andrew agreed. 'We're missing something. I just can't see what it might be yet.'

'What are we going to do if we don't track the engagement ring down?' Lloyd asked.

'Try other jewellers, brokers, maybe auction houses,' Andrew replied.

'Unless the killer kept the ring for some reason, or they've gone out of area – which feels less likely given how connected to here everyone involved is – then the only way to move something that valuable would be through an expert.'

'They got rid of everything else pretty quickly,' Lloyd rationalised, 'so it wouldn't make sense to keep hold of the ring for too long, I guess.'

Andrew gestured for Lloyd to turn left at the junction ahead. 'Let's hope so.'

The car was quiet for a long time as Lloyd concentrated on never even approaching the speed limit. The radio playing quietly in the background was nearly enough to lull Andrew to sleep.

Lloyd only spoke again when they approached the outskirts of Hale village. 'It's nice to actually feel like we're doing something useful for once though.'

'What do you mean?' Andrew asked.

'Well, the Ballroom doesn't usually get the most exciting cases, you know,' Lloyd said, parking just outside French and Son. 'A lot of the stuff we get sent that's even slightly recent-ish has had such shoddy hands on it in the first place that it's almost impossible to know where to begin.'

Andrew tilted his head. 'You're not happy with the way CID's conducting investigations?'

Lloyd wrinkled his nose. 'Well, no offence to you, sir, because you're obviously good at your job, and I bet you were great when you were at CID, but yeah, some of it's been a bit shit, if you'll pardon my French.'

Andrew was still connected enough to his former workplace to feel offended, but he would grudgingly have to admit that from what he'd seen from CID's role in Marnie's case, they had, in fact, been a bit shit.

'How did you end up in the Ballroom?' Andrew asked.

'I requested it,' Lloyd said with a grin. 'I'd heard about it back when I first joined the force and thought it sounded totally made up. I'd met Jen on an earlier case, back when she was Higson's DC, and she made a good case for me to take up her old role when she got promoted.'

'Then how did Jen end up there?' Andrew had wondered about it on a few occasions throughout the week, but it hadn't really come up in conversation.

'That I don't know,' Lloyd replied. 'She's pretty cagey about it.'

'Hmm,' Andrew said. Jen seemed more than capable, so Andrew found it hard to believe that she'd been sent there as any sort of punishment. Then again, despite the changing culture of the force, Jen was still a woman, and Andrew knew plenty of superior officers who still weren't keen on changing the boys' club mentality.

There wasn't time to dwell on any of that now though.

'Shall we?' Andrew gestured towards the jewellers, and they both got out of the car.

The stifling heat of the day before hadn't abated yet, and the sun reflected off the cushions of rings and necklaces on display in the window, temporarily blinding anyone who looked for long enough. Andrew pulled on his suit jacket, instantly grimacing at the sense of claustrophobia.

French and Son had been adorning the wealthy housewives of Cheshire and South Manchester with gold and jewels for nearly a century, and Andrew was desperately hoping that someone here would be able to help in tracking down Marnie's engagement ring.

A small silver bell tinkled gently as Andrew pushed open the door, and he screwed his eyes shut at the sudden change from sunlight to artificial fluorescence. When he opened them again, it was to find an elegant older woman staring at him quizzically.

'Can I help you, gentlemen?' she asked, giving both of them a pointed once-over.

Andrew assumed that they might not look anywhere near as well-heeled as the usual French and Son clientele.

'I hope you can,' Andrew replied, fishing his identification out of his pocket. 'I'm Detective Inspector Andrew Joyce, and this is my colleague DC Lloyd Parker. We have a few questions about an item that you may have been approached to sell.'

The woman's face darkened immediately. 'I'm afraid we don't deal in items of questionable origin, Detective Inspector. Our brokerage service is offered only to a small number of regular clients, and, occasionally, to members of certain societal rank.'

Andrew didn't have to be a genius to assume that he fell squarely outside the definition of 'certain societal rank'.

'Ma'am, I am certainly not suggesting any wrongdoing on your part.' Andrew gave his most charming smile; the one that had definitely got him into trouble in the past. 'The item in question is, in fact, of *significant* value. If you could just take a quick look at this photograph, I would be most obliged.'

Andrew proffered the blown-up image of Marnie's engagement ring towards the woman and kept smiling at her until she took it from him with a quiet *hmm*.

Lloyd snickered next to him.

'Keep talking like that and you'll fit right in with the Swans,' he whispered.

The woman's face soured further. 'Yes, I believe that I do recognise this ring.'

As much as he wanted to jump up and down in excitement and relief, that probably wouldn't do much for his clearly limited cachet here. Instead, he smiled again. 'Wonderful. Would you be so kind as to give us any information that you have on the seller, and indeed the current status of the ring?'

Lloyd looked like he was about to swallow his own tongue in an attempt to avoid laughing. Thankfully the woman was still glaring at Andrew, so she didn't notice. She nodded once and headed off through a locked door in the back corner of the room.

'She absolutely hates you,' Lloyd hissed with a grin. 'But you're too polite for her to yell at.'

Andrew smirked slightly. 'I would have started bowing if I'd thought it was going to get her to cooperate.'

'Oh, here we go,' Lloyd muttered, nodding towards the door to the backroom as it opened again. The woman stopped at the counter and gestured for the two men to join her.

She held a sheet of paper up in front of her and perched a pair of thin-framed reading glasses on her nose before reading aloud. 'One nineteenth-century cluster ring. Two-and-a-half carat, oval cut pigeon-blood ruby. Eight brilliant-cut diamonds. Eighteen-carat yellow gold band. Brought to us for a valuation in February this year.'

'And the name of the seller?' Andrew asked, already feeling the tingle of excitement that came when the chase started in earnest.

'I'm not sure I should just be handing out such information, Detective Inspector. It's confidential,' the woman replied, pursing her lips.

She reminded Andrew of a particularly frightening librarian from his school days.

Andrew nodded, trying to look as pious as possible. 'I'm afraid that this is connected to a murder investigation.'

'*Murder*?' The woman blanched. 'No, no, that can't be right.'

'I'm afraid that the young woman who had accepted a proposal with that ring was killed back in January,' Andrew said, and the words tasted as acrid as they always did. 'That ring is a key piece of evidence in our investigation.'

The woman was shaking her head now. 'I think you may have the wrong piece of jewellery, Detective. This ring is included in the portfolio of a long-standing client. There must be some mistake.'

'There's no mistake,' Andrew replied firmly. It was time to increase the pressure. 'The ring was removed from the body of a murder victim. We want to give that young woman justice and her family closure. We can't do that without investigating every possible avenue.

'Now, can you please confirm if you still have the ring in your possession?'

For a long moment, Andrew thought that the woman might still refuse to reply, but then she nodded once.

'We were requested to find a buyer,' she explained. 'The ring was to remain with us until such time as a sale was completed. A buyer has been arranged, but the terms of payment are yet to be fully agreed.'

'So, you still have the ring?' Andrew asked, aware of how desperately invested he sounded.

'We do,' the woman confirmed and then sighed loudly. 'The ring is held as part of a collection belonging to Mr Rex Hughes.'

* * *

'So, that's actually Marnie's ring?' Jen said in awe, staring down at the open box on Andrew's desk.

'It is,' Andrew confirmed. 'The woman at French and Son wasn't happy about handing it over, and even less happy about agreeing to do so without informing Hughes. We need to make sure that nothing happens to this damn thing, or we're all getting sued.'

'There's a store in the basement,' Jen replied. 'Higson's the only one with a key though, so I suggest you don't take your eyes off it until Monday.'

'That woman from the jewellers would probably skin you alive if you lost it,' Lloyd piped up, dipping another chocolate digestive in his mug of coffee.

The mood in the Ballroom was more jubilant than Andrew had previously known it. Tracking down the ring had boosted everyone's mood, and even Andrew wasn't feeling quite as morose as he had that morning. He still had that strange underlying sense of dread that he couldn't quite shift, but even that had been dulled by their breakthrough.

'So, what now?' Jen asked. 'Do we have enough to bring Rex Hughes in?'

Andrew shook his head. 'Not yet. The woman at French and Son couldn't confirm who actually brought the ring in, only that it was someone who was claiming to act on behalf of Rex himself. They had a signed letter, and the signature does seem to match previous correspondence from Hughes, but it's not enough on its own. Not when all letters pertaining to the prospective sale of the ring were to be sent to an address in Bury that doesn't seem to have any connection to Hughes.'

'We'll get something,' Jen said, optimistic as ever. 'I'm sure of it.'

'It's a bit Lady Di, isn't it?' Lloyd pointed at the ring. 'Different colour though.'

'Well, Rex did seem to treat Marnie like a princess,' Jen said. 'Though it's not quite as impressive as that emerald Peggy's been wearing all week.'

'Oh, is Peggy getting married?' Lloyd asked, frowning. 'Charlie didn't mention that, and I mean, Charlie mentions *everything*.'

'No, she's not getting married,' Andrew said, snapping the ring box shut. Even though he hadn't actually divulged anything, he still felt that this was skirting too close to a subject he'd been told about in confidence. That, and he thought that Lloyd might actually implode under the weight of such shocking gossip if he found out what had happened to Peggy the year before.

'Oh, okay,' Lloyd accepted the answer with a shrug. 'I suppose it's just because she's loaded. I guess owning stuff like that all feels very normal to her.'

'I can't imagine actually having that much money,' Jen added, somewhat wistfully.

'I doubt most people can,' Andrew said, draining his coffee mug. 'Speaking of Peggy, what time does her shift finish?'

'Three-thirty,' Jen said. 'She told me she was going to come straight here like you asked.'

'It's quarter past four,' Lloyd said, looking at his watch with a frown.

Andrew propelled himself out of his chair and was racing down the stairs before Lloyd had finished speaking.

The sound of clattering behind him confirmed that Jen and Lloyd were right on his heels as he tore up the road towards Market Street.

'Why the hell are we *running*?' Lloyd shouted, his voice half lost to the wind.

Andrew skidded to a stop only a hair's breadth from running straight into the side of a passing bus. Lloyd grabbed the back of his shirt to steady him on the edge of the pavement.

'Jesus Christ, sir, have you got a death wish?' Lloyd said, breathing heavily from exertion.

'It's three minutes max from Lewis's to the Ballroom,' Andrew replied, looking for a suitable gap in the afternoon traffic. 'There's no reason Peggy shouldn't have arrived by now.'

'She probably just got held up,' Jen said, placating.

'She probably did.' Andrew sharply gestured for the others to follow him. 'But she's late back the day after Rebecca told Liam Byrne all about the rich girl working in the Perfume Hall. I don't like it.'

Outside the main entrance to Lewis's, Andrew turned to his colleagues. 'Jen, go around to the staff entrance and wait there. Lloyd, head for Cross Street. Charlie picked her up there last night, so just in case, yeah?'

Lloyd and Jen followed their orders without complaint and Andrew forced himself to walk as casually towards the doors as possible, even managing a tight smile for the doorman who greeted him cheerfully.

He was probably overreacting, and he'd be delighted to agree with that assessment as soon as he knew what was going on. Andrew knew what it was like to be too late, assuming that someone was fine when they truly weren't, and he wasn't going to make that mistake again.

Andrew spotted Peggy in under a second. She was standing at her counter, looking harassed as a male customer talked *at* her. Even from this distance, Andrew could see Peggy sneaking furtive glances towards the large clock on the wall. Andrew sagged slightly in relief and immediately felt stupid for racing in so gung-ho. Lloyd was probably going to take the piss for hours.

'Well, hello there.'

Andrew turned at the slightly suggestive greeting and found himself faced with the predatory smile of Janine Turner. He groaned internally.

'Can I help you with something?' Janine asked, sidling closer, proffering a bottle of *Poison* towards him.

'No, thank you,' Andrew replied politely, turning to leave.

'Oh.' Janine pouted. 'Are you sure?'

'Janine, leave the poor man alone!' Rebecca snapped, striding over and placing herself like a human shield between Andrew and Janine.

'I was just asking this gentleman if he needed any help, *Rebecca*,' Janine said icily, staring daggers at her manager.

'This *gentleman* is Peggy's boyfriend,' Rebecca hissed.

Andrew was so thrown that he tripped over his own feet as he attempted to move away. 'Um,' was all he managed to croak out.

'Come on, Andrew,' Rebecca said, steering him away from the Christian Dior counter with a steel grip on his arm. 'I'm sure there are other customers you could be *helping*, Janine.'

Andrew glanced back over his shoulder and briefly wondered whether he was about to witness a murder in the Perfume Hall. Janine looked like she was seriously considering chucking the bottle of *Poison* straight at Rebecca's head.

'Sorry about Janine,' Rebecca muttered as she let go of Andrew somewhere between Calvin Klein and Elizabeth Arden.

'It's fine.' Andrew wasn't sure he could form a longer sentence. Jesus, what was Peggy up to telling people stories like that? He understood that she needed to bolster her cover a little, and he'd played a part in *suggesting* a relationship when he'd spoken to Rebecca, but she could have *asked* him first before actually stating anything explicitly. Besides, he already had a girlfriend.

Andrew wrinkled his nose. Wait, no, he actually *didn't* have a girlfriend anymore. But that wasn't really the point, was it?

'Sorry Peggy's late,' Rebecca said, nodding her head towards where Peggy was now hurriedly gift-wrapping a box of perfume. 'This happens sometimes on a Saturday. April, who was meant to take over at half-three got here a bit late – bus problems - and Peggy was already stuck with that guy over there. Shop policy is that we're supposed to stay with a customer from browsing through to purchase.'

'It's fine, really,' Andrew repeated, wincing as Peggy started *un*wrapping the perfume as the customer picked up a completely different bottle instead.

'It's so nice that you've come to meet her again,' Rebecca said, smiling at Andrew once more. 'Are you both in town for the evening?'

'Maybe for a bit,' Andrew replied, and that wasn't altogether a lie. They *were* going to be in town; just at the Ballroom, rather than the dinner or drinks Rebecca was imagining.

'It's a shame you didn't come along last night, Andrew. Did Peggy tell you that we went out after work?'

'Yeah, yeah, she did.' Andrew nodded, gladly taking the opening for a further avenue of questioning. 'I had to work late last night, I'm afraid.'

Rebecca nodded in understanding. 'Oh, what is it that you do?'

Now, Andrew couldn't be entirely sure, but he thought that there was something slightly off about that question. Rebecca's expression hadn't really changed, save for a slight sharpening of her gaze, but it made Andrew wary.

He forced a smile. 'Honestly, I'm not surprised that Peggy hasn't told you. It's all very boring. I'm in research. History, mostly.'

'Oh, right,' Rebecca's face cleared again. 'Well, I'm sure it's much more interesting than you're making out.'

'It can be,' Andrew agreed.

At that moment, Peggy looked over and flinched in surprise when she saw Andrew standing with Rebecca. *Sorry*, she mouthed silently to him, before taking payment from her customer at last.

'Well, it looks like she's finally free,' Rebecca said as Peggy hightailed it away from the counter before she could get caught again.

'*Finally*! Well, have a lovely weekend, Rebecca.' Andrew's most charming smile appeared for one more outing.

'Thank you, Andrew. Maybe we'll see you two out later tonight.'

Time for just one last question then. 'Oh, have you got plans?'

Rebecca lit up. 'My fiancé is taking me out for dinner. Somewhere special, apparently.'

Andrew's stomach turned. Shit, Rebecca and Liam really were more serious than he'd thought. He looked down at her left hand out of habit.

Rebecca caught the motion and waggled her fingers. 'Oh, it's still very recent. We haven't found the right ring yet.'

Andrew thought of the emerald on Peggy's right hand and sincerely hoped that it wasn't being considered as an option.

THIRTEEN

Peggy was lying on her bed, staring up at the ceiling, and wondering how she could possibly still be awake. She'd already been exhausted by the time she'd finally managed to leave Lewis's, but then her debrief at Tib Street had kept her in town for another hour. Andrew had wanted her to go over everything that had happened on Friday night when she'd gone out with Rebecca. He'd wanted to know everything that Rex had said, and even how he had said it. Then, he'd made her go over it for a second time.

Andrew had been sharper with her than he had been in days, which Peggy thought was quite unfair as it wasn't her fault she'd been late out of Lewis's. He'd looked perfectly happy to be talking and smiling with Rebecca though – *his suspect in a murder case*. Bloody man.

Jen had been the one to eventually take pity on her and gently suggest to Andrew that perhaps there was nothing else Peggy could add to the investigation at that moment. She'd then driven herself home, and the journey had been blessedly quiet and drama-free.

Home hadn't been the peaceful sanctuary she'd been hoping for though. Marnie had been unusually agitated, but she'd still wanted to sit down with Peggy and Emmeline in an attempt to work out why and how she had managed to make herself briefly visible to both Andrew and Rebecca, and then how she had managed to appear clear as day to Charlie the night before.

Peggy had, perhaps naïvely, always just assumed that Emmeline knew everything that there was to know about being a ghost, yet even she still had no clue about how Marnie was doing things that had taken Emmeline decades of interaction with Peggy to even *begin* to achieve. As for how Marnie seemed to be able to travel to locations that had no connection to her, or indeed appear solid to others, Emmeline had even less of an idea.

'Last night she told me that she could *smell* aftershave,' Peggy had whispered when Marnie had been distracted going through Peggy's tape collection searching for songs she liked.

'Are you certain that is what she said?' Emmeline had asked, looking surprised. 'I don't think that would be possible, Peggy.'

'She knew I'd been with Rex.' Peggy's frown had deepened. 'And she knew something that Andrew had said to me. Something he'd said when it was just the two of us.'

Emmeline had then looked so troubled about the whole situation that Peggy had decided to leave the discussion there, which left her no closer to answering the question of just what on earth Marnie actually *was*.

In addition to Andrew's mercurial mood, and Marnie's sheer impossibility of being, Peggy also had another problem in the form of Charlie. First, he'd cried off driving her into town that morning, claiming he had a headache that he needed to sleep off. Then, when Peggy had found him in the kitchen after work, she'd been able to feel the silent accusation radiating off him.

When Peggy had suggested that they have dinner together, Charlie had curtly informed her that he'd already eaten, and then he'd left for town not long after that. Seeing Marnie had given him a real fright, and Peggy could sympathise with that, but it wasn't as though it had actually been her fault.

Well, at least she didn't *think* it was her fault.

She'd finally given up on trying to read any more of her book an hour ago, and so there she was, half listening to see if Charlie came home, and half wallowing in the fact that it felt like she was apparently to blame for everyone else's problems.

The air shifted suddenly, and the hair on Peggy's arms stood on end just before Marnie materialised in the corner of her bedroom looking terribly upset.

'Something's happened,' Marnie said, her eyes wide and shining with tears.

'What do you mean?' Peggy asked in alarm, sitting up and reaching to turn on her bedside lamp. 'What's happened?'

'I don't know,' Marnie replied, worrying her hands together, 'but something's changed, and it feels wrong.'

'Marnie, what are you talking about?' Peggy was baffled.

'It's something to do with Rex,' Marnie said, and her voice shook with fear. 'I think it's something bad.'

'Something's happened to Rex?' Peggy asked, brows knitted. 'How do you know that? Marnie, have you seen him?'

Marnie shook her head desperately. 'No, no, I don't know how I know. I just do. Something bad is going to happen, Peggy. I can feel it. '

'Okay, okay, let me think,' Peggy replied, holding up one hand, hoping that Marnie would give her a second to get her thoughts together. What was the protocol for a hysterical ghost telling you that something bad had happened to their ex-fiancé (who also happened to be a suspect in their murder)?

Andrew.

Peggy grabbed the cordless phone from the other side of her bed and called 192.

'Good evening, Directory Enquiries,' came the crystal-clear voice from the other end of the line.

'Hi, I need Andrew Joyce, Gatley,' Peggy replied, and Marnie sighed in relief.

'Do you have an address?' The operator asked.

'Um, maybe, hang on.' Peggy thought desperately back to when she'd parked behind Andrew's car the other day. She couldn't remember seeing a road sign. 'No, sorry, I don't have it. It's just off Altrincham Road though. Does that help?'

'Hold, please.'

Peggy held. She hoped that would be enough information to connect her to Andrew. She didn't have a clue where Jen or Lloyd lived, let alone Higson, and she really didn't want to have to call Rex Hughes directly. She silently begged the universe that Andrew wasn't ex-directory.

The line clicked open again. 'I have the number, or would you prefer to be connected?'

'Connected, please,' Peggy replied quickly. She could always get the number later if she needed it.

The call rang out.

'Come on, come on,' Peggy whispered into the phone as Marnie watched her expectantly. 'Please don't be out. Please, *please*. Please have absolutely no life and be at home on a Saturday night.'

'What? Who is this?'

Peggy jumped in surprise. She hadn't realised that Andrew had answered. 'Oh, shit, sorry, oh God. Andrew?'

'Who is this?' Andrew repeated brusquely. He sounded tired and more than a little affronted.

Oh good, he was one of *those* people on the phone.

'It's me, Peggy,' she replied. 'Peggy Swan. I'm helping y-'

'Yes, I know who you are, Peggy,' Andrew cut her off, caught somewhere between amused and exasperated.

'Right, yes, sorry, of course,' Peggy replied, cringing at herself. Jesus, had she really been a sociable person once upon a time?

'Peggy, why are you calling me at one am?' Andrew asked drowsily before he inhaled sharply. 'Shit, wait, has something happened? Are you alright?'

'No, nothing's really happened, I'm fine,' Peggy assured him. 'The thing is, though, Marnie's here.'

There was silence for a long moment. 'Right?'

'She's really upset,' Peggy explained, and she did have to admit that she sounded a bit mad calling a Detective Inspector in the middle of the night to tell him that she had a frantic ghost with a gut feeling wailing in her bedroom. 'I mean, she's saying that something bad is going to happen.'

'Bad how?' Andrew asked, and Peggy heard his tone shift again towards professional.

'I don't really know,' Peggy replied. 'She doesn't seem to either, only that it has something to do with Rex.'

Andrew swore under his breath and Peggy could hear the sound of him moving around, followed by the unmistakable sound of keys jangling.

'You're not actually going out at this time, are you?' Peggy asked, wincing when she noticed that it really was after one in the morning.

'Why did you call me if you didn't expect me to do something?'

That was fair. 'What *are* you going to do?'

Marnie gestured wildly from the corner, hissing, 'What did he say? Has he heard anything about Rex?'

Peggy shook her head tersely, bringing her finger to her lips in a shushing motion.

'Who's that?' Andrew asked, and the sharpness of earlier was back.

'Who's what?' Peggy played dumb because there was absolutely no way that Andrew should be able to *hear* Marnie. She waved frantically at Marnie to back off. 'I can't hear anything.'

'I definitely heard someone,' Andrew replied.

Peggy sighed deeply. 'Ugh, fine, it's Marnie, alright?'

'Well, there's no need to lie about it,' Andrew grumbled. 'You could have just told me that it was none of my business.'

'Jesus Christ, I told you who it was because it *is* your business,' Peggy replied, clenching her hand around the phone in annoyance. 'It's not my fault if you don't believe me.'

'Whatever you say,' Andrew replied.

Dear God, he was the most infuriating man on the planet, which, when that planet also included Charlie, was really saying something. Peggy was furious and opened her mouth to give him a piece of her mind.

'Look, Peggy,' Andrew added with another great big sigh before she could even utter a syllable, 'just chalk it up to lack of sleep or the fact that I am desperate for a proper break in this case, but I will go and check out the Hughes house, just in case. Okay?'

Peggy clenched her jaw to keep from swearing at him. 'Fine. Thank you.'

'Just go back to sleep,' Andrew replied, 'or whatever it is you were doing. I'll see you on Monday morning.'

There was no chance to reply before Andrew ended the call.

'Well?' Marnie asked as Peggy held the phone away from her ear and glared at it. 'What did Andrew say?'

'He is so annoying,' Peggy muttered at the handset before replacing it on the base. 'He *still* won't let himself actually believe me, you know.'

'Right, yeah, but what's he doing about Rex?' Marnie asked, brushing aside Peggy's irritation.

Peggy waved her hand and turned off the lamp again. 'He's going to go and check the house.'

Marnie stared at Peggy and raised her hands. 'Well?'

'Well, *what*?' Peggy asked, lying back down on her pillows.

'Well, why aren't you going to get your car?'

Peggy sat up and gaped at Marnie. 'Are you serious? You want *me* to go and check on Rex?'

'No.' Marnie shook her head as though Peggy was the crazy one in this situation. 'I want *us* to go check on Rex.'

'Marnie, no. No, no, absolutely not.'

'Peggy, what if Rex is in danger? He could need my help!' Marnie cried. 'I can't just go myself in case someone sees me! And that's only if I could *get* there anyway.'

'I'm sure Rex is fine. Just let Andrew do his job, okay? There's nothing we can do.'

'I don't believe that. What if he needs us and we're not there for him?'

'Then Detective Inspector Joyce will help him.'

'But what if *Detective Inspector Joyce*-' Marnie paused to roll her eyes as she mimicked Peggy's sudden formality. 'What if he's in danger too?'

'I'm sure he can handle himself, Marnie. He's a police detective, remember? Anyway, it's probably all fine.'

Marnie looked taken aback. 'Wait, don't you believe me?'

'No, no, I do,' Peggy replied, raising her hands placatingly. 'Of course I do, but you said yourself that you don't know what's actually wrong.'

Marnie's eyes filled with tears again. 'Peggy, it's bad enough that I can't be with him. What am I supposed to do if I lose him forever?"

Peggy didn't think it would be wise to point out that Marnie didn't actually *have* Rex and therefore couldn't really *lose* him, what with Rex thinking his fiancée was dead and gone; but that was, you know, apparently a very minor point.

'Peggy, *please*.'

Charlie had always warned Peggy about her bleeding-heart tendencies - as he called them - and how they would get her into trouble. As much as Peggy denied that she was easily persuaded, she could already feel her resolve wavering in the face of Marnie's distress.

'I don't even know where Rex lives,' Peggy sighed in exasperation as she rolled off her bed.

'Well, obviously *I* do.' Marnie looked significantly happier. 'I'll direct you.'

'Oh no, you are *not* coming with me,' Peggy said, pulling on a pair of socks and tucking her pyjama trousers into them.

'But how can I help if I'm not there?'

'This is not about helping, okay? This is me agreeing to just drive past Rex's house to make sure it's still standing and that Andrew still has his all limbs intact.'

'Look, I could just come with you anyway,' Marnie replied, folding her arms. 'I'd prefer if you agreed, but it's not like you could stop me.'

Peggy pursed her lips. 'No, but I could just get back into bed and go to sleep instead.' Touché.

'And then I could stand in the corner and sing every single word of *West Side Story* for the rest of the night.'

'Is that supposed to be a threat?' Peggy asked incredulously.

'You haven't heard me sing,' Marnie replied, arching one eyebrow.

'Oh my God, *fine*.' Peggy threw up her hands in despair as she disappeared into her depleted wardrobe to find her ratty old trainers. 'But we're not getting involved, alright?'

Marnie made a vague attempt at the scouts' honour hand gesture when Peggy reappeared.

Peggy quietly cracked open her bedroom door. She wanted to avoid alerting anyone from Timothy to Emmeline to her movements, and it all felt remarkably like being a teenager trying to sneak out of the house when Marnie followed her down the stairs in complete silence.

She only allowed herself to breathe normally again when they'd left the house far behind them and had the garage doors open.

'Wow, and I thought *Rex* liked cars,' Marnie said, gawping at the collection of vehicles.

Peggy unlocked her own car and gestured for Marnie to get in.

It was impossible to ignore the fact that Marnie then opened the door and buckled her seatbelt as though she weren't the manifestation of a dead woman.

'Really, this one?' Marnie asked, wrinkling her nose at Peggy's small car.

'Yes, this one,' Peggy replied, slowly guiding the car out of the garage. She kept her headlights off just in case and only turned them on when they were halfway down the driveway.

Just before they reached the gatehouse another car turned onto the driveway, coming towards them. It slowed immediately.

'Oh crap,' Peggy hissed, bumping her car onto the grass slightly so that she could pass the other car without stopping at the narrow juncture.

Charlie stared at her through the driver's window, mouth open in surprise as he rolled slowly by.

Peggy kept her gaze straight ahead as they passed each other, but she caught Marnie waving at him out of the corner of her eye. She really hoped that Charlie wouldn't drive into the lake in surprise.

When she looked in the mirror, she saw Charlie's brake lights glowing. 'He's going to follow us.'

'Well put your foot down then,' Marnie replied. 'He'll have to turn around first. We can still lose him. Come on.'

'You're enjoying this way too much, you know,' Peggy muttered.

'I've been dead for six months,' Marnie replied drily. 'Of course I'm enjoying it.'

Peggy couldn't really argue with that, and she didn't slow down until they'd left Butterton far behind and were well on their way to Heald Green.

As they got closer to their destination, however, the reality of the situation started setting in; namely that Peggy was driving to a stranger's house in the middle of the night on the instructions of a ghost. 'If Andrew sees me, he's going to go berserk.'

'Do you want me to pop out and scare him?' Marnie asked as they drove past the train station.

'Please don't,' Peggy groaned. 'Just don't let him see you at all.'

'Fine, I'll try my best. *Oh*, hang on, you need to turn left here, and then right at the traffic lights.'

Peggy did as she was told, and a few minutes later she caught sight of a familiar car parked outside a row of unassuming little cottages slightly further up the road. Peggy supposed that the large, gated house on the corner was their actual destination.

'Park here,' Marnie said suddenly, pointing to the left, right behind the empty Belmont.

'You know that's Andrew's car, right?'

'Well, I think that's *Rex's* car coming towards us, so just do it!' Marnie cried as the streetlights illuminated a red sports car driving slowly up the road.

Peggy pulled over to the kerb quickly, nearly driving straight into the back of Andrew's car in her haste. She killed the engine with a sigh of relief. 'Jesus, Marnie, stop shouting.'

'It *is* Rex's car,' Marnie said, ignoring Peggy as the red car slowed in front of the house. The gates started to inch open.

'Is he in the car?' Peggy hissed. 'Please say 'yes' so that we can go before we get caught?'

'Yes, he's driving,' Marnie said in relief. 'I can't see anyone else in the car with him.'

'Right, Rex is fine, everything's fine, and we're leaving now, okay?' Peggy said, reaching out to put the key back in the ignition.

At that moment, a figure crept out of the farthest cottage's front garden. Peggy couldn't see their face, and they were dressed head to toe in black.

'Who's that?' Marnie asked, tapping Peggy's arm repeatedly. 'Don't you think that looks really suspicious? Oh my God, what if it's someone here to kill Rex?'

Yes, Peggy *did* think it was a bit suspicious, but what was she supposed to do in this situation? Where the hell was Andrew anyway?

'I'm going to have a look,' Marnie muttered.

'No, you're not! You are absolutely *not* to get out of this car!' Peggy commanded. 'What if the person out there recognises you? What if they're the person that killed you?'

'It's not like they could kill me again, is it?' Marnie deadpanned.

Peggy wished that Marnie was slightly less well-adjusted. 'Well, no, but Marnie I'm not sure scaring the living daylights out of someone else is the way to go about this.'

The figure suddenly looked back towards the cars and Peggy wasn't quick enough to duck down. 'Oh no, oh no, oh no.'

The figure started sprinting towards them and Peggy fumbled turning the car key.

'Uh oh,' whispered Marnie before disappearing with a slight 'pop'.

'Marnie!' Peggy yelled indignantly. 'You can't just bugger off now!'

The passenger door was yanked open, and Peggy squealed in surprise. Oh God, she was going to die. Murdered at the side of the road in Heald Green, in her pyjamas!

'Shut up, shut up!' hissed the figure, voice slightly muffled as they clamped a hand against Peggy's mouth. 'Jesus, are you trying to draw attention to yourself?'

Yes, thought Peggy desperately, struggling to turn her head, *that's exactly what I'm trying to do!*

'Stop it! It's me!' snapped the figure, letting go of Peggy and pulling down the scarf that had covered their nose and mouth.

Peggy blinked in surprise at the fury on Andrew's face.

'I thought you were a murderer,' she said, words tumbling over each other in relief.

Andrew stared back at her in complete disbelief. 'What the fuck do you think you're doing here?'

Peggy flinched slightly at the harsh tone. She opened her mouth to reply but was cut off again.

'Is this some sort of twisted game you have going on?' Andrew asked, shaking his head. 'Sending me off on a wild goose chase in the middle of the night, and then, what, you just drive out here to watch me look like an idiot? Is that what everything this week has been about?'

'What?' Peggy recoiled in surprise. 'Do you honestly believe that I would do something like that? Why would I?'

Andrew shook his head tightly. 'I want you to go home right now, Miss Swan. You're lucky I'm not arresting you for wasting police time.'

Peggy was incensed and her hands were shaking. 'Get out of my car, Detective Inspector.'

'Gladly,' Andrew snapped, all but flinging himself out, slamming the door behind him and heading for his own car.

Peggy watched as Andrew unlocked his door, and then frowned at the handle when the door didn't open. He jiggled the key and then the handle again.

He walked around to the passenger side, clearly making an effort to avoid all eye contact with Peggy. The same thing happened again.

'That'll teach him to think twice before he acts like a dickhead again,' Marnie whispered from the back seat.

Peggy snorted despite her simmering rage and turned the key in the ignition. The headlights flared to life, giving her a perfect view of

Andrew's bewilderment. She waved primly before reaching down to put the car into reverse.

A slightly muffled clanking sound stopped her in her tracks. The gate to the Hughes house was opening again. She flicked the headlights off immediately, just about catching Andrew's surprised expression.

'Marnie, you should probably open his car door now,' Peggy hissed, as the gate reached the halfway point. 'Marnie? Seriously, I completely agree that he was being a dickhead, but they'll see him!'

Marnie remained silent, and Andrew remained locked out.

When it became clear that Marnie wasn't here anymore, even though Andrew's car stayed stubbornly locked, Peggy reached over and pushed open the passenger door.

'Get in, you idiot,' she hissed to the floundering detective.

Andrew looked between his car and the Hughes house quickly before turning and hurrying over to Peggy's car. He climbed in and closed the door softly behind him. 'Get your head down.'

Peggy slid down in her seat and thanked her lucky stars that she wasn't parked under a streetlight.

The nose of the red sports car appeared, and Andrew pushed Peggy further down.

'Just pray it turns the other way,' Andrew whispered harshly.

It didn't. The car exited the driveway towards them instead.

Peggy made herself as small as possible and held her breath as the car drove by. It looked like Rex was still alone, and thankfully he kept his eyes on the road as he passed by Peggy's car.

Andrew swore quietly. 'I can't believe I'm about to say this, but I need you to follow that car.'

'Follow Rex's car?' Peggy blinked in surprise.

'That's what I said,' Andrew barked. 'Quickly, before you lose him.'

Peggy reversed slightly before swinging the car around and back out onto the main road. Thankfully there was no other traffic around and it was easy enough to spot Rex's lights in the distance.

'Right, you need to stay close to him,' Andrew instructed, buckling his seatbelt. 'And fasten your seatbelt.'

'Absolutely fine to take my hands off the wheel then,' Peggy grumbled as she awkwardly complied.

'You need to get closer,' Andrew said. Peggy dutifully pressed the accelerator as she followed Rex's car.

When Peggy got within a few car lengths of Rex she could see that he was driving a Ferrari. It was probably the one he'd been enthusiastically chatting about with Charlie when they'd met.

'Not *that* close,' Andrew complained, and Peggy tapped on the brake pedal slightly too forcefully in surprise.

'You said stay close,' Peggy replied waspishly. 'Maybe you need to be a bit more specific. Oddly enough, I don't spend much time tailing other cars.'

'Didn't they cover that when you were training to be a police officer?' Andrew snapped. 'Oh, hang on, that's right, you're not actually a police officer, are you? *Thank Christ.*'

'Well, that's extremely rich coming from the man who couldn't successfully unlock his own car,' Peggy retorted, clenching her fingers around the steering wheel.

'Oh, for God's sake, you need to go a bit faster than this!' Andrew gestured wildly towards Rex's car, which, in Peggy's opinion, wasn't even that far ahead of them.

'Right, that's it!' Peggy growled, bringing the car to a violent halt at the side of the road. 'You can bloody drive!'

Peggy opened her door and stalked around to the other side of the car as she left the engine running. Andrew glared at her as he moved out of the way to let her in before getting in himself and slamming the driver's door.

Peggy badly wanted to tell him off for mistreating her poor car, but thought that if she started yelling at him again she might not actually be able to stop. Instead, she silently fastened her seatbelt again and folded her arms.

Tense silence reigned as Andrew followed Rex's car onto Princess Parkway towards Manchester. Peggy kept her head turned so that she could look out the window, making sure Andrew knew that she was ignoring his existence entirely.

'Where the hell is he going?' Andrew muttered. He pulled back from the Ferrari slightly as they approached a set of red traffic lights, before moving closer again once the lights changed to green.

Andrew then remained stubbornly mute as they drove towards the city centre, but Peggy had no intention of being the one to break the silence either. The dark night and stillness were enough to lull Peggy towards sleep, and she fought to keep her eyes open.

'He's stopping.'

Andrew's sudden comment was enough to surprise Peggy back to alertness. She jerked out of her drowsiness in mild alarm and banged her head against the passenger window. She rubbed her temple as she turned to glare at Andrew.

He wasn't looking at her at all though. Instead, he was watching as Rex stopped the car directly opposite the Haçienda. People were spilling out of the club and right onto the road with very little care for their safety or awareness of their surroundings.

'Closing time,' Andrew muttered. He inched the car forwards carefully, doing his best to avoid running over any revellers as they drove past Rex and parked slightly further up Whitworth Street.

Peggy glanced in the wing mirror on her side of the car. Rex had made no move to get out, but Peggy saw him check his watch with a frown.

'I think he's waiting for someone,' Peggy murmured.

Andrew looked over at her, slightly less sour-faced now, and nodded. He glanced in his own mirror and straightened. 'Hang on, here we go.'

A man was walking across the street in the direction of Rex's car, stumbling slightly as if drunk. He turned and yelled something to a group of young women leaving the club as he walked backwards. His words were too slurred for Peggy to catch, but the group waved back, cheerfully calling out goodnights as they headed up the road towards the taxi rank.

As the man reached the pavement his posture changed entirely. At once he was taller and broader than he had seemed a moment ago. Any hint of stumbling disappeared as he strode towards Rex's car.

'That's...weird,' Peggy whispered as she watched the man get into the passenger side of the car and say something to Rex.

Andrew stayed silent but nodded in agreement as they watched the man take something out of the inside pocket of his jacket and hand it over to Rex.

'What's that?' Peggy frowned. The yellow streetlight near Rex's car was casting odd shadows over the windscreen making it difficult to see anything clearly. 'What did he just give to Rex?'

'I don't know,' Andrew replied quietly, shaking his head. 'Hang on, I think they're setting off.'

Peggy and Andrew turned their heads away, but Rex didn't even slow down as he passed them. Andrew gave it a few seconds and then pulled out after him again.

'Do you recognise that man?' Peggy asked.

'No,' Andrew shook his head. 'Not at all. Do you?'

Peggy decided that Andrew asking a civilised question meant that a temporary truce had obviously been called. 'No.'

'You've definitely not seen him around Lewis's, or when you were out with Rex on Friday night?' Andrew asked as they headed towards Deansgate. 'Bloody roadworks everywhere!'

'Well, I wasn't actually out *with* Rex, was I?' Peggy huffed in annoyance. 'But no, I don't recognise him, and Marnie's not here right now, so I can't actually check with her.'

Andrew looked like he was about to say something, but Rex's Ferrari briefly slowed significantly just ahead of them, and he went back to concentrating on driving.

The loud whispering hit Peggy like a wall as the car stopped to idle outside Manchester Cathedral when the Ferrari reached another red light.

'Jesus,' Peggy hissed in alarm, flinching.

'What?' Andrew asked sharply, slightly flustered as he tried to look at both Peggy and the Ferrari at the same time. 'What's wrong?'

'Nothing,' Peggy said, shaking her head and doing everything she could think of to block out the incessant whispering in her mind. 'Not really. I just forgot that the cathedral was there, that's all.'

'Oh,' Andrew said quietly. 'Jen mentioned that you don't like being near churches. Sorry.'

They lapsed back into silence as Andrew followed the Ferrari along the road as it hugged the curve of the river, and then under the railway bridges to where the landscape of Victorian warehouses was dominated by the twin structures of the Boddingtons' brewery chimney and the looming red brick tower of Strangeways Prison.

'Do you know what that tower's for?' Peggy asked breaking the fragile peace. 'When we were little, Charlie used to be utterly convinced that it was a watchtower so that the prison guards could look out over the city to check that children were behaving.'

Andrew snorted lightly. 'Why am I not surprised that he came up with that? It's not a watchtower though; it never was. It's a ventilation tower.'

Andrew then shivered slightly, glancing up at the ominous structure through the windscreen. 'Still creeps me out though, no matter how many times I see it.'

Peggy was suddenly very uneasy, and her skin prickled almost painfully. She rubbed her bare arms and wished she'd thought to grab a jacket on her way out of the house.

'Hang on, I know where he's going,' Andrew said when Rex turned right onto Southall Street.

As Andrew made to follow the path of the Ferrari round the corner, Peggy reached out and grabbed his arm so tightly he stopped the car in surprise.

'Andrew,' Peggy croaked, her whole body beginning to tremble. 'I can't go down this street.'

'What do you mean?' Andrew asked, shaking his head. 'Peggy, we need to follow him. I think he's going to his warehouses on Empire Street.'

'Let me out of the car then,' Peggy begged, staring sightlessly at the imposing red brick walls of the prison itself. She took a deep breath and tried to calm her racing heart even as she felt her own body closing in around her. 'Please, please, *please*.'

'I can't let you out of the car in the middle of Strangeways!' Andrew protested loudly as Peggy reached over to unfasten her seat belt. He grabbed her hand to stop her. 'Peggy, what the fuck is going on? You are *not* getting out of this car!'

Peggy hadn't realised that she'd started crying until she was taking in great heaving breaths trying to get enough air. She managed to point out the window at the prison. '*That place.*'

'Fuck this,' Andrew snapped, slamming his foot down on the

accelerator.

The car hurtled up the road, faster than they'd gone all evening, and yet Peggy still felt hands clawing at her face and her hair. These ghosts didn't look like people at all though. Instead, they were just yawing dark shapes whispering wickedness or screaming in eternal horror. They grabbed at Peggy, trying to pull her towards them as though she were some sort of salvation.

The car screeched to a stop, and Peggy had just about accepted that the voices were gone when hands grabbed her arms roughly and pulled her out of the car. It took a second to realise that it was Andrew standing in front of her, and even longer to understand that he was speaking to her.

'Peggy, I need you to breathe,' Andrew was saying, softly and slowly, as though he were talking to a terrified child as he grasped her hands tightly between his own. 'If I have to tell your brother that you dropped dead of fright right in front of me, I think he might actually kill me. I doubt he'd make it pleasant.'

Peggy took in another gulp of air before she started coughing; a terrible hacking sound that shook her whole body. She could almost feel her ribs creaking and grating against each other and she pulled her hands free so that she could wrap her arms around her stomach to try and hold the aching at bay.

'That's better,' Andrew said, repeating it over and over again until it became a blurred mantra in the background.

Peggy finally managed to blink enough times that her eyes stopped watering. 'Ow,' was all she managed as she desperately swiped at her face, the tears already drying sticky and unpleasant in the cool night air.

'You're alright, Peg. You're okay. I just need you to sit down for me,' Andrew said quietly, gently pushing Peggy back into the car. 'I have to go and check if Rex is on Empire Street like I think he might be. Can you wait here for me? Lock yourself in, alright?'

Peggy managed to nod as Andrew went and locked the driver's side door before handing her the keys and closing the passenger door almost soundlessly. He waited until Peggy pushed down the locking knob on the passenger door, then he gave her one short nod and sprinted up the street.

Peggy didn't really know where she was, and she watched Andrew until he disappeared into the gloomy darkness.

Even at this time of night - or morning, she supposed - the unmistakable aroma of the surrounding breweries pervaded the air, tickling her nose slightly. Yet still, underneath the pungent scent of fermentation, there was the hint of something darker; something that Peggy had only rarely experienced in her life. It was an almost tangible feeling of malevolence, and she thought that she could sense it rising into the ink-dark sky above the walls of Strangeways, even though it was a few streets away now.

Peggy closed her eyes and hoped that whatever evil was in the air wasn't looking for Andrew.

FOURTEEN

Andrew stopped running when he reached the corner of Wooley Street. He glanced back over his shoulder and could just about make out Peggy in the passenger seat of her car. He hoped to God that his luck would go the right way and that all the recent CID reports of gang activity cropping up around Cheetham Hill were slightly overblown. He couldn't carry on with this endeavour if he thought that he'd left Peggy as a sitting duck. He needed to track down Rex Hughes quickly, find out what was going on, and then get the hell out of there.

He moved more cautiously as he headed down Wooley Street itself. Even though he'd seen Rex turn left onto Empire Street he'd been too distracted by Peggy screaming like a banshee to know if that had been his final destination or not.

What the hell had happened to Peggy back there anyway? Even though part of him still wanted to believe that she was lying about the ghost thing –because, really, the alternative was somewhere far beyond disturbing – Andrew didn't think that he could chalk up her reaction to being near the prison as her being a good actress. Andrew knew what terror looked like, and he certainly knew what it *felt* like, and everything about Peggy's behaviour had clawed at his natural instinct to help and protect. He supposed that he had to face the fact that if there was anywhere in the city that would be haunted by something more than a little malevolent, it would probably be the building rising up into the blackened sky in front of him.

Even though CID was a division that routinely found itself involved in the lives of convicted criminals, Andrew had actually spent very little time within the walls of Strangeways itself since he'd qualified as a detective. A quick interview with a prisoner here or there, and always during the brightest hours of the day, hadn't really made any real impression on him.

He had, however, also been there just once as a child. He was certain of it, even though his mother had denied that it had ever happened until the day she died.

Andrew had been dressed in his best Sunday suit, which had actually just been a hand-me-down from Rob. The shirt collar had been starched and made him itch terribly, but every time he'd raised a hand to his neck his mother had batted it away with her fingers, or, as he distinctly remembered happening once, her bone-handled comb. His chubby little hand had been clamped in his mother's so, so tightly that he'd felt the bones in his small fingers grinding against each other. They'd walked through that Gothic entrance together with Rob in tow, all the while being stared at by that bloody tower.

He'd only seen his father briefly, and he hadn't really understood where he was. His mother had tried to tell him that it was just somewhere new that Daddy was working for a while, but Rob had told him when they got home that their father had been caught doing something bad. When he'd asked his mother about it, he'd been swiftly and soundly reminded why it was best not to ask her questions.

Andrew shook the memory from his shoulders, letting it settle like dust around him as he pressed himself close to the walls of the brewery warehouses and importers as he crossed over the junction with Knowsley Street. He eventually found himself within spitting distance of the eastern wall of the prison itself, right on the corner of Empire Street.

He jumped back in surprise when he heard a loud thud close by, followed by the sound of Rex Hughes swearing.

'I don't care about that. Did you fucking threaten my sister?' Rex asked, voice dangerously low. 'Did you come to *my* house and threaten *my* family?'

'I didn't mate, I swear I didn't, and it weren't Ian either,' an unfamiliar male voice replied.

Andrew supposed that it probably belonged to the tall man Rex had picked up outside the Haçienda, but without actually looking around the corner he couldn't be sure.

'Rex, man, why would I do summat like that?'

'I've already told you that we need to shift this store,' Rex replied, his voice still barely more than a murmur.

'I know, man, I know, I get it,' the other voice replied. 'Look, Ian weren't 'appy about leaving 'ere, we both know that, right? But 'e understands. What with those nonces movin' in on Craigson's patch, it don't make no sense to be in town anymore. Ian's already found a good place over Failsworth way. I ain't been to your 'ouse though, mate, I swear, and Ian 'asn't either.'

'Well, if it wasn't you, and it wasn't *Ian*, then who the fuck put a brick through my window this morning?' Rex's voice was shaking dangerously. 'Who's warning me off selling here? I need the cash for it, or we're all fucked.'

'I don't know who it is, Rex, mate, I *swear* I don't know,' the other man replied. 'Look, you're still king of the 'ill in the 'açienda, right? Same at Rotters. They're the two you wanted to keep, right? I swear to you, boss, the kids there still want *your* stuff, not the fuckin' Byrnes' crap from 'olland. You can run everything from somewhere further out. Gettin' out's a good idea, mate.'

'If I find out that you're lying to me, Johnny, I'll put a bullet in your head,' Rex said, deadly quiet. 'You know I will.'

Andrew couldn't quite believe it. Every suspicion he'd ever had about Rex Hughes was being laid bare just around the corner from him.

'I want your boys on the Byrnes,' Rex added, sounding slightly calmer now. 'Especially Liam. Someone squawked, and now the police know that I nearly took his fucking head off in town.'

'When was that?'

'Months ago, back when he swore to my face that he had nothing to do with what happened to Marnie.' Rex made a slightly choked sound and then coughed loudly. 'I want you to put one of your boys on Athena too, and my mother. If anyone lays a fucking finger on either of them, I'll have you all strung up by your balls, got it?'

'Got it, boss,' Johnny replied. 'We could empty out 'ere and be in Failsworth next week. Paul reckons we can take some stuff up to Blackburn on Friday. 'E thinks we should get in up there as fast as we can. I know Tony agreed to leave up that way alone, but I don't trust that Liam won't try to pull a fuckin' fast one anyway.'

Rex growled. 'The sooner Tony puts his fuckin brother in the ground the better.'

'D'ya really think 'e will?' Johnny asked in surprise. 'Kill 'is own brother, I mean?'

'Tony Byrne would kill his own mother if he thought he'd get something out of it,' Rex replied.

'Crazy bastard. What about Blackburn though, boss? Should I tell Paul to sort it?'

'Fine,' Rex agreed, 'but make sure Paul knows that if he gets nicked outside of the city I can't do anything to help him, and he and I have never met.'

'Oh, e'll know, mate, 'e'll know.'

Andrew shuffled backwards slightly, wincing as his foot caught on a stone, sending it rolling across the pavement.

'What the fuck was that?' Rex hissed.

'I didn't 'ear anythin', boss,' Johnny replied.

'Well, *I* did.'

Andrew pressed himself back into the narrow doorway, hoping that the lack of streetlights and the blessedly moonless sky would give him enough cover.

A door opened, scraping noisily over the ground. Rex appeared around the corner and stared straight up the street. Andrew closed his eyes and held his breath.

'It'll just be bloody rats, boss,' Johnny said, also sounding closer now. 'They're everywhere up 'ere.'

'Whatever,' said Rex eventually. 'Let's just get what we need and get out of here. I'll drop you back in town. I've got some digging I need you to do for me.'

'On what?' Johnny asked.

'I think I've found the answer to our little cashflow issue,' Rex replied. 'There's a new girl working in perfume at Lewis's.'

Andrew let out a shallow breath in surprise but forced himself to stay still.

'What? Some shopgirl's got money?' Johnny asked incredulously, voices starting to fade as they walked away. "ow's that?'

'Rebecca says she's filthy rich,' Rex replied, 'I need you to find out just how rich that actually is.'

'Sure thing, boss.'

Andrew stayed exactly where he was until he heard a door inside the warehouse slam, heart hammering in his ears. He then waited a few more minutes before leaving the shelter of the brickwork columns on either side of him.

As much as he wanted to get into that warehouse, he had the distinct sense that he'd already pushed his luck far enough for tonight. He couldn't go in there after a likely-armed Rex Hughes without backup, and certainly not when the only person who knew his location wasn't even police. He needed to get back to Peggy and then call this into Higson in the morning; he didn't care if it was Sunday or not.

Andrew was certain of one thing as he jogged back to the car; Rex Hughes wasn't getting his hands anywhere near Peggy or her money.

* * *

'We can't bloody well just request a raid on a warehouse, Joyce.' Higson's exasperation was clear, even down a phone line.

'Sir, if it's where Rex Hughes is running his drug operation from w-'

'You have absolutely no proof that's the case,' Higson replied. 'You didn't actually *get* any when you were there, remember?'

'Yes, but I-'

'I know very well what you were doing, Joyce,' Higson said. 'You made the right call getting Her Maj out of there and not getting yourself gutted, but you're not in CID anymore. We don't *do* raids at the Ballroom, alright?'

'Well, what the fu-' Andrew cut himself off to take a calming breath. 'What *do* we do then, sir?'

'We collect evidence to solve old cases,' Higson replied slowly. 'Marnie's death is the old case you've been assigned to; we are *not* aiming to take down a drug empire while we're at it.'

'But they're *connected*. They have to be.' Andrew said, gritting his teeth. Why was Higson being so resistant all of a sudden?

'Joyce, do you think Rex Hughes killed Marnie?' Higson asked simply.

'No, sir, I don't,' Andrew replied, 'but I think she was killed because of his business interests.'

'If Rex Hughes isn't a suspect in Marnie Driscoll's murder, then you are to leave him well enough alone,' Higson said firmly. 'The man's an arse, and I don't doubt that he has friends in very low places, but he is not your concern right now.'

'But sir-'

'Enough!' Higson snapped, and Andrew held the phone away from his ear.

'You are part of *my* team now, Joyce, and I am ordering you to focus your attention on finding Marnie's killer, not on something that you think will have Chambers begging you to come back to CID.'

'That's not what this is about,' Andrew snapped, and it was *mostly* the truth. He'd be a liar if he didn't admit that he'd had visions of bringing down Rex Hughes *and* the Byrnes and then strolling back to Chester House with his head held high, but that wasn't the point.

'Joyce, you can take Swan out of Lewis's, but I want her around in case we need to speak to Marnie again, got it?'

'Got it,' Andrew ground out.

'Now, if you'll excuse me, I'm going back to my bloody weekend,' Higson replied brusquely. 'And if Cusack and Parker are there, you can tell them from me that they better not even *think* about requesting this as overtime.'

The call was abruptly ended, and Jen gave Andrew a sympathetic glance from where she was indeed leaning against the edge of her desk with Lloyd next to her.

Andrew very, very carefully replaced the phone in the cradle, trying hard to control his patience. Then he picked up a stapler and threw it across the room with a frustrated yell.

The stapler bounced rather satisfyingly on the sprung floor of the Ballroom before it skittered across the floorboards and crashed into the skirting board with a dull thump.

'That well, huh?' Jen asked, wincing as a little cloud of white plaster dust rose up from the damaged skirting board.

'What did he say?' Lloyd asked, putting down the pack of Gingernuts he'd brought in with him.

'He's the one who wanted us covertly on Rex Hughes!' Andrew stood up, pulling at his hair with both hands. 'He's also the one who said he wanted to see the Byrnes behind bars, but apparently now he wants us to leave it alone!'

'He said that?' Jen asked, genuinely surprised.

'Our orders are to find Marnie's killer, but leave Hughes out of it,' Andrew replied harshly. 'Peggy's out of Lewis's, but Higson's not done with her yet.'

'I don't understand,' Lloyd said slowly. 'We can't investigate a man who's probably involved in Marnie's death just because we don't think he actually strangled her himself?'

'Higson hates the Byrnes,' Jen added, shaking her head. 'He doesn't think much of Rex Hughes either. Why would he warn us away from an opportunity to get evidence of their drug network?'

Andrew thought back to something Rex had said the night before. 'Jesus, do you think Higson's on the take?'

'*Higson*?' Jen practically shrieked in horror. 'Not a chance. He's a lot of things, but he's not a crook, sir.'

'Why would you even suggest that?' Lloyd asked, clearly judging Andrew for even daring to think such a thing.

Andrew sighed and ran a hand over his face. 'It's just something Hughes said last night. He was talking about what would happen if one of his guys got picked up by police outside of the city; he said that if that happened, he wouldn't be able to help him out.'

Jen nodded slowly, looking grim. 'Which sounds like Hughes has friends in high places.'

She folded her arms. 'Not Higson though. I'm sorry, sir, but no, I refuse to believe that's the reason.'

'That's your decision, DS Cusack,' Andrew replied sharply, 'and I'll respect that for as long as it doesn't impede our investigation. I'll also let you decide whether you're coming with me now, or not.'

Andrew stood up and grabbed his jacket from the back of his chair.

'Where are you going?' Lloyd asked.

'Empire Street,' Andrew replied simply. 'If there's something there that proves that Rex Hughes is involved in moving drugs or any evidence of a connection with the Byrnes then we're going to find it.'

'But, sir, we can't do that,' Lloyd said, glancing at Jen warily.

'Look, we might not be able to pin Marnie's murder on Rex, but he as good as said that he's going after Peggy and her money,' Andrew replied as he stuffed his tie in his pocket. 'We're not going to let that happen, are we?'

'Well, no,' Jen replied, still looking unconvinced. 'But why don't you just call someone at CID? Tell them what you overheard. I'm sure they'd be delighted to take down Rex, and surely they'd happily take the kudos for protecting someone as wealthy as Peggy.'

'Who am I going to call, Jen?' Andrew shrugged. 'Look, I don't think anyone was weeping the day I left. And what did you say the CID investigation into Marnie's murder was like, Lloyd?'

'Er, a bit shit?' Lloyd offered as he thought back to the day before.

'Exactly!' Andrew said, gesturing wildly with both hands. 'So, what if they purposefully didn't look very hard at certain suspects back in January? Come on, we knew nothing about the house in Dover, nothing about the fact Rex had been engaged before. Charlie bloody Swan got more information out of his so-called *contacts* in one morning than CID got in six months. Doesn't that seem a little strange to you?'

Jen nodded slowly. 'You said that CID could never pin anything on Rex Hughes even though they found suspected members of the Byrnes' gang in houses he owned.'

'Exactly!' Andrew said again. 'What if that's because some people don't actually want either Rex Hughes or the Byrnes behind bars?'

'I think he might actually have a point,' Lloyd said slowly to Jen.

'Alright,' Jen agreed with a sigh. 'I'll come with you. Not because I think Higson's involved, mind, but because it's our job to investigate all credible leads, and also because Peggy's one of us.'

'Thank you,' Andrew said gratefully. 'Lloyd?'

'Obviously,' Lloyd replied. 'Though if Higson finds out, I'm going to tell him that you two bullied me into going with you.'

'Fair enough.' Andrew shrugged and led the other two down the stairs and out onto Tib Street. 'But that means you're going out to Heald Green to get my car later.'

In their short drive across the city, Andrew again recounted everything he'd heard the night before for the benefit of his colleagues.

'None of this sounds like he actually wants to be part of the Byrnes' network though, does it?' Jen asked as she drove them past the cathedral.

'It sounds like Hughes wants to keep his operation as it is now,' Andrew agreed. 'I'm not sure how that works when there are known associates of the Byrnes holed up in properties owned by Hughes though.'

'Perhaps he actually *didn't* know who his tenants were?' Lloyd suggested. He sounded somewhat unconvinced though.

'Maybe.' Andrew said as Jen indicated to turn right down Southall Street. He shivered at the memory of Peggy's screams the night before. He hadn't shared that part of the evening with his colleagues, feeling like that might be betraying a confidence.

'Er, sir, I think there might be a problem,' Jen said, gesturing with her head to the road in front of them.

Three police cars were parked at the junction with Empire Street, and a group of ten or so police officers were milling around.

'Shit, do you think there's been a prison break?' Lloyd asked, sounding inappropriately excited about the prospect.

'From *that* place?' Jen said, staring up at the prison. 'I doubt it.'

'Oh Christ, that's Fallon from CID,' Andrew groaned as Jen slowed the car.

'Oh, the moron in the Capri the other day?' Jen asked, twisting her lips in distaste.

'Yes, and DCI Chambers is there too.' Andrew craned his neck trying to see what was happening further down the street. 'If *he's* here then it's something big.'

'Oh crap, they're coming over,' Jen whispered as Fallon waved at the car to stop.

Jen rolled down the window. 'DS Cusack, CRD, sir.'

Fallon frowned, and then immediately grinned when he caught sight of Andrew in the passenger seat. 'Oh, hello again, *Andy.* Is this what you lot do on Sundays? Take little tours around the city?'

'What the fuck's going on, Fallon?' Andrew snapped. God, he hated this guy.

'Nothing to do with you, mate, I'm afraid,' Fallon replied, smiling smugly. 'CRD doesn't investigate active murder cases, does it?'

'No, we're just cleaning up the mess that you lot left in the first place,' Andrew replied tartly.

Fallon scowled. 'Yeah, well you can bugger off because this has nothing to do with you.'

'Warehouse on the corner of Wooley Street?' Andrew tried, just to see Fallon's brows knit in confusion.

'How did you know that?'

'It's connected to a case we're currently working on,' Andrew replied. 'So just lift the tape up like a good boy and let us down there, yeah?'

'Fuck off, Joyce,' Fallon said, shaking his head as he took a step backwards. 'You're not working on any case connected to this.'

An officer came over and tapped Fallon on the arm before whispering something to him. Fallon beamed and turned back to the occupants of Jen's car.

'Because I'm feeling generous on this beautiful Sunday morning, I'll give you some good news to brighten your sad little lives,' Fallon said, smirking. 'The good people of Manchester no longer have to worry about that jumped-up little bastard Liam Byrne.'

'What?' Andrew barked, his stomach plummeting as Fallon's implication set in. 'Why? What's happened to him?'

Fallon slid his finger across his neck, and then just whistled chirpily as he turned away without another word.

'Well, shit,' whispered Lloyd.

Andrew groaned in despair; his head already buried in his hands.

* * *

'Marnie?' Peggy called again. She was sitting cross-legged in the middle of her bed, while Charlie was perched on the window seat pretending that he wasn't shooting concerned glances at his sister every few minutes.

Charlie had been sitting at the bottom of the staircase when Peggy had finally got home after her adventure to Strangeways with Andrew. In the split second it had taken Charlie to realise that his sister was mostly being propped up by the detective at her side his angry expression had free fallen straight into concern.

Andrew had left shortly after he'd delivered Peggy, promising that he'd return her car as early as possible the next day. He'd been very keen to impress upon Peggy that Rex Hughes was not to be trusted, but he hadn't actually shared any of what had happened when he'd left her in the car and gone to Empire Street.

Even though she'd still been trying to get her breathing back to normal after the events outside the prison, she could remember with startling clarity the ashen look on Andrew's face when he'd returned to the car and driven her back to Butterton in almost oppressive silence.

'Do you think that maybe she's gone once and for all?' Charlie asked, looking down the driveway towards the main road.

Peggy shook her head. 'No, I don't think so.'

'She hasn't,' Emmeline added, even though Charlie couldn't see her. 'Although, Peggy, I really think you should start doing those breathing exercises you used to do. Whatever happened last night at the prison has altered you, I can feel it.'

'What do you mean?' Peggy frowned.

'Oh Christ, who's here?' Charlie asked looking around the room with suspicion.

'Aunt Emmeline,' Peggy replied.

'Oh, that's alright. Hi,' Charlie said, and then went back to looking out the window.

'I will never understand that boy,' Emmeline said, making a face that was likely the eighteenth-century equivalent of a fond eye-roll.

She turned serious again. 'Peggy, I think you've left yourself too open, too vulnerable recently. I wonder if it's how Marnie gained such strength in such a short period of time.'

'Perhaps,' Peggy agreed. She'd been off-kilter since everything with Edgar and her mother had happened. The distress and shame she'd felt had affected her ability to filter out the voices and visions the way she normally did, which is why even so much as *looking* at a church these days was enough to set her on edge.

'Do you know where Marnie is?' Peggy asked.

Emmeline shook her head. 'Not right now. She appeared back here last night, not too long after you first went out. She was much fainter than she had been. Did she do something that used lots of energy?'

'Apart from the whole premonition that Rex might be in danger, you mean?'

Emmeline sighed. 'Yes, apart from that.'

'Well, she locked Andrew out of his car.'

'What?' Charlie and Emmeline asked in surprise at the same time.

Charlie then snickered. 'Oh, I bet Joycie *loved* that.'

'Yes, well that's how he ended up in *my* car, so I did not love it,' Peggy replied. She looked down at her watch. It was nearly lunchtime and Andrew still hadn't actually returned her car.

'I think I'm going to have to sit young Marnie down for a little chat,' Emmeline said as she nodded sagely. 'Perhaps I'll be able to help her understand what's happening to her a little better. See if we can't calm her down and aim for a little more consistency?'

Peggy thought that all sounded rather sensible, but she got the feeling that Emmeline didn't quite know what she was in for. Marnie seemed to actually enjoy the freedom being a ghost gave her to move around at will, and she certainly wasn't above using it to her advantage. Or, maybe it was just that Peggy was still feeling sore about how disastrously her evening had gone once she'd agreed to Marnie's plan.

'Well, you might want to see if she has anything to say about the fact that her boyfriend's Ferrari is coming up the driveway right now,' Charlie said suddenly, pressing his face to the window.

'What?' Peggy asked in surprise, jumping off her bed and hurrying to stand next to her brother.

Sure enough, the red Ferrari she and Andrew had followed all the way to Empire Street last night was passing the lake.

'Fiancé, not boyfriend,' Marnie said, popping into existence just to Charlie's left.

'Jesus bloody Christ!' Charlie shrieked, grabbing his chest and staggering backwards before toppling onto the bed.

'Marnie, dear, please do try not to kill Charles,' Emmeline said mildly. 'He's sure to be a frightfully disruptive spirit, and I'm not at all ready for that.'

Peggy looked between the other three occupants of her bedroom and contemplated simply climbing beneath her duvet and just staying there; possibly until the end of time.

'What's he doing *here*?' Marnie asked, looking over at Peggy. 'Did he see us last night? Or at least see Andrew?'

'God, I hope not,' Peggy replied. 'And get away from the window in case he sees you now!'

Marnie acquiesced, although she scowled as she did so. 'He's a good man, Peggy. I don't know why Andrew's so interested in his movements.'

'Because he drove into the city in the middle of the night, picked up a man who was pretending to be drunk, and then drove to a grotty old warehouse next door to a prison,' Peggy replied tartly. 'Come on, Marnie, I know you love the man, but you have to admit that's all a bit suspicious.'

'He's a busy man,' Marnie said, shrugging, although she did look slightly unsure of herself. 'Anyway, I'm sure he was just helping a friend get home.'

'Does Rex have many friends who live in warehouses?' Charlie asked as he clambered back to his feet.

Peggy thumped him with a cushion before Marnie could do something worse.

'Ow,' Charlie whined, rubbing his head. 'Well, Peg, you're going to have to go down there and see what he wants.'

Peggy shook her head. 'Andrew told me, very specifically, not to do anything of the sort.'

Marnie turned to fix Peggy with an icy stare. 'Excuse me?'

Peggy closed her eyes and mentally kicked herself for being so stupid. Sharing the fact that Rex was in any way under suspicion for anything was likely to set Marnie off on a rampage. How they'd got away with her not realising up to this point was nothing short of a miracle.

'What's that supposed to mean?' Marnie asked, tapping her foot on the carpet.

'Look, Marnie,' Peggy sighed, 'just know that Andrew doesn't think that Rex has anything to do with your death, okay?'

Well, not directly, Peggy amended silently, but Marnie didn't have to know the specifics just now.

'Well of course he doesn't!' Marnie looked outraged. 'What sort of stupid theory would that be?'

'Right, exactly, utterly stupid,' Peggy said, crossing her fingers behind her back. 'But Andrew thinks that someone might have killed you to get back at Rex for something.'

Marnie blinked furiously. 'You think I was killed because of something Rex did?' She shook her head vigorously. 'No, no, no way. Absolutely not.'

'No, no,' Peggy said, holding up her hand and hoping that Marnie wouldn't take a single step closer to the window. 'No, more like perhaps Rex wouldn't do something that they wanted him to do, and so they took it out on you as a warning to him.'

Charlie raised his eyebrows behind Marnie and looked at his sister disbelievingly. Peggy pretended that she couldn't see him.

'So, you mean, maybe Liam Byrne, or someone else terrible, wanted Rex to do something for them, and then he refused?' Marnie asked, looking hopeful again as she half-repeated Peggy's words. 'Because he's a good man?'

The fact that Marnie kept repeating that statement still couldn't make it ring true in Peggy's head, but because she wasn't really feeling the need to have her family's ancestral home razed to the ground on a sunny Sunday morning she gave a weak smile. 'Exactly'

'Well, whatever kind of man he is, he is currently parking right outside the door, and I'd say we have about thirty seconds before Timothy is all over him like a rash,' Charlie said to Peggy and then grimaced. 'And you *know* what he's like about 'new money'.'

Timothy was a bigger snob than even their father, and part of Peggy thought that Rex genuinely deserved to be subjected to the butler's particular brand of extraordinarily polite character assassination. But, when all was said and done, Rex was actually a suspected criminal, and it probably wouldn't be wise for anyone to rile him up.

'Can't you just go down and tell him that I'm not here?' Peggy said, already pushing her brother towards her bedroom door. 'Maybe he's here to see you anyway. He was practically salivating at the thought of your car collection the other night.'

'Rex does love cars,' Marnie agreed, nodding.

'Quickly, Charlie,' Peggy hissed as the doorbell rang. 'I can practically hear the sound of Timothy's judgement approaching at speed.'

'Very bloody funny,' Charlie muttered as he bounded down the stairs and opened the front door with a yell of, 'Don't worry, Timothy, I've got it.'

Peggy could imagine the sour look on Timothy's face at that moment because he *really* despised raised voices. She crouched down and peered around her partially open bedroom door with both Marnie and Emmeline looking over her head.

'Oh, Rex, hello!' Charlie said brightly, opening the door as though he were surprised to see the other man there. 'What brings you all the way out here?'

'Charlie,' replied Rex with a smile, holding his hand out to shake. 'Sorry to drop in like this, but I was wondering if your sister was around.'

'Oh my God, is he making a move on *you*?' Marnie hissed, and Peggy shushed her with a sharp wave of her hand.

'Oh?' Charlie made a sort of shrugging motion. 'No, you know what, I don't think Peggy is here right now.'

'Ah, but I think I saw her in an upstairs window when I drove in,' Rex replied, looking up the stairs.

Peggy pushed back, and Emmeline and Marnie also tripped backwards into the room again.

'Really?' Charlie laughed, and it definitely sounded stilted. 'It's so hard to know in a house this big, you know?'

'I bet,' Rex replied, looking around the house in poorly concealed awe.

'Let me just go and check,' Charlie said, smiling tightly. 'You can wait here if you like.'

Charlie made a real show of knocking loudly on Peggy's door, and his sister dragged him in by the collar a second later.

'Would you *please* stop doing that to me?' Charlie whined in dismay, tugging at his shirt. 'You're ruining my clothes.'

'What am I supposed to do now?' Peggy hissed, ignoring Charlie's sartorial dramatics. 'Why couldn't you have lied? Said I was someone else?'

'Peg, I don't think that sort of lie works when the man's seen you with his own eyes,' Charlie replied. 'We should all just be glad he didn't see the extra from *Ghostbusters* over there!'

'Charlie, be serious!'

With a quick glance towards her resident ghosts on the other side of the room, Peggy lowered her voice so that only her brother could hear her. 'I don't know what happened last night, but Andrew wasn't happy at all when he came back to the car. I really don't think I should be going anywhere with Rex.'

'Look, you know what Andrew's like,' Charlie replied, shrugging again. 'But if you're really worried, why don't you just invite Rex in for tea?'

'Tea?' Peggy repeated blankly.

'Yes, *tea*,' Charlie said, rolling his eyes. 'You know what tea is. Come on, Peggy, wake up and think. It keeps him here in the house where we all are too, but it also gives you the chance to find out what he's up to. Surely even Joycie would think that was a good idea.'

Peggy really wasn't so sure.

FIFTEEN

Andrew rolled up the window and climbed out of Peggy's car, slamming the door closed behind him. The heatwave was still in full swing, which had made the drive from town out to Butterton humid and uncomfortable. It had done absolutely nothing to improve Andrew's already sour mood.

Fallon, and every other officer Jen had tried to speak to at the crime scene, had refused to tell them anything more about the circumstances of Byrne's death, and it wasn't too long before a young DC was sent over to not-so-politely tell Jen that she needed to leave.

Andrew had jumped out of the car when DCI Chambers had approached the cordon a second later.

'Sir!' he'd shouted, ignoring the judgemental glances of his former colleagues. 'Sir, can I have a word?'

'Joyce?' Chambers had looked completely taken aback by his former DI's presence. 'What the bloody hell are you doing here?'

'We're following up on a few leads related to the Marnie Driscoll murder case, sir,' Andrew had explained. 'She was the young-'

'Woman murdered in her kitchen just after Christmas,' Chambers had finished, nodding. 'Yes, I remember. That doesn't explain your presence at my crime scene though. Certainly not on a Sunday.'

'Well, sir, the thing is, the warehouse on the corner up there belongs to Rex Hughes,' Andrew had said, pointing past Chambers to where the majority of the officers were congregated.

'Hughes?' Chambers had frowned. 'He was the girl's fiancé, wasn't he?'

'Exactly, sir,' Andrew had confirmed, feeling overwhelmingly relieved all of a sudden. 'And the thing is we're looking into a possible link between Hughes and Liam Byrne.'

Chambers' expression had then darkened suddenly. 'You're doing *what*?' he asked waspishly. 'Might I remind you, Detective Inspector Joyce, that CID already looked into any links between Hughes and Byrne, and we found absolutely no evidence of anything suspicious.'

'Right, sir, I know that, but now Liam Byrne's been found dead in a warehouse owned by Rex Hughes,' Andrew had said. He'd been slightly put out that Chambers was being so resistant to seeing the obvious.

'We've not yet confirmed the owner of the property,' Chambers had replied tightly.

'But it belongs to Rex Hughes, sir, I'm certain of that.'

'You are not part of this investigation, DI Joyce.'

A sudden thought had struck Andrew. 'Sir, DI Fallon was called out to the Hughes house yesterday.'

'Yes, yes,' Chambers had waved his hand, 'I believe a child threw a rock through Miss Hughes' bedroom window.'

'A child?' Andrew had laughed incredulously. 'What kid writes threats about the sale of a warehouse? It obviously had something to do with her brother's business dealings.'

'DI Joyce, I fear that you are getting carried away,' Chambers had said, shaking his head pityingly. 'DI Fallon tracked down the teenager responsible before the end of the day.'

'But, sir!' Andrew wasn't proud of the way his voice had come out as an indignant squawk.

'Enough, DI Joyce,' Chambers had snapped. 'Get out of here before I have you forcibly removed. That would surely do very little to improve your already-plummeting career trajectory.'

Last chance, Andrew, he told himself. He really didn't want to have to divulge the next piece of information to Chambers – it would raise too many questions about how he'd obtained the information – but it was all he had left. 'Sir, I saw Rex Hughes here last night. Not even twelve hours ago. He was talking to a man identified only as Johnny. They were discussing the movement of drugs through the city. Hughes's warehouse is a store for the drugs, sir, I'm sure of it.'

Chambers eyes had been flint as he'd gestured for Andrew to step closer. 'You have evidence of this?'

'Well, no, sir, not *hard* evidence,' Andrew had replied, 'but I know what I heard him say last night.'

'So, *no*, you have no physical evidence whatsoever,' Chambers had concluded sternly. 'DI Joyce, I had hoped that a brief stint with Higson on Tib Street would have resulted in you bringing your CID expertise to a failing department. I had not anticipated that you would lose all common sense in the process.'

'But-'

'That is *enough*, Detective Inspector!' Chambers had barked.

Andrew had clenched his fists as every single person in earshot had then turned to stare at Chambers.

'Get out of my sight, Joyce,' Chambers had snarled. 'Do *not* let me catch you anywhere near this case. I'll be sure to call Higson as soon as I'm back at Chester House. Clearly, he needs to shorten your reigns.'

'Sir,' Andrew had mumbled contritely, but Chambers had already turned away, dismissing him wordlessly.

He'd despondently walked back to Jen's car, hoping that nobody spoke to him. If they had, he'd truly doubted that he would have been able to refrain from punching them as an outlet for his frustration.

Jen and Lloyd had remained blessedly silent as they'd driven back to Tib Street.

Once inside, Andrew had snapped at Lloyd, telling him that he was to get out to Heald Green immediately and bring Andrew's car to Butterton House.

Lloyd had complied instantly, heading off to catch a bus. Jen had left the Ballroom silently soon after, carefully placing a cup of steaming black coffee on Andrew's desk just before she did.

So, what was Andrew supposed to do now? Higson had warned him away from looking into Hughes, and Chambers had done the same with Liam Byrne. Yet somehow they still expected him to be able to solve Marnie's murder.

Had Higson known about Byrne's murder before the Ballroom team had left for Empire Street? Andrew found it difficult to believe that all senior officers hadn't been contacted the minute they suspected that the body in the warehouse was Liam Byrne, and Higson was surely high enough up the food chain. If that was the case, then Higson had purposefully kept that piece of information to himself when Andrew had called him earlier.

Andrew couldn't be so sure that Jen's faith in Higson was warranted but questioning it would mean that Andrew also had to seriously consider Chambers' intentions, which was something that Andrew couldn't bring himself to examine too closely just yet. Chambers had been a good DCI to him for years, and Andrew didn't have the capacity or the energy to sustain a crisis of faith at the current time.

He draped his jacket over his arm and approached the door to Butterton House. He twitched slightly in surprise when the door swung open without warning.

'Joycie!' Charlie grinned. Andrew thought that there was something strained about the joviality though.

'I've brought Peggy's car back,' Andrew said, holding out the key for Charlie to take.

'Oh, thanks, she'll be pleased,' Charlie replied. 'I think she was starting to think you were planning on keeping it.'

'No, something came up that needed dealing with first.' Andrew grimaced at the reminder. 'Look, er, I need to talk to your sister. Could you get her for me, please?'

Charlie looked slightly panicked for just a second. 'Oh, right now? I'm afraid now's not a good time. She's busy.'

Andrew pursed his lips. 'Well, can you just go get her anyway? I really need to speak to her about something. It's important, Charlie.'

'Ah, no, well, you see, the thing is th-'

'Lady Margaret left for another engagement a couple of hours ago,' the butler chimed in as he gave Andrew a smile that was somehow both terribly polite and judgmental in equal measure.

'Right?' Andrew said, looking at the butler. 'Do you know where she went, um-'

'Timothy, sir,' he replied with a slight incline of his head that suggested that, yes, he was indeed far superior to Andrew.

'Right, Timothy, yes. Do you know where I can find Peggy?' Andrew wrinkled his nose. 'Lady Margaret, I mean. Or when she'll be back?'

'Right, *thank you*, Timothy,' Charlie cut in, moving in front of the butler and quickly stepping outside next to Andrew. He then pulled the door closed behind him.

'What's going on, Charlie?' Andrew asked, worry creeping into his tone. 'Where's Peggy?'

'Right, listen, before I say anything you can't blame *her*, okay?' Charlie said, holding out his hands as though trying not to spook a creature he feared may be about to attack. 'And preferably not me either.'

'Charlie, where is she?'

'Rex Hughes turned up here a couple of hours ago.'

Andrew's eyes widened, but Charlie held up a hand and continued. 'Peg invited him in for tea – I thought that was sensible – but he turned her down, saying that he'd promised his sister he'd meet her at the golf club. He wanted Peggy to join them for lunch.'

'And she said *yes*?' Andrew cried. 'Jesus Christ, I *told* her to stay away from him.'

'Right,' Charlie said slowly, 'but he did turn up at our home, Joyce. We weren't expecting that.'

'*I* should have,' Andrew berated himself. 'Right, I need your sister's car key back. Which golf club have they gone to?'

Charlie grimaced. 'That I don't know, I'm afraid. He didn't say which one.'

'How many golf clubs can there be?' Andrew asked, gesturing again for the key, which Charlie handed over this time.

'This is Cheshire, Detective Inspector,' Charlie replied with a shrug. 'We have a *lot* of golf clubs.'

'Christ, what is wrong with you people?' Andrew muttered rubbing his temples; he could feel a blinder of a headache coming on. 'Do you have *any* inkling at all, Charlie?'

'Wilmslow, maybe,' Charlie replied, clearly thinking hard. 'It's probably flash enough for Rex. Oh, no, hang on, maybe Mere if his sister's with him. I think it's a bit nicer there for lunch these days.'

'I don't need a bloody review of the place, Charlie,' Andrew said slightly desperately. 'Which one do you reckon is the most likely? Because they're not exactly next door to each other.'

Charlie tilted his head from side to side quickly. 'Mere, I'd say Mere.'

'Okay, I'll go to Mere,' Andrew said, jogging back to Peggy's car. 'Lloyd will be here in a minute with my car. Can you ask him to go to Wilmslow Golf Club to check if Peggy's there?'

'I could just call both places and ask,' Charlie said, pointing a thumb over his shoulder towards the house. 'Wouldn't that be quicker?'

'Yeah, do that, but be discreet!' Andrew said, unlocking the door. 'I need to go, just in case.'

'Just in case what?' Charlie called. 'What's going on, Joyce? Is Peggy in danger?'

'Yeah, Charlie, this time I think she might be,' Andrew replied, and all colour drained from Charlie's face.

'Well, go then!' Charlie shouted, already turning to head back into the house.

Andrew didn't need to be told twice. He started the car and tore down the driveway.

* * *

By the time lunch arrived at their table, Peggy was fairly certain that Rex's two am jaunt across Manchester was starting to catch up with him. It felt like every few minutes he was hiding yawns behind his hand, excusing himself with a charming smile and an apology each time, and he kept pulling at the collar of his shirt self-consciously. His sister had noticed too, and she kept kicking him under the table.

'Late night?' Peggy asked as casually as she could, reaching for her glass of water. She'd declined the wine Rex had offered as soon as they'd arrived, and all three times he'd asked her since.

'Yeah, just a few work things, you know.' Rex fixed her with another one of those practised grins. 'All very boring, and not how I wanted to be spending my Saturday night.'

'Well, I did say that you should have come out with me and Tina instead,' Athena said, picking at her salad. 'You'd have had much more fun.'

Athena looked over at Peggy and rolled her eyes. 'Is your brother like this, Peggy? All work, very little play? Constantly complaining about how tired he is?'

Peggy chuckled. 'No, I don't think you could ever accuse Charlie of being 'all work'. He discovered the dance floor when he was about fifteen, and he's never really looked back.'

'We *must* have bumped into you both in town before,' Athena replied. 'Surely.'

'I've never really been one for being out past ten o'clock,' Peggy said with a shrug, 'Maybe Charlie though. You'll generally find him at either Rotters or the Troubadour.'

'I *miss* the Troubadour!' Athena lamented, suddenly more animated. 'They used to have the *best* bands on.'

'Oh, do you not go there anymore?' Peggy asked, politely. God, she really did feel like she'd forgotten how to have a conversation. That, and she kept expecting Marnie to just pop up and casually join them at the table.

'No, we haven't been there in ages actually.' Athena frowned and looked at her brother. 'Why is that again? I can't remember what happened.'

'I fell out with one of the guys on the door,' Rex replied, eyes growing cold. 'I don't frequent places that treat their clientele badly. It's just not right, I mean. We're the ones spending the money so that these guys actually have jobs, right?'

Oh God, he's one of those *people*, Peggy thought. When she got back to Butterton she really would need to ask Marnie what it was that she'd seen in Rex, because there didn't appear to be much of anything *good* going on beneath the surface.

'I've been telling Rex for years that he should stop complaining about the clubs of Manchester and just open his own.' Athena grinned, nudging Peggy. 'You should help me convince him.'

'Oh, no, I'm not sure I could do that,' Peggy replied awkwardly. She really wished that she'd just turned Rex's invitation down.

'Excuse me, Mr Hughes?'

The woman who'd greeted them at the main reception when they'd arrived had approached the table and was now wearing an apologetic smile.

'Yes?' Rex looked more than a bit put out at the intrusion.

'I'm so sorry to bother you in the middle of lunch,' she said, courteously nodding her head, 'but I'm afraid there's a call for you at the desk. I did say that you were busy, but I've been informed that this really is urgent business that cannot wait.'

Rex blew a loud breath out between his lips and messily dropped his napkin on the table. 'Alright, thank you, Helen. I'll be right there.'

Helen smiled apologetically once more and left.

'If you'll excuse me, ladies,' Rex said as he pushed his chair back. 'I'll be right back.'

'Busy man,' Peggy commented.

Athena rolled her eyes again. 'Honestly, I don't know what he spends all his time doing, but there seems to be something urgent every five minutes these days.'

'Oh right.' Peggy hoped that she sounded just casually interested. 'What exactly does Rex *do*?'

'Honestly, I have no real clue,' Athena said, laughing self-deprecatingly. 'When our father died, Rex inherited his businesses, lots of properties in and around the city, that sort of thing. I think he spends his life just trying to make it all work, you know?'

'I know that feeling,' Peggy replied, taking a bite of her pasta. Rex had left the table, but there was no point in letting her own food get cold.

'Really?' Athena asked, raising one manicured eyebrow.

Peggy nodded. 'Charlie doesn't really have any head for business. I do the accounts for our father, and meet with our estate tenants and staff.'

'Wow,' Athena said, looking impressed. Then she frowned. 'Although, Peggy, there is one thing bothering me.'

Given that Athena didn't know about Peggy working for the police, snooping on her brother, or the whole talking to Marnie's ghost thing, she wondered what other facet of her personality was causing trouble now. 'Oh?'

'Mmm.' Athena dropped her voice into a whisper as though she were about to divulge a secret. 'Why on earth are you working in a shop?'

'Oh, *that*,' Peggy said, desperately affecting an air of indifference that she'd learned from her mother of all people. 'I had a spot of personal bother last year - you know how these things can be – and I suppose I was a little bored. I thought it might be fun.'

'Fun?' Athena asked disbelievingly. 'And is it, *fun*?'

'No, not really,' Peggy replied honestly, taking another sip of water. 'It's actually really hard work, and I can't wait to fall into bed at the end of the day.'

Athena nodded. 'Marnie used to be dead on her feet by the end of the week.'

Peggy watched as her companion went completely ashen.

'Oh God, what a terrible thing to say,' Athena whispered, her eyes filling with tears. 'I'm so sorry. Sorry, it's just, poor Marnie.'

'I understand,' Peggy said, feeling awkward again. She'd never been very good at consoling people.

'Athena sniffled as she pushed her plate away from her, lunch mostly untouched. 'It really hit Rex hard, you know. Not that you'd suspect most of the time these days, but he's still really cut up about it.'

Her eyes then widened as she seemed to come to her senses. 'Oh God, I'm so sorry, please don't listen to a single thing I'm saying. I shouldn't be talking to *you* about this, should I?'

Peggy blinked. What exactly was that supposed to mean?

'Sorry, no, I mean, what with the fact that Rex has brought you out for lunch,' Athena added. 'No, I mean, oh God, I'm really putting my foot in it, aren't I?'

Peggy laughed despite herself, which immediately turned to choking when she spotted Charlotte Bamford and her horrible husband Matthew being seated on the far side of the restaurant. She then caught sight of Charlotte's mother and heard two very familiar voices laughing loudly.

Oh my God, her *own mother* was here, and so was Edgar.

'Are you alright?' Athena asked, concerned. 'You've gone white as a sheet.'

'Sorry, I'm suddenly not feeling well,' Peggy said, rising onto shaking legs, grabbing her handbag from the back of her chair and hurrying to the toilets without another word of explanation.

She locked herself into the cubicle nearest to the door and sat down on the closed toilet lid, drawing her knees up to her chin. Her heart was beating wildly in her chest, and she really did feel like she might throw up.

'Peggy?'

The hiss of her name caught her by surprise and Peggy jerked, banging her elbow loudly off the cubicle wall. She rubbed the bone frantically. 'Hello?'

'Peggy, it's me,' came the irritated reply, just before a pair of shoes appeared in the gap beneath the cubicle door. They were very shiny, and they also very much belonged to a man.

'Andrew?' Peggy asked in confusion, unfolding herself and quickly opening the cubicle door. 'What the bloody hell are you doing in here?'

'Well, what the bloody hell are *you* doing on a lunch date with Rex Hughes?' Andrew replied, and he was still whispering angrily.

'Firstly, it's *not* a date,' Peggy replied as she went to stand by the sinks, 'his *sister* is here. Also, it's not my fault. He ambushed me at home.'

'Ambushed?'

'Yes, *ambushed*,' Peggy replied stroppily as she gripped the counter tightly. 'And now you're doing the same, which is awful of you considering how everyone else is already clearly out to get me this afternoon. Why can't I just go out for lunch like a normal human being? Why does there always have to be drama? What exactly is it that I've done to deserve this? Is this penance for something? I mean, *really*, Andrew, *why?*'

Andrew frowned at Peggy in open concern.

'Are you alright?' he asked, blinking slowly as he tried to process the torrent of words she'd just thrown at him. 'Because you're rambling.'

'No, I am *not* alright!' Peggy shouted, before lowering her voice. 'My mother and bloody Edgar are out there, okay?'

Andrew looked appalled on her behalf.

That mollified Peggy slightly until she thought about the circumstances, and then she jabbed at Andrew's chest with her index finger. 'And you should absolutely not be in *here*! Get out!'

'I need you to leave with me right now,' Andrew said hurriedly, glancing towards the door in mild panic.

'I can't leave with you,' Peggy replied. 'Athena saw me come in here, and she could come looking for me at any moment. Rex drove me here, Andrew.'

'Peggy, I really need you to listen to me, Rex is-'

'Trying to charm me out of my money?' Peggy replied, deadpan. 'Yeah, thanks for the warning, but I've been dealing with men like Rex since I was about fifteen, alright?'

Andrew managed to look even more horrified. '*Right*, but that's not all.'

'Peggy, are you alright in there?' Athena called from the other side of the door.

Andrew froze, eyes darting around in an attempt to locate a suitable hiding place should Athena actually open the main door.

'Yes!' Peggy shouted, too loud and too desperate. She lowered her voice. 'Yes, sorry, I'm just washing my face. I'll be right out.'

'Okay, but just so you know, Rex has had to leave,' Athena called back. 'He said to tell you that he's really sorry but something really urgent has come up. Between you and me he looked as green as you just did when he came back from his call.'

Peggy watched as Andrew's expression arranged itself into something she couldn't fathom.

'Oh, that's a shame,' Peggy replied, hoping she sounded far more sincere than she felt.

'Right, you're absolutely leaving with me then,' Andrew hissed quietly. '*Right now.*'

'I'll drive you home, alright?' Athena offered. 'I'm so sorry about my useless brother.'

Peggy looked at Andrew and shrugged.

'No!' Andrew whispered harshly.

'Thanks, Athena,' Peggy replied loudly. 'Would you mind if we left now? I'm really not feeling well at all. I'm so sorry.'

'Of course, that's fine,' Athena agreed. 'Rex has already settled the bill. I'll meet you at the front when you're ready. Take your time.'

Andrew looked more wound up than ever as they both waited for Athena's footsteps to fade.

'Peggy, listen to me. Something's happened,' Andrew said tightly. 'I suspect it's what the call Rex just got was about.'

'What?'

'Liam Byrne was found murdered this morning. At Rex's warehouse on Empire Street.'

Peggy sucked in a breath of surprise. 'Christ.'

'I'm just popping to the loo; I'll be right back!' An unfamiliar voice came from just the other side of the door.

Andrew leapt into the closest cubicle, slamming the door and locking it behind him. Peggy turned quickly and splashed her face with water.

The woman who entered barely gave her a second glance, and Peggy was inordinately glad that she didn't recognise her at all.

'Leaving,' Peggy whispered as she passed Andrew's hiding place, heading for the door.

'Um, okay?' The woman in the other cubicle replied, confused.

Peggy practically ran out of the ladies, keeping her head down as she ducked past the restaurant's entrance. Seeing her mother and Edgar from afar had been bad enough; she certainly wasn't ready to see them up close.

'Oh, there you are!'

Peggy looked up in surprise, Athena was standing just outside the main entrance, an unlit cigarette hanging loosely from her lips.

'Sorry, I didn't know how long you were going to be,' Athena apologised, as she plucked the cigarette from her mouth and carefully replaced it in the carton she fished from her handbag. 'Ready?'

'Yes, thanks,' Peggy said and followed Athena across the car park to a gleaming white BMW.

'Rex gave it to me for my birthday,' Athena laughed, as she patted the bonnet. 'And by that, I mean I picked it out, and he paid for it.'

Charlie wouldn't buy Peggy a car under any circumstances, which was completely fine with her. She quite enjoyed seeing what Charlie came up with for last-minute birthday gifts each year. Last time it had been a crumpled Woolworths token and a striped bag of pick 'n mix that had obviously once been full, but lacked any sweets that Charlie particularly liked by the time it was handed over; it had basically just been yellow gummy bears and one candy watch on an elastic bracelet.

As Peggy climbed into the car she noticed that Athena had one of those little tree air fresheners hanging from the mirror. Peggy fleetingly thought that it might actually be a good gift for Charlie's next birthday - a different scented little tree for each car.

'You'll have to direct me, if you don't mind,' Athena said, as she buckled her seatbelt. As she reversed out of the parking space she pushed the cassette back into the tape player and the sound of Tears for Fears filled the car.

'Oh, I like this one,' Peggy said, as the next song started.

'Me too,' Athena agreed with a grin. 'Did my brother have you listening to that terrible drone music on the way here?'

Peggy actually quite liked The Cure, so she hadn't actually minded that Rex had played their songs on the way to Mere. She made a fairly non-committal sound in reply.

'Urgh, he did, didn't he?' Athena said, perching her sunglasses on her nose as they drove away from the Country Club towards the main road. 'I don't know why he thinks anyone else would find that naval-gazing nonsense appealing.'

Peggy laughed lightly as Athena turned onto the main road. She surreptitiously glanced in the wing mirror to see if there was any sign of Andrew following them but the coast remained clear.

Truth be told, Peggy felt unsettled. Liam Byrne being found dead the night after Peggy and Andrew had tracked Rex to the scene of the crime didn't sit well with her at all. She wondered if anyone had thought to try and get hold of Rebecca. She suspected not.

'What is this guy doing?' Athena said, swearing loudly as a black car sped up behind them when they turned up the hill in the direction of Butterton a minute later. 'Jesus, what is wrong with people? I preferred it when Sunday drivers meant old ladies driving at two miles per hour.'

Peggy shrieked in surprise as the car was suddenly buffeted forwards.

'Oh my God!' Athena shouted as the car behind them drove into the BMW's bumper again. She looked in the rear-view mirror and gestured wildly in terror. '*What are you doing?*'

Athena fought with the steering wheel as the car was rammed again. The little green air freshener tree was spinning wildly in circles and Peggy couldn't take her eyes off it.

'Peggy, we're going to crash!' Athena screamed shrilly as the BMW was finally knocked from the road.

As the car hurtled towards the field in front of them all Peggy could do was squeeze her eyes shut and hope that Andrew wasn't too far behind.

SIXTEEN

'Well?' Charlie asked, throwing his hands up. 'Where is she?'

'What do you mean?' Andrew asked, getting out of Peggy's car in front of Butterton House for the second time that day. Charlie and Lloyd were both standing at the top of the steps looking at him quizzically.

'Peggy,' Charlie said slowly, as though Andrew was a particularly dense toddler. 'She was at Mere, wasn't she?'

'Yeah, she was,' Andrew turned in a circle, surveying the grounds, as though by looking hard enough he could make Peggy appear through sheer force of will. 'Hang on, are you saying she's not back?'

'I thought that's what you were doing,' Charlie said, clearly exasperated now. 'Bringing her back.'

'She left with Athena Hughes,' Andrew replied slowly, looking around again. 'You're sure she's not here?'

'We're certain, sir,' Lloyd said, nodding his head. 'When we were sure she wasn't at Wilmslow we waited here. Nobody's come up that drive other than you.'

'They left a good hour before I did,' Andrew replied. 'I stayed to see if I could get anything useful out of the staff.'

He left out the part where he had unsuccessfully attempted to get a glimpse of Peggy's mother and Edgar too.

Andrew held his hands out to Lloyd. 'My keys?'

Lloyd threw the keys to the Belmont down the steps and Andrew caught them as he headed towards his car.

'Which way did you come back?' Charlie asked.

'Main road until just before the village,' Andrew replied. 'Why?'

'That's probably not the way Peggy would go if she were driving herself,' Charlie explained. 'She'd have come back up the hill. Old habit. Maybe she directed Athena that way instead.'

'What do you want me to do, sir?' Lloyd asked.

Before Andrew could reply, the front door opened and Timothy appeared.

'I'm sorry, sir,' he said to Charlie with a small bob of his head, looking somewhat troubled, 'but there's an extremely urgent telephone call for you in the library.'

Timothy barely had a chance to step aside before Charlie barrelled past him. Andrew and Lloyd followed a split-second later, chasing Charlie down the corridor towards the room they had been shown into when they'd first arrived.

Charlie snatched up the receiver and pressed it to his ear. 'Hello?'

Andrew couldn't hear what was being said on the other end of the line, but the basic facts of the situation were being laid bare in Charlie's increasingly panicked expression anyway. Whatever had happened, it wasn't good.

'Well, is she alright? How did it happen?' Charlie demanded.

Andrew and Lloyd looked at each other in alarm.

A moment later Charlie sagged slightly. 'Okay, thank you. Yes, okay, I understand, thank you.'

What Charlie did next was not what Andrew expected.

'Marnie!' Charlie yelled, spots of colour suddenly high on his cheeks. 'Marnie, where the hell are you?'

'Marnie?' Lloyd asked Andrew quizzically, raising one eyebrow.

'Charlie?' Andrew tried after the other man shouted for Marnie again. 'Charlie, what are you doing? Where's Peggy?'

'I want to speak to Marnie!' Charlie snapped. 'I want to know more about this godforsaken fiancé of hers and why bad luck seems to follow his family around.'

'Charlie, I need you to explain what's happening,' Andrew said carefully, lowering his voice and keeping it even, just as he'd been taught to do in high-stress situations. He needed to get Charlie talking, and quickly.

'My sister and Athena Hughes are both currently at Wythenshawe Hospital,' Charlie said, crossing his arms and glaring at Andrew. 'Thankfully both have only minor injuries.'

Andrew felt his stomach plummet. 'What? Why?'

'Well, the very nice man on the phone just now said he thinks that they were run off the road by another car.' Charlie's tone was icier than Andrew had ever heard it. 'You were supposed to bring my sister back safely, *Detective Inspector*.'

Andrew wanted to argue with him, he really did, but Charlie was entirely correct, wasn't he? Andrew had known that Athena Hughes was being targeted by someone – regardless of whatever story was being spun by CID – and yet he'd still let Peggy drive off with her. He shouldn't have let her out of his sight.

'I'm sorry,' Andrew said, and he meant it. This was his bloody fault.

'I don't want apologies, Joyce,' Charlie replied, and he was obviously livid. 'At this very moment, Timothy will no doubt be informing my father that we've just received a phone call from the hospital. I need to go and deal with *that* situation before too many questions are asked. *You* are going to go and fetch Peggy because it's the absolute least you can do for her right now.'

Andrew thought it probably wasn't wise to give any more of a reply than a polite nod.

Charlie seemed to agree as he left the room without another word.

* * *

Peggy felt like an idiot.

She'd banged her head on the passenger window when Athena's car had met a gatepost and abruptly come to a halt. Apparently, she'd then been seeing just the right amount of stars to warrant concerned glances and whispers of possible concussion from the hospital staff.

Andrew had told to her stay away from Rex Hughes, but she hadn't listened, and now here she was, sitting on a cold, plastic chair waiting for Charlie to come and pick her up. She knew the hospital had called the house, and she'd made sure to tell them to ask for Charlie. Although she suspected that her father probably knew all about this little episode by now anyway, she hoped that she could buy herself a little time before she'd need to actually speak to him.

Right now, she just wanted to get out of the hospital and get home without encountering anyone else in her family, which was unlikely. Then she was going to ask Marnie some fairly serious questions about just what in the hell Rex had got himself into.

Peggy rubbed the side of her head self-consciously, wincing as her fingers brushed against a particularly tender spot. She assumed that the mother of all headaches was going to catch up with her later when she didn't have any of the shock of the crash itself to stave off the worst of it.

Even though she didn't actually have a concussion, the fogginess was enough to drown out any faces or voices trying to get her attention. That was more than a small mercy as hospitals were always particularly difficult places for her to be.

The double doors at the end of the corridor opened noisily and Peggy sat up straighter in surprise when it wasn't Charlie who appeared, but Andrew looking even more dishevelled than he had at Mere. He was also somehow managing to convey both anger and relief at the same time as he strode towards her.

'Where's Charlie?' Peggy asked when Andrew stopped in front of her.

'Are you alright?' He asked gruffly, ignoring her question.

Peggy shrugged, not quite meeting his eyes.

'Peggy, *are you alright*?' Andrew asked again, and his tone was noticeably softer this time.

'I'll be fine,' Peggy replied quietly. 'Sore head, bruised ribs. That's all.'

For a moment Peggy thought that Andrew might push her for more of an answer, or at least something a little more truthful, but in the end, he just ran a hand through his hair with a tired sigh.

'Are you okay to leave now?' he asked. 'Do you need to speak to anyone first?'

Peggy held up the sheet of paper in her right hand. 'They've already signed me out. The doctor said the police were on the way though, and that they'd want to speak to me and Athena. Do I have to wait?'

'Christ, no.' Andrew shook his head vehemently. 'Not a chance are you waiting here. If anyone from CID wants to speak to you, they'll have to go through me first.'

Peggy frowned. She'd met Andrew less than a week ago, and for the entire time she'd been working under the assumption that even though Andrew had left CID for indeterminate reasons he was desperate to get back there as soon as possible. Suddenly though, in the fluorescent glow of an antiseptic-tinged corridor that conclusion didn't sit quite right.

Andrew looked down the long corridor, craning his neck. 'Do you know where Athena is?'

'No,' Peggy replied. 'They told me that she's fine though; just a few bumps and bruises.'

'Good.' Andrew held out a hand to carefully help pull Peggy to her feet. 'Look, I want you out of here just in case Rex turns up.'

'I haven't seen him since he took that phone call at lunch,' Peggy replied as they walked slowly down the corridor towards the exit. 'Do you know where he sped off to?'

'Not for certain,' Andrew admitted. 'But I'm guessing it was to go and check that he was being told the truth about Liam Byrne.'

They were quiet as Andrew led the way to his car, which was less *parked*, and more abandoned diagonally across two spaces with the front left wheel of the Belmont up on the edge of the kerb.

'I thought you were all about law and order,' Peggy said, raising one eyebrow, shuffling towards the passenger side.

'Not when I'm worried about someone,' Andrew replied immediately with a small shrug.

Peggy ducked her head, mildly embarrassed at the honesty, and opened the car door. She hesitated slightly but forced herself to sit down and close the door behind her.

'Okay?' Andrew asked, waiting to start the engine until Peggy nodded her consent.

'Listen, I expect that it's the last thing you want to think about right now, but I need to talk to you about what happened with Athena,' Andrew said as he reversed, 'and I have a few things I need to tell you about Marnie's case. If I take a statement from you about the car accident I can probably keep CID out of your hair for a bit longer.'

'Alright,' Peggy agreed. Her heart sank at the thought of facing her father. 'Any chance we could go somewhere that's not Butterton?'

'I thought you wanted to go home,' Andrew said, frowning as they reached the car park exit.

'I don't want to have a conversation with my father just yet,' Peggy replied, gingerly touching her head again. 'Or Charlie, for that matter. How pissed off is he?'

'With you? Not at all,' Andrew replied. 'On the other hand, I'm definitely off the Christmas card list.'

Peggy winced. She knew what Charlie was like when he slipped into the role of protective brother, but she also knew that he'd be feeling guilty about his own involvement in what had happened.

'Look, my house is about ten minutes away,' Andrew said. He seemed to then think about the words that had left his mouth and frowned. 'Right, okay, that didn't sound professional at all. Sorry. I mean-'

'Your house is fine, Andrew,' Peggy said, trying not to laugh at the constipated look on the detective's face. 'I trust you.'

Her reply seemed to pacify Andrew as he indicated right and drove them away from the hospital.

'How's your head?' Andrew asked a few minutes later.

'Not too bad yet. Although they did say that it's probably going to feel worse later. At least it's not a concussion. Charlie would probably relish the thought of getting to come and yell at me every few hours to make sure I wasn't dead.'

Andrew's forehead wrinkled and Peggy realised that she probably shouldn't be casually bringing up the concept of her demise after giving quite a few people a bit of a fright that afternoon already.

'Have you always lived in Gatley?' Peggy asked quickly, trying to lighten the mood and reaching desperately for any safe topics she could think of.

'Yes,' Andrew replied slowly, clearly aware that Peggy was trying to avoid talking about herself for a while. He allowed it. 'I live in the house I grew up in, which is both a blessing and a curse, I suppose.'

'Well, I know what that feels like,' Peggy replied wryly.

'How long has your family lived in that house?'

Peggy waved her hand mock-airily. 'Oh, you know, only since about thirteen-fifty.'

'*Thirteen-fifty*? Are you joking?'

'No,' Peggy laughed. 'Deadly serious. The house as you see it now has been around for about two-hundred-and-fifty years or so, but the land has been in the family since the fourteenth century.'

Andrew blinked a few times. 'You know, I don't think I've ever had anyone say that to me before.'

'That's probably for the best,' Peggy replied as the car stopped outside the house on Acacia Road.

Peggy looked up at the house, thinking again how well-tended the front garden was, which was sort of surprising as Andrew didn't quite seem the type. Then again, she didn't really know him all that well, did she?

The slight smudges in the upstairs left-hand window slowly merged into the shape of a person. Peggy lurched forwards in surprise and nearly cracked her head on the car window.

'What?' Andrew asked worriedly, looking between her and the house. 'What's wrong?'

Peggy couldn't take her eyes off the upstairs window. A boy, maybe twelve or so, was staring back at her in amazement. He was wearing a faded blue t-shirt that might have been a football kit, but he was slightly too hazy to tell for sure. It was like Peggy was looking at him through a greased lens. His hair was dark and messy, and it reminded her of the way Andrew's looked when he got frustrated and ran his hands through it. Come to think of it, the child in the window had very similar features to the man in the car next to her.

'Peggy?'

Peggy jumped at the soft use of her name. She turned her head and saw that Andrew was looking back at her in slight panic.

'Peggy, what is it?'

Andrew looked genuinely worried about what her answer was going to be, so she thought it probably wasn't the right time to ask Andrew if he knew that he was being haunted by a child.

'Nothing,' Peggy said, forcing a small smile, 'nothing at all. Do you think we could maybe go for a walk somewhere instead? I think I could do with the air.'

Peggy was certain that Andrew looked directly up at the window before he said, 'Yeah, sure. Pub?'

'Head injury,' Peggy said, pointing at herself.

'Beer garden,' Andrew replied as he produced a notebook and pen from the glove box. 'I'll get you a soda water, and you can get your air.'

'Alright,' Peggy agreed, keeping her eyes on the ground as she climbed out of the car and turned away from the house.

'You're sure everything's okay?'

'Yep,' Peggy said as brightly as she could manage. 'Lead the way.'

Andrew acquiesced, and it was only a few minutes before Peggy found herself sitting at a table tucked into the corner of the busy beer garden at Andrew's local with a glass of iced soda water in front of her. It looked like Andrew had ordered the same for himself.

'Sorry about this part,' Andrew said as he opened the notebook, 'but I do actually need you to tell me what happened in the car with Athena.'

Peggy shrugged. 'I can't tell you that much, I'm afraid. We'd just turned up the hill towards Butterton when a black car came right up behind us. I think it might have been a Vauxhall, but I can't be sure. Athena wasn't very happy about how close the driver got in the first place, but then the car drove straight into the back of us.'

'Could it have been an accident?' Andrew asked, although his tone suggested that it was more of a question he *had* to ask, rather than one he wanted to.

Peggy shook her head. 'Even if that first bump had been somehow accidental, which I would have found hard to believe anyway, the second one definitely wasn't.

'Athena was shouting and gesturing in the mirror towards the driver. He was wearing sunglasses, so I couldn't really see much of his face. The car hit us again, much harder that time, and we went off the side of the road into a field. The car hit a gatepost and we stopped. I don't really remember much else until the ambulance arrived. The farm manager saw what happened from his office, so he called for one immediately.'

Andrew looked like he might be about to snap his pen in half. His lips were pursed. 'So, you don't think you've ever seen the driver of the car before? He wasn't at Mere when you were having lunch, maybe?'

Peggy held up her hands in apology. 'I honestly couldn't say. I'm really sorry.'

Andrew shook his head. 'You have nothing to be sorry for.'

'Apart from the bit where you told me to stay clear of Rex Hughes and I ended up going out for lunch with him instead?' Peggy said grimacing. 'Oh, and the part where you said that I shouldn't leave with Athena, but then did that anyway.'

'Yeah, okay apart from those things.' Andrew allowed himself a small smile. 'You're like a magnet for chaos and crisis.'

Peggy frowned as that reminded her of something Athena had said at lunch. 'Athena mentioned that Rex has had a lot going on recently.

Apparently, he seems to be dealing with crisis after crisis.'

Andrew turned solemn again. 'I'm not surprised. There's obviously something serious going on.'

'Do you think he killed Liam Byrne?' Peggy asked quietly.

'Either that, or he had some hand in it at least,' Andrew replied. He sighed and leaned his elbows on the table. 'Look, that brings me to the thing I have to tell you. Byrne and Hughes have both been a little too interested in you and just how much money you have.'

'I already told you that's just what life is like, Andrew.' Peggy tried hard not to let her frustration show.

'No, seriously, Peggy, I know you think that everyone just sees you and goes straight to what they can get from you, but that's not true. The fact that these two *very dangerous* men even know your name is something that I'm not even a little bit comfortable with.'

'What are you saying then?' Peggy had a feeling that she knew what was coming.

'I've already spoken to Higson, and he agrees,' Andrew replied quietly, skirting the point for a second. 'You're out of Lewis's, effective immediately.'

'What? No!' Peggy shook her head. 'But what about Rebecca? And Janine? Don't you want to know more about them?'

'I think we need to be concerned about the fact that we started this with one murder, and we're now at two.'

Peggy's face fell. 'Oh God, poor Rebecca. Do you think anyone's told her?'

'*Poor* Rebecca?' Andrew's eyebrows shot up in surprise. 'Are you serious? She was engaged to a criminal.'

'Her fiancé is still dead, Andrew,' Peggy snapped. 'Have a bit of compassion. She might not have known what he was really involved in.'

'I think you're giving her too much credit.'

Peggy narrowed her eyes. 'Well, I think I can safely say that sometimes men *lie* to the women they supposedly love. You know, it really pisses me off the way everyone always blames the woman.'

Andrew looked suitably chastised when he realised what Peggy was getting at. 'I didn't mean that, Peggy. You know I didn't.'

'Look, just let me have one more day. Even if it's just to let me check that Rebecca is alright, because I guess CID won't even know to speak to her, will they?'

'Peggy, no. You could have been killed today, and I can't have that.' Andrew shrugged. 'I *won't*.'

'Marnie's going to think that you're not looking into her murder properly,' Peggy muttered.

'Of course I am!' Andrew's eyes widened. 'Actually, that's something I needed to ask you. Back at Butterton, your brother was yelling for Marnie. I thought he couldn't do your, you know, *thing*.'

'*Thing*' Peggy mouthed with an eye-roll. 'He can't, but apparently, he *can* see Marnie, even though he can't see anyone else in the house.'

'How many bloody ghosts do you have in that house?'

'Fourteenth century, Andrew. Work it out for yourself.'

'Why do you think Marnie is so different then?' Andrew asked instead, trying not to think too hard about how often he might be surrounded by things he couldn't see.

'I don't know. I wonder if she's maybe tied to something here, or perhaps it's just that she *really* wanted to live. She had a lot to live for.'

'What do you mean 'tied to something'? Like an object?'

'Maybe. Emmeline – that's my great aunt – knows of a few ghosts who remained until an item of theirs was discovered or moved.'

'Emmeline?' Andrew frowned again. 'So, hang on, this ghost thing you can do is a family trait?'

'What? Oh no, sorry, I said great aunt, but really there are quite a few more 'greats' in there,' Peggy admitted.

Peggy watched as Andrew parsed that information and eventually realised that Peggy was referring to a long-dead relative. He took another gulp from his glass, and Peggy wondered if he was now wishing that he'd ordered something stronger.

'Right. Dead aunt.' Andrew coughed and reached into his jacket pocket to pull out a box. 'Do you think Marnie might be tied to this?'

Peggy took the black box and opened it. She then shot Andrew a wry look. 'You know it's bad form to propose to near-strangers, right?'

'Funny,' Andrew replied drily.

Peggy inspected the ring. It was quite a spectacular piece of jewellery now that she could see it up close, and it had obviously cost Rex an absolute fortune. 'It's definitely the same ring Marnie has on her finger now, so she probably died wearing it.'

Andrew nodded grimly. 'So, maybe she's attached to it because nobody knew where it was? Maybe finding it is the closure she needs?'

'Maybe.' Peggy closed the box. Movement caught her eye over Andrew's shoulder. 'Andrew, why is there an irate woman heading our way?'

Andrew turned, before whipping his head back in Peggy's direction, expression one of complete panic. 'Shit. Oh God, I'm really, *really* sorry.'

'Andy!' The woman barked, stopping at their table. She crossed her arms over her chest and gave Andrew a look so dark Peggy was certain that if looks could kill Andrew would have just been annihilated.

'Kate! What a surprise,' Andrew replied, and, *oh*, Peggy knew that tone. That was guilt.

'Don't '*what a surprise*' me, you absolute tit,' Kate said, and then she set her sights briefly on Peggy before turning back to Andrew. 'And who exactly is this?'

Peggy had a good idea of what was going on here, and she really wasn't in the mood. She certainly did *not* need Andrew to answer for her. 'Peggy Swan,' she replied with as much civility as she could muster. 'I'm working with Andrew at the moment. And you are?'

Kate looked slightly put out that Peggy didn't seem even remotely cowed. 'Kate Simpson. Andrew's *girlfriend*.'

'Andrew's *ex*-girlfriend,' Andrew supplied indignantly. 'Which, incidentally, was your idea.'

'Yes, because you're a cheating arse.'

Peggy shot Andrew an appalled look.

'I am not!' Andrew snapped at Kate. Then he looked at Peggy. 'I'm really, really not.'

Kate laughed coldly. 'Right, sure, and you're 'working' with Miss La-di-dah over here.'

Peggy didn't know this woman, and she really didn't want to have an argument with her.

'Right, I think I'll take that as my cue to leave.' Peggy stood up abruptly. 'Andrew, thank you for coming to get me earlier, I appreciate it. I think I'll leave you two to it.'

She gave both Andrew and Kate a short nod before heading for the exit. She was almost free when she realised that she was still holding the ring box in her hands. As much as she didn't want to have to go back to the table, she couldn't exactly walk off with a piece of key evidence.

'Bugger,' she muttered, turning and heading back towards the table.

'It's been *four* days since we broke up, Andy. I saw you give that woman a ring!' Kate hissed as Peggy approached.

Peggy *almost* felt sorry for Andrew but given how wound-up Kate was she suspected that at least some of the ire might be warranted.

'Yes, you did,' Peggy said loudly, making Kate and Andrew jump in surprise. 'It's actually a beautiful engagement ring, and Andrew is currently doing an exceptional job of trying to find out who murdered the girl it belonged to.'

'M-murdered?' Kate blanched.

'Yes. Horribly murdered.' Peggy felt a slightly shameful satisfaction at how alarmed Kate looked. She then gave her one final tight smile and left the beer garden again.

There was only a minute or two before she heard Andrew calling her name behind her. She stopped just at the end of Acacia Road and waited as he walked towards her.

'What exactly was that?' Andrew snapped. He didn't look pleased.

'What?' Peggy asked crossly.

'Oh, you know, the part where you just casually announced a detail of a case to someone unconnected to the investigation,' Andrew replied. He actually looked quite angry now that he was level with Peggy.

Okay, she *had* done that, that was true. 'Well, I'm actually sorry about that.'

'That wasn't alright, Peggy.'

'No, it wasn't, but I wasn't expecting to be accused of being 'the other woman' by your ex-girlfriend,' Peggy sniped.

'There is no other woman!' Andrew growled in frustration, throwing his hands up. 'Kate got the wrong end of the stick the day I came home from Lewis's covered in perfume. Jesus, I was a crap boyfriend, but I'm not actually a complete arse, alright?'

Peggy's head was starting to ache. 'I don't actually care, Andrew, to be honest. It's none of my business.'

Andrew huffed, all good cheer and relief from earlier snuffed out. 'Fine.'

'Fine,' Peggy sighed in agreement. 'Look, would you mind just taking me home now, please?'

Andrew didn't say anything but started walking towards his house anyway. Peggy glared at his back but followed him down the road.

She looked up at the house without thinking and was relieved when there was no figure in the window. She blew out a noisy breath in relief. Maybe she'd hit her head harder than she'd realised. Why would Andrew be haunted by a child?

Peggy turned her head as she reached the car and the child appeared in front of her, right at the edge of the garden. The scream of surprise erupted from her lips before she could even think about trying to tamp it down.

Andrew spun around so quickly he lost his balance, one foot slipping off the kerb so that he had to reach his arms out and steady himself against his car. 'Jesus Christ, Peggy, what the fuck?'

Peggy held a hand to her chest, as though trying to keep her racing heart contained. The boy was staring at her, unnervingly unblinking. His mouth was moving, but she couldn't hear what he was saying.

'Peggy, what?' Andrew barked, and even through Peggy's stupor she could hear that there was a real thread of fear under his irritation.

Andrew caught Peggy's wrists and ducked down so that his head was blocking the view of the boy. '*What*?'

Peggy had to clear her throat twice before she could get a sound out. 'Nothing.'

Andrew didn't let go of her. 'No, you were weird when we got here, and you're being even weirder now. What the hell is wrong with my house?'

'There's a boy,' Peggy whispered against all better judgement.

Andrew let go of her arms immediately, looking around wildly. He obviously couldn't see anything.

'You're lying,' Andrew said through gritted teeth.

Peggy frowned. She knew Andrew had a hard time believing in any of this stuff, but she thought he'd actually made fairly decent progress for someone who'd had less than a week to get used to it. Outright accusing her of lying was something he hadn't really done since the day they'd met. 'I'm not.'

'Yes, yes you are,' Andrew said, sounding slightly desperate. 'Who told you? *Who*?'

'Who told me what?' Peggy asked helplessly. 'Nobody told me anything.'

'Don't lie to me!' Andrew was shouting now, and Peggy could see an old lady peering out of her window across the road.

Peggy looked at the boy, who hadn't moved an inch. He was still speaking soundlessly.

'He's about this tall.' Peggy said quietly, holding her hand up near her shoulder. 'Dark hair. Freckles.'

'*Who* told you?' Andrew stomped towards her, and Peggy took a step back in surprise. 'Don't lie to me again, Peggy.'

'I'm not lying to you!' Peggy was angry now too. Who the hell did Andrew Joyce think he was trying to intimidate her like that?

'There's a boy in your garden who looks an awful lot like you, *Detective Inspector*. He looks so much like you that I'm guessing you know exactly who I'm talking about.'

'I'm not kidding, Peggy.' Andrew's voice was shaking with suppressed rage and something else that might have been sorrow had it not been sharpened into a weapon.

'Who is he, Andrew?'

Peggy knew that was the wrong question when Andrew's face immediately contorted into a sneer.

'What? Can't you just ask him yourself?'

Peggy took a deep breath, and she knew that she should just walk away from this argument. It was pointless and unnecessary, but then again, she wasn't feeling anywhere near the best version of herself given the day she'd had so far.

She closed her eyes and forced herself to concentrate on the image of the boy in her mind. If she could figure out who he was then maybe Andrew would believe her.

'What the hell are you doing?' Andrew asked furiously, reaching for Peggy's wrist again.

Her eyes flew open, and she wrenched her arm back quickly. 'Get your hands off me,' she snapped, and her voice was devoid of any suggestion of warmth.

Rob, came the voice in her head.

'His name is Rob,' Peggy said, clenching her jaw against the sudden urge to cry that had come out of nowhere.

Andrew staggered backwards slightly, and he clamped a hand over his mouth in surprise.

'And he says-'

'Peggy, stop,' Andrew pleaded, wide-eyed. His anger had dissolved, leaving only desperation. 'Stop. *Please*!'

'*And he says* that you were supposed to come and find him,' Peggy added.

Peggy could see the split-second where those words took the knife she'd already wielded and twisted it viciously somewhere deep inside Andrew. He crumpled entirely, his back sliding down the car door until he was caught somewhere between crouching and sitting on the pavement.

It was cruel, and she knew it even without knowing the details of *why*. It hadn't given her even the tiniest flare of satisfaction, and the instant the words had left her mouth she'd regretted them.

Andrew said nothing and just stared back at her as though he'd never seen her before in his life.

Well, that was the end of that then. There wasn't a chance she was going to be allowed to help find out who'd killed Marnie now. *Well done, Peg*, she chastised herself, *well done*.

'Goodbye, Andrew,' she said, at a loss for anything else, and turned away.

As she walked up Acacia Road in search of a bus, she refused to give in to the urge to look back over her shoulder. She wasn't quite sure what she'd do if she saw that little boy again, or what she'd do if she had to see that terrible expression on Andrew's face again.

A bus pulled into a nearby stop as she turned the corner onto the main road. She jogged gently towards it, hoping that she'd make it before it pulled away.

She couldn't care less where it was headed.

SEVENTEEN

It was four o'clock the next morning when the week-long heatwave finally exploded in a spectacular display of thunder, lightning and torrential rain.

The power had been completely out by six am when Andrew finally hauled himself out of bed after yet another night of virtually no sleep.

He'd then opened the silent fridge to discover that he had run out of milk, and he'd only just resisted the urge to thump his forehead repeatedly against the door. Instead, he'd leaned his head against it and tried to will himself back in time to a week earlier.

If ghosts existed, then why couldn't time travel be real?

The hairs on the back of his neck stood on end again, just as they had done a few hundred times since the night before; ever since Peggy had told him that she could see Rob.

Rob.

The thought that his older brother was somehow trapped in this house, a place he'd been so unhappy, was enough to make his stomach turn. But it had been Peggy's words, delivered with the frostiness he'd surely deserved at that stage, that had made him dry heave more than once overnight.

He said you were supposed to come and find him.

His brain had somehow created a terrifying, repetitive chant of those words, but in an unnatural combination of Peggy's clipped tones and the memories Andrew held of the way Rob used to speak. He'd had to close his eyes and concentrate on the cool fridge door against his cheek just to stave off the rising tide of nausea.

When dodging the rain on the way to the car, Andrew had put his foot straight into a puddle on the last step of the garden path and the tepid rainwater had sloshed over the rim of his shoe, soaking through his sock in seconds.

Then the Belmont had refused to start.

Andrew really should have taken all of that for the omen it was.

So, it wasn't, therefore, any great surprise that when Andrew hammered on the door at Tib Street it was opened by Dolly, eyeing him darkly while smoking yet another cigarette.

'Not a good day for you to be late, Pretty Boy,' Dolly said in lieu of any greeting. Her voice was somehow even raspier than usual. 'Not a good day at all.'

Andrew sniffed loudly, deciding that making curt comments had got him into enough trouble recently. He kept his head down, carefully stepping past Dolly, mindful that at any moment she might reach out with those bony hands and accost him.

As Andrew's sodden shoe touched the bottom step of the staircase, Dolly sucked in a large, noisy breath, clearly readying herself to unnerve him further. He paused, but he didn't turn around.

'I thought I told youse to worry about the creepy girl,' Dolly murmured from behind him. 'You haven't.'

'I *was* worried when I needed to be,' Andrew replied stiffly, still refusing to look over his shoulder. 'She's not here anymore, so there's actually nothing to worry about.'

'That's what youse think, is it?' Dolly whispered, her voice cracking on the final word. A great hacking cough escaped her chest, and Andrew could imagine her bent almost double, propping herself up with one hand on the wall.

'It's none of your business,' Andrew said shortly and began ascending the stairs again. There was a distant, occasional thumping sound coming from upstairs.

'I thought youse already had enough regret to last a lifetime.'

Andrew whirled around on the landing to give Dolly a piece of his mind, but she was already disappearing off down the corridor behind the staircase.

'Mad old biddy,' Andrew muttered, trying to shake the shadow of trepidation that Dolly seemed to have left in her wake.

As he rounded the final staircase, he realised that the thumping sound was accompanied by Higson yelling, and what sounded like Jen and Lloyd trying to pacify him.

'…it wasn't exactly like that, sir,' Jen was saying as Andrew pushed open the double doors.

All three occupants of the room stopped to stare at Andrew as he crossed the room to drape his sodden jacket over the back of his chair.

The squelching that accompanied every second step was obscenely loud in the otherwise silent room. With the windows closed for the first time in a week, it was almost impossible to hear the traffic beyond the walls.

'What makes you think you're still welcome here?' Higson barked.

Andrew scowled. 'I didn't think I was particularly welcome in the first place, *sir.*'

Jen had the decency to look surprised at Andrew's outburst, but Lloyd just whistled loudly as though he were ten years old and two of his classmates were readying themselves for a playground fistfight.

Higson smacked his lips together. 'Well, we *are* in a strop, aren't we? It sounds like Chambers wasn't lying when he said you were acting like a right little prima donna down at his crime scene.'

Higson narrowed his eyes and took a step towards Andrew. 'You know the one I mean, right Joyce? That crime scene on Empire Street; somewhere I think I'd already told you that you had no business being.'

Andrew wished that he hadn't already thrown his stapler, because Higson was looking like a pretty good target now. 'I was doing my *job*, sir. Which is something that *some people* don't seem to want me to actually do.'

'What exactly does that mean?' Higson barked, folding his arms across his fairly substantial stomach.

'You know exactly what I mean,' Andrew replied angrily. 'You want me to solve a murder, but I'm not actually allowed to investigate key suspects. You put more stock in the testimony of a *ghost* than you do in my ability to scrutinise the facts that we have.'

Andrew threw his hands up in irritation. 'Oh, *and* when I actually get close to anything useful, I'm shut down immediately. What the fuck is actually going on with the police in this city? There's something dirtier going on here than just Marnie Driscoll's murder, and I'm starting to wonder exactly who is involved.'

Lloyd gasped dramatically and Andrew glowered at him.

Higson stood up straight for the first time all week, and Andrew realised that he was actually a hulking great giant hiding underneath all that poor posture and pastry crumbs. Andrew would not be intimidated though; he hadn't got to where he was by standing back and taking crap from people he didn't fully trust.

'Are you accusing me of something, Joyce?' Higson asked evenly.

'Do I need to, *sir*?' Andrew snapped. 'It's obvious to anyone with eyes that Rex Hughes and the Byrnes are connected, but apparently there's no evidence. What else do we need? A third body? Because we came close to two more yesterday!'

Andrew saw Higson's face twitch in surprise. Ah, maybe he hadn't expected Andrew to fight back then. *Oh well*, Andrew was on a roll now.

'What do you think Rex Hughes would do if his sister was killed *after* the threats to her safety were discounted as being the work of teenagers by an investigating officer?' Andrew asked, and he'd started pacing in front of his desk now, his left shoe still squelching noisily. 'What the hell would *we* do if Peggy had been killed? She has no business being tangled up in all of this. How exactly would you explain her involvement?'

'Joyce, sit down,' Higson said calmly as Andrew continued to move restlessly.

'And that's another thing!' Andrew ploughed on, barely even noticing that Higson had spoken. 'What the hell is this department doing putting civilians into potentially life-threatening situations? That can't be GMP policy. That can't be *any* force's policy!'

'Joyce, sit down!' Higson tried again a little louder, but Andrew didn't stop.

'The very fact that you actually get away with doing things like-'

'Joyce!' Higson bellowed. Andrew stopped pacing in surprise.

'Sit down!' Higson added sharply.

Andrew pursed his lips and folded his arms, but he deigned to slowly perch on the edge of his desk, ready to start pacing and shouting again as necessary.

Out of the corner of his eye, Andrew could see Jen and Lloyd looking at each other and shrugging. Clearly, they had no idea where this was going either.

'As you have so *astutely* pointed out, Detective Inspector Joyce, something is rotten in the state of Denmark,' Higson said as he mirrored Andrew's position across the Ballroom.

'Denmark?' Lloyd repeated, confused.

'It's from *Hamlet*,' Andrew replied, his eyes firmly on his DCI.

'Why are we talking about Shakespeare?' Lloyd added, and Jen immediately shushed him.

'Very good,' Higson replied. 'Then again, you're quite the clever clogs aren't you, Joyce?'

Andrew bristled.

'I didn't say that was a *problem*, did I?' Higson said, cutting off any argument Andrew had been about to make. 'Well, not a problem for *me*, anyway.'

'What's that supposed to mean?' Andrew asked. He hated it when people were cryptic.

Higson leaned back a little, rubbing a hand over his beard. 'Do you know why I requested a new DI?'

'Yes,' Andrew shrugged. 'You needed a replacement for DI Benson.'

Andrew did *not* look towards the wall where Benson had last been seen standing.

'Correct,' Higson confirmed. 'But why did I specifically request that Chambers send me somebody with an eye for detail?'

'Because he owed you a favour,' Andrew replied, scratching his head in frustration. 'Is there a point to this, sir?'

'The *point*, Joyce, is that Chambers had three options when I asked him for a DI. He could have sent me someone decent, you know, good at their job; or he could have sent me someone useless that he wanted to get rid of.' Higson raised his eyebrows. '*Or*, he could have sent a spy.'

'A spy?' Andrew asked, disbelieving. 'You think I'm a spy for CID?'

'No, Joyce, I do not,' Higson replied. 'I also don't think that Chambers sent me a general dogsbody who shouldn't have made it to CID in the first place. Which leaves only one option.'

'Look, sir, he said you were decent and good at your job,' Lloyd chimed in, beaming at Andrew. Jen shushed him again.

'I've seen your file, DI Joyce. You're just the sort of detective CID needs. So, why would Chambers, who thinks this department is a waste of time and space, send me a detective with a track record of solving cases quickly and efficiently?' Higson asked.

Andrew frowned. 'What are you getting at?'

Higson rolled his eyes. 'I'm going to take back what I said about you being decent and good at your job unless you speed up here. Chambers wanted you out of the way.'

'But why?'

'When you first got here you said that CID couldn't find any link between Hughes and the Byrnes,' Higson explained. 'You thought that they should have had something by then, and by my reckoning, you're exactly the sort of man who wouldn't let that idea go.'

'So, what? You think everyone over at CID is bent?' Andrew asked, and even though he'd come to a similar conclusion himself, it still made him feel sick.

'Not everyone, certainly not everyone,' Higson replied with a shrug. 'The point is, it wasn't a coincidence that Jen had come across the Driscoll file just as you got here. I wanted to know what was going on in CID. Seeing who Chambers sent me, and then watching how you then behaved was all I needed.'

'So, you actually *did* want me to investigate Rex Hughes?' Andrew asked, stunned. 'What was that phone call then?'

'No goon of Chambers' would have even dreamed of going to Empire Street in the first place,' Higson replied. 'The fact that you went back there against my order – which, you will *not* do again, by the way – proved that you had no reason to want to cover up any link between Hughes and Byrne. If you were being fed information, you'd have already known that Liam Byrne was dead before you got there.'

'Jesus,' Andrew said, and he thought that it was completely fair that his head felt like it was spinning.

'Marnie Driscoll's murder is the closest we've ever come to a likely link between Hughes and the Byrnes,' Higson added. 'Even with Rex Hughes being the one trying to keep the case open, something wasn't right. All three of you have seen just how shit the initial investigation was. I want to know *why*, but first, we need to solve the Driscoll case.'

The phone on Jen's desk rang, and everyone looked over at it in surprise.

'I hope that's not Marnie,' Lloyd whispered. Andrew rolled his eyes.

'DS Cusack,' Jen said as she answered. Her eyes widened momentarily a second later. 'Could you please just hold on for one second?'

Jen covered the mouthpiece and lowered her voice before speaking to her colleagues. 'It's the manager of French and Son. Apparently, Hughes' representative, whoever that is, has been in contact this morning because they've agreed to the sale. The prospective buyer for Marnie's engagement ring is coming in this afternoon to make the purchase, and they're paying in cash.'

'*Cash*?' Andrew hissed. 'Seriously? How much?'

Jen nodded, looking alarmed. 'Half a million pounds.'

Lloyd all but fell over in surprise. '*How much*?'

'Sir?' Jen asked, looking to Higson. 'They can't go ahead without the ring. Do I tell them they need to postpone because of the investigation?'

'What do you think, Joyce?' Higson asked.

Andrew stood up properly. 'I think we let them think it's going ahead. One of us inside the shop, the rest outside. We watch who arrives to approve the sale and take the cash. Then, when the handover happens, we go in.'

'Very good,' Higson replied. 'Cusack, tell the lovely lady on the phone that we're hoping to conduct a little sting operation in her establishment this afternoon.'

'Er, alright,' Jen agreed hesitantly. She then relayed the information calmly despite the shrieking she was receiving in response from the other end of the line.

'Joyce, Parker,' Higson said, nodding at each man in turn. 'You two take the ring to French and Son now. I'll follow on with Cusack.'

'Backup, sir?' Andrew asked. 'We don't know who's going to turn up. It might be Hughes, but it could easily be an associate of Byrne. Given Liam's death, they might be a bit *twitchy*.'

'I know a few people out that way,' Higson replied. 'I'll make sure none of this gets back to CID. This is *your* investigation, Joyce, so I expect this operation to be successful.'

Andrew swallowed heavily. It probably wasn't the right time to mention that he wasn't feeling particularly proud of himself or his abilities after the night before. 'Sir.'

'Ready, sir?' Lloyd asked.

Andrew checked that the ring box was still tucked in the inside pocket of his soaked jacket. He handed his car keys to Lloyd. 'You can drive.'

Lloyd grinned and took the keys. He bounded out of the room and down the stairs.

Andrew followed more slowly, carefully checking each turn of the staircase for Dolly before making his way down. He breathed a sigh of relief only when he was safely in the passenger seat of his car, with the door closed firmly behind him.

As Lloyd navigated the car out through the narrow roads surrounding Tib Street, Andrew did a double take when he saw a DeLorean parked around the corner from the Ballroom.

There was only one person he could think of who'd so casually park a car like that in this part of the city. He just really, *really* hoped he was wrong.

* * *

Andrew wasn't wrong.

'I hate that car, Charlie,' Peggy complained as she looked down at the overly milky tea the waitress had deposited in front of her a few minutes ago.

'I know,' Charlie replied, blowing lightly over the coffee in his own mug. 'You've only told me about four hundred times since we left the house.'

Peggy stuck her tongue out and fiddled with the corner of a sugar packet she had no intention of opening.

'Hey, this was your idea,' Charlie protested. 'You could have stayed at home.'

'Well, yes,' Peggy agreed. 'But if I'd let you come in by yourself, you'd have probably just murdered Andrew by now.'

'And he'd have deserved it,' Charlie said darkly.

'Don't say terrible things, Charlie,' Peggy replied, shaking her head. 'There have been too many terrible things this week already.'

'He let a concussed woman get on a bus by herself!' Charlie protested. 'Not to mention the fact that it's his fault that you were concussed in the first place.'

'Not concussed!' Peggy corrected her brother and sighed. 'And I probably shouldn't have said what I said.'

'What did you say that was so bad?' Charlie shrugged. 'Joyce didn't even tell you who it was you'd seen.'

'Right, but you didn't see his face, Charlie,' Peggy replied. She swore quietly as she accidentally tore through the packet, sending little granules of sugar bouncing across the tabletop.

'Well, I *would* see it if you'd just let me go round the corner now, wouldn't I?' Charlie grumbled.

'I'm not kidding, Charlie,' Peggy protested. 'It was the same look on Marnie's face last night when she thought I was accusing Rex of something.'

'To be fair, Peg, you *were* accusing Rex of something.'

Peggy closed her eyes and slumped down in the slightly sticky booth.

When Peggy had eventually made it back to Butterton the night before – after two bus rides and a taxi – Charlie had been incandescent with rage at the thought that Andrew had abandoned his sister. It was only the combination of Peggy bursting into tears and then Marnie popping up on the staircase that had diverted his attention away from the detective and the myriad ways he was going to make him pay.

Marnie had been horrified to hear what had happened to Peggy and Athena, and she'd made Peggy go over the whole sorry affair twice before she'd been satisfied that she had every detail. Peggy hadn't shared the news about Liam Byrne's murder. She'd also left out what had happened with Andrew and the mysterious Rob, knowing that it would be bad enough to share that with just Charlie later on.

'You've actually seen my ring?' Marnie had asked, with an excited little squeal.

'Yes,' Peggy had replied tiredly as she'd kept her distance from the others. 'Andrew's keeping it safe for you.'

'Do you think he'll give it back to me?' Marnie had asked hopefully.

Charlie had opened his mouth, but Peggy had cut him off before he could escalate the situation. 'I'm not sure, Marnie. I think it depends on what happens with the case. It's still evidence until they've solved it.'

Marnie had seemed to accept that, and Peggy had hoped that the ghost would take that as her cue to leave and let Peggy reflect on her terrible day.

She hadn't left though. Instead, Marnie had wanted to theorise on just who had been behind the accident.

It had reminded Peggy of something she'd been meaning to ask Marnie since Athena mentioned it at lunch. 'Marnie, did you and Rex used to go to the Troubadour?'

'Ooh, I like the Troubadour,' Charlie had chimed in happily.

Peggy had rolled her eyes at her brother. 'Yes, I know. Marnie?'

Marnie had looked surprised at the question. 'Um, yes, we used to go there a lot. Rex liked it because they used to have good bands on, and they'd always make sure that we had a nice table in the corner when we went in a group.'

'So, what happened?' Peggy asked. She hadn't entirely bought Rex's story about a disagreement with the bouncer.

Marnie had looked thoughtful and then taken a seat next to Charlie. If Peggy had been feeling better, she would have laughed at how her brother had tried to awkwardly shuffle further away.

'I remember that we went there on a Friday,' Marnie had started. 'At least I think it was a Friday. Athena came with us because her boyfriend back then – Danny, very boring – had gone home after dinner. Rebecca and Joan from work were there too. Did you ever meet Joan?'

Peggy had said no, impatient for Marnie to continue the story.

'Shame, I think you two would have got on. Anyway, what was I saying? Oh, yes, so we were all there having a nice time when one of the bouncers who'd been on the door came over to say that he needed to have a word with Rex.

'Rex didn't seem to think this was weird, even though I did. He went off somewhere, and then a little while later Rebecca spotted Janine across the club. She was there with Liam Byrne.'

Peggy had perked up. 'What were they doing?'

Marnie had looked at Peggy as though she were mad. 'Dancing? Drinking? What else would they be doing? Anyway, Rebecca pointed them out just before the shouting started.'

'Who was shouting?' Charlie had suddenly become quite invested in the story now that there was the potential for a dramatic moment.

'Rex,' Marnie had said. 'Which was unusual, because he wasn't the shouting type, you know? He was never one to raise his voice. But there he was, shouting and swearing at this bouncer. He was saying something about being ripped off, and how he didn't like people stealing from him. I guess Rex was being accused of something he hadn't done, and he was absolutely furious.'

Peggy had been certain that Rex was definitely not as innocent as Marnie had believed him to be.

'So, he came back to the table and told us that we were all leaving and not coming back again,' Marnie had continued. Then her eyes had grown almost comically wide. 'Oh, and then the funniest thing happened. Rex whirled around and his arm knocked into Janine – she and Liam had come over towards us when Rex started shouting – and Janine spilt her drink all over her dress. She ran off to the ladies shrieking something terrible.'

Peggy hadn't thought that was particularly hilarious in any way, but Marnie had been highly amused at the memory.

'Oh, and *then* Rebecca said she was going to go and help Janine,' Marnie had added, looking baffled. 'What was that about? Oh, *wait, wait,* what if she didn't stay for Janine? What if that's when she started going after Liam and lying about everything?'

Marnie's mirth had completely dried up at that thought.

'Was it after that night that Rebecca started behaving oddly?' Peggy had asked carefully.

'Yeah, now that I think about it, it might have been,' Marnie had replied. Then she'd frowned. 'Why are you even asking me this anyway?'

'Oh, no reason, I was just wondering,' Peggy had said as casually as she could.

'Right,' Marnie had replied slowly. Then her eyes had narrowed. 'So, now that your detective's got my ring and the police are trying to find out who's threatening Athena, are you going to leave Rex alone now?'

'Yes,' Peggy had agreed. She'd then taken a deep breath and steeled herself. 'Marnie, look, the thing is, I think you might want to prepare yourself to find out some things that you don't want to know.'

'What do you mean?' Marnie had snapped. Charlie had stood up immediately and pretended that he had a desperate urge to look out the window.

'Just that maybe Rex was a wonderful man to you, but that perhaps he really had got mixed up in something that he shouldn't have done,'

Peggy had replied carefully.

'Oh, not this again!' Marnie laughed humourlessly. 'Come on, Peggy, just give it up, alright? Some people actually have good relationships you know.'

'What does that mean?' Peggy had asked, even though she'd had a horrible feeling that she already knew what Marnie was going to say.

'Emmeline told me a bit more about what happened to you and your fiancé,' Marnie had said, crossing her arms.

Peggy had felt cold all over at the betrayal.

'Not everyone picks terrible men, you know!' Marnie had added spitefully.

'Now, hang on one second,' Charlie had cut in angrily.

'No, you're right, Marnie,' Peggy had replied woodenly, shrugging as she stood up. 'You're right, not everyone *does* pick terrible men. The problem is that I'm not the only one here who has done just that. Despite what you think, Rex is *not* a good man.'

'Don't you dare say things like that!' Marnie had shouted, and the air around her had started growing hazy.

The sensible part of Peggy had obviously been clubbed over the head too hard that day because she'd felt herself unable to stop from replying to Marnie. Just as she'd done to Andrew earlier, she'd known that she was about to say something that would really, truly hurt.

'Your fiancé is at war with the Byrnes over drugs, Marnie,' Peggy had snapped. 'He doesn't want them muscling in on his territory. Even now, even after what happened to you, he can't bring himself to stop hurting people. And for what? More money? Power?'

'Stop it! Stop it!' Marnie had shrieked, and the large sash window, which had been propped open to battle the suffocating heat, slammed shut like a guillotine.

'Er, Peggy?' Charlie had said, looking horrified as objects on Peggy's dressing table began rising into the air untouched.

'No!' Peggy had cried in frustration. 'I've had enough of everybody blithely believing lies, and then not believing me when I'm telling them the bloody truth! Rex is probably the reason you're dead, Marnie, and I am so sorry for that, but this is *his fault*.'

Peggy had been expecting the apocalypse at that stage, but Marnie had just looked as though she'd been shot, and that Peggy had been the one holding the gun. Her face had crumpled, and big fat tears had started rolling down her cheeks before she'd popped out of the room with a deafening crack.

'Peg?' Charlie said, and Peggy was pulled back into the café.

'Sorry,' Peggy replied, turning to stare at the raindrops meandering down the window. 'I'm fine. Just thinking.'

'Lewis's will be open now,' Charlie said, looking down at his watch. 'Are you sure you don't want me to come with you?'

'I'm sure,' Peggy replied, pulling herself to her feet and sweeping all the sugar she'd spilt into her hand before dropping it into her untouched tea. 'I just want to see if Rebecca's there.'

Charlie reached out and grabbed his sister's sleeve before she left. 'Peg, I know you think you should do this, but you still don't know that Rebecca isn't involved in all of this somehow. Just be careful, okay?'

'I'm only going to Lewis's, Charlie,' Peggy said, forcing a smile. 'What's going to happen there?'

It was only when Peggy was turning a slow circle in the Perfume Hall ten minutes later that she was forced to consider whether she should have kept that thought to herself to avoid jinxing anything.

Peggy had been forced to fend off a few interested enquiries into why she'd been replaced over on Estée Lauder before she got anywhere near Rebecca's usual station. When she finally made it to the centre of the hall she was no closer to learning anything about Rebecca, other than nobody had seen her that morning.

'Peggy!'

Peggy whirled in surprise when she heard Rex call her name. Oh God, he wasn't supposed to be here.

'Peggy, are you alright?' Rex asked, gathering her up in a hug. 'I was so worried.'

Peggy kept her arms by her sides and did her best to wiggle away from the unwanted contact.

'Are you alright?' he asked again when he finally let go of her.

'I'm fine, honestly, so no need for you to worry,' she replied. 'How's Athena?'

'Terrified of leaving the house,' Rex replied, shaking his head. 'I can't imagine how frightening it must have been for you both. I can't even believe you're here this morning.'

'Oh, no, I'm not,' Peggy replied. 'I mean, I'm not at work. I just came in to apologise to Rebecca.'

'Rebecca? What for?'

Now, was it Peggy's imagination, or did Rex look more stressed than usual?

'Just to apologise for not being here at such short notice,' Peggy replied, choosing her words carefully. 'But she's apparently not here today.'

'Oh, right, of course.' That was definitely relief in both Rex's voice and on his face.

'Why are you here?' Peggy asked.

'Oh, I came looking for you actually.' Rex rubbed the back of his neck sheepishly.

Peggy wrinkled her nose. Rex had come looking for her at work? The day after she'd been run off the road with his sister? Why had he even assumed that she was here if Athena wouldn't even leave the house? He'd definitely sounded surprised when he'd spotted her.

'Yes, I know,' Rex replied, looking caught out. 'Wishful thinking on my part. Mad, right? I mean, you shouldn't even be here, should you? You should be at home getting a good rest before you come back to work.'

'I've actually handed in my notice,' Peggy replied. 'So, I'm not coming back. Anyway, I need to be off, but it was nice to see you, Rex. Send my regards to Athena, please.'

'Let me take you out for lunch,' Rex said, sounding desperate.

'Rex, it's barely past breakfast time. No, thank you.'

'Brunch then!' Rex suggested loudly. 'It's the least I can do given what happened to you yesterday.'

'I really don't need brunch,' Peggy replied. 'Goodbye, Rex.'

Rex grabbed her arm and Peggy's heart rate sped up. 'Peggy, please, I need someone to talk to. I'm really worried.'

'About what?' Peggy asked, trying to keep her voice calm. They were in the middle of the shop floor, Rex couldn't be a threat in here, surely.

'Everything,' Rex said, and his eyes were truly wild now. 'What happened yesterday. *Rebecca.*'

'What about Rebecca?'

'Something's not right with her,' Rex said. 'She's been acting strangely, and now you've said she's not at work. She was Marnie's best friend, Peggy. I need to find out what's going on with her, and she seems to get on well with you. Has she told you anything I should know?'

Peggy thought this was all a bit odd. 'Rex, I barely know her.'

'Just come with me, Peggy, *please.*'

Every instinct Peggy had told her not to agree, but with Andrew saying that he wasn't allowed to investigate Rex anymore maybe this was the final chance to get something on him. She couldn't stomach the thought that Marnie wouldn't get justice, and maybe it was also a little bit because she didn't like the idea that Marnie would continue to think that Peggy was a liar.

'Alright,' Peggy sighed. 'Can you just give me a second, please?'

'Why?' Rex frowned.

'I just want to leave a note of apology for Rebecca,' Peggy replied as calmly as she could manage. 'My mother always told me to leave a message if the person I wanted to see wasn't available. You know how it is.'

Before Rex could reply, Peggy turned on her heel and strode across the hall to where she could see Janine watching her interaction with Rex curiously.

'Peggy!' Janine said, beaming at her. 'How are you? I was so surprised when they said you weren't coming back to work.'

'Fine, Janine, thanks,' Peggy said hurriedly. 'Look, is there any chance you could do me a favour? I'd be so, so grateful to you.'

She was laying it on a bit thick, but she figured Janine would respond best to this tactic.

'Oh, of course,' Janine agreed just as Peggy had thought she probably would. 'What can I do?'

'Can you please call this number as soon as you get a chance and ask for Andrew?' Peggy replied, pulling an old receipt from her handbag and scribbling the number for the Ballroom on the back of it.

'Oh, your boyfriend, right,' Janine said, nodding. She managed to look slightly put out.

'Yes, fine, sure,' Peggy said, deciding it wouldn't be worth the hassle to correct her. 'Can you ask for Andrew and tell him that I might be a bit late because I'm having a quick brunch with Rex Hughes?'

'You're doing what?' Janine asked, eyes growing wide as though she were being told some great salacious story.

'Can you please just tell Andrew?' Peggy asked, hoping she didn't look too desperate. 'Oh, and can you just tell him that Charlie will probably be looking for me too.'

'How many men do you have on the go?' Janine asked, with far too much awe. 'How do you have *time*?'

Peggy ignored the question and shoved the receipt at the other woman. 'Thanks, Janine, you're a lifesaver.'

Peggy turned back to Rex and plastered a smile onto her face. 'Okay, sorry about that.'

'That's fine,' Rex said, and he was looking quizzically at Janine. 'Are you sure she can be trusted to pass on a message?'

'I hope so,' Peggy muttered as Rex held the main door open for her. 'Right, where to?'

'I'm just here,' Rex said, opening the door of a nondescript car parked right in front of Peggy. 'It's raining, so we'll just drive up the road.'

Alarm bells were ringing in Peggy's mind. 'Actually, Rex, I've changed my mind. I don't actually feel very well after all.'

Rex's face transformed instantly. Instead of the affable, charming expression he so often wore, his face was devoid of anything but snarling annoyance as he opened the rear door of the car instead. He moved towards Peggy quickly.

Peggy only managed to take one step backwards before Rex grabbed her arm and pulled so forcefully that she practically stumbled into the backseat of the car before he gave her a final push, slamming the door behind her.

She didn't even have the chance to unfold herself from the inelegant sprawl before Rex started the engine and began driving them away from Lewis's.

'What the hell do you think you're doing?' Peggy shouted. 'Rex, let me out of this car right now!'

'I'm sorry, Peggy, I can't do that,' Rex replied evenly. 'I came looking for Rebecca because I heard that she'd got herself involved with someone she really shouldn't have. But she's not here, and I think you're my only hope now.'

'What are you talking about?' Peggy reached for the door handle and Rex put his foot on the accelerator in response.

'If you try and get out of the car, you'll kill yourself,' he said, horribly calmly, speeding through a red light and narrowly avoiding another car.

'Jesus Christ, slow down!' Peggy yelled as Rex weaved through traffic, bouncing two wheels up onto the kerb to pass down the left side of waiting cars. Peggy's head throbbed uncomfortably.

It was then that Peggy heard the beginnings of whispers. *No, no, no,* she thought as she glanced through the windscreen only to see the cathedral coming up ahead, just as it had done when she'd been in the car with Andrew on Saturday night.

Oh my God, Andrew was absolutely going to kill her. Well, if Rex Hughes didn't do it first, that is.

The car flew down the road, screeching past the cathedral and around the river. Peggy instinctively knew where they were going even before she caught sight of the prison's ventilation tower.

'Rex, let me out of the car. Please just let me out of the car,' Peggy begged desperately, and in that moment she was more terrified of what was about to happen in her head than anything Rex could do.

'I can't do that, Peggy, I'm sorry,' he replied as he turned onto Southall Street. 'Just stay calm and everything will be fine.'

Whether she wanted to comply or not, Peggy knew that it was going to be impossible. The car turned right, and Peggy screamed until the darkness won out.

EIGHTEEN

'Lloyd?' Andrew shook the radio in his hand again. '*Lloyd*? Can you hear me?'

The radio finally crackled in response. 'Yes, sorry, sir. I've just been getting a lecture on how I'm not actually allowed to touch anything in here.'

Andrew smirked. 'Alright, well just do what the nice lady tells you.'

'Any movement outside yet?' Lloyd asked. The hint of excitement in his voice was obvious even now. He'd told Andrew on the drive to Hale that he'd never been part of anything like this before.

'Nothing yet.' From where Andrew sat in his car, slightly further up the road from French and Son, he had a perfect view of the front door, and of the car that contained Jen and Higson on the opposite side of the street.

Andrew picked up the radio again as a black sports car shot past his window before screeching to a halt outside the jewellers. 'Hang on, Lloyd, I think the buyer might be here.'

A man got out of the black car, dark hair almost to his shoulders, with a pair of sunglasses perched on top of his head. Andrew rolled his eyes. It had only stopped raining a few minutes earlier, and the sun hadn't made even the briefest of appearances.

The man checked his reflection in the window before sauntering into the shop, and Andrew had to tamp down the petty little shock of joy at knowing that this man was about to get quite the surprise.

'I see him,' Lloyd muttered in reply.

Only a minute or so later, a very familiar red Ferrari parked just up from Andrew's car.

'Here we go,' Andrew whispered to himself. All he needed was for Rex Hughes to get out of that car and they would almost have enough to haul him in for questioning over Marnie's murder. He'd wait, of course. Nobody was going to move until the money had been exchanged for Marnie's ring.

The driver's door of the Ferrari opened, and a leg appeared. It was an obviously feminine leg wearing a pair of fancy-looking heels. Not Rex

Hughes then. Rebecca, perhaps? Or Janine?

The leg gradually became a whole person, and Andrew waited for the woman to turn towards him. From this angle, he could see that she would be fairly short without the shoes, and the skirt she was wearing seemed like it had probably been designed with someone taller in mind. Then again, what did Andrew know about fashion?

Her face was obscured by large, dark sunglasses and Andrew swore loudly when he realised that he didn't recognise her at all. Andrew allowed himself to entertain the snide little fleeting thought that at least Peggy might finally be happy about something, given that it didn't look like Rebecca was involved here.

Whoever this woman was, nobody had ever looked into her as a suspect. She perfectly matched the description of the woman who'd returned Marnie's presents to Kendals, but who the hell was she?

'Incoming,' Andrew muttered into the radio.

'Affirmative,' Lloyd replied quietly. 'I'll let you know as soon as the contract is signed and the money's been handed over. The manager here just counted all half a million in front of me. It doesn't actually look like very much, you know, considering how much it *is*.'

Andrew did know. He'd seen so much discarded money following robberies gone wrong that he'd learned pretty quickly that what seemed like a staggering amount of money never really looked quite as exciting as you'd imagined it would.

He gave it a minute and then signalled to Higson and Jen.

They started getting out of their car and Higson then gave his own vague wave to the two police cars that Andrew knew were parked on an adjacent residential street. Sure enough, the nose of the first car appeared at the corner of the main road a few seconds later, just as Jen and Higson took up their position outside the jewellers.

Andrew closed his eyes for just a second and took a deep breath. After the most bizarre week of his entire life, he was finally going to get the answers he needed.

'Sir, it's done.'

At Lloyd's words, Andrew practically threw himself from his car and burst into French and Son.

'Police!' Andrew announced loudly. 'Nobody move!'

The buyer stood up from where he'd been seated at a small marble-topped table, looking miffed. Lloyd casually clamped a hand on his shoulder and pushed him back down.

'I think you should do what he says,' Lloyd grinned at the man. '*Sir.*'

Andrew was going to have to have a little chat with Lloyd about the appropriate level of glee to show during an arrest.

'Ma'am, I'm Detective Inspector Joyce, and now I need you to identify yourself,' Andrew said calmly as he approached the table. The woman was still wearing those damn sunglasses inside.

She was also tightly grasping a bag that was lying on the table, and Andrew assumed that it was the payment for the engagement ring. She didn't say anything, but she was shaking her head wildly.

'Ma'am, please,' Andrew said. 'Identify yourself.'

The woman took off her sunglasses. Her bottom lip wobbled, and she took a great gulp of air before she spoke. 'My name is Mary. Mary Parish.'

Mary Parish? Andrew ran the name through his head a few times, but nothing useful came back.

Then. *Wait.*

Someone, somewhere along the way had been called Mary, but who the bloody hell had it been?

'And how did you come across the ring that you've just sold, Mary?' Andrew asked, still thinking desperately. 'Because it doesn't belong to you, does it?'

Mary was still shaking her head. 'No, no, it's not mine. It belongs to my employer.'

Mary. Andrew remembered where he'd heard that name before.

'You're the Hughes's housekeeper,' Andrew said, already certain that he was correct before she nodded. 'How did you get this ring? Be specific, Mary, because I'll know if you're lying to me.'

'It was left out on the kitchen counter a few months ago, next to a list of jobs that Mr Hughes wanted me to do on top of my usual responsibilities,' Mary said, and her voice was still shaking. 'He often leaves notes for me if there's something he wants doing connected to work.'

'Such as what?'

'The family owns lots of property,' Mary explained, repeatedly clasping and then unclasping her fingers on the table in front of her. 'So, if they've got tenants moving in and out at short notice, he might ask me to go and clean if they haven't got time to get the usual girls in. He does pay me a nice bonus when I do that though. Am I in trouble?'

'Yes,' Andrew replied simply.

Mary looked only seconds away from bursting into floods of tears, and Andrew did actually feel like a bit of a git.

'So, he asked you to bring the ring here?' Andrew looked over to where Higson was speaking quietly to the two uniformed officers who had just entered the shop.

'He did. I was supposed to have the ring valued, and then leave it here until a buyer was found,' Mary said, trembling. 'I didn't steal the ring from him, I swear!'

Andrew ignored the denial for now. 'One last question, and then I'm afraid we're going to have to take you to the station.'

'What? No!' Mary protested, and then she actually was crying, and Andrew really did feel sorry for her.

'I'm sorry, Mary, but that ring was taken from the scene of a murder.'

'What?' bellowed the man across the table.

Lloyd tightened his grip to keep the buyer from moving.

'No, no, it wasn't,' Mary said desperately. 'It wasn't. Mr Hughes had given it to that dear girl Marnie, God rest her soul, before Christmas. The police would have given it back to him after she died. I wasn't to speak to him about it, the note said. I suppose it would have just upset him too much.'

'The police didn't find that ring at the scene of the murder.' Andrew shook his head. 'Look, Mary, can you please tell me if Mr Hughes asked you to return anything to Kendals back in February? Maybe around the same time you were given instructions about the ring?'

Mary frowned but nodded slowly. 'Yes, Mr Hughes left a bag out in the kitchen, right there with the jewellery and things at the same time as the ring. I was supposed to take everything back to Kendals for a refund, but he wanted it in cash rather than for it to go on his credit account. I got terribly upset when they wouldn't take back some earrings, so I took them to a jewellers up the road. Should I not have taken them somewhere else? Oh God, I thought I was doing the right thing!'

Andrew looked over at Higson who gestured for him to continue.

'Did Mr Hughes tell you why he wanted you to return the items?'

'No, he didn't, and I didn't have any reason to ask. I took everything back as I was told to do. I even wore the clothes he left out. He said he didn't think they'd take me seriously if I wore my usual things,' Mary replied with disconcerting earnestness.

Her face crumpled entirely. 'I didn't steal anything, I swear. I left all the money on the kitchen counter as he asked, and I took everything back. Everything. I went back and forth between different places until I could get him the best price for those earrings too. I've worked for that family for eight years, and my mother was there for twenty before me. I would *never* steal from them.'

'Alright, Mary, that's it for now,' Andrew said, gesturing to the two uniformed officers. 'You'll need to go and answer some questions for me, and I'll come to see you again later, alright?'

'Well, what do you think?' Andrew asked Higson as Mary was led from the shop.

'She's not our murderer, Joyce,' Higson said, lighting a cigarette even as the manager protested loudly from behind the counter. 'But you already know that.'

'Do we have enough to bring Hughes in?' Andrew asked, running a hand through his hair in frustration. 'There's just something about all of it that still doesn't feel right. By the sounds of it, Rex has never actually spoken to Mary about any of it. And notes? I doubt she'll have kept any of them, which means we still have no useful, physical evidence.'

'Can I take my ring and go now?' The man at the table asked, clearly irritated.

'Sorry, that ring is part of an active murder investigation,' Andrew replied, pushing the bag of money back across the table towards him. 'But do hang around for a minute, I'm sure one of my colleagues would like to have a quick chat with you about your terrible parking.'

The man stood up so suddenly that he broke free of Lloyd's grip and lunged at Andrew.

He stopped short when Higson grabbed the back of his shirt as though he weighed nothing. 'I wouldn't do that if I were you, sunshine.'

The phone behind the counter rang shrilly.

'Can I answer that?' The manager asked, shooting Andrew the same sour look she had when he'd first enquired about the ring. 'I do still have a business to run.'

Andrew glanced over at Jen. 'I'd prefer if DS Cusack answered the phone right now, thanks.'

Jen's smile lent the manager just a hint of an apology before she picked up the receiver. 'Good afternoon, French and Son.'

'Do you reckon it's Hughes, sir?' Lloyd asked, nodding towards the phone. 'That would be pretty good, wouldn't it?'

'It would,' Andrew replied slowly, watching Jen's face as it changed from polite indifference to pure surprise. 'But I don't think it is.'

'Yes, yes, I can confirm that the contract of sale has been signed, and the money received by your representative,' Jen said, sounding only marginally hesitant. 'Yes, in cash, as agreed. Okay, thank you. Good day.'

Jen put the receiver down and stared at it as though it held the secret to life.

'Well?' Andrew asked, impatiently. 'Was it Hughes?'

'Kind of,' Jen replied, still shell-shocked.

'What do you mean, 'kind of'?' Andrew and Lloyd looked at each other in confusion.

'Well, sir, it's just that it wasn't *Rex* Hughes. It was *Athena*.'

'Athena?' Andrew asked dumbly, not entirely sure that he'd heard Jen correctly.

'Yes, sir, I'm absolutely certain,' Jen said, and really Andrew had absolutely no cause to doubt her.

'Shit,' Andrew said, staring at the floor. '*Shit*.'

'Anything else to add to that, Joyce?' Higson asked, coming over to stand in front of the other man.

Andrew scrubbed a hand across his face. 'How did we miss that she was involved?'

'Because she's a very good liar,' Higson said plainly. 'So, what are you going to do?'

'We need to get to the Hughes house right now,' Andrew replied, already heading for the door. 'They'll be expecting Mary back with the money, surely.'

'Right, everybody out,' Higson shouted. He pointed at the manager. 'You will not touch that phone, you will lock this shop up, and you will go home for the day, and then *maybe* I won't need to look more closely into where you're getting your stock from.'

He turned his attention to the furtive-looking buyer. 'And *you* are a very, very lucky boy. Get your arse out of my sight.'

The man, quite sensibly, scarpered, almost tripping over Lloyd as he whipped past him and out onto the pavement.

'Joyce, we'll be right behind you,' Higson added.

'Sir.' Andrew inclined his head respectfully then turned and ran towards the car, Lloyd close behind.

'Sorry, Lloyd,' Andrew said as he clambered quickly into the car and started the engine. 'I'm driving this time.'

* * *

For one blissful moment, Peggy thought that she must have fallen asleep on the sofa at home, but as she cracked her eyes open, she realised that she was staring up at an unfamiliar ceiling.

She swallowed heavily and winced as her throat burned. Jesus, what had happened?

Peggy's eyes grew wide and she sat bolt upright, running her hands over her head, her hair and her arms to check that she was intact. She had a disturbingly vivid memory of feeling like she was being smothered, with sharp, claw-like hands scratching her skin as she'd been pulled further and further down into darkness. The words that had been screamed at her in her mind had been foul, violent thoughts of evil and annihilation, and she would have sworn that she'd felt her own soul trying to rip itself away from her just to be free of the malice.

Rex. He'd driven her straight past the prison, and it had been a million times worse than it had been when Andrew had just sped them to safety on Saturday night. Even now, Peggy was sure that she could hear whispering, but her head was pounding too hard to be sure.

She realised that she was likely in the warehouse on Empire Street. The room she was in was small and furnished like an office, with a paper-strewn desk pushed against the wall opposite to where she was sitting. There was a filing cabinet next to the door, and piles of white envelopes everywhere. There wasn't a window in sight.

How could she have been so stupid? How many times was she going to ignore all the signs and just throw herself into a situation that she knew was probably going to be a terrible idea?

She hoped with everything that she had that Janine had passed on her message. It was far from ideal that she was placing all her trust in a person she'd spoken to a grand total of five times.

Though what good would it actually do her? It would let Andrew know that she'd run headlong into a precarious situation again, and that was about it. She had no way of telling anyone where she was, or what had happened after she'd left Lewis's.

Peggy knew that she had to get out of there, and she needed to do it quickly. She knew she wouldn't be able to go back past Strangeways, so she'd have to head in the opposite direction until she got far enough away to be able to find a way of contacting Andrew or Charlie. She had only herself to rely on right now, and that was going to have to be enough.

She was so tired though, and every muscle screamed in protest as she pushed herself up to standing on unstable legs. At least she wasn't wearing heels, and really, she'd take what she could get in the way of good luck right now.

Peggy forced herself to walk as quickly as she could towards the door. She couldn't hear any sounds coming from the other side, but she wasn't stupid enough to think that Rex had brought her here and then just left her entirely.

She pressed her right hand against the back of the door to steady herself and put her left on the handle.

She paused just before she pressed down. Maybe she wasn't entirely alone.

'Marnie?' she called softly. 'Marnie, can you hear me?'

Peggy's call was met with silence, but part of her still clung to the hope that Marnie was just royally pissed off with her after the night before, rather than she was too far away to hear her.

'Marnie?' she tried again. 'Please. Marnie?'

Peggy screwed her eyes shut for just a second and tried to accept that

Marnie wasn't coming. Then, she pushed down on the handle, pulled the door open, and peered carefully through the slowly widening gap.

The office led straight out into the main warehouse space, and as far as Peggy could see, there was nobody else around.

It was obviously still raining because water was pouring through the gaping holes in the ceiling and puddling all over the floor. There were three doors evenly spaced on the wall at her back, and she hoped that if Rex was behind any of them, he hadn't heard her sneaking out.

Peggy crept forwards, walking on her tiptoes through the rust-tinged water, lest she make the slightest sound by splashing too hard. There was a pair of large green wooden doors directly in front of her. What looked like a piece of police tape secured only on one end was fluttering slightly in the breeze that was coming in alongside the sliver of daylight where the doors met. There was a hole in the brickwork directly above the doors and Peggy shivered when she caught sight of that bloody ventilation tower again.

As she got closer to the doors, the whispering in her ears grew louder and the back of her neck prickled in warning. She felt like she was caught right on the edge of a shiver, but her body was refusing to give in to the temptation.

The proximity of the prison was going to be a problem.

A door opened behind her, and Peggy didn't even turn around. Pushing away the increasingly frantic whispers, she bolted for the green doors as quickly as she could, her feet skidding on the slick ground. Her shoulder hit the door heavily, jarring her bones and stealing the breath from her lungs.

'Hey!'

Oh God, who was that? Peggy thought as she pulled on the doors desperately. They noisily grated inwards an inch or so, but then stopped dead with a rattle and a thunk of finality. She realised then that they must have been chained shut from the outside.

A hand roughly grabbed the back of her cardigan and Peggy cried out hoarsely in surprise as she was spun around to face Rex. He was pressing his fingers tightly into the top of her arm, hard enough to bruise and Peggy knew that there was no way she could wriggle free this time.

'Let go of me!' she croaked.

'I can't do that, Peggy,' Rex barked, and she could smell alcohol on his breath, turning the air between them sour. 'Now, come and sit down like a good girl and you'll be fine.'

Rex put his hand between her shoulder blades and pushed until she started walking back towards the office again, stumbling over her own feet as she tried to keep her balance at the awkward angle.

'What the fuck is she doing out?' The man whose voice she hadn't recognised snapped angrily.

'Nothing to worry about, Tony,' Rex replied, tightening his grip on Peggy again in silent warning. 'She's just going back in the office again.'

'Hughes, I swear to God, if you're lying about how much money we can get for her, I'll shoot you in the head before you've had a chance to blink,' Tony said with eery calm. 'Both of you.'

Peggy was close enough to see the look of panic cross Rex's face, and her own heart was hammering in her chest at the threat. She didn't think Tony was the kind of man to make jokes.

'Oh, for Christ's sake, Rex, what have you done *now*?'

Rex spun around in surprise at the new voice, pulling Peggy so quickly after him that they both nearly tumbled to the floor in a heap. Peggy held out her hands to try and steady herself as Rex's feet grappled with the over-rotation.

'*Athena*?' Rex asked in a strangled voice as his sister walked towards them slowly. Peggy was fairly certain she'd never heard anyone sound more shocked.

'What are you doing here?' Tony asked. He didn't sound surprised to see Athena at all.

Athena was staring at her surroundings, nose wrinkling more with each step. 'I see you're here too, Tony. It's a wonder the place is still standing.'

Tony Byrne. Peggy knew nothing about the man beyond the fact that he was Liam Byrne's older brother. Liam Byrne, who'd been killed in this very warehouse only the day before.

Peggy struggled against Rex's hold again. His grip had slackened with the distraction of Athena's arrival, and he didn't resist when Peggy wrenched her arm away from him. She took a couple of steps backwards until she was almost in line with the door to the office.

'Oh, and Peggy's here,' Athena said, shooting her a saccharine smile. 'That's helpful actually, because I've been wanting to ask you exactly what it is that you think you're up to.'

Peggy shook her head. 'I'm not up to anything. Your brother threw me in his car and brought me here. Ask him what *he's* up to!'

'Oh Peggy, come *on*,' Athena laughed sharply. 'Why not just tell the truth?'

'What truth?' Rex asked, looking between Peggy and Athena.

Tony took a step towards Rex. 'This better not be me finding out that she's not swimming in cash, Hughes.'

'No, no, she *is* filthy rich,' Athena said, tilting her head to survey Peggy in a way that made her feel very much like she was in the sights of someone much, much more calculating than they'd ever been given credit for. 'She's even got a title. But Rex is missing part of the story here.'

'What?' Rex asked, still looking baffled.

'Rex, why don't you just go home?' Athena sighed, and she sounded almost pitying. 'You're only in the way at this point.'

Athena then turned her attention to Tony. 'I thought I told you that I wasn't interested if you were going to involve either of our brothers.'

'Well, *my* brother's no longer an issue.' Tony smirked. 'But, unfortunately, *your* brother owes me quite a lot of money.'

'What?' Athena snapped sharply, looking surprised for the first time since she'd arrived. 'How much money?'

'Just 'cos it's you, I'll round it down,' Tony replied, scratching the back of his head hard enough that flakes of dandruff rained down on his collar. 'Rex here owes me two hundred thousand.'

'*Two hundred...*' Athena trailed off, now in obvious shock.

'So, you see, I need to get that back before I can move on with our own little agreement,' Tony shrugged, waving his hand between his chest and Athena.

Athena's face morphed into a murderous expression as she turned her attention back to her brother. 'You stupid bastard! You borrowed money from *him*?'

'Your brother reckons we can get enough money from *her* –' Tony pointed at Peggy, '– to more than cover what he owes me.'

For just a second, Peggy thought that Athena was going to physically attack her brother, but in the end she just shook her head at him again and then sneered at Tony Byrne.

'Did my idiot brother tell you that your hostage has a boyfriend?' Athena asked, pulling herself up to her full height again, all hint of that momentary slouch disappearing in an instant.

'No, she doesn't!' Rex argued.

'Why would I care about her boyfriend?' Tony frowned. Then he brightened slightly. 'Wait, is he rich too?'

'No, I shouldn't think so,' Athena replied, and she smiled at Peggy again. 'Do you want to tell them, or should I?'

'I have no idea what you're talking about!' Peggy shook her head vehemently.

'Oh, fine,' Athena sighed wearily. She looked between her brother and Tony Byrne. 'Her Ladyship over there has her very own Detective Inspector at home.'

'No, I don't!' Peggy protested. Jesus, seriously, *why* did nobody ever believe her when she actually told them the truth?

'What the fuck, Hughes?' Tony asked tersely, reaching towards his jacket pocket and taking a step towards Rex. 'Are you a grass?'

'Stop it, Athena!' Rex barked at his sister, eyes wide in panic. 'Stop lying!'

'I'm not lying,' Athena said as calmly as though this were nothing more than a lovely, casual chat between friends over a cup of tea. 'You've even met him, Rex. In fact, he's been in our house. Don't you remember? He told you how he was going to solve Marnie's murder only a few days ago. Very earnest, doesn't trust you one bit.'

'I don't have a bloody boyfriend!' Peggy cried as Rex turned on her. 'She's lying!'

'Andrew Joyce, Peggy. Does that ring a bell?' Athena added in a sing-song voice. 'I saw you together at the hospital.'

Shit. Peggy hadn't even considered that Athena might have seen her with Andrew.

'The policeman who came to ask me questions after the crash?' Peggy asked with a shaky laugh, desperately hoping that she sounded bewildered enough to be believable. 'You're joking, right?'

'Do I look like I'm joking?'

No, Athena didn't look like she was joking at all. She looked like poise and venom, and also like she was devastatingly certain that she had Peggy caught in a lie.

Athena shrugged one shoulder. 'And then there's the fact that on Friday night Rebecca told me that your *Andrew* had come to meet you after work, and wasn't that terribly sweet? *Such* a nice man, apparently. Oh, and terribly handsome even if he is a little dull. Works in *research*.'

Under any other circumstances, Peggy would have laughed at hearing Rebecca's review and then would have delighted in sharing it with Andrew after the fact. She wasn't laughing now though.

Athena pursed her lips. 'Maybe I should have worked it out then. Rebecca never was a very good judge of character.'

'You've got it wrong, I swear,' Peggy said, but she already knew that she'd soon have to accept that arguing with Athena about any of this was going to be futile.

'Stop lying!' Athena snapped.

'Are you setting me up?' Tony roared, this time grasping at Rex's shirt with his fist.

Rex, not quite expecting the attack, stumbled to the side. He caught the heel of his left foot on his right shoe and toppled backwards pulling Tony Byrne heavily down with him. The crash reverberated through the warehouse.

Peggy took advantage of the commotion and darted backwards into the office, slamming the door behind her. She threw herself bodily at the filling cabinet and her breath whooshed out of her in surprise as her ribs hit the metal frame. She thanked anyone still listening that it was just enough force to topple the cabinet, blocking the door.

She knew it wouldn't give her much time, but maybe just a few seconds to formulate a plan was all she needed.

Oh God, who was she kidding? How was she supposed to get out of a windowless room when all other ways out of the building were blocked by three people who had no intention of letting her leave? She was fairly certain that at least one of them had a gun.

Peggy stumbled around the room, her legs still shaking. She knocked over stacks of envelopes and opened drawers, looking for anything that she could use to defend herself. She wasn't going to just sit there and wait for them to force their way in.

The first thud of a body against the other side of the door gave her such a fright that her hand slipped on the desk, sending a pile of paper fluttering to the floor.

Her eyes followed the tumbling bundle and Peggy then had to quickly blink a few times to check that she wasn't seeing things. There, sitting on the floor by the skirting board was a green rotary telephone.

'Oh my God,' Peggy mumbled, dropping to her knees and snatching up the receiver. She swore in relief when she heard a dial tone, desperately trying to remember the Ballroom's number. She usually had no problem with recall, but her thoughts were still muddled enough that she had to abandon her first attempt at dialling and start again.

'Oh please, please, please, pick up,' Peggy muttered, closing her eyes and pulling her knees to her chest. 'Please, please, *please*!'

The sudden click in Peggy's ear almost had her crying in relief, but then the recorded message kicked in.

There was another thump against the door, and the shouting outside ratcheted up in volume as the filing cabinet creaked and groaned, scraping slowly across the floorboards, gouging deep fissures in the soft wood.

Finally, the message ended, and Peggy heard the beep she'd been waiting for.

'Andrew!' She didn't quite know whether she was whispering or shouting louder than she'd ever done in her life. All she knew was that she was running out of time, and this was the only scrap of a chance she'd get.

'Rex took me to Empire Street! Tony Byrne's here-' she cut herself off with a yelp of horror as the filing cabinet moved again, much more significantly this time as Tony Byrne's cursing grew even louder.

'Athena's here! She's working with Byrne! I'm sorry. I didn't know! She knows I know you, but she thinks we-'

Peggy cut herself off with a yelp as there was another thud and suddenly the doorway was wide enough for Tony to force himself through.

'What the fuck are you doing?' he shouted, practically vaulting the desk to get to her.

Peggy whimpered at the undisguised rage in Tony's expression. She clung onto the phone like the lifeline she desperately hoped it was, even as Tony lunged towards her. 'Andrew! Tell Charlie not to give them a penny!'

Tony shoved her roughly to the floor, wrested the telephone from her grasp and then hurled the entire thing against the wall.

Peggy threw her arms up over her head as sharp shards of green plastic rained down around her.

Then, for the first time in years, Peggy closed her eyes and prayed.

NINETEEN

'Where do you think they've gone, sir?' Lloyd asked just as the junction with Tib Street came into view. He'd been unusually quiet for most of the journey, which Andrew found unsettling.

'I don't know,' Andrew replied tightly. His knuckles were white from the way he'd been gripping the steering wheel since they'd found the Hughes house locked up and without a single car on the driveway an hour earlier.

He might not have been a big believer in the paranormal, but Andrew trusted gut feelings, and his gut was telling him that the reckoning he'd been expecting was on its way.

'Mary said that she was instructed to bring the money back to the house,' Lloyd said, 'so they must be planning on coming back soon.'

'They,' Andrew repeated, flicking the indicator harder than necessary.

'Yeah,' Lloyd replied slowly. 'Rex and Athena. Sir?'

'Just thinking out loud,' Andrew said. 'Ignore me.'

'Alright, sir,' Lloyd agreed chirpily as they turned into Tib Street.

Andrew glanced up the street and groaned when he caught sight of someone in a horribly familiar purple blazer leaning against the *Cheryl Richard* nameplate.

'Oh, for Christ's sake, what's *he* doing here?' Andrew grumbled as he parked the car and valiantly tried to ignore how the glare Charlie Swan had fixed on him was genuinely quite menacing.

'Well, sir, you *did* say that you'd abandoned his sister when she had a concussion,' Lloyd said, wincing slightly.

'I didn't *abandon* anyone,' Andrew replied crossly, which was technically true. 'And nobody had a concussion!'

'You don't have a sister do you, sir?' It was more of a statement than a question.

'No,' Andrew replied, unbuckling his seatbelt. 'Why?'

Lloyd sighed loudly. 'I have three. All older than me, and all of them drive me nuts. The thing is, though, I'd still kick anyone in the bollocks for upsetting them, and I'm sure they'd do the same for me.'

Andrew didn't have time for sibling politics. He already felt like an arse for not making sure that Peggy had got home safely in the first place, but he'd have to atone for that sin once he knew where the hell the Hughes siblings were. He climbed out of the car while Lloyd rummaged in his pocket for his door key.

As Andrew climbed out of the car, Charlie's glare slowly faded into apprehension, and that worried Andrew far more than the tirade of accusations he'd been expecting.

'Peg's not with you?' Charlie asked Andrew as Lloyd unlocked the door.

'Why would Peggy be with me?'

Andrew shook his head when Charlie rudely pushed past him into the building.

'Because she's not with me,' Charlie replied crisply as the three of them traipsed up the stairs, 'and she wasn't at Lewis's when I stuck my head round the door half an hour ago.'

Andrew stopped dead halfway up the second set of stairs. 'What?'

'Don't worry Joyce, she didn't go behind your back and show up for work,' Charlie called back without stopping. 'She went in on the off chance that Rebecca might be there.'

Andrew shook himself out of his stupor and bolted up the stairs into the Ballroom, arriving just as Charlie was in the process of flinging himself dramatically onto the sofa.

'I don't bloody believe this,' Andrew snapped, stomping towards his damned desk and throwing his damned jacket over his *damned* chair. 'I specifically *told* her to stay away from there!'

'Right,' Charlie shot back darkly, 'but the thing is, Joyce, you don't actually have the right to tell Peggy what she should or shouldn't do. You lost that privilege when you relieved her of her association with your case, and, let me be clear here, *Detective Inspector*, the only reason that I haven't decked you yet is because Peggy asked me not to. She's a far, *far* better person than I am.'

'Children, please, shut the fuck up,' Higson barked as he entered the Ballroom, Jen at his heels. 'Lloyd, uniform at the Hughes house are going to check in every half an hour. Go get coffee, and then sit over there until they call in.'

'Sir,' Lloyd agreed. 'There's a message on the machine. Do you want me to check that first? Could be uniform if they couldn't get us on the radio.'

Higson waved his hand, which didn't seem to be either agreement or otherwise as far as Andrew was concerned, but Lloyd just shrugged and pressed the button to play back the messages.

Andrew pointed at Charlie. 'What did Peggy say she was doing exactly?'

'She said that she was going to go and see if anyone had heard from Rebecca, given that the poor woman might be upset about her fiancé being murdered over the weekend,' Charlie replied irritably. 'Peg was worried that Rebecca might not even know that something had happened to Liam Byrne, and would have just shown up to work as normal. You lot didn't seem too bothered about making sure Rebecca knew anything, after all.'

'If Peggy was going to Lewis's, why did you think she would be *here*?' Andrew asked, ignoring Charlie's final comment for now. Something was wrong, he could practically smell it.

'I thought maybe she'd finally come to her senses and decided that she *did* need to come and give you a piece of her mind after all,' Charlie replied, folding his arms.

'Hey!'

Everyone turned at Lloyd's startled shout.

'What?' Andrew asked, folding his arms as Lloyd pointed at the answering machine.

'There's a message from Janine Turner, you know, from Lewis's,' Lloyd explained. 'I didn't get to the end, but I've rewound it because you need to hear it. It's a message for you, sir.'

Andrew gestured for Lloyd to press play. 'Turn the volume up.'

The machine beeped, and a woman's voice filled the Ballroom, growing louder as Lloyd twisted the dial.

'Oh, wait, is this the right number? Did that message say this was the police? Oh, well, this is the number I have. So hi, Andrew, if you're there. It's Janine.'

'Oh, no surname?' Charlie scoffed over Janine's next words. 'Friend of yours, *Andrew*?'

'Shut up, Swan!' Higson snapped and Charlie shrank back looking apologetic.

'-so, Peggy came in to see Rebecca, but she's not in today. She said that I had to tell you that she's gone out with Rex.'

Andrew had reached for his jacket before he'd consciously realised what he was doing. He snatched up his car keys and headed for the door, even as Janine continued talking.

'- she did say someone called Charlie might be looking for her too. She didn't look very happy to be going, to be honest, which is weird, because Rex is lovely. Oh, not that you're not lovely too!'

'Sir, hang on!' Lloyd called as the message ended with a cooing goodbye. 'There's another one. It might be important.'

Andrew didn't stop though. He was halfway down the stairs with no real plan in mind when Higson bellowed his name. The DCI's tone was far harsher than it had been even when he'd been yelling at him the day before, and it had Andrew sprinting back up the stairs again immediately.

'What?' he asked, stopping in the middle of the room when he realised that everyone - even Higson - was staring at him in horror. Charlie was standing next to Lloyd and looked like he might be about to be sick.

'Um, we've only heard the beginning, but...um...' Lloyd said, quickly pressing the rewind button on the machine before clicking 'play' again.

'Andrew!'

Andrew nearly dropped his keys in surprise at the sound of Peggy's voice floating out of the answering machine. He recognised that quality to her voice; it was the same as when she'd begged him to let her out of the car before they drove past Strangeways.

'Rex took me to Empire Street! Tony Byrne's here-'

There was the sound of metal scraping against something, and Peggy made a noise of distress. Andrew let out a low string of creative expletives.

'We need to get to Empire Street now!' Jen said, grabbing her own car keys from her desk.

'Athena's here! She's working with Byrne! I'm sorry. I didn't know! She knows I know you, but she thinks we-'

There was another thud on the message, this one much louder than the last, and Jen pressed a hand over her mouth in utter dismay.

'What the fuck are you doing?'

Andrew assumed that the new voice was Tony Byrne, and he barely registered the tip of his car key pressing into his palm as he balled his fists in rage. He looked at Charlie's pale face and shaking hands, and he knew exactly how he felt.

'Andrew! Tell Charlie not to give them a penny!'

Peggy's desperate plea was punctuated with a yelp of surprise, followed by a roar of anger that was abruptly cut off as the message ended.

The machine beeped and there was absolute silence in the Ballroom.

Andrew's heart was thudding in his chest, and he had to swallow down the bile that was trying to force its way up his throat.

'Sir? Come on, let's go!' Jen said, pushing past where Andrew was standing stock still.

'She won't be there anymore, Jen,' Andrew said quietly. 'They'll know she called me, so they won't have stuck around.'

'We have to *check*, sir!' Jen protested. 'Please!'

'No. Joyce is right,' Higson said, rising to his feet. 'The Hugheses aren't stupid, they've shown that repeatedly, and Tony Byrne may be as thick as two short planks, but he won't take the chance of losing his hostage.'

'Then where do we go?' Lloyd asked. 'We know they're not at the house.'

'I'm going to look for her!' Charlie, who was now even paler than he had been a moment ago, headed for the door.

'Charlie, wait.' Andrew reached out and tried to grasp Charlie's arm as he walked by.

Charlie rounded on him, white-hot fury burning in his eyes. 'This is on you, Joyce. If anything happens to Peg, I'll kill you myself. Don't think I won't.'

'I know,' Andrew replied seriously. 'And you're right, it *is* on me. But running off to Empire Street isn't going to help anyone. Peggy's not going to be there, I'm certain of it, but it doesn't mean that they won't have someone there, just waiting for us to arrive.'

'We can't just sit here!' Charlie's anger had slipped towards desperation.

Andrew closed his eyes and pressed his fingertips hard against the lids. Charlie was right; they had to do *something*.

'Do we need to contact CID, boss?' Jen asked, and her question was obviously directed at Higson.

'I believe that would be the prudent thing to do under normal circumstances,' Higson replied plainly.

Andrew's eyes flew open, and he stared at his DCI in disbelief.

'But these aren't normal circumstances,' Higson continued, almost rolling his eyes at Andrew. 'In fact, I think the exact circumstances we find ourselves in would benefit from no further interference from DCI Chambers.'

Higson then shot Andrew an appraising look. 'Well, Joyce, come on then, *astound me.*'

Higson had said the same thing to him almost a week earlier. Had it only been a week? Surely not.

Andrew grabbed at his hair and tugged the strands hard enough to hurt. He needed to think.

A week earlier, he hadn't really thought that this place existed, he'd never heard of the Swans, or known the ins and outs of shopgirl gossip. A week earlier, he certainly hadn't thought ghosts existed.

Wait.

Oh, Jesus, was he really about to do what he thought he was about to do?

'Peggy's going to take the piss until the end of time,' Andrew mumbled into his palms.

'What?' Higson raised an eyebrow.

'We should ask Marnie,' Andrew suggested, the words feeling strange as they rolled off his tongue. It felt like telling the absolute truth even though you thought you might actually be lying.

'Marnie?' Jen asked. 'But Peggy's not here.'

'No, I know that, but she's not the only one who's seen her,' Andrew explained, and then he looked over at Charlie. 'Peggy told me that you've spoken to Marnie this week, even though you can't normally do that sort of thing.'

'Seriously?' Lloyd asked. Unsurprisingly, he still managed to look delighted underneath the fear.

Andrew groaned despairingly, and he had to swallow every ounce of pride he had left as he added, 'I might have seen her too.'

'No way!' Lloyd shrieked as he pointed at Andrew in amazement.

Charlie shook his head and studiously ignored Lloyd's gawping. 'We only saw her because of Peggy.'

Andrew pursed his lips, reached into his jacket pocket, and then handed over the small velvet box. 'Maybe it's not *just* because of Peggy. Go on, see if you can get hold of Marnie.'

Charlie looked like he really wanted to tell Andrew that he thought he was behaving in a way that was more than a bit insane and that if his sister's life wasn't at stake then he probably would have just come right out with it.

'It's worth a try, Charlie. Peggy thought Marnie might be attached to an object; maybe it's this ring.'

With a sigh, Charlie took the box and looked around the room. 'Marnie? Marnie, can you hear me?'

There was no reply.

'Come on, come on, come on,' Andrew muttered, his hand tapping nervously against his thigh as Charlie called for Marnie again.

'I don't think this is going to work,' Charlie said despondently when Marnie still didn't respond.

'No, it *has* to. It has to!' Andrew mumbled, snatching the box back out of Charlie's hand. 'Otherwise, what is the fucking *point* of all of this? What is the *actual* point?'

Andrew gripped the box tightly in his palm. 'Marnie! Marnie Driscoll!'

He started pacing around the Ballroom, purposefully avoiding catching anyone else's eye. If he did that, then he might have to accept what he was doing, and there was no way he could cope with that just then. 'Oi! Detective Inspector Benson! Any other bloody ghosts that can hear me? Literally *anybody*! Come on!'

'Sir, are you alright?' Jen asked carefully as Andrew headed back towards the desks.

'Marnie!' Andrew shouted at the ceiling this time. 'Stop being so fucking selfish! Seriously, *talk to me*, or I'm taking this bloody ring and throwing it in the canal. Then you can spend the rest of your eternity searching for it yourself!'

'That's a bit harsh,' Charlie said quietly.

'I am *trying* to find your sister!' Andrew snapped. 'Marnie, I swear to God, I'll do it.'

There was still no reply.

'Alright, fine!' Andrew threw his hands over his head. 'Canal it is.'

Andrew had made only one step towards the door before there was a slight popping sound. A split second later, Marnie Driscoll appeared right in front of him.

Every muscle in Andrew's body tensed, and he had to tamp down his natural instinct to see Marnie as a threat.

Jesus Christ, *there was a dead woman standing in front of him.*

Andrew turned at the sound of commotion to see that Lloyd had stumbled off the edge of the desk where he'd been sitting, sending a stack of paper files flopping to the floor. His mouth was open, and he was staring wide-eyed at Marnie.

Jen, as could be expected, was dealing with Marnie's appearance with significantly more aplomb than Lloyd.

Higson looked positively ecstatic.

'You know, Peggy told me you were a bit rude,' Marnie said, tapping her foot on the floor as Andrew turned back to look at her. 'And I saw the way you behaved towards her that night outside Rex's house.'

Andrew had the distinct impression that he was being judged when Marnie folded her arms.

'*And*, despite what I said to Peggy before, I'm not actually sure that the handsomeness makes up for the bad attitude,' Marnie added, narrowing her eyes. 'No, Peggy was right, it doesn't.'

'Now, hang on one second, I-'

Andrew's protests were stopped when Charlie cut in. 'Maybe we should focus a bit more?'

'Marnie,' Andrew said tightly when she continued to glare at him, 'do you know where Peggy is?'

Marnie smacked her lips together, clearly irritated. 'She's probably off stealing someone else's fiancé if she's got bored of mine.'

Andrew was outraged on Peggy's behalf. 'That isn't fair!'

Marnie's eyes zeroed in on the small box in Andrew's right hand. 'Is that my ring?'

Part of Andrew – the very, very immature part that he usually kept locked away – dearly wanted to say 'no' and then just hide the ring behind his back. 'Yes, it is.'

'Can I see it?' Marnie's tone had shifted towards hopeful curiosity.

Andrew lifted his left hand to open the box, but when Marnie just leaned over and plucked the box from him, as though that were a perfectly normal thing to do, he almost lost the will to live.

'What the hell just happened?' Jen asked, staring at Marnie with nothing short of fascination.

Andrew was less fascinated and was looking down at his now-empty hand in horror instead.

'She was doing stuff like that all weekend,' Charlie said quietly. 'Peggy doesn't understand how.'

Peggy. God, they needed to not get side-tracked by the fact that they had a ghost in the Ballroom. Well, one they could *see* anyway.

Andrew thought it might be time to adopt a more sensitive approach. 'Marnie, we really need you to help us find Peggy.'

Marnie wasn't listening though. She was staring down at the open ring box, and her face was contorted in a mask of terror. 'Oh my God, oh my God.'

'What is it, Marnie?' Jen asked carefully, making the very sensible executive decision that she was far better placed to deal with the visibly upset woman than any of the men currently around her.

'I was in the kitchen,' Marnie whispered hoarsely, still staring at the box. 'Rebecca was late.'

Andrew stiffened. Peggy had said that Marnie hadn't been able to remember the details of the night of her death, but maybe that was finally changing.

'Rebecca was late,' Marnie repeated, and even though she was right in front of them she sounded far away. 'She's always late for things these days.'

Jen looked at Andrew, wide-eyed, and Andrew gestured in a way that he hoped translated to 'Please, keep her talking'.

'That's right,' Jen agreed quietly. 'Do you remember what happened, Marnie?'

'We were supposed to be going to Janine's party,' Marnie continued. 'I don't even really know why we were going when Janine was always horrible to both of us. Everyone else from work was going though, so I suppose it would have been bad form to say no.

'Rex had asked me to go to an event with him on the same night, and I'd hated that I'd had to turn him down. It would have been nice to go to something together. He'd been so busy all the way through December. I think it's why he kept sending me presents, you know. He felt guilty.'

Marnie shook her head slowly. 'I don't know how many times he sent Athena into Lewis's, or over to my house with something for me. She must have felt like the postman!'

'Athena brought all the presents to you?' Jen asked carefully.

'Yes.' Marnie shrugged. 'I suppose she probably bought them all too. Rex always did say that he was terrible at buying gifts.'

'He did say that, sir,' Jen said, turning to Andrew.

'He did.' Andrew agreed quietly. 'And if Athena bought all the gifts, then that would explain how somebody would be able to find out which items had been given to Marnie as gifts without asking Rex.'

He slowly approached Marnie, careful to keep his movements small and controlled. 'Marnie, were you alone the night Rebecca was late?'

'Yes,' Marnie said, and now that she was looking directly at Andrew he could see that her eyes were shining with unshed tears. 'I was watching *Top of the Pops.* Dad normally watched it with me – even though he didn't have a clue who anybody was – but he'd promised to take Mum to the pictures.

'When Rebecca didn't arrive, I decided it would probably be alright to sneak a bit of Mum's vodka,' Marnie continued. 'I'm not a big drinker, but I knew that everyone was going to be asking me a million questions once they found out that Rex had proposed over Christmas. A bit of liquid courage, you know?'

'I know,' Andrew replied quietly. He had to tread very carefully here. They needed to know exactly what had happened to Marnie on the night she died, but they also needed to track down Peggy, and quickly.

'Marnie, what happened when you went into the kitchen?' Andrew asked, voice barely above a whisper.

Marnie shook her head and a tear managed to escape. 'I don't know. I don't *want* to know. Please don't make me.'

Andrew steeled himself and tentatively took another step closer to Marnie. 'I know it's terrifying, and I'm sorry that you have to even think about it, but I need to know what happened to you so that we can find the people responsible. You deserve that, Marnie.'

Marnie let out a sob and pressed the ring box to her lips to stifle the sound. 'There was nobody in the kitchen. I shouldn't have had the vodka, and I just wanted some water. Part of me was ready to tell Rebecca that she'd just have to go to the party on her own.

'I was filling up my glass at the sink and then there was something around my neck.' Marnie sobbed again, louder this time.

Andrew felt like an utter bastard for doing it, but he needed to push her a little more. They were *almost* there. 'Marnie, did you see anyone? Did you see who it was in the kitchen?'

'There was a scarf,' Marnie replied dazedly. 'I tried to pull it off with my hands. It was wool. I remember that.'

'Jen, there was nothing about wool fibres in the report, was there?' Andrew asked as quietly as he could out of the corner of his mouth.

'Nothing, sir,' Jen confirmed. 'Nothing at the scene, and nothing under Marnie's fingernails. Which seems highly unlikely if it were a wool scarf.'

It was worse than unlikely. It was yet another example of someone not doing their job properly, either by accident or, more likely, by design. The thought that CID had been so convinced that either Rex or the Byrnes were involved that they'd just cantered through the investigation as quickly as possible with no intention of giving Marnie's family closure made Andrew's blood boil.

'It was nicer than just wool,' Marnie said suddenly. Her hand unconsciously pressed against her throat. 'Softer, I mean. Cashmere, or something else. It was expensive.'

Andrew's stomach twisted unpleasantly. Expensive engagement rings, expensive cars, expensive murder weapons.

Marnie sank to her knees suddenly, and a sound so inhuman came from her lips that Andrew was savagely reminded that he was asking someone to relive the exact moment of their murder.

'I can see!' Marnie wailed. 'I can see, in the window!'

'Sir, that's what you said. You were right,' Lloyd piped up from his side of the room. His voice was shaking. 'The *reflection*.'

'No, it can't be!' Marnie cried. 'It can't be. It *can't* be!'

'Who is it, Marnie?' Andrew asked, and he was very aware that the windows seemed to be rattling gently in their frames. He really hoped that they weren't about to have an experience like he and Peggy had lived through in Lewis's. A wall of windows shattering inwards was likely to cause far more catastrophic damage than the perfume bottles had.

Marnie looked directly at him, and Andrew felt like she was staring straight into him and beyond him at the same time. It was unnerving and terrifying, and Andrew fleetingly wondered if this was how Peggy felt all the time.

'It was Athena,' Marnie said, and her voice had been reduced to a brittle croak. 'Athena did it.'

Andrew's heart sank. He should have been pleased that they actually *knew* who'd killed Marnie, but truly knowing that Athena was capable of murdering her own brother's fiancée suddenly made Peggy's position seem even more precarious.

'Oh, Marnie,' Jen said, and she was crying herself. She hurried over to the girl slumped on the floor and hesitantly reached out a hand to press against Marnie's back.

Andrew watched Jen's face morph into confusion when her hand appeared to rest between Marnie's shoulder blades just as it would have done if Marnie were alive.

Marnie let out a cry of surprise, but before Jen could pull away with a hurried apology Marnie had thrown her arms around Jen's neck and was bawling into her shoulder.

'Fuck me,' Lloyd whispered in awe.

Andrew decided that he was going to let that one go because he was thinking the exact same thing.

'Joyce, *please*,' Charlie said softly. He was looking at Marnie pityingly, but Andrew knew, and understood, that his primary concern had to be for his sister.

Andrew nodded and went to crouch by Marnie and Jen. 'Marnie, I need you to help me with something.'

'No, please, no, please don't make me think about anything else,' Marnie said, burying her head further into Jen's shoulder. Jen nearly toppled over and had to put one hand down on the floor to steady them both.

'Just one more thing, Marnie. I need you to help me find Peggy.' Andrew had to choose his next words carefully. 'Marnie, she's in danger.'

Marnie leaned away from Jen to look at Andrew with a tear-stained face. 'What? She really *is* in trouble? You weren't just saying that to get me to come here?'

Andrew shook his head. 'Marnie, do you know a man named Tony Byrne?'

Marnie scrunched her face up. 'No, but is he related to Liam?'

'Tony is Liam's older brother,' Andrew explained. 'We thought that he might have been behind the car accident that Peggy and Athena had yesterday, but I think we were slightly off on that. I need you to think really carefully, Marnie. Are you sure Rex never mentioned someone called Tony?'

'Never. Rex is a *good* man,' Marnie replied stubbornly.

'He kidnapped my sister!' Charlie snapped.

Marnie looked appalled. 'No, he didn't. He wouldn't do that. I kept telling Peggy that she was wrong. She *is* wrong. You're *all* wrong.'

'Are we?' Higson asked brusquely. He reached over and pressed a couple of buttons on the answering machine.

Andrew barely had time to brace himself before Peggy's message played again. Marnie's face twisted in confusion, and she kept shaking her head, faster and faster as the message continued.

'Marnie, please help,' Charlie implored, as the message finished. 'Peg's the only real family I've got.'

'I can't!' Marnie was getting more agitated by the second. 'I said something terrible to her last night and I haven't seen her since.'

Andrew could feel their chance slipping away from them. 'Marnie, listen, I know you don't think that you can help, but I do. And you're not the only one who said something unforgivable to Peggy last night, alright?'

Marnie remained unconvinced.

Andrew sighed. 'Without her, we would never have been able to speak to you, and without you, we wouldn't have been able to solve this case.'

Andrew shuffled over so that he was right in front of Marnie. 'Marnie, please try. I know you don't want anything bad to happen to Peggy.'

'I don't know what I'm doing,' Marnie replied tearfully. 'I'm crap at being dead. Peggy and her auntie keep talking about how I'm doing things wrong.'

'Marnie, I don't believe in ghosts,' Andrew said plainly, almost laughing at the absurdity. 'Except, maybe now I do. I know that you're the only one who can help us now.'

'I'll try,' Marnie replied with a loud sniffle. She closed her eyes.

Andrew looked up and saw Higson giving him an approving look.

Bugger, that meant Andrew had finally gone native. He'd bet everything he owned that this possibility had never even crossed Chambers' mind when he'd sent Andrew to the Ballroom.

'I can't get to her,' Marnie said suddenly, startling Andrew. 'It's like she's too far away, or something.'

Well, that was that then, wasn't it?

Andrew sighed again and dropped his face into his hands in dismay.

'But I think I can hear the sea?' Marnie added, looking confused. 'That can't be right though, can it?'

'The sea?' Lloyd raised one eyebrow.

'Yeah, the sea,' Marnie said, sitting up straighter all of a sudden. 'Peggy's not on her own. Oh my God, Rex is with her. He's *hurt*!'

Andrew didn't particularly care about the end of that statement. 'Is Peggy alright?'

'I think so,' Marnie said slowly. 'I think she's asleep.'

The best Andrew could do with that information was accept that asleep was better than dead, and that was all they could hope for just then.

'Can you see or hear anything else?' Andrew asked, feeling both his hope and his patience fraying.

Marnie shook her head and looked ready to burst into floods of tears again. 'I'm sorry.'

'It's okay,' Andrew said quietly. It wasn't though. He was under no illusion about what would happen to Peggy if they didn't find her soon. He heaved himself to his feet and turned to face Charlie.

'You have no idea where she is, do you?' Charlie asked miserably.

Andrew was about to say 'no' when he caught sight of the bright yellow pencil case still sitting on the edge of Jen's desk. Some planning documents and a road atlas rested nearby, and Andrew nearly tripped over his own feet as he threw himself across the room.

'What are you doing?' Charlie asked in surprise as Andrew whirled around again, this time clutching a piece of A4 paper covered in typed lines.

'Rex Hughes has property all over the city, right?' Andrew said, looking down at the list he was holding, focussing on the two handwritten scribbles at the bottom of the page.

'Right, but last time I checked, Manchester wasn't at the seaside,' Higson said wryly.

'No, but the Hughes holiday camps were,' Andrew said, holding out the paper to Charlie, who took it hesitantly. 'Charlie, you told us that there were two houses the family had kept when they sold the parks.'

Charlie's eyes widened when he realised that Andrew actually had a pretty damn good idea of where Peggy might be.

'Dover's too far away,' Charlie said slowly.

'Exactly!' Andrew said, turning to Higson. 'Sir, I think they've taken Peggy to a house that they own over in Wallasey.'

'Rex was going to sell that house,' Marnie interjected suddenly. 'I think there was another one he wanted to get rid of too.'

'What?' Andrew looked over at where she was still sitting on the floor.

'He told me at Christmas,' Marnie continued. 'He wanted to sell it so that he could give the family house to his mum and Athena when he and I got married. He was going to build us a house of our own. I don't think Athena was very happy about the idea of being stuck in the house alone with her mother, but it's not like she had anywhere else she could go.'

For Andrew, everything clicked together abruptly.

'Christ, that's it!' Andrew announced, looking wildly around at the others. 'Peggy was right; it's always about money.'

'What *are* you on about?' Lloyd asked, looking at Andrew sceptically. 'Er, *sir*.'

'I don't think Athena and Rex are in this together at all,' Andrew explained. 'I don't think they ever were.'

He shot Marnie an apologetic glance. 'I think Athena killed you because she was jealous.'

'Seriously?' Lloyd still looked unconvinced.

'Right, hang on, look.' Andrew pointed at Charlie. 'How much of your father's estate do you get when he dies?'

Charlie didn't look too bothered by the thought of his father's death, so Andrew assumed he'd be okay with answering the question.

'Nearly all of it,' Charlie replied with a shrug.

'And Peggy?' Andrew asked. 'What about her?'

'Peg will technically get whatever my father leaves her in his will, which

I doubt will be very much after what happened last year,' Charlie added.

'What happened last year?' Lloyd perked up again.

'Nothing,' Charlie, Andrew and Marnie replied in unison.

'Where's this going?' Charlie asked, frowning at Andrew.

'Even though Peggy is older than you, you still inherit everything by the very virtue of being the only son.'

'That doesn't seem very fair,' Lloyd added, wrinkling his nose in distaste. Andrew thought that Lloyd's sisters should be quite proud of their younger brother.

'Oh, it's not,' Charlie agreed wholeheartedly. 'I've already told Peg that she'll get half of everything when our father eventually dies.'

Andrew turned to Higson again. 'Sir, I think Athena Hughes has been unable to accept that her younger brother inherited the vast majority of their father's fortune. She resented how much Rex was spending on Marnie because she saw that money as her rightful share.'

Andrew started pacing again. 'Think about it. The returns made to Kendals were exchanged for cash, and today the money from the sale of the engagement ring was also all meant to be paid in cash.

'I don't think Athena has access to her own money, and I think she finds it humiliating to ask her brother for things when she's watching him splash out on a whole driveway full of cars, or when he's selling property for his own gain, rather than hers. Especially when I don't think he's as flush with cash as he wants everyone to believe.'

He paused and pointed at the box Marnie was still holding. 'Marnie, did Rex ever tell you how much that ring was worth?'

'No,' Marnie replied, looking down at the enormous ruby, 'but it was obviously expensive.'

'Athena was about to sell it for half a million pounds,' Andrew said. He watched as Marnie's mouth fell open in surprise.

'Jealousy is a great motivator,' Higson muttered, shaking his head.

Wasn't it just? thought Andrew. He thought of how Kate had been inexcusably rude to Peggy at the pub; how his mother had resented him and Rob for their 'freedom'; and how Marnie had behaved when she'd thought that Rebecca and Rex had gone behind her back.

'Go on. What else?' Higson gestured for Andrew to continue.

'I think Athena knew full well what sort of 'business' her brother had got himself into in Manchester, and I think she found out that Rex has been losing territory to the Byrnes,' Andrew explained. 'What if she saw the bigger picture though? Fighting the Byrnes hadn't been doing Rex's finances any favours, and it sounded like he was being forced out of the city entirely.

'We know that Rex was angry about selling Empire Street when he still had dealers in clubs in town, but whoever he owes money to has him over a barrel by the sounds of things. What if Athena could see that Empire Street was far more valuable as part of a deal with the Byrnes than it would be as part of a quick sale to a property developer?'

'So, the note and the accident were setups?' Jen asked.

'I think so, but until we've found them, and we know that Peggy's safe, this is all just speculation,' Andrew said, picking up his car keys from where he'd abandoned them on his desk. 'We mustn't forget that Athena Hughes still thinks she made half a million today, and I don't think she'll be very happy when she finds out that the sale fell through.'

'How does this end though, sir?' Jen asked worriedly. 'I can't see Rex Hughes just ceding control of everything to his sister, can you?'

Andrew swallowed heavily. 'No, I think that's where Peggy comes in.'

'What do you mean?' Charlie asked.

Andrew sighed, bracing himself. 'We know that both Rex and the Byrnes have been interested in how much money your family has, and Rex said that Peggy could be the answer to his cashflow problems, right? I think his long game was to try and wheedle his way into a relationship with her, which is why he turned up to take her to lunch on Sunday.'

Both Charlie and Marnie immediately began shouting over him in a racket of alarm and protest.

'Quiet!' Higson barked. 'Both of you. Carry on, Joyce.'

Andrew nodded his thanks. 'I think that plan changed when Liam was killed. Remember what Peggy said about how Rex left lunch early? He was *surprised* by the phone call about Liam. A murder in the building he's trying to sell is likely to put a buyer off anyway, but then, that same afternoon his sister is run off the road, after receiving a note warning Rex off selling the warehouse.'

'So you think all of that was to scare him into pulling out of the sale?' Jen asked.

Andrew nodded again. 'But now he needs another way to get cash quickly. He hasn't got time to waste on trying to get Peggy to part with her money.'

'So he kidnapped her instead,' Jen concluded.

'Right, but Peggy said that Athena and Tony Byrne are working together,' Andrew continued, trying not to think about the terror in Peggy's voice. 'I don't think Rex is pulling the strings anymore, and I think they'll only keep him around for as long as he's useful to them.'

Andrew left it at that. He couldn't bring himself to voice what that would likely mean for Peggy. Tony Byrne wouldn't just let her go, whether Charlie paid up or not.

Marnie made another sound of distress.

'We need to go to Wallasey,' Charlie said, voice wavering. 'We need to go and get Peggy now!'

'I know some of the old boys over in Merseyside,' Higson said, standing up and shrugging on his jacket. 'I'll get some blues and twos to come in after us.'

Charlie handed the list of addresses over to the DCI.

'Marnie, I need you to see if you can get to Peggy,' Andrew said, holding out his hand. 'And I'm sorry, but I'm going to need your ring back.'

Marnie sniffled again and handed over the ring. 'Please help Rex too. I know you think he's a terrible man, but I still love him, Detective Inspector, and I don't want him to die.'

Andrew was making no promises, so he gave Marnie a tight smile which she could interpret however she wanted to.

'Charlie, I think you should go back to Butterton,' Andrew said. 'The Hugheses might call the house.'

'Not a fucking chance!' Charlie snapped, entirely as expected.

'Alright, I tried,' Andrew conceded with a shrug. 'Right, let's go.'

They all hurried down the stairs together, pausing at the bottom when their path was blocked by Dolly.

'I always did like the seaside,' she said with a beaming smile. 'One of youse better bring me back a stick of rock.'

She stared hard at Andrew for a long moment, eyes narrowed, before she gave him a nod and moved out of the way, turning her full attention back to the cigarette in her hand.

Andrew gave her as wide a berth as possible. He opened the door and the group flooded out onto the street.

'Shit! Look!' Jen pointed at the end of the street where there was a bin lorry making a collection.

Andrew unlocked his car and wrenched open the door. He leaned in and pressed his hand hard on the horn until the binmen looked back down the road curiously.

'You need to move!' Andrew yelled. 'Now!'

'Can't do that, boss!' One man shouted back. 'You'll just 'ave to wait!'

'It's Police business!'

'I don't care if it's the Queen's business, mate!' The man sent Andrew a very creative hand gesture.

Andrew growled in frustration and seriously considered just hijacking the bin lorry and moving it himself.

'Give your keys to Lloyd!' Charlie barked, snatching the keys from Andrew's hand anyway and then turning to throw them to an alarmed Lloyd.

'You're coming with me,' Charlie added to Andrew, turning on his heel and practically running down Tib Street.

Andrew swore loudly and tore off after Charlie.

'See you in Wallasey, sir!' Jen yelled after him.

Andrew rounded the corner and stopped when he saw where Charlie was standing. The suspicion that had niggled at Andrew's mind earlier that day was confirmed when the steel gull-wing door of the car rose into the air.

'You have got to be fucking kidding me,' Andrew muttered to himself as he jogged towards the DeLorean.

'Get in, Joycie!' Charlie barked, before climbing into the car.

Andrew bit back the terse reply on the tip of his tongue, reminding himself that Charlie was as worried about Peggy as he was.

Andrew climbed into the car as the engine turned over, and he'd barely closed the door behind him when Charlie accelerated up the road.

When it came down to it though, Andrew didn't really care whether they arrived in a DeLorean or on a bicycle.

All that mattered was that they weren't too late.

TWENTY

Peggy's eyes snapped open mid-shout. She could still feel the phantom pressure tightening around her throat, and her fingers clawed at her neck as she desperately gasped for air.

She was alright, she was alive. She wasn't lying on a cold tiled floor in a small kitchen, no matter how much her body tried to convince her that she was. Her heart continued to beat frantically even as her brain began to recognise that she'd been dreaming.

No, *not* dreaming. That definitely hadn't been a dream. Peggy had the disconcerting feeling of being smothered by a sense of pure terror that she knew wasn't her own. It was just how she'd felt when she'd first encountered Marnie at Lewis's, except this time the feeling came with a soul-deep certainty that Athena Hughes had been the one who'd killed Marnie.

Peggy bit her lip and wiped at her damp cheeks as she stood up, leaning her head back against the wall. It didn't look like anything had changed in the time she'd been asleep, at least not inside anyway. Rex was still slumped in the opposite corner of the empty room, exactly where he'd fallen when Tony Byrne had balled up his fist and delivered a swift blow to Rex's head. Peggy hoped to God that he wasn't actually dead, but she couldn't quite make herself go over there to check.

Now that the torrential rain had stopped, Peggy could hear the sound of the waves rolling towards Wallasey Beach. Athena and Tony had made absolutely no effort to disguise where they were driving Peggy and Rex to, which worried Peggy enormously.

She knew that they planned to demand money from Charlie for her release, but Peggy was under no illusion that they were intending to just simply let her go when this was all over. She worried her hands together and hoped that Andrew had received her message; and that he also just so happened to have a miracle at his disposal.

A sudden groan of discomfort startled her, and Peggy watched as Rex slowly pushed himself into a sitting position while he cradled his head in his hands. When he eventually glanced at Peggy he flinched in surprise.

'Are you alright?' Peggy asked quietly. Charlie was right, she clearly did have bleeding heart tendencies.

'No,' Rex grumbled, rubbing the side of his face, wincing as he found a particularly tender spot.

Peggy shook her head and turned her face towards the large window that overlooked the beach. When they'd first arrived, she'd spent a long time vainly struggling to open it, but the sash had remained stubbornly fastened in place. Even if she had managed to open it and shout for help, the heavy rainstorm had kept anyone from walking the length of the beach. It was still early on a June evening, but with the persistent threat from the heavy clouds, she knew that she'd well and truly missed any chance of raising the alarm.

'Why have you been lying to me?' Rex asked, startling Peggy.

Peggy thought that was a bit rich coming from the man who'd been planning to palm her off to a criminal for money under the guise of taking her out for brunch. 'Because I wanted to find out who killed Marnie.'

Rex's face lost all hints of confidence and he stared open-mouthed at Peggy.

'She doesn't know what you're really like, you know,' Peggy added, shaking her head. 'She's still convinced that you're clever and charming, and that the police are completely wrong about you.'

'What are you talking about?' Rex asked, and there was a thread of irritation weaving through his words now.

'I'm talking about *Marnie*,' Peggy snapped. 'I'm talking about how you lied your arse off to that poor girl about who you really are. What was your plan, Rex? Just hope that she kept looking the other way for the rest of your lives?'

'You know *nothing* about Marnie!' Rex growled. His voice was shaking with suppressed anger and Peggy was glad for the distance between them. 'How dare you even speak her name when you don't know anything about her, or about *us*.'

'Oh, I know a lot more than you think, and I know that Marnie *will* find out the truth,' Peggy replied, and she was just as angry as he was, but for Marnie, and for herself.

'Marnie is *dead*!' Rex roared, slamming his fists down on the floor.

'You can't know what Marnie thinks because she's dead!'

'I know she is! Your sister is the one who killed her!'

Peggy stalked towards Rex, trepidation leaving her as she watched him go stock still and completely bloodless. She pointed a shaking finger in his face. 'But you're to blame as well.'

Rex dived towards Peggy, and if he hadn't still been recovering from Tony Byrne's attack he probably would have ploughed straight into her. As it was, she side-stepped him easily and he crashed harmlessly to the floor nearby.

Before Rex had a chance to right himself, the door to the room swung open and Athena Hughes appeared looking absolutely livid. Tony Byrne sauntered in behind her, glancing between Peggy and Rex in concern.

'What the *fuck* is going on in here?' Athena screeched. She looked far less put together than she usually did, and her eyes were wild as she looked between Rex and Peggy.

'Get this psychotic bitch away from me!' Rex barked at his sister. 'If you don't, I'm going to break her neck before I come after you two.'

Athena's mouth slowly morphed into a smirk, with only the slightest quiver at the edges. 'Oh, really Rex? And what has Her Ladyship done to upset you so much? Has she turned you down again?'

Peggy glowered at Athena. 'I just told him what really happened to Marnie. He doesn't believe me.'

Athena tilted her head and raised her eyebrows. She reminded Peggy of an owl.

'And what exactly did you tell him?' Athena asked with a shrug.

'I told him that you killed her,' Peggy replied simply. She got a slight perverse pleasure out of seeing Athena's surprise creep onto her face.

'And how exactly did you come to that conclusion?' Athena asked tightly. Next to her, Tony Byrne looked ready to pounce if anyone said even one wrong word.

Peggy took a deep breath and squared her shoulders. 'I saw it.'

'You *saw* it?' Athena laughed loudly. 'Jesus Christ, Rex, you're right, she is psychotic.'

Peggy narrowed her eyes. 'Pink scarf. Very soft. Probably quite pricey. Am I right?'

Athena stumbled backwards as though Peggy had physically struck her.

'Who the fuck have you been talking to?' Athena hissed, still keeping her distance. 'How do you know that?'

'Athena?' Rex's voice was so small that Peggy almost found it in herself to feel sorry for him.

Athena marched towards Peggy and clamped her hands tightly on her shoulders. Manicured nails dug sharply into Peggy's skin even through the layers of her clothing, but as she tried to pull away Athena only tightened her grip. She was a couple of inches taller than Peggy even without her ever-present towering heels, and Peggy would be lying if she said that she wasn't afraid.

'Who have you been talking to?' Athena repeated. '*Who*?'

'Marnie,' Peggy replied.

Athena's fingers spasmed and Peggy winced.

'Tell me who's been talking to you, and maybe I'll make sure your death's quicker than poor Marnie's was,' Athena snapped. 'It's not your little boyfriend – he doesn't know jack. So, who is it?'

'Marnie,' Peggy repeated, and the slap to her face, when it came, wasn't that much of a surprise.

'You killed Marnie?' Rex asked, still in that desolate tone of voice.

'It wasn't personal.' The shrug that followed Athena's statement was all the more brutal for its genuine casualness. 'Not really. I probably wouldn't have actually done it if you'd just given her some cheapo diamond ring like you had the other two, or maybe if I hadn't seen the receipt for just how much you paid for it.'

Athena shook her head, shoving Peggy violently away from her. 'Why did she deserve that? She was *nothing*, Rex, and you'd fallen all over yourself trying to impress her.'

'She wasn't *nothing*!' Rex cried. He was pulling at his hair in frustration. 'Fucking hell, Athena, *please* tell me this is some sick joke. Please tell me that you didn't actually kill Marnie.'

'I should have got half of everything when that old bastard died,' Athena spat at her brother. 'But no, as always, Rex gets *everything*.'

Athena laughed grimly. 'And then I find out that you're selling another two houses so that you can go live the good life somewhere else while you leave me in that goddamned little box with the old crone.'

Peggy had only seen the Hughes' house from the outside, but she wouldn't have described what she'd seen as a 'little box'.

'You're not selling the warehouse, Rex,' Athena said, shaking her head vehemently. 'It's worth a *lot* more than you're getting for it, and we're going to need it.'

'We?' Rex looked horrified. 'You think I want anything to do with *you*?'

Athena laughed again. 'Not me and you. Me and Tony. Despite your utter incompetence, I've been able to persuade Tony to reconsider the possibility of a partnership.'

'A partnership?'

'Yes,' Athena smiled widely. 'It turns out I've got a knack for business.'

'But he tried to kill you!' Rex protested. 'He ran you off the road!'

'Oh, for God's sake, Rex, catch up.' Athena looked despairingly at her brother. 'I was never actually in any danger. After Tony got rid of the Liam problem, it needed to look like there was a little tit-for-tat going on. It helped muddy the waters.'

Peggy glanced out of the window hoping that someone, *anyone*, would be in view, but the beach remained stubbornly empty.

Rex laughed, and, God, it was somehow darker than Athena's mirth had been. 'You honestly think I'm just going to let you get away with this?'

'Yes,' Athena replied plainly. 'Well, you'll be dead, so you won't need to worry about it.'

'I was wrong,' Rex said, pointing at Peggy but keeping his eyes on his sister. 'She's not the psychotic bitch here after all. You are.'

Athena just rolled her eyes. 'Right, sure. Look, Rex, you've got until we get hold of someone willing to pay us for *her*, and then when she's dead it'll be your turn. The police will think it's a kidnapping gone wrong. I'll be so upset when they tell me that my darling younger brother killed himself.'

'Andrew knows it was you!' Peggy said, rooting around for any bravery she had left. 'You won't be able to walk away from all of this.'

Athena smirked and Peggy dearly wanted to throw something at her.

'Oh, Peggy, sweetheart, you told Andrew that you were at Empire Street, didn't you? I bet he ran straight round there, all dashingly courageous and ready to save his girl.'

Athena pushed out her bottom lip in a grotesque impression of a pout. 'It's such a shame that he'll have found a few of Tony's friends waiting for him when he arrived. I doubt he got even two steps from his car.'

'What?' Peggy whispered, and her heart was thudding in her ears.

'You should have just kept your mouth shut like a good girl,' Athena snapped. 'It's your fault.'

Peggy was doing her best not to hyperventilate. If Athena was telling the truth and Andrew had listened to that message, then surely Peggy had sent him to his death.

'You really don't have much luck, do you?' Athena crowed.

Rex, taking advantage of Athena's distraction, let out an animalistic snarl as he ran towards his sister.

Tony Byrne stopped him by grabbing Rex's arm and twisting it behind his back.

'Do you want to talk about how you still owe me two hundred thousand quid, mate?' Tony asked, almost jovially. 'Because if you want, we can go over that in detail before I kill you later.'

'Fuck off, Tony!' Rex spat in the other man's face.

Tony immediately reached into his jacket and pulled out a gun that he pointed at Rex's head a split-second later.

Rex immediately lost all bravado and stepped back from Tony with a frightened whimper.

'Not *yet*!' Athena barked at Tony. She grabbed his arm and pulled the gun from his hand.

'Why are you doing this, Athena?' Rex snivelled. 'You could have just asked for anything, you know? I would have *given* it to you.'

'Why should I have to ask *you* for anything?' Athena sneered, waving the hand holding the gun around in a way that made Peggy spectacularly nervous.

'You didn't have to kill Marnie!' Rex thumped a hand against his chest.

'I was *sick to death* of buying all that crap because you were too lazy to do it yourself!' Athena cried. 'Thousands and thousands of pounds wasted on that little tart, and you had the *nerve* to use me as your own private delivery service! Well, Rex, thanks for that, because at least I knew where to find the fucking back door key!'

Rex's expression was blood-curdling in its intensity. 'If it came down to the money or her, Athena, I would have chosen *her*. Every time.'

Athena scoffed at her brother, fury replaced by cold indifference. 'Well, as heartrending as that really is, poor old Marnie will never know because she's as dead as a doornail.'

Peggy was still reeling from the shock of Athena's announcement, so she very nearly missed the moment the room felt charged all of a sudden. The back of her neck prickled in anticipation, and she watched as the air in the space between Rex and Tony shimmered ever so slightly.

'Hello, Athena.'

Marnie's disembodied voice heralded the arrival of the woman herself a second later.

Athena let out a high-pitched scream of horror at the apparition in front of her. She raised her shaking hand and shot wildly in the direction of Marnie.

Peggy threw herself to the floor and started crawling towards the door, hoping that Marnie would be able to keep everyone distracted for another few seconds.

A sickeningly dull thud caused her to look behind her. Tony Byrne lay face down on the floor, blood pooling around his head. One of Athena's indiscriminate bullets had obviously found a home.

Rex and Athena were both staring at Marnie in open astonishment, and Rex was making small abortive movements with his arms as though he couldn't decide whether he wanted to try to reach out and grab her or not. He also looked like he was about to be violently sick.

Peggy pressed her face as close to the floorboards as she could and continued to shuffle out of the room.

Once she reached the landing she clambered to her feet and turned to her right, remembering that was the direction she'd been pulled from when Tony had manhandled her from the car into the house and up the stairs.

At the top of the staircase, Peggy stalled. A man she didn't recognise was hurrying up the stairs towards her. He cried out in surprise as he spotted her, and all Peggy could do was turn tail and run back in the direction she'd come from.

'Oi!' The man shouted from behind her. '*Stop*!'

Peggy didn't stop. She didn't even slow down as she ran as quickly as she could manage, aiming for the door right in front of her at the end of the hallway. She desperately hoped that she wouldn't find it locked when she reached it.

The man's footsteps thundered behind her, and Peggy whimpered in relief when she saw that the door had been left open a crack.

She barrelled into it with the full force of her body, spun on her heel and slammed it shut. Her hand groped against the back of the door and found a sliding bolt. She cried out in relief as the barrel easily slid closed between the door and the architrave. It wasn't much, but hopefully it would hold for long enough for her to plan how to get out of this house.

There was a thump on the other side of the door as she dropped her hand, pressing her shaking fingers to her lips as she stepped backwards.

'Open the fuckin' door!' the man yelled.

Peggy continued to back away, looking around her. She was in a bathroom with old black and white marble tiles laid in a chequerboard pattern on the floor. There was an ancient claw-foot bathtub in the corner of the room, and in the dim evening light, the walls were a faded shade of salmon pink that had probably been terribly fashionable once upon a time.

The window was enormous and looked not over the beach, but instead over a tarmacked area with a few wooden sheds congregated in one corner, along with what looked like the semi-ruined remains of a shower block. There were two cars parked there: the black Vauxhall that Tony had driven them to the house in, and a smaller, red car that Peggy assumed belonged to the man who'd chased her up the stairs.

Peggy's heart sank as she realised that she wasn't going to be able to get this window open either. At some point, someone had secured a wire mesh over the glazing. The frame of the mesh was screwed to the wall around the window and Peggy had no way of breaking through it.

There was another crash against the door, and Peggy cried out as the wood protested loudly but continued to hold.

Jesus, she did *not* want to die cowering in a filthy old bathroom with freedom only a pane of glass - and a two-storey drop – away.

'What the hell is going on?' That was Athena.

'The girl's 'iding in the bathroom!'

Peggy pressed her back against the wire mesh and told herself to stay calm. Marnie had arrived, so maybe she wasn't completely out of hope. A brief high-pitched wail sounded in the distance, and Peggy cocked her head to the side, straining to hear it again.

'Well, get her out of there!' Athena squawked. 'There's fucking funny business going on here and I want out. I don't know how she's doing it.'

'Where's Byrne?'

'Tony's dead,' Athena replied coldly, as though it was just a fact of life that she'd had no part in. 'And I think my brother's about to drop dead from shock.'

'What?'

'Just get her out of there, Johnny!'

Peggy's head turned to the window, a shocked gasp flying from her lips as the wail sounded again. This time it didn't stop at one staccato blast, and Peggy had never been more relieved to hear the whine of police sirens slice through the evening stillness.

'What the 'ell is that?' Johnny said, quieter this time. 'Shit, it's the fuckin' dibble!'

Athena let out an unholy scream of frustration, and Peggy was so thankful that there was a door between her and the other woman. She couldn't be in any way certain that Athena wouldn't just kill her the first chance she got.

'We need to get out of 'ere, Athena,' Johnny snapped.

'Help me look then!'

Peggy frowned as she heard the sounds of shuffling on the landing. What the hell was going on out there?

'Here!' Athena announced triumphantly. 'Take it.'

'Then what?' Johnny asked.

'Torch the place,' Athena replied. 'Let's go.'

Peggy felt her blood run cold as she heard the unmistakable turning of a key in a lock. Then, Athena and Johnny's voices moved further away until they finally became unintelligible.

When she thought she heard movement from downstairs she tiptoed across the bathroom and gingerly slid the bolt backwards as she put her hand on the door handle. She pushed down and pulled the door towards her, but it didn't budge. She rattled the handle violently and dropped to her knees to peer through the keyhole when it still didn't move.

Sure enough, there was the head of a key blocking her view.

'No!' Peggy cried, hammering on the door. 'Let me out!'

She looked around wildly. Maybe she'd missed something when she first ran in here.

Nothing. The bathroom remained stubbornly empty.

She pressed down on the handle again and pulled with every ounce of strength she had. Maybe the lock would be old enough that she'd be able to dislodge it.

After a minute, Peggy had to accept defeat and sobbed loudly, just once.

The sirens were getting louder, but they still weren't close enough. Not when she thought she could already smell smoke.

'Marnie!' she called out desperately. 'Marnie? Are you still here? Please help!'

Just like back at Empire Street, Marnie remained stubbornly silent.

Peggy rushed to the window, hands flying around the edge of the metal frame as she tried to find somewhere she could get some purchase. She could just about get the tips of her fingers through the gaps in the wire grid, but there wasn't then enough space for her to be able to grip tightly and pull.

Her fingers slipped free and the skin around her nails tore painfully. Peggy let out a tearful cry of frustration and sat heavily on the edge of the bathtub.

A door slammed shut downstairs, and Peggy knew that she'd just been left behind to die.

* * *

'Come on, come on, come on,' Andrew repeated, drumming his fingers nervously on his thighs as Charlie accelerated up the road leading to the seafront.

He'd seen neither hide nor hair of the promised Merseyside Police backup yet, and the others from the Ballroom hadn't caught up. This didn't surprise him entirely, knowing that Lloyd was behind the wheel of the Belmont, but it did make him nervous.

He hadn't heard from Marnie either, so he could only hope that she'd been able to reach Peggy and let her know that Andrew was coming for her.

The situation that they were heading into could be described as 'volatile' at best, and on the drive over from Manchester he'd been trying hard not to think too much about the hostage survival statistics he'd had to study the year before.

Charlie had also been disconcertingly quiet for the entire drive.

Andrew had been expecting to bear the brunt of Charlie's ire – not that he didn't think that he would have entirely deserved it – but other than a few mumbled requests for directions he hadn't spoken. Andrew certainly wasn't going to say a word about how far over the speed limit they'd been travelling as they'd covered the miles in a blur.

'Left up here,' Andrew said as the sea came into view. 'Based on where the holiday park used to be, I expect the house will be set as close to the beach as they could get.'

Charlie complied, barely slowing to turn the corner. 'Do you think she's still alive?'

Andrew's throat closed up slightly at the abruptness of the question. 'Yes.'

'Really?' Charlie asked, taking his eyes off the road for just a second to look at his passenger.

Andrew looked out the window. 'I think you need to take this right.'

'Seriously, Joyce,' Charlie said, swallowing heavily as he followed the direction onto a sandy track. 'What the hell do you think we're about to walk into?'

'Athena needs your sister,' Andrew replied, and the words felt like sandpaper in his mouth. 'Without proof that Peggy is still alive, Athena knows she runs the risk of you refusing to give her any money.'

'What if I just offer to pay?'

Andrew sighed. 'Peggy doesn't want you to do that.'

'Would you?' Charlie asked, just as the distant whine of a police siren cut through the still air. 'If you were in my position, what would *you* do?'

Andrew found that he couldn't answer that question. Not when he knew that his official, professional position on how to handle a hostage situation wasn't necessarily the same as his personal view on how he'd behave when the situation involved someone he cared about. A week ago he might have had a better idea of exactly what he was going to do once they reached the house.

'We're going to get her back, Charlie,' he offered eventually.

'You swear?'

For the first time in their acquaintance, Charlie seemed almost as young as Lloyd, and Andrew found that he missed the brash, garish Charlie Swan of the past week, even as annoying as he could be at times; *most* of the time, in fact.

'Joyce?' Charlie prompted, worry plain on his face.

Shit. Andrew was going to have to lie. '*I swear*, Charlie.'

The answer pacified Charlie enough that he gave a single nod, even as the promise turned to ash on Andrew's tongue.

Charlie gestured towards the beach in front of them. 'That's the house then.'

The enormous Victorian building loomed up into the dusky June sky like a forgotten relic. What might once have been cheerfully painted wood above the windows was faded and flaking, and the whole place looked like it was only a few good gusts of sea breeze away from falling straight into the water. Even still, Andrew could easily imagine how it once could have been the jewel in the crown of the Hughes empire; the family up at the house, lording it over the 'commoners' staying in the shabby holiday huts below.

Andrew narrowed his eyes and then blinked a few times just to check that he wasn't seeing things. 'Jesus Christ! Charlie, I need you to put your foot down! *Now*!'

Charlie didn't question what had brought on the sudden yelling, but the DeLorean sped even faster towards the house, both passengers bouncing around uncomfortably as the car failed to even out the bumpy road beneath them.

Andrew knew when Charlie finally spotted the flames too because he swore loudly and screeched the car to a halt in what was actually a fairly impressive handbrake turn, almost blocking the narrow road. Andrew felt every bone in his body rattle as the car stopped moving before the webbing of his seatbelt pulled taut against his chest.

Charlie was up and out of the car before Andrew even had a finger on the door handle. Andrew cursed the stupid doors and rolled out of the car, knees crashing heavily onto the sandy path.

'Charlie, get the hell back in the car!' Andrew hissed as loud as he dared when Charlie started racing towards the house. 'You don't know who's here!'

Andrew knew that technically he shouldn't be making any noise at all, as it might give away their position to anyone waiting for them. Then again, he could not only hear a whole orchestra of sirens by that point, but could also see a flock of blue lights distantly speeding into Wallasey. Any attempt at true subtlety had already gone out of the window.

'Charlie!' Andrew whispered angrily. 'You're going to get yourself bloody killed!'

As if the universe thought Andrew's point required some punctuation, a gunshot rang out from somewhere near the house.

Charlie was on the ground a second later, and Andrew hoped that it was because he'd thrown himself there by choice. Andrew hastily tucked himself behind a ramshackle building that was probably once a shower block for the camp, if the chipped, white-tiled internal walls were anything to go by.

'For fuck's sake,' Andrew muttered, half in horror, but also in irritation. What the hell was he doing in the middle of an active hostage situation without a single armed officer? Not to mention the fact that his only current backup equated to a single person; a person who also just happened to be the hostage's brother and had zero police training of any kind.

Oh, and there was also a *fire*, lest he forget.

When this was over, Andrew was going to the pub. Possibly for a solid week.

He cautiously crept out from behind the building.

Almost immediately, there was another shot. It came from a different position this time, but whizzed off harmlessly into the evening.

Andrew sighed again, because while it was useful to know that they weren't dealing with a crack shot here, it also meant that the risk of a twitchy trigger finger was far higher.

He heard a car approaching from behind, and Andrew glanced over his shoulder to see Jen parking behind the DeLorean. Higson was in the passenger seat looking astonishingly unconcerned.

Lloyd then appeared in Andrew's Belmont only a few seconds later.

Andrew looked back towards the house and swore under his breath when he realised that Charlie had disappeared.

Andrew turned and hastily jogged back towards the cars. 'Get out but stay down. We've got at least two people on the grounds, both armed. I haven't identified either yet, but based on the poor shots I'd say we haven't encountered Tony Byrne yet.'

'Oh my God, the house is on fire!' Jen hissed in alarm. 'Is Peggy inside?'

'I don't know for certain,' Andrew replied, 'but I think it's highly likely.'

'I thought Athena wanted her as a hostage though,' Lloyd said. He frowned. 'And where's Charlie?'

'I think Athena's cutting her losses - I don't know why. As for Charlie, he's off trying to get himself shot,' Andrew replied, exasperated. 'I need one of you to find him and get him back up here. He's no use to anyone if he's dead. His dad would probably have us all thrown in jail for good measure.'

'I'll go,' Lloyd said, already moving towards the house in search of the wayward Swan.

'Plan, Joyce?' Higson asked, and it sounded like he *was actually* interested, rather than trying to put Andrew on the spot this time.

'Uniform will be here in a minute,' Andrew spoke quickly. 'They need to get the fire brigade here immediately. We might need an ambulance too.'

Andrew really hoped that wouldn't be necessary.

'I'll see if I can go around the back of the house from the beach,' Jen suggested. 'If I come up behind them, we might have the element of surprise.'

Andrew nodded in agreement and turned his attention to Higson.

'Sir, I need to get into that house as quickly as possible. If Peggy's inside I've got to get her out.'

'I'll go with Cusack,' Higson said, 'then get the Scousers to follow us.'

'Sir,' Andrew said with a nod and looked back at the house. The flames that had been barely visible before were now tongues of fire licking their way into the front room on the left of the house. Without any knowledge of the building's layout, he was just going to have to get in there and take his chances.

'I'll try and distract them on my way up to the house,' Andrew said.

'Don't get shot, Joyce.' Higson clapped him hard on the shoulder. 'I can't be arsed looking for another DI, alright?'

That was probably as close to a compliment from Higson as Andrew would ever come, so he just kept his mouth shut and headed back towards the house.

'Athena Hughes!' Andrew called, and, *Christ,* he really hoped he didn't actually get shot. 'This will all go a lot better for you if you just give yourself up, alright?'

'I haven't done anything!' Athena shouted back from somewhere in the shadows, an affected shake in her voice. 'My brother made me come out here. Please, just help me get away from him. None of this has anything to do with me!'

'Yeah, and I'm Tom Hanks,' Andrew muttered to himself. He needed to draw her out if he was going to get anywhere near the house. He raised his voice again. 'So, that wasn't you who called French and Son earlier?'

Dead silence followed, and Andrew knew that Athena still thought that she'd made a successful sale that afternoon.

'No?' Andrew tried again. 'Alright, then you won't mind me letting you know that your housekeeper is currently in custody, and Marnie's ring has been confiscated.'

'It's *my* ring!' Athena screeched, almost immediately bursting out from where she'd been crouching behind a black car. She was pointing a gun at him. *Great.*

'No, it was definitely Marnie's,' Andrew replied, keeping his hands at his sides. 'And you stole it from her when you murdered her, didn't you?'

'She never deserved it!' Athena barked harshly, and God she really was intimidating. 'She never deserved any of it. I just took back what was mine!'

'But Marnie deserved to die, did she?' Andrew could hear the sirens growing louder now. He only had a few seconds. 'Did you kill her, Athena?'

'Yes!' Athena shrieked. 'Yes, I did, because the worthless little cow was swanning around covered in jewels that should have been *mine*!'

The sound of police cars getting closer was enough of a distraction that Athena took her eyes off Andrew. He took the opportunity to tear towards the house, hoping that anyone else with a gun would be far more focused on the incoming police cars than on him.

Andrew hit the front door at a run and was surprised that it opened easily when he turned the doorknob. He tried not to think too hard about what it meant for Peggy that the door hadn't been locked.

Acrid smoke billowed into the entrance hall and Andrew covered his mouth with his arm. He looked around wildly, trying to decide where would be the best place to start looking.

'Peggy!' He shouted as loudly as he could, already unnerved by the volume of the crackling flames in the next room. 'Peggy, where are you?'

Andrew needed to think.

If he were a murderous, money-obsessed kidnapper, where would he stash his hostage?

It would need to be somewhere he could get away from quickly if he had to make an escape, so, that ruled out basements or attics, or anywhere that involved unnecessary climbing. Downstairs would probably be too easy for the hostage to try and climb out of a window. Kidnapper Andrew would likely decide that his best bet was a room upstairs.

'Peggy, if you can hear me, I'm coming to find you!' Andrew yelled, coughing slightly as he did so. 'And then we're both getting out of here very, very quickly!'

I hope, he added silently.

He made his decision and hurried up the staircase.

TWENTY-ONE

Peggy was trying to pull the door open again when she heard the unmistakable crack of a gunshot from outside. She rushed over to the window to peer through the mesh and did a double-take when she spotted a horribly familiar purple blazer.

'Oh my God! Charlie!' Peggy cried in terror when she saw her brother lying on the path outside the house. 'Please don't be dead, oh my God, please don't be dead!'

To Peggy's immense relief, Charlie stood up moments later, threw his hands over his head and hurried in the direction of the beach. Peggy gave herself a second to remember how to breathe and then launched herself back at the door again.

She had to get out of there before her brother tried to come into the house to find her. The smell of smoke had been getting stronger over the past few minutes, and Peggy was acutely aware that her chances of escaping the house alive were dwindling with every second that passed.

There was another gunshot from outside, and Peggy jumped in surprise. She pressed down on the handle again, leaning as far back as she could, pulling and pulling. Her hands slipped off the handle and she crashed back onto the tiles with a cry of frustration.

She got to her feet almost immediately, swiped angrily at her damp cheeks, and stalked back towards the door. She was *not* going to just sit and wait for the flames to come to her. She was getting out of there.

With her feet planted firmly on the tiles, Peggy pulled the door handle with every ounce of strength she had left, shouting curses as it refused to budge.

Peggy paused briefly, hands slipping back to her sides. Had she just heard someone calling out? Surely Charlie wouldn't be stupid enough to run towards the burning house!

Peggy struggled harder with the door as the volume of the sirens increased.

With a shout of dismay, she turned away and ran back to the window. If she could just get that bloody panel off the wall, she'd at least have a chance to break the window and warn Charlie away before he got himself killed.

She forced her fingertips through the steel grid again and settled her right foot on the wall beneath the window to give her something to brace against. Peggy tugged as hard as she could until the muscles in her arms and shoulders were screaming in protest.

'Peggy! Peggy, where the hell are you?'

Peggy spun towards the door in astonishment. That wasn't Charlie. Her knees nearly gave out in relief when she realised who it was.

She ran towards the door, hands flying free to hammer on the wood with her fists. 'Andrew! I'm in here!'

'Peggy?' Andrew called again, followed by a loud cough.

'End of the hallway!' Peggy knocked on the door again.

The key turned in the lock and the door burst open a second later.

'You're not dead!' Peggy said, staring at Andrew in disbelief.

'Neither are you,' Andrew replied, and he looked about as surprised as Peggy felt.

Andrew held out his hand and Peggy took it with a rush of gratitude. 'We need to get out of here right now.'

Peggy couldn't agree more, and let Andrew pull her out of the room. The landing had already begun to fill with smoke and Peggy rubbed at her eyes with her free hand as they headed for the staircase.

As they passed the room she'd been in earlier, Peggy tugged on Andrew's hand urgently until he stopped.

'What? Peggy, if we don't get downstairs right now there won't be a downstairs to get to!' Andrew shouted hoarsely.

'Athena shot Tony Byrne.' Peggy pointed at the closed door. 'In there.'

'What?' Andrew cried. 'Is he dead?'

Peggy shivered. 'I think so, but we should check, shouldn't we?'

Andrew looked like he was arguing with himself. 'Shit. Fine, you're right. Stay behind me, though, and if anything happens you need to run as fast as you can, whether I'm with you or not, alright?'

'Alright,' Peggy agreed evenly, despite having absolutely no intention of sticking to that promise if it came to it. She tightened her hold on Andrew's hand just in case he had any vague intentions of doing something utterly daft in the name of being heroic.

Andrew gave her a look that suggested that whily he knew exactly what she was up to he didn't have time to do anything about it just then. He cracked open the door carefully, making sure that Peggy was tucked behind him as he looked into the room.

'Fuck,' Andrew hissed, pushing open the door fully. He let go of Peggy's hand to squat down next to Tony Byrne's lifeless body.

'Oh my God, Rex!' Peggy shrieked as she turned away from the body, and immediately caught sight of the man sitting almost behind the door with his head in his hands. She approached him carefully.

'Rex?' Andrew looked over in surprise. His expression darkened as he stood up and strode over to immediately act as a barrier between Rex and Peggy.

'Get up!' Andrew snapped at the other man.

Rex looked up at them as though he barely recognised them. His right eye was almost swollen shut now, but the left was puffy from crying. *Oh*. Peggy had forgotten that he'd seen Marnie.

'Get the fuck up!' Andrew demanded, reaching down as though he were about to haul Rex to his feet.

Peggy stopped him. 'He saw Marnie.'

'Marnie!' Rex snivelled, and Peggy found that she actually still did have it in her to feel pity for him.

'I don't care if he saw the bloody Angel Gabriel,' Andrew barked, and he shrugged Peggy off to yank Rex to his feet. 'We need to leave!'

A loud crash from downstairs startled all three of them. Andrew released his hold on Rex and ran out onto the landing. Peggy heard him swear loudly before he hurried back into the room, slamming the door behind him.

'What's happened?' Peggy asked worriedly as Andrew ran to the window.

'We can't get down the stairs anymore,' Andrew said, not looking at her as he struggled with the sash window.

'It's jammed,' Peggy said. 'I couldn't open it earlier.'

'Well, imminent certain death is a great motivator,' Andrew griped as the window refused to budge. He looked across the room. 'Hughes, get over here now!'

Rex didn't move.

Andrew growled angrily, and Peggy smacked her open palm against his chest to stop him from launching at Rex.

'Wait,' Peggy said quietly. 'He's had a shock.'

Andrew was outraged. 'And we're all going to die if he doesn't get his arse over here right now!'

'Yes, thank you, I hadn't noticed,' Peggy muttered mulishly. She turned away from Andrew and went over to Rex.

'Rex, can you come and help?' she asked quietly. 'We're not going to get out of here unless you do.'

'I don't want to go,' Rex said miserably. 'It's my fault Marnie's dead. *My* fault. I should stay here. It's all I deserve.'

'Hughes, come and help me, or I'll throw you through the window,' Andrew called threateningly. 'Two birds, one stone.'

'Andrew!' Peggy cried in outrage. She turned her attention back to Rex. 'Rex, Marnie wouldn't want you to do this. She doesn't want you to get hurt.'

'How do you know?' Rex wailed.

'Because she told me,' Peggy said simply. 'She's told me a lot of things.'

Rex blinked a few times. 'You *have* seen her, haven't you? That really was her earlier, wasn't it?'

'It was,' Peggy affirmed, and she held a finger up in warning to Andrew when she saw him open his mouth. 'Rex, I know that Marnie wants you to get out of here.'

'Can I speak to her?' Rex asked desperately. He grasped Peggy's hands and Andrew moved so quickly towards them he practically teleported. 'I need to speak to her!'

'I can try,' Peggy replied, ignoring Andrew's steely glare. 'But not until we're all outside.'

Rex nodded his agreement immediately. He let go of Peggy and hurried over to the window.

'Well?' Peggy said to Andrew, pointing towards the window.

Andrew rolled his eyes and went to help Rex.

There was another crash out on the landing, and this time something hit the door. Wood splintered as the frame buckled in the wall, allowing enough space for black smoke to trickle into the room and give a glimpse of the flames beyond.

Peggy backed towards the window as Andrew and Rex continued in their struggle to open the window.

'It's moving!' Rex shouted triumphantly, and with one almighty cracking sound the sash ripped free from where it had been bonded to the frame.

'We need to go quickly,' Andrew said, looking back towards the fire. He turned to Peggy. 'You're going first, don't even think about arguing.'

Peggy closed her mouth and only nodded with a resigned sigh.

'Right, climb down onto the roof of the bay,' Andrew instructed as Peggy stood next to him, pointing to the felted flat roof below. 'Be careful though, I don't know how sound it is. When you get to the ground, stay as close to the wall as you can and wait for me. Athena might still be out there.'

'You haven't got her yet?' Rex asked sharply. 'She's got a fucking gun. She's going to try and kill me! Again!'

'What happened to 'staying here is all I deserve'?' Andrew snapped. 'Plus, trust me when I tell you that you're right at the bottom of the list of people I'm worrying about right now.'

Peggy hooked one leg over the windowsill and awkwardly ducked her head through the gap. She looked down and was relieved to see that the flat roof didn't seem too far away.

'Ready?' Andrew asked.

When Peggy nodded, Andrew held his hands out for her to take. 'Right, hold on and I'll lean out. You won't have to jump as far.'

Peggy did as she was instructed, trusting that Andrew wouldn't drop her as she hauled her other leg over the ledge. She squeezed her eyes shut briefly as she let herself drop a little and then looked down again. It was only a couple of feet to the roof beneath her, but she didn't want to go straight through the felt into the room below.

She looked up at Andrew and nodded once before she let go of his hands.

Peggy tried to land on her tiptoes, just in case that would help, and when she felt herself stop, she reached out her arms to steady herself against the wall of the house.

'Alright?' Andrew asked.

'Alright.' She looked around and called back up softly. 'I can't see anyone.'

'Stay out of sight anyway,' Andrew instructed.

Rex nudged Andrew out of the way to try and climb through the window, but Andrew grabbed his arm tightly. 'Hey, whoa, hold it. Wait until Peggy's on the ground.'

Peggy crouched down and clambered over the roof until she was holding the edge of the bay window with her fingers. It was wet from the earlier rain, so Peggy's grip slipped away sooner than she'd anticipated, and she landed as an ungainly heap of limbs in the garden.

'Peggy!' Andrew hissed loudly in alarm. 'Are you alright?'

Peggy gingerly waved an arm in response. She had damp, sandy grass in her mouth and her hands were scraped to ribbons, but she was no longer in a burning building or at the mercy of a crazed kidnapper, so she'd take what she could get.

Rex hopped down next to her a few seconds later, just as Peggy was pulling herself to her feet.

'Can you get Marnie for me?' Rex asked immediately, eyes slightly wild.

'In a minute, Rex,' Peggy replied tightly, looking up to where Andrew was coming through the window himself. 'We're sort of in the middle of something right now, aren't we?'

Andrew was still holding onto the window ledge when the glass above him blew outwards, followed by a ball of flames that reached out into the evening air, insatiably seeking further fuel.

Peggy instinctively ducked and covered her head with a shriek of surprise as the glass rained down around her. After a second, she opened her eyes and looked up at the house, but Andrew was nowhere to be seen.

'Andrew!' Peggy shouted in horror as she looked around. '*Andrew*?'

She turned her head up at a slight groaning sound, just as Andrew's face appeared over the edge of the flat roof, squinting down at her. His hair was a disaster, and the previously white collar of his shirt was indelibly blackened, but he was still breathing and that's all that mattered.

'Oh my God, are you alright?' Peggy asked, as Andrew very

inelegantly climbed down from the bay window, dropping to his knees with another hacking cough once his feet finally touched the grass.

'That's the second time something's blown up when you've been around,' Andrew croaked when Peggy crouched down next to him. 'I told you, you're a magnet for chaos and crisis.'

Peggy laughed despite the circumstances, and Andrew grinned mildly in return. Maybe everything would be fine, after all.

'Well?' Rex demanded a second later.

Yet again, Peggy was faced with trying to understand what Marnie had ever seen in this man. Most of the time he was actually an insensitive prick, and that fact remained even if you chose to overlook the whole criminal activity thing.

She rolled her eyes and held up her right hand when she'd got to her feet again. Honestly, if Rex got too close to her, she wasn't going to even bother trying to stop Andrew from lamping him. She might even be forced to do it herself.

'Marnie?' Peggy called quietly. 'Marnie, can you hear me?'

'How the *fuck* did you get out?'

Peggy and Rex both whirled around in unison at the sound of Athena's snarl. She was coming towards them, gun held out shakily in front of her.

'Don't even think about it,' Andrew warned her, as he staggered to his feet. He had his arms wrapped tightly around his ribs and Peggy winced in sympathy when he coughed again.

'Oh, shut up,' Athena snapped, waving the gun in Andrew's direction.

'Marnie, now might be a really good time to come say *hi*,' Peggy said quietly.

'*What* did you just say?' Athena rounded on Peggy.

'Marnie's coming,' Rex spat at his sister. 'And I don't think she's going to be very happy with you, do you?'

Peggy dearly wanted to tell Rex that Marnie wasn't anything like a character from a horror movie. Then again, if Peggy had the opportunity to scare the living daylights out of her murderer she'd probably take it, and Marnie had already shown herself to be the dramatic type.

'Marnie is dead!' Athena yelled. 'Shut your fucking mouth, Rex, or you'll be joining her sooner rather than later.'

'You won't get away from here,' Andrew said, clearing his throat. 'I'd say you've got well under a minute before twenty officers come around that corner.'

'Plenty of time to get rid of at least one of you then, isn't it?' Athena sneered.

'Marnie, seriously!' Peggy called, looking around. 'I'm sorry I was rude about Rex, although he actually is an utter arse!'

'Stop it!' Athena screeched at Peggy.

Peggy watched dismayed as Rex made a break for it, running for the beach as he decided that saving his own backside was more important than a final chance to talk to his dead fiancée or to help the people who'd just saved his life.

'Marnie!' Peggy yelled, slightly hysterical now, and this time she was rewarded with a familiar popping sound.

Marnie materialised about three feet behind Athena. She was shimmering in the twilight, with only the coast behind her. Peggy thought she looked like an avenging angel, and she was absolutely bloody delighted to see her.

Marnie gave Peggy a small wave before tapping Athena on the shoulder.

Athena whirled around with a shriek of surprise.

'Boo!'

Athena screamed, firing the gun uselessly in Marnie's direction.

Marnie just continued to glare steadily.

'I'm going to haunt you until the end of your days,' she said dangerously as she took a step towards Athena. She then smiled, sickly sweet. 'You should know, I really like to sing.'

'Where the fuck is Jen?' Andrew hissed to Peggy, hunched in on himself as he crept towards her. 'I'm going to have to try and take Athena down. Peggy, I need you to be somewhere else, alright?'

Peggy looked at the bedraggled man standing next to her. Andrew looked utterly destroyed, and as though it hurt quite a lot to just stand there and breathe.

Peggy couldn't let him go after Athena in such a state. His luck wouldn't hold out forever.

'I thought by now you'd have realised that I hardly ever listen to you,' Peggy said, slightly apologetically as she wrapped her fingers around Andrew's wrist and squeezed once.

Andrew frowned, so Peggy gave him a strained grin before turning and running full pelt towards Athena, who was still facing Marnie.

Peggy closed her eyes tightly as she crashed into Athena from behind with a loud squeal, toppling them both onto the wet grass.

Athena went down like a tonne of bricks, and the gun flew out of her hand to skitter down through the sloping garden towards the sandy dunes below.

Andrew swore loudly somewhere nearby, but Peggy barely had time to register what she'd done before Athena scrambled to her knees and grabbed Peggy painfully by the hair.

'Ow!' Peggy yelled, slapping at Athena, not caring where she hit. 'Get off me!'

'Get her, Peggy!' Marnie shouted, in what Peggy assumed was supposed to be encouragement.

Peggy should have expected it, but still, the press of a hand to her throat came as a sickening surprise. Athena looked dementedly determined, and Peggy hoped that someone was planning on intervening at some point soon.

'Peggy!' Someone yelled her name, but she wasn't sure who it was over the sound of blood rushing in her ears.

The pressure on her neck vanished as suddenly as it had appeared, and Peggy sucked in a desperate gulp of air. She scrambled back onto her elbows and watched in fascination as a screaming Athena was hauled to her feet in tandem by Marnie and Jen.

'You can't be here!' Athena roared at Marnie as Jen restrained her, snarling viciously as her arms were held behind her back. 'You can't be! You're dead!'

Marnie shrugged as she came to stand in front of Athena. 'You're right, I am dead, and I'm going to make sure that you never, *ever* forget that.'

'Peggy!' Andrew snapped, dropping heavily down on the grass next to her with a grimace. 'What the hell was that?'

'Next part of my police training?' Peggy aimed for levity, but it was ruined by the fact that she now sounded even hoarser than Andrew did.

Andrew looked positively outraged as he stared at her, and the pained grin slid off Peggy's face.

'Never, ever do anything like that again,' Andrew said eventually, closing his eyes and lying back on the grass with a sigh of relief.

'Not planning on it,' Peggy replied, pulling her knees up to her chest and wrapping her arms around them. 'Trust me.'

'Not to interrupt, but we need to get away from this building,' Jen said, as four uniformed officers swarmed around Athena. '*Now.*'

Marnie reached down and wrapped her hand around Peggy's.

Peggy looked at their joined hands in surprise; Marnie felt just as real as Peggy did.

'I'm guessing that's another weird thing I can do,' Marnie said sheepishly looking down at her hands once she'd pulled Peggy to her feet.

'Yeah,' Peggy replied, wide-eyed, unable to say anything else.

'Now,' Marnie said as she looked down at Andrew, who was struggling to his knees. 'Will you let me help you up, Detective Inspector Joyce, or are you going to be rude to me again?'

Andrew gave Marnie's hand a wary glance before looking at Peggy questioningly. She just scowled at him.

Andrew sighed and cautiously allowed Marnie to help him stand up, grumbling and swearing in discomfort the whole time.

'Thank you,' he said somewhat begrudgingly. Marnie just grinned maddeningly at him.

'Come on,' Peggy said. She gently pulled Andrew's left arm from around his ribcage and draped it over her shoulders. 'Try not to die between here and the ambulance I hope someone's already called, alright?'

'What makes you think I should listen to anything *you* say?' Andrew grumbled, but he did lean slightly into Peggy anyway as they slowly moved away from the house with Marnie tagging along beside them.

'Sir!'

Peggy and Andrew looked down towards the sand where they could see Lloyd hurrying towards them. He wasn't alone. He was pushing a handcuffed Rex Hughes in front of him, and Charlie was sauntering beside them rubbing the knuckles of his right hand.

'You're all alright!' Lloyd said cheerfully as he reached them. He then nodded his head towards Rex with a glare and pushed him towards the car park. 'Just going to get this one comfy in a police car. Probably not as nice as that fancy Ferrari, I'm afraid!'

'Peg!' Charlie threw himself at his sister in relief, wrapping his arms around both her and Andrew at the same time. 'And Joycie too. Thank God!'

'Are you alright, Charlie?' Peggy asked, as her brother crushed her uncomfortably against Andrew.

'I'm fine.' Charlie squeezed them both tighter until Andrew hissed in pain. 'Oh, shit, sorry, Joycie!'

'Mmhmm,' Andrew replied vaguely, quite obviously trying to be as stoic as possible in the face of pain.

'And Marnie too!' Charlie added delightedly as he waved at her. 'Although, I should probably apologise to you. We caught your fiancé trying to abscond, so I punched him in the face. Not very hard, mind.'

'Jesus Christ,' Andrew grumbled, and Peggy couldn't stop the slightly hysterical giggle that burst from her lips.

'*Ex*-fiancé,' Marnie said desolately, and Peggy stopped laughing instantly.

Marnie was watching Rex as Lloyd led him away. Rex kept trying to turn around, but Lloyd kept pushing him lightly to make sure that he stayed on course.

'Do you want to talk to him, Marnie?' Peggy asked quietly.

Marnie shook her head. 'No. Not yet anyway. I know he didn't-'

She cut herself off, but the unspoken '*kill me*' was clear enough.

'Maybe one day,' Marnie finished sadly. She sighed and turned away from Rex to focus on Peggy. 'Look, I'm sorry about what I said yesterday. It wasn't fair, and I can't really judge anyone for making stupid choices for people we think we love, can I?'

'It's alright, Marnie,' Peggy replied softly. She'd really prefer not to have an audience of Andrew, her brother, and a small selection of uniformed police officers around for this conversation.

'Friends?' Marnie asked, and it was probably the most hopeful Peggy had ever heard anyone sound.

'Friends,' Peggy agreed immediately.

Marnie smiled wickedly. '*Now*, I've just realised that nobody else here knows that I'm dead. I could talk to any of them, and they wouldn't have a clue, would they?'

'I don't think that's a great idea,' Peggy argued, wincing, but Marnie was already walking away.

'Peg, she's just found out that her fiancé is a criminal and her ex-future-sister-in-law – *bugger, that's complicated* – murdered her over a piece of jewellery,' Charlie said, patting Peggy on the shoulder. 'I think you should probably just let her have her fun for a bit because she's probably going to need your help to get through all this, you know.'

Peggy did know, and it worried her, but that's what friends were for, right? Even for dead women with inexplicable amounts of power.

'Where's Higson?' Andrew asked suddenly, trying to look around.

'I don't know,' Charlie replied, craning his neck to try and spot him. 'I haven't seen him.'

'Shit,' Andrew replied, looking disturbed. 'There was a second gun. Peggy, who else here with you? Other than the Hugheses and Byrne.'

Peggy looked alarmed. 'Oh my God, I forgot! There was another man. Athena called him Johnny.'

'Johnny!' Andrew's eyes widened. 'Rex had someone called Johnny working for him. He picked him up from the Haçienda on Saturday night.'

'He was definitely with Athena rather than Rex though. Loyalty didn't seem to be particularly important to anyone in that house,' Peggy said, her stomach turning as she remembered that Tony Byrne was lying dead in the inferno behind them.

'Charlie, do you know if Lloyd had apprehended anyone else by the time he got to you?' Andrew asked quickly.

'He didn't say,' Charlie replied. 'Why? Do you think something's happened to Higson?'

Peggy spotted movement up ahead, and a familiar hulking figure stopped next to Charlie's ridiculous car. 'No, wait, *look*. I think he's over there.'

Higson, bathed in the flashing blue lights of the assembled police cars, had Johnny by the scruff of the neck with one hand. His other hand lifted a cigarette to his lips.

'Okay, he's actually pretty fucking cool,' Charlie said in utter wonder.

As if he'd heard him, Higson looked over and waved cheerily with his cigarette. 'I caught this rat trying to flee the sinking ship!'

'Sir,' Andrew said, tilting his head in greeting towards his superior officer as they all reached the DeLorean, doors still flung open.

'Nice work, Joyce,' Higson said, nodding in approval as he looked around him. 'It's been ages since we've had an interesting end to a case. Bonus points for the enormous fire and for getting a whole other police force involved.'

'Thank you, sir?' Andrew shuffled slightly. 'I think.'

Another siren joined the chorus, and Peggy looked down the hill to see two fire engines speeding towards them, with an ambulance following closely behind.

'Right!' Higson announced, dropping his cigarette butt on the ground and crushing it with his shoe. 'Let's get you to jail, Johnny boy. I'm sure your old friends will be delighted to see you back inside.'

Higson looked down at the DeLorean. 'Oh, and Swan, move your car before that house comes down. GMP won't reimburse you for any damage.'

Jen and Lloyd approached the group, and they all turned to watch the flames consume the old Hughes house. It was a morbidly spectacular sight as the flames reached higher and higher into the sky, as though they too were trying to remove themselves from the grip of the Hughes family.

Peggy shivered.

'Cold?' Andrew asked quietly, still pressed against her side.

Peggy shook her head. 'Mostly just glad I'm not dead.'

Andrew snorted. 'Yes. The true sign of a successful day.'

'Thanks though,' Peggy said, and she wondered once more if she'd always been so awkward. 'For coming to find me, I mean. Oh, and for the running into a burning building part too.'

'Just don't do anything like that again,' Andrew said, repeating his earlier plea, and wincing slightly as he readjusted his arm around Peggy's shoulders. 'I mean it.'

'I won't,' Peggy replied, and she thought that she might actually listen to him, just this once.

TWENTY-TWO

16th July 1986

Andrew pushed the stack of files away from him with a sigh and looked at his watch, surprised to see that it was already six-thirty.

They'd been getting absolutely nowhere with anything all day, and everyone else had scarpered long before four o'clock. First out had been Higson, straight to whichever pub he usually sequestered himself away in, and then Jen and Lloyd when Charlie Swan had bounded up the stairs with an enormous grin.

'Are you sure you don't want to come with us, Joycie?' Charlie had asked, waving the paper tickets in Andrew's face. 'I *know* people, you know. I could get you in.'

Andrew had declined for what had felt like the tenth time that week. 'Still no, Charlie. Thanks.'

'Your loss!' Charlie had replied brightly, before clapping his hands at Jen and Lloyd. 'Chop-chop, you two. I want to be close enough to see every single curl on Brian May's magnificent head!'

'Bye, boss!' Lloyd had been even more enthusiastic than usual as he'd plopped a mug of black coffee down on Andrew's desk. Over the past month this had become a Pavlovian response to any time Andrew looked less than pleased about something.

'See you tomorrow, sir,' Jen had said with a smile. She wasn't as outwardly exuberant as Lloyd and Charlie, but Andrew could see excitement simmering just beneath her ever-present professionalism.

Andrew couldn't bring himself to judge them all for skiving off to go to the Queen concert, and if he'd been in a good mood he might have even agreed to go with them.

He wasn't in a good mood though.

It had been just over a month since Wallasey Beach, and if Andrew was honest with himself, nothing had been quite right since that night.

The morning after the fire, Andrew had hauled himself into work, leaving the house spectacularly late for the first time in his life. Then, once he'd reached Tib Street, it had taken a solid ten minutes to convince his aching body to climb out of the car. Jen had already been waiting in the open doorway when Andrew had finally shambled over, trying to keep any sign of discomfort from his face.

'Sir, what are you doing here?' Jen had asked, clearly surprised to see him. 'I thought you'd broken a rib. Shouldn't you be at home?'

'Bruised, not broken,' Andrew had replied tersely. 'I'm fine, Jen, honestly. We've got a lot to do.'

He hadn't actually been fine at all. The very little sleep he'd managed to get after Lloyd had finally dropped him off in Gatley at some godforsaken time of the morning had been filled with images of fire and death, and he'd woken up with the terrible, unshakeable feeling that he was being watched.

Andrew hadn't had much time to dwell on any of it though, as within an hour of him arriving at Tib Street, DCI Chambers had stalked into the Ballroom, Fallon on his heels like a lost puppy.

'Joyce!' Chambers had bellowed, and Andrew had stumbled to his feet in surprise.

'Ah, Chambers,' Higson had greeted the other man with a cold smile. 'I thought we'd be seeing you soon enough.'

Chambers had ignored Higson entirely and rounded on Andrew. 'I believe I gave you a direct order to stay away from anything to do with the Byrnes.'

'Hold up there now, Chambers,' Higson said, clapping a hand on Andrew's shoulder hard enough to earn a grimace. 'Joyce is *my* DI, so his orders come from me.'

'He is on *loan* to you, Higson,' Chambers had replied snippily. 'And actually, I think it might be best for all involved if DI Joyce returned to the fold at Chester House. He's clearly a poor fit for this department.'

Andrew had felt a little like he was in the middle of a custody battle, and he'd almost laughed at the absurdity of the situation. He'd spent so much time thinking about how to get back to CID when he'd first come to the Ballroom that he couldn't quite believe the level of apprehension he now felt at the possibility of going anywhere near Chester House.

'*Transferred*, Chambers, not loaned,' Higson had corrected chirpily. 'I've got all the paperwork that says Joyce belongs at Tib Street until such time as either he, or *I*, decide otherwise. You sent it all over with him, remember? All in order, with those little tags to show me all the places where you'd signed your name.'

Chambers' glare had intensified as he'd stared at Andrew. 'Well, Joyce? What will it be?'

Andrew had double-checked with himself that it wasn't just the lack of sleep, the smoke inhalation, or even the bruised ribs that were herding him towards a glaringly obvious answer. He'd quickly concluded that it wasn't, in fact, any of those things.

'I'm going to stay at the Ballroom,' Andrew had said, and he'd thoroughly enjoyed the way Chambers' and Fallon's eyebrows had shot up in synchronised surprise. '*Sir.*'

'Are you mental, Joyce?' Fallon had asked in disbelief before Chambers had silenced him with a glower.

Lloyd had obviously been ready to start cheering, and Andrew had desperately hoped that he'd contain his excitement just this once. He'd been able to tell that Jen wouldn't have hesitated to pounce if Lloyd made so much as a peep, though.

'Well...' Chambers had trailed off looking like he'd swallowed something particularly foul-tasting. 'I'm terribly disappointed to hear that, DI Joyce. You could have made a real name for yourself at CID.'

Oh, I'm sure that's the reason, Andrew had thought. He'd suspected that it was much more likely that Chambers was increasingly concerned about any connections Andrew might find between the Byrnes, the Hughes' operations, and anyone at CID.

'Not to worry,' Chambers had continued with a cold smile. 'CID has oversight of the Hughes and Byrne cases now that there is a proven link to serious drug crime in the city. We'll take it from here.'

Andrew had opened his mouth to protest that this was *the Ballroom's* case, but Higson had tightened his fingers on his shoulder, and Andrew had taken that as the extremely obvious '*shut the fuck up*' that it was meant to be.

Chambers had then given them all one final disdainful look before heading out of the Ballroom with Fallon. Andrew had sincerely hoped that Dolly had hexed them on the way out.

Since then, the Ballroom team had been working on much more mundane cases than Marnie Driscoll's murder, and Andrew had taken it upon himself to start looking through every unsolved serious crime from the previous few decades to see if there was a pattern of poor investigation from CID, and even from the department that had existed before the current incarnation. It didn't help that the 'stack' of unsolved cases actually amounted to three entire rooms on the first floor. So far, he hadn't managed to find anything interesting or concrete enough to go to Higson with, and it was driving him mad.

It was also driving him mad that he'd almost instantly realised that what he'd really missed was the unpredictability of the Driscoll case. A few days after Chambers' visit, Jen had explained to him in no uncertain terms that they didn't regularly have the opportunity to chat with murder victims, and that most of the time there was an awful lot more scouring through files and re-interviewing witnesses.

Andrew had taken his disappointment all the way to the pub that evening. Morose and lonely, he'd known it was time to just go home and try to sleep when he'd reached a point where he'd seriously considered calling Kate just to have someone to complain to. She'd have just told him to piss off anyway, which, he'd had to admit, would have been entirely fair.

Things hadn't improved much in the following weeks, and Andrew had been left wondering if he'd made a terrible mistake in not accepting Chambers' invitation to return to CID. Not because he wanted to actually be part of Chambers' team again, but because maybe he'd have been able to get more done from the inside, rather than clutching at the occasional straw he uncovered at Tib Street.

Andrew looked out at the sun still blazing down on the city and decided that he might have to finally accept that it was time to get out of the Ballroom, even if he didn't want to go and spend another evening at home, perpetually feeling as though there was someone just over his shoulder, *almost* close enough to touch.

He got up with a tired sigh and made sure that all the windows were firmly closed before grabbing his jacket from the back of his chair and closing the Ballroom doors behind him.

He'd just made it to the bottom step when Dolly appeared like a wraith.

'Jesus Christ!' Andrew's hand flew to his chest in surprise.

Dolly laughed throatily. 'Amen.'

Andrew gave her a short nod, which he hoped telegraphed both a farewell and his intention to get as far away from her as quickly as humanly possible.

'Youse might want to fix that 'air of yours before youse go out there, Pretty Boy,' Dolly rasped, waving the eternally primed spray bottle of bleach towards Andrew.

Andrew's hands flew to his hair before he realised what he was doing. He pursed his lips in annoyance as he withdrew his fingers as nonchalantly as possible.

Dolly just laughed again, and Andrew was sure that he could actually hear her bones creaking in time with each exhalation of amusement.

'Alright, don't listen to little old me then. She probably won't mind too much anyway,' Dolly added, grinning unnervingly at him. 'Nighty night, Detective Inspector Joyce.'

Andrew kept his eyes on her as he shuffled sideways towards the front door as though he were an exceptionally hesitant crab, before he absolutely did *not* run out of the door and slam it behind him in relief.

'Mad old bat,' he muttered to himself as he unfolded his jacket from over his arm in an attempt to locate his car keys.

'Hi.'

Andrew looked up in surprise and found Peggy leaning against the *Cheryl Richard* plaque.

'Peggy?' he greeted, disconcertingly hesitant considering that it was *obviously* Peggy standing in front of him, and there was really no need to question that. 'Hi, I mean.'

'You work ridiculously late, you know,' Peggy said, frowning at him. 'I've been waiting out here for an hour.'

'An hour?' Andrew blinked a few times. 'Why didn't you just come upstairs?'

'Oh.' Peggy made a face. 'Well, I think I'm a bit scared of your cleaning lady?'

Andrew laughed at Peggy's half-question. 'Everyone's scared of her, except maybe Jen. Oh, and your brother.'

Peggy smiled slightly. 'I just wanted to come and apologise. I should have done it weeks ago. I've been a bit busy.'

'I understand,' Andrew replied.

Andrew had heard via Lloyd, who'd obviously been speaking to Charlie, that Peggy had taken herself off to a little house somewhere else for a few weeks. Charlie had been cagey about the reasoning, but Andrew was willing to bet that it was a combination of too many ghosts and too many people Peggy wanted to avoid running into.

A couple of weeks earlier, when Charlie had popped into Tib Street looking for Lloyd, Andrew had quietly asked him if the Countess of Acresfield and a certain *Edgar* were still in the area. The sour expression on Charlie's face had been enough to answer that question.

Andrew then thought about what Peggy had just said and frowned in confusion. '*Wait*, what are you apologising for?'

'For everything I said to you after you picked me up from the hospital,' Peggy replied, looking sheepish. 'I had no right to behave like that, and I really am sorry that I upset you.'

'I don't think either of us did particularly well that night,' Andrew said, grimacing.

Peggy's words had cut him to his soul, true, but he'd realised in his many post-mortems of their conversation that evening, that he'd also been terribly unfair to her, and that maybe his guilt over Peggy being hurt had been easier to deal with by lashing out at the very person he'd failed to protect.

Peggy hadn't done any more than he'd asked, really. He'd goaded her into telling him who it was she'd seen at the house, even though he'd known that he wouldn't actually want to hear the truth. He knew now that he owed her a serious explanation, and maybe being out here, miles away from Acacia Road, and under a canopy of summer sunshine, it was the time to offer the beginnings of one.

Andrew took a deep breath to calm his nerves. 'He's my brother.'

'What?' Peggy asked, entirely wrong-footed.

'Rob,' Andrew clarified, shrugging as casually as he could when talking about something he'd fought not to mention since he was a child. 'Rob's my brother. He died when he was twelve. I was nine, which is - *Christ* - nearly twenty-five years ago now.'

For a long moment, Peggy just stared back at him, looking almost as heartbroken as Andrew felt.

'I'm so sorry, Andrew,' Peggy said quietly, and she sounded truly regretful.

Andrew sniffed once. 'It was a very long time ago.'

'I don't think that makes a difference,' Peggy said, shaking her head. 'I'm still sorry that it happened to your brother, *and* to you.'

Andrew hadn't been gracious in accepting sympathy when Rob had died. He'd been an angry, confused child, blaming himself entirely for what had happened. He'd screamed and railed at the stream of condolences from his mother's nameless friends and thought that maybe if he'd just refused to accept his brother's death then Rob would have had to come back to him.

In that way that only children are capable of, Andrew had truly believed that he could will his favoured narrative into life. Rob was supposed to be Andrew's big brother; he couldn't possibly have been gone. He must have just stayed out too late past bedtime and got lost in the dark. He could come back. He *would* come back.

Andrew had ripped his mother's Saint Anthony pendant out of her hands on the night of the funeral and cast it into the open fire of the living room. He'd screamed for God to either bring Rob back or to just strike Andrew down where he stood for his sins. What was the point in having a patron saint of lost things if he couldn't even find Andrew's only big brother? His only *friend*?

Perhaps, one day, if Andrew could ever bring himself to feel that white-hot combination of self-righteousness and foolish courage again, then maybe he'd be able to ask Peggy more questions about his brother.

For now, though, Andrew could be gracious as he hadn't been before, in the face of a woman who understood loss better than anyone he'd ever met.

'Thank you.'

He knew that he should probably say more, but he was a coward, and he wasn't ready to lay himself open for scrutiny just yet. Rob's constant presence in the house felt like enough of a penance for now, acting as a more powerful reminder of his brother's death, and his own part in it, than any headstone or idolised Mass Card ever had.

Andrew let the quiet settle for a second before he smiled broadly. 'So, I've heard from Lloyd that you seem to have a permanent houseguest at

Butterton these days.'

Peggy snorted. 'That's one way of putting it. It's more like Marnie's installed herself as Lady of the Manor. She actually had a whole conversation with Timothy the other day, and he didn't have a bloody clue who she was.'

'No sign of her disappearing into the aether then?' Andrew asked and then frowned. 'Is that what they're supposed to do?'

'Some do,' Peggy replied with a shrug. 'I think most spirits fade away eventually, perhaps when there's nobody around to remember them, or at least *talk* to them. As for Marnie...who knows? I still have no idea what we're dealing with when it comes to her.'

'Are you worried?'

'No.' Peggy sounded confident enough. 'I think she just wants to 'live' her life as far as that's actually possible for her.'

'There's a little rumour floating around that Athena Hughes has been screaming about ghosts in her cell.' Andrew raised an eyebrow in question.

Peggy shrugged. 'I wouldn't know anything about that, Detective Inspector Joyce. You must be mistaken.'

'Really? I could have sworn I heard something about every song from *Chicago* being belted out at four in the morning,' Andrew added, trying to keep a straight face.

'I mean, Marnie *did* warn her about the singing,' Peggy said under her breath. She looked somewhat surprised at herself when she chuckled.

'Is it horribly morbid that we're laughing about this?' Andrew asked after a second.

'Maybe laughing about it is the only way to get over it all?' Peggy suggested. 'It's a very human way of dealing with grief, don't you think?'

'I do.'

'Charlie told me that you're staying here,' Peggy said, gesturing up at the Ballroom.

'For now, at least,' Andrew replied. 'Though I'm not sure how much use I'm being at the minute.'

Peggy opened her mouth to reply but was cut off as a battered, red car pulled up next to them, coughing and sputtering as it came to rest at the side of the road.

'Joyce, what the bloody hell are you still doing here?' Higson asked as he climbed out of the car. It was then that he noticed Peggy and he grinned. 'Oh, I see.'

Peggy's face went pink, and she looked quickly down at her shoes.

'Miss Swan, you haven't actually answered my question yet,' Higson said, waiting where he stood until Peggy glanced up at him again.

'What question?' Andrew asked, frowning between them.

'I have a few cases tucked away in the safe that I think Miss Swan would be able to help us with,' Higson explained. 'She's not yet given me an answer on whether or not she'd be willing to lend her services to the Ballroom on an indefinite basis.'

'As I said the first time you asked, DCI Higson, I'm not terribly sure that I'd be much help to you,' Peggy replied, diplomatically.

'And, as I said to *you* the first time you answered, I think you would be invaluable to us.' Higson raised his eyebrows. 'Anyway, I'll leave DI Joyce to try and convince you that I am entirely correct. Now, if you'll both excuse me, I need to get my house keys, or I'll be sleeping in the pub again.'

Andrew and Peggy watched Higson waddle towards the Ballroom.

'I don't understand that man at all,' Peggy commented as Higson struggled to open the door.

'Nobody does. Though, maybe you should think about what he said anyway,' Andrew said before he could stop himself.

'What?' Peggy asked, surprised. 'Are you serious?'

'Of course I am.' Andrew flinched as Higson slammed the door behind him, just as he always did. 'We'd never have solved the case without you or Marnie.'

Peggy raised her eyebrows. 'Did you hit your head harder than I thought when you fell out of that window? I thought you'd be desperate to be away from all of this stuff by now.'

'So did I.' Andrew shrugged. 'But maybe I've realised that it's all a bit boring without it.'

'Andrew, I'll be honest, you've always struck me as the sort of man who quite likes 'boring',' Peggy said, and she was definitely laughing at him. 'You were so convinced that I was lying to you when we first met that you told me that you were going to record every single word I said so that you'd have proof of me being a fraud.'

Andrew winced. 'I did say that, didn't I?'

'Look, I've told Higson that I'll *think* about it,' Peggy replied. 'Maybe when everything with Marnie settles down a bit more. We'll see.'

Andrew had always thought that 'we'll see' was just another way of saying 'no'.

'Alright, but why don't you let me try and convince you now instead?' Andrew asked, as casually as it was possible to ask such a loaded question.

Peggy looked at him sceptically. 'I already said *maybe*, Andrew.'

'Yes, you did,' Andrew agreed mildly, 'but I'm sure I can come up with ten very good arguments for why you should just say yes to Higson now.'

'Really?' Peggy asked doubtfully. '*Ten*?'

'Yes,' Andrew replied, and he was already confidently formulating a list in his head. He realised that he probably shouldn't have set himself a specific target of ten, but he'd get there eventually.

'In fact, I'll tell you the first one over a drink in five minutes,' he added with a self-satisfied smile.

Peggy laughed loudly. 'Unbelievable.'

Andrew shrugged, then sobered. 'Oh, unless you've already got plans that is. Sorry, I didn't mean to assume that you'd just come all the way into town to see me.'

'I didn't, actually,' Peggy confessed. 'Not entirely anyway. I wanted to pop into Lewis's to see Rebecca.'

Even though it was all over, and Peggy was no longer in any danger from anyone connected to the case, Andrew still couldn't quite shake the apprehension he felt at her words.

Peggy either didn't notice, or chose to ignore it. 'She was okay. Well, as okay as you can possibly be after the year she's had. She told me that you'd explained everything to her.'

'Not quite everything,' Andrew said, hoping to make it clear that he hadn't shared the details of Peggy's very particular role in the whole situation.

Peggy nodded her acceptance. 'She said that she's thinking of moving to Liverpool. I think she wants to get away from anything connected to

Marnie, or Liam Byrne.'

'Wouldn't *you* want to?' Andrew asked. He knew that he certainly would have run for the hills if he'd been in Rebecca's position.

Peggy sighed. 'And what about Marnie's parents? Charlie told me that you'd been to see them.'

Andrew nodded grimly. 'I'm not sure they'll ever be able to come to terms with what happened. They were talking about moving away too.'

'Sometimes distance is the only thing that helps,' Peggy said quietly, and her expression twisted into something a little melancholic.

Andrew thought that he probably shouldn't ask her what she was thinking about, even if he really, *really* wanted to. He owed her that much, at least.

'Drink then?' he asked instead, trying to recapture the lighter mood of a few minutes ago.

'Alright.' Peggy made a disgruntled face. 'I promised Charlie that I'd pick him up from Maine Road later, so I'll need something to get me through his Freddie Mercury impression the whole way home. It's *terrible*, by the way, in case you were wondering.'

Andrew chuckled and squinted up at the sun. 'How about dinner instead then?'

There was enough of a pause that Andrew started to think that he'd overstepped. But then:

'Dinner sounds good. What were you thinking?'

'*Well*,' Andrew said as they started walking down Tib Street, 'I do happen to know a very good Indian restaurant just up the road.'

He grinned at Peggy as they stopped at the edge of the pavement on Market Street. 'And what's even better, is that I know we can add anything we want to your brother's tab.'

Peggy laughed as they crossed the road together, and Andrew thought that the afternoon sunshine bathing their corner of the city in golden light was just about enough to burn away all thoughts of death and ghosts.

At least for tonight.